BRANDY ROW

BRANDY ROW

Shelagh Mazey

Matador
9 Priory Business Park,
Wistow Road, Kibworth Beauchamp,
Leicestershire. LE8 0RX
Tel: (+44) 116 279 2299
Fax: (+44) 116 279 2277
Email: books@troubador.co.uk
Web: www.troubador.co.uk/matador

ISBN 978 1780882 451

British Library Cataloguing in Publication Data.
A catalogue record for this book is available from the British Library.

Typeset by Troubador Publishing Ltd, Leicester, UK

Matador is an imprint of Troubador Publishing Ltd

Printed and bound in the UK by TJ International, Padstow, Cornwall

In loving memory of my mother and father: Roma and Pat Farrell and my older brother Terry.

TABLE OF CONTENTS

CAST

*MAIN CHARACTER: Violet Allen: (1814)
   Daughter of fishing and smuggling family

FAMILY: Father: Robert Allen (1768)
   Mother: Mary Allen (1772)
   Siblings: Thomas, Edward and Robert junior

*MAIN CHARACTER: Matthew Stone: (1811)
   Fisherman and smuggler

FAMILY: Father: Edward Stone (1787)
   Mother: Elizabeth Stone (1791)
   Siblings: Hannah (1815) and John (1825)
   Grandfather: Jabe Stone (1755)

*MAIN CHARACTER: Richard Dryer: (1804)
   Preventive man

*MAIN CHARACTER: Molly Byatt: (1813)
   (Barmaid, Cove House Inn (Violet's friend)

*MAIN CHARACTER: Annie Shaddick: (1810)
   Young woman of easy virtue

*MAIN CHARACTER: Ikey Shaddick: (1815)
   Annie's wayward brother

FAMILY: Father: Alex Shaddick (1779)
   Mother: Susan Shaddick (1783)
   Siblings: Bill, Henry, Tom, May, Eddie, Joseph,
   Jane, Lilly

SUPPORTING CHARACTERS

William Stone: (1796) Annie's husband (Matthew's uncle)
Auntie Sarah Gibb: (1765) Herbalist and midwife
Elsie & John Motyer: Innkeepers at the Cove House Inn
John Pearce: Molly's boyfriend
Robert Comben: Hannah's boyfriend
Jacky Sparrow: Smuggler
Nick Way: Smuggler, and family
Jack White: Smuggler, and family
Thomas Atwool: Smuggler
Letty White: Neighbour
Mr Seaward: Neighbour
Susan Atwool: Annie Shaddick's friend
Mr Gundry: Rope Mill owner
Mrs Hodden, Eliza and John: Family at Chideock
Miss Bennett: Haberdashery owner
Silas Jones: Sailor
Josiah Morrisey: Sailor and blackmailer
First & Second maid: Buck and Doe Inn, Bridport

SECOND GENERATION

*MAIN CHARACTER: Joshua Dryer: (1832)
    Son of Violet Allen & Richard Dryer

*MAIN CHARACTER: Benjamin Stone: (1832)
    Son of Annie Shaddick & Richard Dryer

*MAIN CHARACTER: Rebecca Stone: (1838)
    Daughter of Violet Allen & Matthew Stone

EXTRAS

Rival gang of smugglers
Dorset Coast Fencibles (Soldiers)

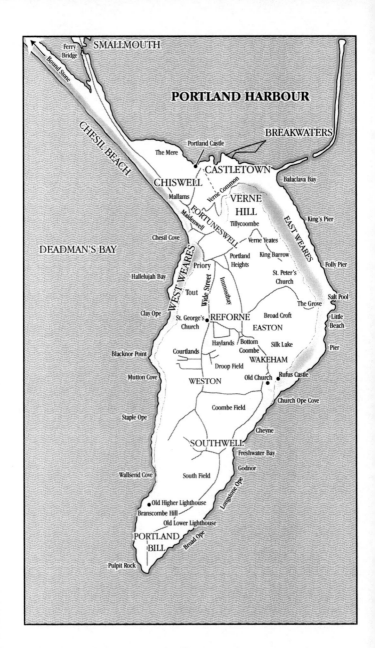

CHAPTER 1 *(July 1830)*

THE KIMBERLIN

It is early morning. The beach is still naked after the
night. Matthew Stone pauses from his work and
scans the smooth contour of the Chesil bank and
the undulating hills of the Dorsetshire mainland.
The causeway appears to be deserted. The sky, a
golden glow to the east, just hints at the rising sun
and the seagulls soar on the gentle breeze.

Matthew has found he can work for hours whilst
relaxing on a pile of sacking. He sits with his broad
back supported by the wooden seats of the lerret,
propped up on its end and resting on its stern,
forming a concave shelter under which he labours
in comfort and yet in the open air. As he mends his
nets and surveys the ocean for mackerel his hands
work automatically, leaving his thoughts free to come
and go. He will never tire of this vast sea and the
wild stretch of beach that lies before him. It has
broken the backs of many of the brave little vessels
that have dared to risk the elements and floundered
there, but its expansive, unassailable arc forms the
natural harbour of refuge and its strength has
protected the islanders for centuries.

Whilst he works he hears the crunch of shifting
pebbles as someone approaches from behind him.
He pauses and listens. Is it a man or a woman? The
noise draws nearer. He continues with his work, but
suddenly she is passing by and, as he hoped, it is
Violet. They were both born in cottages with their

1

foundations rooted in this great beach and have grown up together, but she doesn't notice him as she looks out to sea. He wants to call out but hesitates as the breeze catches at her thick, dark hair and instead he simply watches her until her tiny figure is finally out of sight. She has become a lovely young woman, a fine catch for any man. I will wait here and talk to her on her return, he decides and he continues with his work, though his thoughts remain with Violet.

By the time he can make out the blue of her dress in the distance the early morning sun is like a large red ball, low in the sky and silhouetting the masts and rigging of a ketch moored in the Portland Roads to the east. As she draws nearer he can see her skirt swinging heavily from side to side over several white petticoats, casting a shadow on the pebbles, glowing pink in the mellow light. How can such a slight figure support so many weighty layers of material? But this is Violet. Other girls might still wear the low-cut empire line dresses of the Napoleonic times, but Violet's mother is a dressmaker and her father a smuggler, and who can blame them if bolts of rich Spanish and French material reach the south coast, and the free-traders make good use of it?

Matthew is impatiently observing her progress when he hears another passer-by. This time the sound comes from behind him, but it is from the eastern slope of the causeway. It is the dull thud of a shod horse as it moves from Mere Common and onto the rough sandy track that runs the length of Ham Beach, bordering the harbour of refuge and leading to the ferry crossing.

The rider moves into view and Matthew stiffens

at the sight of a Kimberlin. His pleasure at seeing Violet alone is replaced by anxiety, for he suspects the real reason for those weighty, voluminous petticoats, and this man is a stranger, someone not to be trusted.

He hardly breathes as the paths of the Kimberlin and Violet converge. He stares as the stranger raises his tall hat and Violet drops a slight curtsey. His eyes strain to detect the meaning of the glances that pass between them, but it is too great a distance. Does the man notice anything untoward? The rider proceeds northwards to the mainland whilst Violet continues on her return journey towards Matthew.

As she draws near, stumbling over the large, loose pebbles, he is filled with foreboding. There is an uncertainty in her walk now. Has that Kimberlin noticed anything or was he too taken with Violet's charms? He looked a handsome figure astride that chestnut mare. His hands tighten on the netting. Maybe she has flashed those deep blue eyes at him. He shakes his head, angry at himself for feeling such jealousy. This pain is new to him, he is shocked at its intensity and he is frightened for her.

A brisk breeze is stirring but Violet barely notices. It is typical she should meet someone, today of all days. Her heartbeat was so violent that she feared the pulsing must surely have been visible. Did he notice her unease? She pauses, turning back, her eyes following the stranger. He is weaving his mount along the eastern slope of the causeway, nearing the large patch of green where the sea pinks grow. At his approach the terns rise in the air in a frenzy of angry screeching. She senses that same fear. Now he pauses. Violet stiffens, but he continues unconcerned across their nesting ground, and finally onto the rough track of the causeway.

It is only now that Violet turns and as she climbs higher up the ridge the pebbles move and slip beneath her buttoned boots slowing her down. She tries to hurry but if she stumbles the heavy bottles concealed in the folds of her petticoats will bump and bruise her legs. She throws back a glance, and then relaxes. The stranger is far distant.

She lifts her skirts before her. The sea breeze plays with her hair and the fabric of her dress as she crosses the rise of the beach and she feels like laughing with relief. She stops. It is a beautiful morning and she can see the propped-up lerret ahead, and Matthew, his strong young hands repairing the seine. He seems so safe, so dependable. Had he seen her fear, her relief? Will he understand her confusion?

At her approach he looks up, his head held questioningly to one side, the sunlight on his tanned face. Violet slows. He is so handsome, she suddenly feels shy and unsure and she hesitates. What should she say to him? Sounding as casual as she can and as if not intending to stop, she calls "Morning Matthew".

Matthew, ignoring her greeting, asks her immediately, "What did that Kimberlin have to say to you then?"

She pauses. "Nothing. He just said, 'Good morning' and took off his hat to me." She demonstrates with an imaginary hat and grins. Matthew smiles and she savours this moment watching him carefully, his fine eyebrows raised slightly, the twinkle in his eyes and the soft brown wavy hair just touching his neckerchief.

"You wouldn't be so cheerful if he'd noticed what you were up to."

She observes the dexterity of his strong hands

as he continues weaving his bone needle through the mesh. Again she smiles and the tension is gone. "Ah, but he didn't, did he?"

"No you are lucky, but what if he'd a sudden urge to bed a pretty maid, as is the way with them Kimberlins?"

Her cheeks flush, but provocatively she takes up his challenge. "Do you think I'm a pretty maid then, Matthew?" she asks.

Matthew laughs, but his voice is stern as he speaks, "Don't stray from the subject, I'm serious." Again his eyebrows are raised as he emphasises each word. "You were quite isolated out there and if he'd a mind to bed you, you'd have been done for." His glance falls to her hemline, slowly moving up to look her in the eyes. He holds her gaze as he adds, his voice low, "He'd have discovered what other delights you have hidden among your petticoats."

She feels her face flush, his words and his eyes confusing her. One minute Matthew is serious, the next he is larking about. She doesn't know what to make of him, but responding to his mood she turns her face to the breeze to cool her flaming cheeks, and says dramatically, "I wonder which would be worse, to be ravished, imprisoned, or transported."

"Don't you be too flighty, Mistress Violet, 'tis not only you as 'ud pay the price," he warns.

"Don't you concern yourself on my account, Matthew, I'm not a child no more, I'll soon be seventeen and I know how to look out for myself." Again she flashes a smile.

"That charming smile of yours will get you into trouble just as quickly as it will get you out of it, you know. I shouldn't like to see you come a cropper, Vi," he says softly. "You don't seem to admit to anything bad in folk and there are those who will do you harm, make no mistake."

Violet is unsure of what he is trying to say. Is he jealous and warning her against the charms of the Kimberlin, or is he simply concerned with the safety of the smuggling fraternity? She feels a little indignant that he should be preaching at her in this way. "What on earth are you prattling on about, Matthew? You talk like you're a man of the world, but you're only three years older than I am." She sees by the look in his eyes that her scornful words have hit home.

His voice again low and his eyes penetrating her own, he speaks seriously, "I might surprise you one day, Violet. I could teach you a thing or two, don't you worry." He pauses, adding very quietly, "You might even enjoy it."

She looks thoughtfully into his big brown eyes. "I might even look forward to it," she replies, feeling her heart race at the thought of the challenge. An uncomfortable silence falls between them then and she knows she has gone too far and can stay no longer. "Anyhow I can't tarry here all day, me Ma'll wonder where I'm to. I'll be seeing you, Matthew."

Aware of Matthew watching her, she swings her heavy dark hair over her shoulders and, picking up her skirts, she promptly leaves him. She can sense his tawny brown eyes following her as she reaches the inhabited part of the causeway, and adopts a jaunty gait in order that he might think her carefree. She is not ready for the feelings that he stirs in her, not sure that she could cope if he was to respond too quickly to her teasing.

She skirts a row of lerrets and a family group of fisherfolk just beginning their various daily tasks. Violet knows them well, as she does all of those living in Chiswell, and hopes that they will not notice her rosy, hot cheeks. They acknowledge her as she passes, and she bids them good morning. She leaves the beach via Big Ope and at the bottom of the slope turns right up towards Brandy Row.

The small hamlet where she lives is set slightly apart from the rest of the village, threading its way towards the cove, where the highest of the buildings have a view of the open sea. Her family live in the end cottage; thatched and built of the white Portland stone, it has an archway leading through the ground floor, which gives access to a number of courtyard cottages behind. She is still trembling as she enters her home, clinking and clanging, as her heavy skirts knock gently against the doorway. Inside, the kitchen is empty, and she calls out for her mother to come. Will she notice the change in her?

"Can you help me, Ma, please … with the bottles at the back?"

Her mother comes in immediately from the yard, wiping her hands in a worn towel, and Violet busies herself with the large pockets, stitched at measured intervals all the way round the underside of her petticoats, containing bottles of French wine. One by one they draw them out and at last, free of their weight, Violet stretches and relaxes. "I was obliged to curtsey to a Kimberlin out on Chesil, and I was so afraid the bottles would clang against the shingle, it was a considerable relief when he passed on his way." Violet nervously rubs her hands together, but smiles all the while in an attempt to allay her mother's fears.

Her mother sighs and speaks sternly, "Violet, 'tis no game we're playing. It could mean prison or worse for a good many of us, if any one of us were caught, so don't you treat it like just a bit of fun."

"I wasn't, Ma. I said I was scared, but he didn't see nothing, so I was a bit pleased with myself, that's all." She looks at her mother's anxious face. How can she explain to her something that she really doesn't understand herself? That these confrontations, whilst on the one hand they actually terrify her and make her feel sick with anxiety, at the same time they make her feel so alive that the rest of her life seems dull in comparison. Perhaps until today, because today was different, Matthew was different. But still her mother would not understand. How could her gentle contented mother have any inkling of her feelings? "Don't worry about me, Ma. I'm careful enough."

Her mother shrugs her shoulders in resignation, and shaking her head she mutters, "I hope so, Vi, I hope so."

Together they move a small sideboard away from the wall, and lifting out a loose block of stone, they place the bottles into the concealed hiding place, carefully replacing the sideboard and the lamp and odds and ends that had been stood upon it.

Violet breathes a sigh of relief. "Thank goodness that's out of sight. Now we can relax."

"No, Violet, that's where you are wrong, we can never relax. Times are changing and since the more desperate Venturers have become so violent, it isn't as easy as it used to be. A lot of folk have turned against us, which makes it a much more risky business. Also there are the new coastguard men to watch out for. You have to be more careful than ever before."

"Ma, you mustn't worry yourself. You don't understand the thrill I get from each adventure. But I am no feather-head, and I have too many tricks up my sleeve to get caught, have no fear on that score." For a moment she thinks her mother is going to burst with exasperation.

"Violet, you are so young and cocksure of yourself. How do you know what I will or will not understand? Do you think that I was never young like you?" She grabs up her towel and marches off to the backyard. As far as she is concerned the subject is closed.

Later that morning Violet picks up the basket of white linen that her mother has washed, and takes it down to the cove to lie on the pebbles to bleach in the sunshine. She is weighting the edges with larger pebbles, and feels the hot rays on her back. It is mid-July and the sea and sky are very blue. High above her, towards the cliffs of West Weares, a skylark is hovering, serenading its mate with its beautiful lyrical song. There is not a cloud to be seen and Violet is, for the moment, carefree. She stands, enjoying the heat.

Her thoughts are broken by a fisherman's shout. "In Ope! … Mackerel Straying! … In Ope! … It's swarming with 'em." The man is running and panting hard. "There are masses of 'em." He gestures to another who has joined him.

Her eyes lift northwards, her hands shielding them from the bright reflection of the sun, and she can see the familiar sign where a fustian jacket has been laid over the top of an oar, pushed down into the pebbles far enough to stand up.

The seine crew is assembling from all directions and the boat is quickly launched. Violet can see the turbulence created by the shoal as they flurry by in the sunlight and as she watches she tries to pick out Matthew among the men who are busy in their endeavour to trap the mackerel in their nets.

Then she sees him. He is in the boat with her father and three brothers. Matthew's grandfather, Jabe, and his sons are with the 'shore-arm'. The lerret crew row round the shoal in a wide semicircle and she watches her father paying out the seine as they go, until they have encompassed the shoal and the boat is ready to beach some way south of the other shoremen.

Violet is just completing her task as the boat approaches her, and the men leap ashore, quite used to the unavoidable soaking. Matthew is in the lead as they pull the boat to safety, and then heave on the seine, and the two crews labour towards each other, battling against the tide. She watches him carefully. He looks so fit, his muscles rippling as he heaves with the others on the heavy netting and she cannot help wondering how it would feel to have him hold her in his strong arms.

The net is coming in fast and furious, and as it comes nearer the shore there arises within it a frantic flurrying of silver-backed fish. The sunlight is glittering on their writhing wet bodies and there is jubilation all around; they must have got most of the shoal.

Violet's father calls her over, "Come and give us a hand, Vi."

She is delighted, able to enjoy again the company of Matthew, but also thrilled because at last her father has given her a chance to prove she can be as useful as the boys. She joins the men on the sun-baked shingle loading the fish into baskets to be humped up over the winter ridge for the fish tout.

The seabirds screech overhead and the hot sun scorches down on them. Occasionally a flagon of cider is passed around and Violet has her swig along with the men. Matthew remains silent.

The morning wears on and Violet's slim brown hands work speedily, the silver scales decorating her bare arms.

Nick Way, her father's friend, calls, "That's good work, Vi."

"It is an' all," another calls. Her father smiles, they all smile, except for Matthew.

She picks up a fully laden basket and moves it out of the way, up the beach further, returning with another empty one and settling this time right next to Matthew.

"Oh ah, prefer his company to mine do 'ee?" says Grandfer Stone.

Violet laughs, but feels her cheeks burning again. "'Ere, I think you'm got sommat there," says Violet's older brother Tom, nudging Bob beside him.

Matthew watches Violet's colour deepen and Bob adds, teasingly, "You been keeping that quiet, Matt."

Matthew retorts good-naturedly, "Leave off will ya, I ain't been keeping nothing quiet," adding only just above a mumble, "Chance 'ud be a fine thing."

Only Violet hears, and she is not sure she has heard right. She glances sideways at Matthew whose hands are working feverishly, but who, at last, returns her glance with a smile. She smiles back shyly, feeling so happy that she could suffer this back-breaking task even if it were to take all day. Nevertheless, the job is nearly finished and it is a relief to stand up and stretch the stiffness out of her limbs. It will be good, too, to wash the pungent smell of fish from her hands and change her stained pinny.

Violet leaves the men to carry the catch up the beach and she returns home with her empty wash basket feeling his eyes on her. She turns back but he has looked away, then he looks back again and his smile is gentle.

She spends the rest of the day doing chores for her mother and can hardly wait until tea is cleared away and she is free. She removes her apron and buttons her boots, and is off like a bird out into the fresh early evening air.

11

Even though it is nearly six in the evening the sun is still warm and the cloudless sky a deep blue. As she passes the chapel the small congregation are in full voice and the joyful music sings in her heart. She turns into Big Ope and sees her friend Molly Byatt, the barmaid at the Cove House Inn, running down the slope to greet her. Leisurely, they stroll up the slope between the fishermen's homes on the one side and the inn and cottages on the other. As they pass those lower down the slope they both smile to see a black and white cat sitting cleaning herself, discarded half-eaten fish heads lying around her while her three tiny kittens play hide and seek behind the tubs of geraniums and amongst the lobster pots.

Letty White is kneeling on her top step, her round rear twisting from side to side as she vigorously scrubs the steps of her cottage. Violet calls out cheerfully, "You need plenty of elbow grease there, Letty."

"Too true, Vi. I wish my Jack had got Oyster Cottage when he had the chance. I'd exchange their three steps for these eight any day."

"Maybe so, Letty, but you won't be saying that next November when the sea comes over again," says Molly.

"You're right there, Molly. I'll be only too glad of them then." Letty nods her head in agreement and returns to her task with renewed vigour.

Violet is thoughtful and saddened. "I wouldn't want a cottage built on the beach like these. I will want to go higher up out of harm's way."

"You'll get no argument from me, Vi. I lost my whole family the last time. 'Tis risky enough in the Cove House Inn, but at least once the shutters are closed the sea just washes right over us there. The memory of us all being trapped by the floods and then the house collapsing on us and killing both my parents still gives me nightmares. I was so lucky to be rescued alive."

"It doesn't seem possible that that was only six years ago and so many of our friends and neighbours were lost. The rescuers were all so brave, I remember watching Matthew's father as he carried old Mrs White to safety. I can still picture him as I watched from my bedroom window, striding up the slope and out of the flood, the huge waves still crashing all around them."

"I would have had to go to the poorhouse if it hadn't been for John and Elsie." Molly nods in the direction of the inn and as they both pass it they can hear the pots and pans being tidied by the kitchen maid.

"They were kind to take you in, Moll, but you do earn your keep and so they benefit too."

Having climbed the ridge, they can see the sea breaking gently against the pebbles and they both run down to the water's edge. Molly is a tall, slim girl, with unruly, curly blonde hair and blue eyes. Her features are not striking, but she has a special charm in the little creases of her smile and around her eyes which reflect a pleasant disposition. When standing side by side, Violet only reaches Molly's shoulders, but as she sits down next to her friend there is not much difference between them.

"I'm so tempted to bathe my toes in that cool, white water. I've been on the go all day," says Molly gazing at the breaking waves lapping at their boots.

"Well, go on then. It'll probably do them the world of good," giggles Violet.

Molly thinks for a second and then starts to remove her boots almost feverishly as if her life depends on it, making Violet laugh and then follow suit. They both squeal as their feet first touch the icy cold water, and then as they get used to it they delve deeper into the pebbles with their toes and enjoy the refreshing coolness as it washes over them.

"That's much better," says Molly, leaning back on her elbows and relaxing. "I've been looking forward to this all day."

"I know what you mean," says Violet, "It's lovely to be free of the chores at last." She too relaxes beside her friend.

"Moll, you didn't happen to see a Kimberlin about this morning, did you? A tall, well-dressed gent with dark hair and eyes?" She remembers his eyes particularly; they seemed to say so much. "He passed me by on a beautiful chestnut mare, when I was returning along the beach carrying loot from over Ham."

"You never were? Oh I've seen 'im all right. We've had him staying at the Cove House since Friday. He made me go all of a dither when he looked at me, him being so polite and handsome, but he didn't look at me very often," she giggled.

"What is he doing here?" asked Vi.

"He were after lodgings or summat." Molly pauses, "John Motyer reckons he's the new preventive man," she says with an air of importance.

"No," says Violet incredulously, "I might've guessed." So she had been right to be alarmed and the fear comes flooding back, but again she thinks of his eyes and they are suddenly so vivid in her mind it startles her.

She breathes deeply, and slowly the words come. "So he is destined to become the enemy. Father'll be interested in that," she says, pushing away the disturbing image. "I wonder when he'll be back."

"Dunno, time'll tell," says Molly resignedly, and they both lapse back into thoughtful silence.

"'Have you seen John Pearce and Robert Comben lately, Vi?" asks Molly.

"No I haven't, why?" says Violet, glad of the change of subject.

"Well, I saw them in Fortuneswell the other day, and they were making eyes at me. They were saying how pretty I was, and John carried my basket up to the dairy shop for me. I think maybe John is sweet on me, 'cause he were ever so nice." Violet has known for ages that Molly has a soft spot for John Pearce, but she had said nothing.

Molly has become flushed, "I told them I come up most days on errands for Ma'am, and I hope I'll see them again, 'cus Robert works for John's father in the mill and they was delivering flour down Underhill and gave me a ride back home in horse 'n cart. Must've saved me a half-hour."

Violet gives Molly a squeeze, "You lucky thing, Moll. You'll soon be walking out." They both laugh. "May I have the pleasure of your company this evening, Miss Molly?" Violet pretends she is John Pearce, and puts on a posh accent, as she imagines he might do. They both begin to giggle, when suddenly a voice makes them jump.

"Evening, Miss Violet, Miss Molly."

It is Matthew again, he looks so tall, standing on the ridge above them and they can see he is laughing at them. "Hello Matthew," says Violet, at the same time hearing the echo of Molly's greeting, and feeling foolish.

She watches him as he approaches and sits down close behind them, his eyes warm with amusement, but still scanning the ocean for that telltale patch of disturbed water where the mackerel will be found 'straying'. He picks up a pebble and lazily flicks his wrist. The flat stone skims the sea's surface jumping off it several times before its journey ends. "Saw the

Pearces going into chapel just now." The remark is over-casual and the look in his eyes betrays the fact that he has overheard their conversation.

Molly does not mind. She smiles. "Were John with them?" she asks.

"He were," says Matthew, with a grin.

"What's so funny?" laughs Molly, as she dries her feet in her petticoat.

Matthew shrugs, "Nothing that I know of," he says, still smiling.

Molly must have thought that two could play at that game for Matthew has not come alone to sit with them without some ulterior motive. As she puts on her boots she says, "Anyway I'm not staying here playing gooseberry. I've got to go and see your sister Hannah about summat. I'll see you tomorrow, Vi." She jumps up, adding mischievously, "Don't do anything I wouldn't do," and giggling, she leaves them both.

As soon as Molly has left them alone together, Violet suddenly feels overwhelmingly shy and, carefully avoiding Matthew's gaze, turns her attention to wiping her feet dry.

Matthew moves forward to sit beside her. Can he see how she is trembling? She feels him observing her as she lowers her eyes, engrossed in her task, and then he grows serious again. "Robert Comben were there too, if you're interested?"

"No, not I," she says, "I hardly know them, they live up top o' hill, they only know Molly 'cus Robert's her cousin."

"You know I well enough," says Matthew, his eyes looking directly into hers, saying far more than those few words had done.

Blast it, she is blushing again. She looks away, trying to hide it from him. It is easy enough to flirt with the boys, but what do you do when they respond? Still she feels his eyes on her, seeking out her own. She busies herself by attending further to her feet until eventually, feeling compelled to break the silence, she says the first thing that comes into her head. "Don't you think 'tis strange that the pebbles here are as big as potatoes and they're gradually smaller as we go along the beach, till they're just like gravel at West Bay?" Her observation is blurted out and her voice sounds tense even to her. Has he noticed?

Matthew grins, "Aye, it's a mystery all right, but I'm glad 'tis so. There's many a pitch black night I've put ashore and 'twas my only clue as to where we were to."

He moves even closer to her. So close that she feels the heat rise in her cheeks, her heartbeat becomes erratic and it is as if butterflies are fluttering in her stomach. She must pull herself together. She is being silly. There is no reason to be nervous of Matthew. She's known him always. Whatever has come over her? She concentrates her thoughts on the incessant noise of the breaking waves but they become louder and louder until they seem to roar inside her head. She fumbles for a flat pebble in order to play ducks and drakes, as Matthew had done. Her first pebble skims the waves and she faintly hears Matthew saying, "That were a good'n." Her hand closes over another. His hand covers hers and he pulls her towards him and kisses her tenderly.

It is her first kiss. She hadn't expected it and yet she'd been filled with anticipation. He is stirring feelings in her that are new and magical. She thinks that this must be what falling in love is all about and as she looks up into his eyes she is trembling.

He kisses her again, moving even closer and she feels his arms around her. She trusts him. Her eyes close excluding all else around them. Has Matthew closed his eyes too? She doesn't want to open them to reality, she wants to stay in this dream forever. His lips are soft and tender, her whole being fills with love, she returns his kisses willingly and when they stop her body is still crying out for more.

Some children come down to the shore to play. Matthew kisses her again gently, and then looking at the children, he turns to her smiling, a softness in his voice as he says, "Remember when we used to play tag?" His voice is husky. She cannot trust her own and so she just nods, conscious of his body close to hers. She listens as he talks of the morning's catch, but not of their feelings for one another and she is glad, it is too new and fragile a thing to put into words. Violet feels the gentle heat of Matthew's body through the fabric of his shirt, contrasting with the hard cold pebbles on which they sit and she leans against him, enjoying the manly feel of his muscles against her.

She listens to the rhythmic, tidal splashing of the breaking waves, swishing to and fro, accompanied by the squeals of delight from the children a short distance along the beach. The sun with its lingering warmth casts long shadows behind them. She feels safe and thinks again of the earlier events of the morning when Matthew had watched her encounter with the stranger.

She turns to look up at him. "You know that Kimberlin nearly frightened me to death this morning, I were concentrating so hard on where I trod I never heard him coming. He didn't half make me jump."

"I thought you were making light of it," says Matthew, studying her carefully. She lowers her eyes under his steady gaze, reluctant to show the extent of her conflicting feelings. "I have heard he might be the new riding officer, so for heaven's sake, Vi, be careful."

"That's what John Motyer said to Molly."

Matthew is silent for a while. "If he's coming back here to stay, we'll have to get more organised. Why, only last week there was an open battle in the Cove House Inn, between the Minister and a bloke from top o' hill." He chuckles as he pictures the irate man. "This bloke was fair put out 'cus he'd carefully balanced his keg of brandy inside his tall hat, all the way up the hill home from chapel, and when he finally relieves himself of his burden, he finds it is gone off! You know, 'stinkibus', so he is really indignant and is telling the Minister in no uncertain terms what he thought of him."

Violet is laughing as she pulls on her boots.

"I know it sounds funny but the thing is no one in there showed any caution at all." He looks serious now. "We're all too cocksure of ourselves. We got too used to old Taggart being a pushover. But this here Kimberlin don't look like no pushover to me. He's used to giving orders and having folks obey. My guess is we're in for a battle of wits, but he's going to have to be something special to get one over on us. I reckon we can show him a thing or two."

"He didn't say much to me, but I don't think he do miss much neither," says Violet. "Although he didn't discover my bottles he really looked hard at me, as if trying to see if I'd anything to hide." Again she remembers those eyes, so seductive and yet so sharp.

"Well," says Matthew, "we'll have to be ready for him if he's coming back to stay. We can't afford any blunders."

That is something she cannot bear to think of. Too many of her loved ones are at risk. They fall silent for a while, then Matthew stands up and holds out his hand for her, pulling her to her feet with ease, but even the feel of his fingers around hers cannot quieten the fear.

"Don't take any chances, Matthew. You must warn the others to take special care."

"We'll tread carefully, Vi, don't fret. No Kimberlin's got the better of us in the past and the sport can only sharpen our wits for the future. You'll see."

CHAPTER 2 *(November 1830)*

THE PREVENTIVE MAN

One morning early in November Violet is staring wistfully out of her bedroom window when she hears a knock at their front door, then her mother ushering Molly in and calling up to her, "Vi, Molly's here to see you."

"Tell her to come on up, Ma."

Violet is covering her bed with her patchwork quilt as Molly enters. "Hello Mol, just let me tidy this up then we can sit down." They both sit on the edge of the bed and Violet picks up her rag doll and fiddles with it.

"It is a lovely sunny morning out there, Vi, and surprisingly warm for the time of year."

"I know and I am really weary of doing boring chores in this fine weather while everyone else is outside enjoying the fresh air. I sometimes wish I had been a boy because my brothers get all the excitement and adventures."

"Oh Vi, I am so glad you were not a boy, besides if that was the case you wouldn't have fascinated Matthew, would you?"

"Maybe not, but I would be able to spend more time with him, wouldn't I?" They both laugh.

"How are you two getting along?"

"Oh Mol, he makes me so happy I cannot tell you. I feel excited whenever I see him and there are times when I actually tingle as he touches me. It is just so lovely believing that someone is always thinking of you and that somebody truly loves you."

"I have noticed and I am so pleased for you both. You look so happy when Matthew's around and he seems to have a more confident air about him too. Folk are bound to put two and two together."

"I think they have already. Me Ma and Pa have guessed since the boys started teasing me, and 'tis only a matter of time before the whole village knows."

"I have heard a few people gossiping, people like Auntie Sarah and some of our neighbours." Molly lowers her voice to a whisper, "Have you thought about doing 'you know what'?"

Violet gives a puzzled frown. "What?"

"You know." Molly's look is meaningful. "Following the custom, making sure you are well matched."

Violet blushes. "No! Not yet! I am too young to be caring for a baby, besides Matty wants to wait until he can provide for me."

"Well, this is the time to test him. Then if you fall you can get married. I wouldn't be hanging around with a catch like Matthew," Molly adds with a smile. "I am sure you could persuade him."

"A baby would be lovely." Violet smiles wistfully. "But I would really be tied down then. No, we are too young to start a family. Matthew's right, we need to get some savings behind us and a home of our own before we risk that."

"Well, I'm surprised that Matthew is in no hurry to claim his rights, but I suppose you do have plenty of time."

"In any case, he has already said to me that he has no doubts as to our being well suited. He just wants to provide a home for us first and I must say it is nice that he cares so much for our future and that he is trying to be sensible and doesn't want to take advantage of our island custom."

"That may be so, but I don't think I would hang around with John given the chance!" They both laugh at Molly's enthusiasm.

"Have you heard any more about the new preventive man?" asks Violet, eager to change the subject.

"No, not a mention, though I have noticed in the Cove House that the smugglers are all uneasy not knowing where they stand, and some have been laughing and joking in the hope that the government has forgotten that the Customs and Excise laws are not being properly enforced on Portland."

"Well, I must say 'tis odd."

"Well, at the moment I think they are all making hay while the sun shines," says Molly.

"I don't blame them."

Violet's mother calls up to them, "Would you and Molly like a something to eat?"

"Yes please, Ma." They both go downstairs.

The following morning there is a new wintry chill in the air. Violet is fetching the day's water and as she approaches the well she sees that Auntie Sarah, as everyone calls her, is filling her buckets, and Susan White and Annie Shaddick are also already waiting. These are two girls with whom Violet shares no affection. They are both three and four years her senior, and have always jeered and teased her as a child. They stick together like limpets, even out-doing each other in their spitefulness, seeking and finding the weak spots, though why it is she who has been their target she has never fully understood.

Today, as she fears, they are at it again, huddled together whispering and giggling, until Violet thinks she must have a mark on her face. Self-consciously she runs her hands through her hair, it is somewhat unruly as she has just washed and dried it by the fire before breakfast and it is as if it has a mind of its own. They smirk on seeing her unease, but she turns away.

Auntie Sarah looks at her sharply, then at the two girls. "Pay them no heed," she says quietly, "They're just jealous of thee, always will be; older than thee and no Matthew in sight for them. With your comely looks to compete with they know they don't stand a chance. You're like a thorn in their sides. Why, there's not a …"

The sound of hooves clattering on the cobbles cuts her short. All around silence falls. Violet watches as the horse stops at the well. It is so close that she can smell the leather of the saddle and the reins the rider holds loosely in his hands. Soft gentleman's hands with fingers long and fine.

"Would you mind telling me where I might find the Cove Cottages?" he asks the group. His voice is deep and earthy.

She shades her eyes from the glare of the sun. Now she can see his face and she recognises the man from the beach. As his eyes meet hers she feels a heat rise in her, a heat which grows fierce. She can see nothing else, and she can hear nothing else. There is only his eyes on hers, eyes that seem to penetrate the soul. She can hardly breathe, her legs feel weak.

Then Annie Shaddick pushes her aside. "I can show ya' if ya' like, 'tis only just round back o' here," she blurts out.

The stranger's dark eyes do not move from Violet. "Could you spare a little water for a thirsting man?" he asks her and as he speaks his eyes linger on her lips.

Almost without knowing she lowers her bucket into the well. Her hair falls across her face as she hauls back the bucket, heavy with water, and now her breathing is more even; the heat is dying. Her hand shakes as she fills her ladle and passes it up to him. All the time he watches her.

"Thank you," he says. Then his lips are on the ladle, his throat moving as he swallows, but his eyes still hold hers, and then he asks her name. The other women remain silent.

"Violet Allen, Sir," she says, her voice not sounding like her own.

"Thank you, Violet Allen," he says, handing back the ladle. "Richard Dryer's the name; I'm so pleased to make your acquaintance." He lifts his tall hat as he had done that morning on the beach and only now does he turn to the others, and she feels the loss of the moment as his attention leaves her.

Dryer strokes his horse as he asks Annie and Susan, "Which of you two young ladies know the Cove Cottages?"

"Why, we both do, Sir," says Annie, moving closer to him, shouldering Violet aside. "But I can show ya just as quick as tell ya, 'tis this way, Sir." She takes the horse's reins, lifts her skirt and leads the way through Brandy Lane and up to the cottages above and behind Violet's home.

Richard Dryer does not turn to Violet again but she watches him until he disappears from view. Susan says, lifting her yoke, "There's folk who'll want to hear of this," and she hurries off with the news.

Violet breathes deeply. What is happening to her? She looks at the ladle she still holds and touches the rim where his lips have been.

Auntie Sarah speaks then, and her voice is grave. "I fear he brings trouble, that one. I'd be giving him a wide berth, if I were thee. Annie Shaddick'd give her eye-teeth to get a man like him, but he were eyeing thee not she, so beware."

She tries to brush the matter aside, to make light of her feelings, "He were only acting curious, that's all, Auntie Sarah, it don't mean nothing." But she really doesn't want to let go of the memory of his eyes on hers, his soft lips, or the heat which has all but consumed her.

"Maybe so but I should keep out of his way if I were thee. He looks like a gent who's used to getting what he wants. Anyways, I'll be seeing thee. Remember me to ya Ma and Pa," and she too, turns to home.

Violet watches her walk along the road past the familiar cottages and it all seems so normal. She looks back to where Richard Dryer had ridden and it is as if she has imagined it all. But her heart even now beats speedily.

Maybe it is the fear of what the stranger represents that sets her pulses racing. Yes, that must be it. She picks up her pails and sets off home. She must see Matthew and tell him, but then she looks over her shoulder again and knows that she longs to feel again as Dryer has made her feel, and hates herself for her disloyalty.

On reaching home, Violet takes the water inside to the kitchen. She has left her mother boiling crabs and 'long oysters' in the backyard, and the pungent smell hits her as she enters the cottage. "They're ready, Vi," calls her mother.

He'll think I'm a common fishwife if he gets a whiff of this lot, she thinks. She doesn't remove her bonnet and cloak, but fills her big basket and covers it with a white cloth, and her mother gives her a florin.

"Get us a quarter peck loaf of bread, half a peck of pecked apples, some flour, a pat o' butter, some dripping and six candles on your return with the empty basket, Vi," instructs her mother, "and be careful with the change."

"I am always careful, Ma." Violet smiles. She is making for the door when she says, making an effort to sound casual, "Oh Ma, that Kimberlin's back, and he was looking for Cove Cottages. Seems he's taking Taggart's old place. I think he must have remembered me from the beach in the summer because he didn't half stare, but anyway he was very polite. You should have seen Annie Shaddick breaking her neck to show him up to Taggart's cottage. She nearly knocked me to the ground in her haste." Violet chuckles to herself as she turns to leave.

Her mother looks up at her, surprised at the animation in her daughter's face as she tells her this latest bit of news. "That man is a bit too close for comfort." She nods in the direction of Taggart's old house above and behind their cottage where she can see Mrs Shaddick cleaning the salt deposits from the windows. "I suppose poor old Annie Taggart's been put in the poorhouse now. 'Tis what many of us 'll come to no doubt."

"Annie didn't waste any time, did she?"

"Well, good for them, Mrs Shaddick has a lot of mouths to feed."

"I don't know how she will manage this new job as well as the laundry she takes in," says Violet.

"Well, that lazy Annie will have to do a bit more to help her, won't she?"

"I am sure she will have no hesitation in

volunteering for that! Anyway I must get on, I will try not to be too long."

Violet's mother shakes her head sadly as she turns, tiredness showing in her movements as well as in her eyes. Her hairstyle, essentially practical, is drawn into a knot at the nape of her neck, emphasising the lines of age on her brow. The romance and vitality of youth has long left Mary Allen, who is well into her fifties. She fingers a swathe of deep red material. Her husband would occasionally surprise her with a little gift of perfume, or some material he'd come across, usually French, but Mary never asked questions, though a little glint would come into her eyes and she might plant a reserved peck on his rough cheek. This is the only hint of their once vibrant emotions, now dulled with poverty, hard work and the natural erosion of time.

She hangs up the dress she is making for Mrs Motyer. A dressmaker on a small scale, she has been teaching Violet since she was tiny. It is a great help having Violet so good with her hands too, but now when they work together in the evenings they will have to keep an eye out for Dryer, and when the men are on a trip they will have to make sure the signalling candles are near to hand. She continues her cleaning and then begins baking some dough cake to try and distract herself from the thought of the risks that they constantly take.

Her Violet has often lit the three warning candles at her bedroom window when Taggart was about, and when they thought the riding officer was abed a single candle was left, to show that it was safe once more.

She'd go before sunrise, sometimes alone and sometimes with help, and haul in the rafted casks of spirits, which were strung along a weighted rope and then sunk in shallow water, with markers to show the place. A French sloop named 'L Aimable Vertu' of about 35 tons, with a master known to them as French Jack, usually used this method and left the contraband at an agreed place along Ham, the eastern beach of the causeway, bordering the Portland Roads.

Otherwise Violet met her father as he beached off the West Bay and hid as many pounds of Bohea tea, ells of pepper and even pounds of coffee berries about her person, in the pockets of her petticoats and in the lining of her padded corsage, as she could. These tasks were once accomplished by Mary herself, now she only worries until Violet returns safely.

Many of the Chiswell fishermen, including Matthew's family and her menfolk, actually row over to France, or they may rendezvous with the French sloops out at sea, but they always stand off until the coast is clear in all respects, depending on an elaborate system of signalling and absolute loyalty and secrecy; never making any method too much of a habit.

The casks are often taken straight to the Cove House Inn, and it is there that much of the dealing is done. John Motyer, the landlord, takes what he wants for his stock and with any strangers free to come and go at will he is able to carry on an illicit trade with a perfect cover. It certainly isn't John Motyer who takes most of the risks, though he surely takes most of the profits. Mary pokes the fire with more force, raising the temperature of the oven.

When Violet returns home it is past noon. They

divide some bread and cheese between them and with a flagon of cider they enjoy their meal, sitting together by the fire. "It's turned real chilly, Ma," she says. "The wind's getting up a good'n."

"Ay, 'tis typical, they're expecting a good haul tonight too. They're planning to stand off in the Roads ready and waiting for Jack. He's due to meet them about nine."

"Well, I suppose 'tis one good thing, the new man won't be expecting a run on a night such as this," says Violet, "that is if the wind hasn't dropped none."

"True," her mother agrees. "You didn't say much to me earlier. What's he like, this Kimberlin?"

Violet stares into the flames. The very mention of the man sets up such confusion. She struggles to keep her voice steady. "Well, he introduced himself to me as Richard Dryer." Her voice is barely above a whisper, "But as you know, both times I've met with him he has been looking down at me from his horse and so he looks to be very tall."

She swallows and still doesn't look at her mother. "I think he's rather quick-witted and so our men must be on their guard." She pauses, and for a moment instead of Dryer she clearly sees Matthew, but then it is Dryer again and she forces herself on, her voice still quiet.

"He has dark hair, almost black, and sharp, dark eyes – must be brown, I suppose. He has a wicked grin too, like a gambler with something up his sleeve. You know what I mean. His clothes are of the best-quality materials, and he wears a tall hat and soft leather riding boots – no whip – he doesn't use a whip, and he has a very low, soft voice." She glances up.

Her mother is smiling to herself. "Hmm, you took it all in then," her mother says.

"Well, I have met him twice now, Ma!" she says defensively.

"Yes, well with any luck he'll be resting after his journey, and won't start in earnest 'til the morrow." Her mother gets up to put more fuel on the fire. "At least then they'll only have the old enemy, the weather, to worry about." Some smoke puffs out into the room as the cold clot lands with a gust of air. "You'd best be collecting more shen for the fire tomorrow, we be getting low." The two women spend the rest of the afternoon sewing dowlas shifts for the poorhouse girls.

At about seven o'clock Violet dresses for the cold, takes up her lantern and leaves to go to Matthew's house, which is set at right angles to Brandy Row, alongside the chapel. She is making a lace cap for her mother's Christmas present, and as Matthew's mother is an expert lace maker she has agreed to help her. This evening Matthew is attending a Court Leet meeting with his father at the George Inn at Reforne, but she wants to see him, and so she leaves earlier; but Matthew and his father are already on their way to the meeting.

"Why, there's a sight for sore eyes," says Edward Stone, with a grin. She blushes. She still cannot get used to the older men treating her as a woman, she has been 'little Vi' so long.

"Thank you, Mr Stone," she laughs, as though he has made a joke. "You're not going to the meeting already, are you?" She looks sadly at Matthew and wonders if he has heard about the return of the Kimberlin.

"I'm afraid so."

"Maybe we'll see you later."

"I doubt we'll be back in time, Vi, but I'll call

on you tomorrow." He grins, obviously uncomfortable with his father standing by, and then he gives her a wink and they part reluctantly.

"Bye," she calls, and lifts her lamp higher. It is getting very windy and her cloak and skirts are flapping so wildly that she is relieved when Matthew's sister, Hannah, answers her knock and lets her in.

"Gosh, 'tis blowing a gale out there," Violet says, as the door closes on the howling wind.

Hannah takes the lantern, "I'll hang it up."

Violet removes her cloak and follows Hannah into the warm and cosy parlour, where she is greeted cheerfully by Johnny and his mother. Hannah lifts the cat off the sofa and puts it down on the rug beside Johnny, where it stretches lazily.

"There you are, Vi, you can sit next to Ma now."

"Thank you," says Violet, as she settles herself down next to Mrs Stone in front of the fire and takes up where she had previously left off with her lacework. Hannah stirs the driftwood into flame and then returns to knitting the Guernsey for her brother. Mrs Stone is busy with her own lacework but ready to help should Violet get into difficulties.

They have all been expecting her and Hannah cannot wait any longer before telling Violet her news. "Vi, I saw Robert Comben this morning and what do you think of this? He has asked me to go to the Fair at Reeve Plot with him on Thursday. John and Molly are going together too. I asked Matty, and he says he's going to ask you, Vi."

"Well, of course he will," interjects Mrs Stone. "Who else will he be going with, when they are walking out together?" she says, chuckling to herself.

"I only meant it will be nice for all of us to go together, Ma," says Hannah, a little peevishly. "It'll be good fun, won't it?" she says excitedly to Violet.

"I wouldn't miss it for the world," says Violet, infected with Hannah's enthusiasm.

"Remember last year, when old Dappy went to see Madame Christabel, and she said he were going to move house, and he were telling everyone it were rubbish, and when he got home drunk as a Lord his missus had chucked all his belongings on doorstep, and locked him out. He were hopping mad."

They are all laughing now, remembering his purple face, and how he had been staggering about under the bedroom window. "Then his wife emptied her wash bowl over him, and shouted, 'Stop yer hollering and bugger off, you ain't stopping here no more,' and slammed the window shut." Their laughter becomes uncontrollable.

"He just stood there, dripping wet," blurts out Hannah, between giggles, "With everyone staring at him as they went home from the fair. It were the funniest thing I ever saw." She sighs, hand on her heart where her laughing has given her a stitch.

"Never could hold his drink, couldn't Dappy," says Mrs Stone, "but it never made no difference. He's still the same, and she had him back after a week with his sister."

"She were right though, weren't she? ... Madame Christabel," says Violet with a serious expression. "He did move house." Then she bursts out laughing again, adding merrily, "For a week."

They are all smiling again at the picture it presents. "It always is loads of fun, everyone lets their hair down and enjoys themselves, children and all can join in, can't they, Johnny?" Violet winks at young Johnny, who is still sitting on the hearthrug quietly whittling a piece of driftwood.

"'Tis time you are to bed, young man," says his mother. "You'd best be getting some supper now."

Violet looks apologetically at Johnny for drawing attention to him, knowing how it felt to be dismissed when company was around, but he just smiles and does as he is told.

Hannah goes to fetch some mead while Johnny is preparing for bed. Mrs Stone asks Violet, "Have you and Matthew made any plans for your future together?"

Violet blushes, "No, Mrs Stone, not really. Matthew wants to save up his money so we will have a good start in life when we do get wed."

"That's just like our Matthew; everything has to be done just right. He won't make a move 'til he's certain of the outcome, always been the same he has. Even when he were just a nipper he'd save up all his pocket money all year and divide it up equally between all the family to make sure he'd have enough come Christmas time. You would not believe the pleasure he got from working it all out. I don't know who he gets it from 'cus neither me, nor his Pa's the same … We've never got two ha'pennies to rub together, that's the problem." She chuckles again and Violet smiles.

"He's a good boy though, Violet. He'll make you a good husband. He wouldn't hurt a fly wouldn't our Matthew. I don't know how his Pa would've managed lately without his help. He's that proud of him. Why, only yesterday they came in after a long day's work and Ed says to me, "He's a damn hard grafter that son of ours. He hasn't stopped since sun-up. We've got a bumper catch to show for it and all," he says.

Violet nods, it is one of the things that attracted her to Matthew. He is more of a man that the other lads, who spend their time larking about and drinking too much ale. She knows he has ambition and that he knows the only way he'll ever get anywhere in this life is by his own hard labour.

Hannah brings in their glasses of mead, "I wonder how the meeting's going?" she says, as she hands them around.

"I bumped into Matty and his father on my way here," says Violet.

"Talking of bumping into folk, I ran into that Kimberlin in Fortuneswell today. He'd been shopping I guess, 'cus he were all loaded up with pots and pans and stuff and Annie Shaddick were tagging along behind him carrying a wooden yoke and pails filled with candles and a lamp and all sorts. She looked as proud as you like, even though he were treating her like some skivvy – silly ha'p'orth."

"What did you think of him?" asks Violet, looking up from her lacework.

"Well, he's obviously a toff and far too handsome for my taste. I wouldn't trust him an inch if he were my man, that's for sure."

They all laugh.

"Well, good looks don't necessarily go with a good brain, so let's be hoping he don't turn out to be too clever for his own good," says Mrs Stone sagely.

"Oh blast, I've gone wrong now," says Violet.

"Let's see then, ducky," says Mrs Stone. Violet hands her lacework to Matthew's mother. "Don't fret, there's nothing what can't be put to rights." Mrs Stone sorts out the problem and then they spend the rest of the evening chatting and anticipating the events forthcoming. It is about nine o'clock when Violet has completed one corner of her work and her eyes ache.

"A cup of tea and some cake?" asks Hannah, laying aside her work.

"That will be lovely. Then I must go."

Half an hour later Violet closes the front door behind her and steps out into the wind. As she turns towards her home someone steps out of the shadows of Brandy Lane.

In the cottage that Richard Dryer is renting, there is a coal fire burning and some kind of order is now apparent.

The two Shaddick women have been cleaning and working in the cottage all day and the girl Annie has helped him stock the place with necessities. He has purchased candles and holders, some coal and a tinderbox, an old oil lamp, with which he is particularly pleased for it is similar to one that his mother always used to read by; also a lantern, a wooden yoke and two pails, some bedding and a jug and bowl set, and lastly, an assortment of cooking pots and some food.

The wagon of furniture arrived four hours after he had, and the waggoner helped him in with it. It was very basic – for the bedroom, a double bed with brass bedstead and a feather mattress, a Spanish oak armoire, and a tallboy and coffer, both also in oak. He places the coffer under the window-ledge and on it he rests his jug and wash bowl; then he puts a small brass carriage clock and a chamber stick upon the tallboy, and he gazes at the clock, lost in thought, before finally going downstairs.

He enters the living room through a latched door at the side of the large fireplace and bread-proving ovens. Standing there, he studies the layout of his parlour, and is almost satisfied with the overall effect, but something isn't quite right. He adjusts the angle of the two armchairs in relation to the fireplace, then flicks a duster over the surface of the gateleg table and the davenport in the corner.

"There, that's better," he murmurs aloud.

Dryer sits in an armchair smoking his pipe, with his feet resting on the fender. Yes, it is better. The dancing flames create shadows on the wall and the carved wood of the oak dresser behind him. He relaxes. The fire crackles and now the violet-eyed beauty from the beach comes into his mind. He looks across at the empty chair opposite and feels restless. He sucks on his pipe; then looks again at the chair. God, it was as though he could not drag his eyes from hers this morning. He leans back in his chair closing his eyes, picturing her. A log spits. He pushes his hand through his hair and gets to his feet, unable to sit still. He walks across to his davenport, opens the drawer and takes out an ornate casket. Placing it beside him he sits down again by the fireside.

On one side of the larger container there is a separate mahogany box that is locked, and after he has sorted through the smaller items he finds the key. He removes one of a pair of Henry Nock flintlock duelling pistols. The walnut stock has a chequered grip with a rounded butt. It feels heavy in his hands and lovingly he runs his fingers over the barrel and the leafy gold engraving on the lock plate. Carefully he returns it, laying it opposite its twin and relocking the case.

He then thumbs through the other items, letting the memories back into his life, into his new home: a beautifully engraved pocket watch, a lady's diamond cluster ring, two locks of hair, and some kind of receipt. There are also some hand-crafted enamel buttons, and an old penknife. His expression saddens further as he takes out two folded sheets of paper. He studies the letters written in a neat hand, and having read them several times he returns them to the sanctity of the box. He sighs and swallows, trying to dispel the pain of the lump in his throat, to no avail.

Eventually he gets up from his seat and returns the casket to the bottom drawer. He knocks out his pipe into the fireplace and puts it in his pocket. Having poked at the fire, he goes into the kitchen, takes down his lantern and lights it. He dons his cloak, tall hat and scarf, and taking up his lantern he leaves, heading for the Cove House Inn. He has to dispel this melancholy mood somehow.

'My God it's blowing tonight,' he thinks, as he braces himself against the wind that is whistling up through Brandy Lane. The fine salty mist that it carries numbs the flesh on his face, and he hangs on to his hat with his free hand as he goes. On entering Chiswell, he sees immediately the billowing cloak and petticoats of a woman as she too enters the same street, by the chapel. He pauses. It is the girl from the beach. He turns to follow.

Violet recognises Dryer immediately and her footsteps falter, her heart races, the wind tears at her and the sea seems to roar inside her head. A chill of fear paralyses her. She must delay him, for her father's sake, and all else flies from her mind. She slows her pace, allowing him to gain on her, and then she turns; she will have to shout in this wind.

"Good evening, Sir," she cries, as loud as she can.

"Why, it's Miss Allen is it not?" says he, "what brings you out on a night such as this?"

"I've been visiting," she answers. "You seem to have lost your direction, Sir. There is nothing beyond Brandy Row. Can I help you?"

"I was looking for the opening that leads on to

the beach and to the Cove House Inn, but I must have taken the wrong turn. Fortunately I see now that I have not chosen unwisely, just delayed a little my original destination." He moves closer to her because the wind is snatching their words and spiralling them upwards into the night, and he adds, "It's not wise for a lovely young maiden like yourself to be out unescorted at this time of night. However, it will indeed give me great pleasure if you will allow me to see you to your home."

Violet has visions of her father and brothers struggling in this terrible wind with the latest haul and the helpers that could get caught red-handed if he were to arrive at the inn right now. She takes the arm that he offers for the small distance to her home.

"Thank you, Sir, though there's no real need to fret on my account. I'm quite safe among friends here. 'Tis only Kimberlins that bring trouble to our island."

"Kimberlins?" he queries.

"Strangers, Sir; sailors and such like, mostly over to Castletown. They don't often get around this way." She thinks it wise to change the subject. "Have you settled yourself in, Sir?" she asks.

"Yes, I am greatly pleased with today's progress, Violet; I have most essentials arranged, although I need a couple of rugs and some cutlery, and I will have to get some curtains made as soon as possible."

Violet goes quiet as she thinks about this. Should she, or shouldn't she? Her heart begins to thump. "Well, begging your pardon, Sir, but me Ma and I, well we could make your curtains for you, if you'd consider it, Sir."

Dryer cannot believe his ears, "Yes, indeed I will. I should like that very much. Maybe I could discuss it with your mother?" He stops and is looking at her expectantly.

"What, now, Sir?" she says with dismay. "Tonight, Sir?"

"Well, it is rather urgent, Violet, but if it is inconvenient I could call tomorrow."

Violet considers quickly. She must keep him away from the beach. "No, it will be all right. Mother won't mind. I see the lamp's still lit. Come on in. She is waiting up for me."

They pass two more doors and then Violet stops. "This is our house, Sir."

Violet opens the front door. "Mother, I've a visitor," she calls from the hallway, taking off her cloak and bonnet, and hanging up the lanterns. "Ma, it's Mr Dryer," she warns as she opens the door from the passage.

Violet's mother stands up as Dryer enters the living room. She looks flustered as she puts her scissors and pincushion into her box and says, "Pleased to meet you, Sir. I didn't expect callers at this time of night, won't you take a seat?"

Mrs Allen gives Violet a strange questioning look, and her daughter shakes her head slightly. "I bumped into Mr Dryer a minute ago, Ma, he took the wrong direction for the Cove House, but he were saying he were needing some curtains made. So I thought he'd better come in and see you, Ma."

Her mother smiles, understanding in the look she gives Violet; then she turns to her guest. "Well, Mr Dryer, I could call round sometime tomorrow, and measure the windows …"

As they discuss the details, and while Dryer is talking to her mother, Violet is able to study him. She guesses he must be around six and twenty years, his dark hair is wavy and, she had been right, he is at least six foot tall with broad shoulders, his muscles those of a mature man. She is not surprised everyone quite naturally addresses him as 'Sir', a gentleman by birth, he has that kind of an air about him. But what brought him to this island alone?

"… Fine, ten o'clock tomorrow morning then, sorry to intrude late in the evening, but I am sure you understand I am eager to get the cottage sorted out. Thank you for your trouble and goodnight to you, Mrs Allen."

He is turning to Violet and she opens the door to the passage, where he takes up his lantern and steps out into the darkness.

"Goodnight, Violet, thank you for your help." He smiles at her.

She says simply, "Goodnight, Mr Dryer," and closes the door behind him, then pauses to compose herself. Her mother calls, "Remember the candles."

She runs upstairs to light the candles in the window and watches the dim light bobbing along Brandy Row. Then her heart jumps, because just behind it is another lantern, and two shadowy figures. It is Matthew and his father. They must have seen Dryer leaving their cottage. Whatever will Matthew think?

Matthew is boiling with indignation. "What in hell's name is he doing at our Violet's at this time of night?" He is furious.

"Steady now, lad," says his father. "We don't know much about the man, but we know Violet better than to think bad of her, so just you hold your horses and come on with me now. I think we deserve a drink after all that talking, don't you?"

Matthew narrows his eyes and watches Dryer as he strides up Big Ope ahead of them, feeling his father's restraining hand on his arm. He watches the shaft of light appear and disappear as Dryer enters the Cove House Inn.

"I'll kill him," he curses.

"Now you keep a still tongue, d'you hear me," says his father. "Just watch and learn, and say nowt 'til you've got good reason. You don't want an enemy without good cause, Matthew. If there's good cause you'll have plenty behind you."

Matthew bursts open the door with the wind and his father behind him, and Edward Stone has trouble closing the great heavy door against the gale.

The bar is full of the menfolk of Chiswell. The atmosphere is smoky, both from the fire and the clay pipes several of the men are drawing on. There is a group in one corner playing shove ha'penny, Jabe Stone and the older men, still dressed in their working smocks, in another group playing cribbage. Jabe's web-footed dog Skipper is lying at his feet. The men drinking at the bar are chatting and Dryer is ordering himself a pint of ale.

They all look up as Matthew and his father enter. Skipper gets up to greet the two fishermen, nuzzling them until they pat him affectionately, then he returns to lie down beside his master again. Joseph Flew and Violet's father, who are at the bar, ask how the meeting went.

"Same as usual," says Mr Stone, cynically, "a lot of jawing and nothing doing; talk about fund raising, and complaints about the tolls and the danger of the crossing, and the like, but it's not enough on its own. We need government support, and we won't get it without proper recognition."

Matthew remains silent. He watches Dryer down half of his pint, and he orders one each for himself and his father. "What you having?" he asks Robert Allen and Jo Flew.

"Same again please, John." They hand their mugs to John Motyer, across the bar.

Dryer moves over to the fireplace and starts a

conversation with Captain Dick and old Tom Comben. Molly is going among the tables with a cloth, collecting the empty mugs and wiping the tabletops. Matthew smiles and gives her a wink and she puts the mugs on the bar and leaves by a side door.

A few minutes pass and Violet's brothers burst in through the front entrance, and Bob leans his back against the door to close it against the November wind. They join those at the bar and are soon deep in conversation with Mr Stone. Matthew takes this opportunity to step across to the fire and warm his hands.

"Evening. Dryer, isn't it?" says Matthew, in a low voice.

"Yes?" Dryer answers warily.

"I believe I saw you leaving the house of the Allen family as I were returning from the meeting up top o' hill?"

"So?" His tone raises a little.

"Well, might I ask you what your business is with them at this time of night?"

"What's it to do with you?" Dryer is angry now.

"I happen to be intending marriage with Violet, and I don't like what I saw."

"Now you just watch your tongue, young fellow; I was conducting personal business with her mother, and I don't like your inference." His voice is raised now and has caught the attention of the men at the bar.

Matthew points at Dryer and says, with emphasis, "You just make sure any further business you have in that quarter is conducted in daylight, got my meaning?" and he stalks back to the bar.

Well, damn your impudence you young upstart, thinks Dryer, disappointment and fury surging through him. She belongs to another man who has just had the last say in front of the whole bar. He looks around the room. The groups are resuming their previous conversation and occupations, but Dryer senses they are keeping a watchful eye.

Well he, Richard Dryer, is a fool. He has trodden on that lad's toes and now there is no hope of the slightest pretence of friendship with any of them, least of all with Violet. He cannot let that snip of a lad get away with this. He needs an ally, but this scene has alienated them on two fronts and surely must have put paid to any hope of that.

Then he notices a man sitting apart from the rest. He is small and vulpine to look at, and is even more shabbily dressed than the others. He has been trying unsuccessfully to light a clay pipe, obviously with inferior tobacco, and he has a nearly empty glass, which has been so for some time. Dryer thinks, he could be the weak link I'm looking for, it's worth a try. He sits down near at hand and offers the man some tobacco from his pouch.

"Thank 'ee kindly, Sir," says the humble little fellow, apparently used to servility.

Dryer knows he must be careful not to make anything too obvious, and thinks, 'I'll make my approach out of view of these cunning fellows'. He sits for some time watching and listening, determined to remember names and faces and linking families and friends. When eventually he empties his tankard he boldly walks out and calls, "Thank you, Landlord," over his shoulder.

He turns up his collar against the wind, having finally managed with both hands to pull the door closed, and taking up his unlit lantern he walks around the side of the inn.

The moon is casting changing shafts of light across his path as the fleeting clouds rapidly hide and then reveal it. He stands hidden in the shelter of a partly demolished building he has noticed further along the beach and watches the men leaving for their beds, when the inn gradually empties.

He does not have to wait long before the shabby little man leaves, and Dryer follows at a safe distance. He is making for the north end of Chiswell, and Dryer is about to make his presence known when he turns into Dark Ope. Ideal, he thinks, and hurries after him.

Dryer sees the man ahead of him, pushing on between the narrow walls of Dark Ope, which cut out the noise of the wind. Dryer kicks a stone. The man presses his body back against the wall and freezes.

Dryer creeps quietly forward, and rushes at the last minute, clasping a hand over the man's mouth, whispering, "I mean you no harm, just thought it might be worth your while if you could give me any information that a customs official might find worth paying for, just between you and me mind. I'm sorry if I caused you any anguish, it's just that I could do with a friend in the camp, so to speak, do you understand my drift?"

Dryer releases his grip. The man takes a deep breath saying, "How can I help 'ee, Gov? I know nothing."

"Well, just think on. If you do get to hear of any unlawful shipments being landed, there's a golden guinea in it for you, for any tip that leads to a haul. Is it a deal?"

"Oh, aye, Sir, I'm your man, Sir," says the thin croaky voice.

"I've taken Taggart's old place, but I'll not want you coming there. If you've anything to tell me, be sitting at the fireside in the Cove House, and knock your pipe out on the hearth like this." Dryer examples five knocks to a rhythm. "I'll meet you within a quarter of an hour here, in this passageway. I'll be in there most nights just in case you've anything." And

45

with that he says, "Goodnight to you," and carries on through Dark Ope and into the Square.

Dryer turns right towards his home and, stumbling over the potholed cart track, he thinks bitterly of Violet in the arms of Matthew Stone. He cannot let that happen. He grimaces as he makes a silent vow that he will not let that happen. "I'll pay you back in more ways than one. Just you wait and see, Matthew Stone. I'm not as stupid as I look and you've got 'Smuggler' written all over you."

Jacky Sparrow, the little fox-like man, is always in need of money. He has a family to support and like the other quarrymen of Portland he too gets paid annually, for a good deal of the year living on credit, paying higher than market prices for his flour, and owing money from one year to the next.

He is in debt at the inn too, but on the fourth of November it is pay day, and John Motyer is an understanding man if you are fair with him. He doesn't mind you running up a bill; he knows who he can trust, and Jacky Sparrow is one of them. In three days' time Jacky will settle his debts, and on the fifth of November, with everyone else, he will pay his quit rent to the Reeve, a year in advance and who knows what the following year might hold? Maybe another boat will come in, but not this one; this one isn't for him.

He re-enters the Cove House by the side door, and two hours later he leaves the same way. He is going to enjoy this game. That land shark Dryer is a poor judge of character, and Jacky Sparrow is not a little offended by it.

"I'll show him I'm no turncoat," he mutters, angrily.

CHAPTER 3 *(November 1830)*

THE REEVE FAIR

Violet awakes the following morning feeling anxious. Had Matthew recognised the stranger leaving their house last night and if so, how has he reacted? She jumps out of bed and covers it with the blankets and patchwork quilt that she helped her mother to make. Hastily she washes, dresses and runs downstairs for breakfast.

Her mother, who has already cleaned out the grate and lit the copper, is cooking some porridge. Violet puts the kettle on the fire to make a pot of tea, and is laying out the cups when her father joins them. He has on his baggy black trousers with the braces hanging down, but he is bare-chested. She wonders if he knows about Dryer's visit.

He gives her and her mother a quick peck on the cheek each. "Morning," he says and goes out into the yard for a cold swill from the water butt. He returns moments later, picks up a towel, dries himself and puts on his flannel vest. Then he puts his arms through his braces, over the top he throws on a light-grey sailcloth smock and he sits down to his bowl of oats. Violet relaxes.

"I believe Matthew fell out with our friend the Kimberlin last night," he says.

Her stomach churns.

"Oh, what was that in aid of then?" says her mother, as she dishes up a bowl for Violet.

"I dunno, the boys said it was all over in a jiffy,

but it weren't too friendly, that's all I know." He takes a mouthful of food and Violet sits down beside him, but cannot drink her tea. Whatever has happened between them?

Three more bowls of steaming porridge are laid on the table as her brothers join them.

"That Kimberlin called here last night to ask if we'd do him some curtains," says her mother. "He met our Violet returning home from Matthew's and she was clever enough to keep him talking and bring him back with her to keep him away from the beach."

Her father looks expectantly at her. An explanation is called for.

"Well, it was about nine-thirty and I was worried he'd bump into you at an awkward time, so I sort of went along with him to delay him, but … I think it is that what upset Matty … 'cus he saw him as he was leaving our house."

Her father frowns. "I'm not surprised. Have you taken leave of your senses?"

She remains silent.

"Whatever came over you, Violet?"

"She was only trying to help, Robert," says her mother.

"That's not the point. We don't know this man. We don't know what he is capable of and until we do, I think it wise that you don't leave home after dark unless accompanied by myself, or one of your brothers, or since you are courting, Matthew. Is that understood?"

"Yes, father," she says. "I'm sorry; it was on the spur of the moment. I didn't think about what folks 'ud make of it."

"It's not what folks make of it," says her father with exasperation. "It's what kind of trouble you could get yourself into. Don't you see, you're a young girl, and a temptation to any man, let alone a Kimberlin."

Violet looks at her father, at his weather-beaten face, his thick salt-and-pepper, greying hair and bushy sideburns and his troubled blue-grey eyes, and she knows he is genuinely worried for her, "I'm sorry, father, it won't happen again, but what would you have done if you had been me?"

"I would probably have tried to distract him in some way too, but I'm in a different position because I'm not a young woman."

"And that's why it wouldn't have worked half as well," laughs Tom.

Their father shrugs. "I know you were only trying to help, love, but I'm not just laying down the law, it's for your own good and you know that really, don't you?"

"Yes, of course I do, Father, but don't you worry, it won't happen again."

She finishes her breakfast and goes out into the backyard to fetch her yoke and buckets; then wraps her shawl around her, buttons her boots and goes to fetch the day's fresh water. If Matthew actually had words with Richard Dryer, she is in real trouble.

There is no one at the well and she is glad that she doesn't have to stand in line, it is so cold. As she lowers her buckets, she sees Matthew approaching and feels uncomfortable for the first time since she has known him. He is eager for a confrontation, his eyes searching her face, and she braces herself.

"Morning, Violet." His voice is civil, but he is unsmiling.

"Morning, Matthew," she replies. She continues with her task, adding, "How did the meeting go last night?"

Annoyed, he pulls at her and the rope slips from her hands. She hears the bucket hit the water and his voice rises, "I want to talk to you, Vi." He is angry now and he has her full attention.

"Well, go on then," she says. Shivering and folding her arms, she stands straight before him.

"It's about last night. I saw that Dryer bloke leaving your house nigh on ten o'clock, when I was returning from the meeting." There, he'd spat it out. She waits for more, but he waits too.

"Yes?" she finally says, unsure of which way to reply.

"Well, what was he doing?" he demands.

"He was seeing our Ma about making some curtains for his cottage, that's all. Why, Matthew, is something wrong?"

He appears to deflate before her, but rather than lose all impetus he continues indignantly, "Well, it's never decent calling on two lone women at that hour and I don't like it, Violet, I don't like it at all."

"Matthew, I met him by chance as I was leaving your house. He'd lost his way and I thought I'd detain him a while 'cus Father were unloading stuff about then and I was worried about them. Mr Dryer …"

"Mister Dryer is it now?" he interrupts, mimicking her.

"Mr Dryer …," she repeats with emphasis, "… started talking about settling in the cottage, and how he wanted some curtains made, and I took the opportunity of delaying him further and asking him in to see Mother about it." She pauses, looking at him, challenging him.

"He didn't stay long, but it was just long enough for the men to beach and unload between nine and ten. At nine-thirty, if he'd gone to the inn he might have sniffed out something, so I took the chance."

Matthew's shoulders slump in resignation. His tawny eyes are troubled and his expression grave, and she takes pity on him, "But it won't happen again, I promise. I don't care for anyone but you, Matthew, you know that, but if I don't act natural with Dryer, he's going to suspect I've something to hide and become suspicious of me, or our menfolk. So I'd rather be a bit friendly to him, just to keep him happy, no more than that."

She returns to her task of hauling up the buckets of water.

"I'd rather you didn't speak to him, Violet," says Matthew. "I don't trust him with you."

Whilst heaving on the rope she reasons with him. "I can't be rude to him now Mother and I are making his curtains. Be fair, Matthew, I swear I'll never give him any chance to make anything of it. But you have to trust me or it won't work between us."

"All right, Violet, but I laid me cards on the table to him last night. He knows we're courting, so don't let him take any liberties at all, or we'll be through, Violet. I can't help it, I don't like it."

She unhooks the rope. "You shouldn't have worried, Matthew; there is no need for you to say anything to Mr Dryer. You've probably done more harm than good. I've told you before I can look out for myself." She picks up the yoke and attaches the buckets, and then Matthew helps her to steady them across her shoulders.

"I'm sorry, but I don't like the fellow and I cannot bear to think of him ogling at you. Anyway, let's forget about him, there is something else I wanted to ask you before you go. I want to take you to the fair. Will you be able to come with me and the others, Vi?"

"Of course I can. Hannah mentioned it last night so I was already looking forward to it, but I must go now, Matty. I'm frozen." She puts her hand on his arm and with eyes wide and innocent she asks him, "Will you call for me on Thursday?"

"Yes, I'll come for you at around six of the clock. That's when Hannah and Molly are setting off too. See you then." He bends and kisses her cheek gently and whispers, "Bye."

"Bye." She smiles and they part. Relieved that she has sorted that out with Matthew, and also pleased that he is actually jealous enough to show it, she hums a little tune as she hurries home.

Violet is glad when the day of the fair turns out to be mild. The previous few days of high winds have banished the heavens of all clouds and the sky is bright and clear. Now that the wind has dropped, she will be able to wear her new best dress after all. Of all the things her mother has made, this is her favourite. It is fresh blue poplin, with long full sleeves. It is trimmed with satin bows and she has a warm blue and white shawl for the evening. She looks in the mirror. Yes, her best poke bonnet matches perfectly and the little white lace cap showing underneath looks crisp and clean against her dark hair.

Although she knows the latest styles are designed with skirts slightly shorter, Violet sticks to the old fashion of the long skirt because she cannot afford the square-toed, lightweight shoes, and prefers to hide her practical buttoned boots. Anyway, being quite small, it suits her better by creating the illusion of a little height.

Matthew is so impressed he lets out a whistle when she answers his knock. Flattered, she slips her arm through his, and he draws her closer. She enjoys the smell of him and the warmth of his body against her, as he holds her hand firmly in the crook of his elbow. She is proud and happy to be at his side as they join the procession weaving its way up through Fortuneswell to the annual site of the fair. They take this route because it is part of the ritual to follow the Reeve Staff up to the top of the hill.

Matthew's little brother Johnny runs along beside them and catches hold of Matthew's free hand as they go. "Tell me again, Matty, why did King William make us on Portland special?"

Matthew laughs, "I have told you time enough, I'd have thought you'd tire of hearing it."

"You know how I love hearing of our old tales and customs. Please, Matty, tell us again."

"Very well," Matthew sighs. "We on Portland were excused military service many years ago by King William, who thought that it was more important that we defend our island. Portland is in a very unique and important position." Violet smiles as Johnny proudly puffs out his chest and marches alongside his older brother.

"You see, the black death had killed off so many on the island, coming as it did through the port of Weymouth, that our population dropped dramatically and there were not enough men to defend the coastline. So he decreed that instead we should pay a land tax, what we call 'the quit rent', as a substitute for serving in the militia."

"How does the King know who pays?"

"Well, whoever owns most land pays the most and he or she then becomes the Reeve. There is one Reeve for each Manor, and they are in charge of collecting and recording the quit rent. Each Manor has a sign which is scored on the staff, and payment is shown by the notches and scratches." Matthew points out the Reeve who is carrying the huge staff before them.

"And that is why we have been free from time

immemorial." Johnny repeats the expression they have all heard so many times sitting at their firesides on winter evenings.

"You should be very proud of this special privilege, Johnny," says Violet. "It's our right and we must never give it up."

"Yes, there's many would have us forget it, and we have often been forced to stand firm and remind them of our immunity under the Admiralty Seal," continues Matthew. "You have heard our Pa talking of when the press gangs came and they were fought off by angry Portlanders, up top o' hill."

Of course he remembered. "You mean when the two quarrymen and the blacksmith were shot?"

"Yes, that's right. Well, Richard Bennett and young Mary Way were also wounded. She died within two months, but our folk defended themselves with muskets and pistols that had come off the wrecks of the military transport ships eight years earlier, and they wounded nine of the marines so seriously that they had to be discharged from the service."

"So we stuck up for ourselves."

"Yes, Johnny, we did, but that tragedy should never have happened. It only occurred because the press gangs disregarded the royal statute."

Violet squeezes Matthew's arm. "Let's not think of that on a beautiful day like today. Look, Johnny," she says pointing ahead to a group of Mummers. They are wearing a variety of animal heads or masks and cavorting about the roadway, making the young folk laugh. Everyone is walking in the same direction, lured by the gay music of the hurdy-gurdy wafting down off the common.

Hannah and Molly eagerly look out for Robert and John as they near the entrance, where the variety of colours, noises and smells are intoxicating.

Morris Men dressed in costume, with straw hats and ribbons of red and white, and little bells on their wrists and ankles, dance and shake their tambourines to an impromptu band of violins, trumpets, kettledrums and hautboys.

Violet and the others stand watching and listening as they wait for John and Robert, whilst the sheep and other stock pass by, along with people of all ages and sizes.

The Morris Men begin another tune, and with batons clashing in time with the music they lay them on the ground and do a variation of a Scottish sword dance.

Some of the children are preoccupied with funny little wooden monkeys that climb up and down on sticks, and Johnny and his mother go off in search of one. Many have won or bought wooden whistles and several dance past them playing like the Pied Piper and weaving in and out amongst the stalls.

Shrieks of delight come from somewhere within, where a group are watching a puppet show, and the high-pitched, odd voices that represent each character ring out above the other noises.

Suddenly Molly jumps in the air and waves. "Here they are," she says, and she calls to them, "Over here," and they all move forward to meet up with the two boys.

This is what they have been waiting for. Excitement surges through Violet as, at last, they move with the flow, into the fair.

Above the noise of the puppeteer they hear the loud clang of a bell as it is struck, and as they round the crowd of children they see a group of men cheering and 'Ahhing' as their companions succeed or fail in their various attempts. The challenge is to bang the peg with an enormously heavy hammer in order to shoot a bolt upwards and strike the bell at the top of the shaft.

"There's not many who don't hit the mark, are there?" says Violet, as they watch.

"Well, it's not surprising with all our quarrymen having a go, is it?" returns Matthew.

The man in charge has overheard them. "In some areas I have to employ someone to prove that it's actually possible to strike the bell, but not here," he says.

He begins calling on smaller members of the gathering and challenging them to try. Soon they are watching poor old Dappy, who comes forward reluctantly, but more out of self-consciousness than any doubt of his ability. He staggers a little as he balances the hammer over his right shoulder, before swinging it in a wide circle and letting it drop. The bolt shoots up like a rocket and hits its target, Clang!

"Whoopee!" everyone yells, and old Dappy beams from ear to ear.

"Poor man. He didn't expect that, did he!" murmurs Violet, noting the stallholder's expression of despair. Is he considering closing the game? But as she walks on through the maze of faces, she can hear again the 'Ahs' of failure as unsuccessful attempts are made.

"Oh look, it's the Coconut Shy," says Hannah. "How much is it?"

"A farthing for six tries," says the woman with the money wallet. "Win a bottle of Eau de toilette for your sweetheart, boys?" she asks the men.

"Let's all have one go each," says Violet.

"All right, let the girls go first," says Matthew. "Go on, Vi, have a go."

Violet picks up the ball and aims at the biggest coconut, she holds her breath as it wobbles precariously, but it doesn't drop.

Then Molly and Hannah both have their turn and miss; Robert makes one wobble, but John hits one clean off its cup and they all shriek with the fun of it. The last to go is Matthew but he also misses and is very serious about it.

"It doesn't matter," whispers Violet tenderly, noticing his disappointment, "it's only a bit of fun and we did get our money's worth, 'cus Molly has some scent. Let's go and find something else," and Violet takes his hand, as they all go on to the next gathering. It is a boxing ring.

"Oh no, I don't want to watch fighting, Matthew," says Violet.

"Oh go on, Vi, it's a laugh," says Robert. They gather closer to the fighters. The lads are really getting involved, and even Molly and Hannah are joining in with the shouting and jeering.

Violet watches the blows land. One of the men is struck above the eye and falls to the ground, he shakes his head as he struggles, unable momentarily to regain his feet, and blood spurts into the sawdust. It is quite revolting. Unable to bear it for a moment longer, Violet says to Matthew, "I'm just going on a bit further to see what's next."

He is going to go with her but she says, "No, you stay, I know you are enjoying it. I'll be back in a minute." She works her way forward through the crowd, peeping between elbows and standing on tiptoe to see over the shoulders of the onlookers. She passes the bell-ringers, the fire-eater, the sword swallower and the bearded lady. Then she spies, set apart from the general hubbub, a small ornately painted booth. There is a veiled lady, the signs of the zodiac, gaming cards and a crystal ball painted around the walls of the booth and as she passes around to the front, there is Madame Christabel sitting outside on the steps!

Violet avoids eye contact, for she does not dare to go and see the famous Madame Christabel. But nevertheless she hears the woman calling after her. "You ought to come inside for a reading, my dear, for I can sense that your life is about to be turned upside down."

"No thank you," she says still avoiding eye contact.

"As young as you are, I can see that you have two suitors and a decision must be made." Violet's blood runs cold. She pauses in her tracks. Could this woman read her mind?

She turns and looks at her. The woman is dark and foreign looking, with piercing, shrewd green eyes, and her untidy hair is partially covered in a brightly patterned headscarf.

"Things are going to be very difficult for you my dear, times are going to be hard." She is tapping her long jewelled fingers over a pack of tarot cards. She continues regardless, "Beware! There is danger and death shadowing you."

Violet rushes away from the annoying woman feeling confused and frightened. Her parents have always told her to take what gypsies and fortune-tellers say with a pinch of salt, but this gypsy woman spoke with such confidence. How can she just brush aside what she has just said? She daren't tell the others about it.

She shakes her head trying to clear her mind, wanting to find Matthew and her friends. She hurries towards the boxing ring and stands on the perimeter of the crowd, searching wildly among the faces. There is no sign of them. She walks slowly on, past the fairings and peddlers, glancing back, but still she cannot see him.

She feels the tears building. Where are they? Why did she leave Matthew? Why had she even considered going off on her own? She hurries on again but still she sees none of them. Then, set back to one side of the main path, she notices two more large groups of men. One group is gathered around the Reeve and the others are playing some kind of game with a peg in the ground at which they are aiming horseshoes.

Between the two, and standing out from the other men, she immediately recognises Richard Dryer. He is wandering aimlessly among the crowds. Her heart races, and she dives into the crowds again, not wanting him to see her while she is unaccompanied. She hurries on. Matthew, where are you?

The quack doctor tries to delay her with his sales patter but she brushes him aside firmly and presses on. Then she spies Matthew. Briefly she catches a glimpse of his green sleeves as he jumps in the air and shouts, "I did it!" The canopy of the coconut shy flutters behind him. She runs to him.

He turns and sees her. "Look, I won it for you." He thrusts the bottle of perfume at her and then his arms are around her, hugging her. At last she has found him. She is safe in the warmth of his embrace, but out there somewhere in the crowd, Richard Dryer is lurking. She struggles free, saying, "Oh, thank you, Matty, it's lovely," and he squeezes her hand in his.

Then Matthew drags her along, dodging the geese and poultry and flitting from one sideshow to the next, and soon they are laughing again. They admire the acrobats and as they watch the juggler the sun goes down. They must have seen everything that there was to see. Eventually their energy dwindles and a tired Hannah suggests, "Shall we go and watch the Mummers now before we go back home?"

"That's a good idea," says Molly, and they make their way towards the large stone-carrying trailer that is acting as a stage for the village players.

They stand in their couples. Tired out, Violet leans back against Matthew and he encircles her in his arms. She feels secure, with Matthew's love and her friends around her. She laughs to see people that she knows well looking so comical, and although the story is quite ridiculous it gives everyone a great deal of pleasure watching their neighbours acting the fool. They all laugh and applaud loudly at the end of the performance, while a peculiar rabbit and a ferocious-looking lion go round among them with a hat for contributions.

The night sky is now dark, but the gay lights of the sideshows and a full moon mean that not many have even noticed. The animal noises of the daytime marketing are now silent, and the childish voices of the young ones are no longer heard as Violet and Matthew link arms with their friends and start their own sing-song as they march home.

"Where be thic Blackbird gone, I know where 'ee be, 'Ee be in thic wurzelgrove, and I be after 'ee, When 'ee sees me, and I see 'ee …"

Dryer returns home from the fair to his silent, empty cottage. The gay music and happy united families have only served to sharpen his loneliness to an unbearable degree.

He spotted Violet at the fair; he saw the sunlight strike her hair, her eyes bluer than the sky, her body lithe as she ran into the arms of that darn Matthew Stone. He slams the door in frustration. If it wasn't for Stone she could be his for the taking.

Yesterday, he had watched her from his bedroom window, carrying driftwood back from the beach, with a strong wind at her back and he had longed to hold and steady her as she went. She looked so tiny and precious that one big gust would have taken her forever.

Tonight he followed them home, hearing their laughter and their local songs; if only his arrival here had not been delayed. He pours himself a tot of brandy and sits down in his armchair.

"Women have always been my downfall," he mutters under his breath, gazing through the golden haze of brandy … Why does he need them so?

He has a sudden yearning for his mother, why did she have to die so young from that dreadful illness? He misses her even now. He had needed her desperately last year, for she would have understood about Martha and the child, but not father, not his bigoted, puritanical Lord of a father. Angrily he swirls the brandy round and round and then drains the glass.

"Oh, Martha. Why did you and the child have to suffer, because of me?" He pours himself another tot of brandy and as the remaining embers of the fading fire warm him, and the brandy soothes him, he eventually falls asleep.

Annie Shaddick lets herself in at six o'clock the following morning and finds Dryer as he has fallen asleep, fully dressed and with his stockinged feet resting on the fender. She has entered the room quietly and has not disturbed his slumber. For a moment she gazes at him and then she goes into the kitchen to light the copper.

Dryer awakes to the sound of the nicking of a piece of steel on flint. When he enters the kitchen he smells the sulphurous odour of the tinderbox, as the home-made wooden match held by Annie finally ignites and she puts it to the fuel beneath the copper. She stands up and their bodies brush as he walks past to fill the kettle.

It is strange but he just accepts Annie as part of the furniture. He has been alone with her for five days now, as together they have cleaned and arranged the cottage. They might be married, but for the night-times when she goes home and yet still he pays her no attention. Now she stands and regards him, pointedly staring mistily into his eyes, and he recognises at last what she has been trying to convey.

He walks towards her and lays his hands on her shoulders. Her eyes do not change their expression of challenge but hold his gaze, and a little smile appears at her mouth. Dryer is in no mood for teasing, he feels his body responding. She has started something now, and if she's willing, that's her look-out. He hasn't had a woman in a long while. His right hand moves upwards to her neck and under her hair and his mouth is hard on hers. Hungrily he samples her gift to him, before eagerly pulling her up the stairs to his bed. He cannot help himself. He feels his frustrations ease, as Annie pleasures him, as he enters her, brutal in his urgency. With each thrust he pushes the image of Violet from him, burying the pain until he falls back exhausted on the bed.

Sounds of life are evident in the surrounding cottages and the sun is shining as Annie rolls over and, partly covering him with her body, says, "What else can I be doing for thee today, Sir?"

"Go and make a pot of tea, Annie, please," he says, and grinning, he slaps her behind as she gets up to do as he asks.

He feels less fraught this morning. Annie is not the answer to all his prayers but her willingness does prove something. That deep yearning for Violet Allen remains, but maybe he can remedy that. After all, he does have a way with women and 'faint heart never won fair maiden'.

Some days later when Mary Allen has finished making the curtains and Violet has bought and sewn on all the rings, she is sent round to Dryer's cottage to hang them for him. Annie Shaddick frowns as she lets her in.

Dryer stands behind her. "Go for bread, please, Annie," he says. Annie flings him a look.

"We need bread, Annie."

Annie grabs up her shawl and shoulders past Violet, slamming the front door behind her.

Embarrassed, Violet says, "I've brought the curtains."

"Thank you, Violet. Please, sit down."

"No, Sir, I must get on." Her hands are trembling as she begins to unpack her parcel.

"Would you like a cup of tea, Violet?"

"That would be nice. Thank you, Sir." She makes a start on the kitchen window whilst he prepares the tea.

"I must say, you were very quick making these up and the workmanship is excellent. Please thank your mother for me."

"Yes, Sir, I will," she says, her voice low.

Silence falls between them as they both occupy themselves with their tasks. Violet is uncomfortable with this, but can think of nothing to say. She is in his house alone with him. How could she have let this happen?

She works swiftly, eager to be finished and safe back home with her mother; she masters her trembling and completes the kitchen window. Glad to be away from him, she goes into the living room to continue with her work.

When, later, he enters with the tea things he finds her standing on his footstool, silhouetted in the light of the window, arms stretched and trying with difficulty to hook the wooden pole back into place. He stands and stares, then realising her difficulty he quickly puts down the tray and comes to her aid.

"Here, let me help you," he says, and climbing also upon the same small stool, he takes the pole and sits it easily in place.

His body is so close and warm behind her. She suddenly feels hot, her heart races and then her head swims when she looks down. She puts her hand to her head. Is it the stretching? She feels his strong hands helping her down. "Are you all right, Violet?" he asks with concern.

"Oh, yes … thank you. I just felt a bit dizzy, that's all," she mutters hazily.

He moves even closer then and holding her firmly against him leads her to one of the armchairs. He smells pleasantly of cologne. "Here, sit for a while and have your drink."

She sits quietly taking deep breaths and he passes her a cup of tea. She feels his eyes upon her as she drinks. The tea is very hot. She looks up at him and smiles, self-consciously; he smiles back and she immediately looks away again, taking some more sips of the hot tea. Gradually her heart rate returns to normal.

"I feel better already thank you, Mr Dryer."

"Good, I was quite anxious for a moment, I thought that you were about to faint," he says gently. "And you looked so well yesterday. Did you enjoy yourself at the fair?"

She flushes crimson. So he did see her after all. She hopes that it wasn't when she was ducking and diving to avoid him. She finds her voice, "Yes, we had great fun. We were lucky with the weather too." She takes another sip of tea. She must make conversation somehow.

She clears her throat, "Did you hear about the floor collapsing at the Sun Inn in the middle of the mazey dance and all those folk tumbling into the cellar below?"

"Yes," he laughs, "Annie told me. She was passing by when it happened and, like she said, it was a miracle that out of nearly two hundred people no one was hurt. Apparently the only casualty was a violin."

She smiles, and drinks some more, "You make a good cup of tea," she says, not wanting to dwell on the discomfort she is feeling.

"I'm learning." He smiles. "At home there were always servants to perform such tasks. We …"

"Where …?" she stops short. They have both spoken at once.

"Go on," he says.

"I was just going to ask, where is your home?"

"Here now," he answers, but still there is no explanation.

"Have you travelled far?" she persists.

"No, thirty miles or thereabouts, from my father's estate in Somersetshire." He draws up a chair and sits down close by her. "You would have loved it there, Violet. It was so grand; I had always believed that nothing could have induced me to leave, until last year."

"Why, whatever happened?" she asks, growing bolder.

He sighs heavily. "It was my father. I simply realised that I could not stand living with his hypocrisy any longer." He stops and says nothing more.

Sensing a reluctance to expose his feelings and

therefore unable to pry any further she puts down her empty cup, and rises. "I think I'd better get on, Mr Dryer, 'cus me Ma says not to be long. I've only got the big front door curtain and the two bedroom windows to do."

"Of course," he says. "I'll show you upstairs."

He stands up and takes the curtains from her, indicating that she should go first, and then follows, close behind her, up the narrow curving stairway.

Her legs are unreliable and as she grips the banister, the wood feels smooth and cool to her clammy fingers. She enters the bedroom and the very nearness of the bed makes her all the more aware of Dryer's proximity. He seems to stand so close to her. Nervously she adjusts the curtains and all the while her heart races recklessly.

When at last the front window is hung with the rich velvet material, she turns her attention to the window at the back.

Dryer tests the smooth running of the rings. He draws the curtains shut. "I want to see if they meet," he says. He makes no attempt to reverse the procedure.

In the semi-darkness a swell of panic swamps her. The ceiling is lower upstairs and there is no need for a stool. She is stretching to complete the back window when she sees his reflection behind her. She turns quickly.

"Oh Violet, why are you so nervous of me?" He takes her hands in his and puts them to his lips.

She goes weak all over. His tender voice is tempting her, and his hands … and his lips. "Oh!" Is it a groan or a murmur? It comes from deep within her. She should never have come; it was a big mistake.

Overcome with confusion, she looks up at him and their lips are suddenly together. His arms are wrapped around her. She can feel his hands all over her back, stimulating her senses to an extent she has never dreamed possible.

"No … no!" Is she speaking aloud? "Oh, no!" She makes a feeble attempt to push him away.

"Oh, please don't," he begs, enfolding her more firmly in his strong arms.

She feels dominated, wonderfully dominated, and needed, so desperately needed. But no, it is wrong. She is Matty's and he would not be able to bear the thought of it.

Dryer kisses her again with a passion she has never before experienced and in spite of herself she feels her heart racing, her eyes closing.

Suddenly the front door slams and she stiffens. She feels his grip loosen. Annie is back.

Dryer is forced to allow Violet to compose herself. He helps her to complete the final window and then she follows him downstairs.

"Thank you, Violet, thank you very much," he is saying as they cross the living room.

She is trembling so much, she finds it hard to answer with a steady voice. "Don't mention it, Sir," she manages, in polite reply.

"Allow me," she hears him say as he helps her on with her cloak, his hands lingering on her shoulders. "Let me see you out." Her mind is in turmoil; her heart seems split in two. Whatever would Matthew think if he found out about this?

Out of earshot of Annie, Violet's composure disintegrates. Her eyes fill with desperation as she pleads with him, "Please, I beg of you, don't mention any of this. You took advantage and it mustn't happen again. I am betrothed to Matthew."

Dryer smiles and says softly, "Don't worry, Violet, I shall not tell a soul." But he thinks to himself, you may be betrothed to Stone, but the flame within you burns for me, I know it.

He closes the door and as he enters the living room Annie holds out another length of velvet. "What's up with this 'un then?" she asks sullenly.

"Oh, we forgot that one. Thank you, Annie." He takes it from her and hangs it against the front door. "There, that's more cosy, isn't it?"

She is frowning, so he gives her a pat on the buttocks and says, "What's up with you? You look like you found a ha'penny but lost a groat."

CHAPTER 4 *(November 1830 – September 1831)*

TWO BIRDS WITH ONE STONE

Since the incident at his cottage, Dryer has had no excuse to speak with Violet and she has been successful in her many endeavours to avoid him. Christmas is approaching and she is spending more time at Matthew's house, determined that her mother's lace cap will be completed in time. It is here that she learns of the run planned for early December.

She sits silently, working with Matthew's mother, and listens as the men discuss the details. She is supposed to feel privileged just to be there but not expected to contribute to the conversation.

"We are all agreed on the date and time, but what about Dryer?" asks her father.

"I have arranged a diversion to lure the waterguard and Dryer to the east of the island," says Jacky Sparrow. "That's all in hand, no need to worry on that score, but we don't want all and sundry getting wind of it. There's a limit to the number of families the run can support."

"I hear Ikey Shaddick's already sniffing around," says Jack White.

"Well, we definitely don't want him involved," says Matthew immediately.

"I don't know, it might be safer to have him with us rather than against us," says Jacky Sparrow.

"No, absolutely not, he's too hot-headed. I agree with Matthew," says his father.

"They should all agree with Matthew. It's quite

obvious," Violet whispers to his mother, who nods in agreement.

"It's worth thinking about, Matt. After all, having him involved will ensure his sister's silence," says Nick Way.

There are mutterings among them, and then her brothers are arguing.

Matthew speaks again. "Annie will never betray us to a Kimberlin, at least she never has yet."

"There's always a first time," someone says.

"Well, I think we should have a vote, bearing in mind that Ikey is already suspicious," says Jack White.

Violet wants to speak up. Her heart begins to thump, but it is none of her business and the men will not like her interference. She looks at Matthew's mother who is silently twisting her bobbins, as the men in the room raise their hands in favour of Ikey taking part. Catching her attention, Violet rolls her eyes to the ceiling to show her opinion of their foolhardiness.

Poor Matthew, he seems convinced that Annie will never betray them. It is true that her parents, with all those mouths to feed, depend as much if not more than any other family on the success of the free-traders, but if it was up to her they'd both be kept in ignorance.

Matthew is therefore uneasy when, a week later, the crop is swiftly and silently dispersed among the men and he keeps close to Ikey as they leave the exposed area of beach and move into the shadows of Chiswell's lanes. They cover a short distance, pause and listen, move forward cautiously and pause again, progressing carefully from cover to cover. Then they hear the sound they all dread, the lookout's signal.

"Careful," he hisses, "the waterguard, they're here."

Loaded with contraband, they are at their most vulnerable. Any abandoned cargo stumbled upon by the revenue men will only confirm their suspicions and so they are reluctant to dump the crop and run. The weight of two ankers of brandy could mean the difference between three hours of merriment and three months of hard labour, but no one wants to give the land sharks any excuse for extra vigilance. They cling to their spoils as best they can and make haste to find cover at the earliest possible moment. It is every man for himself, but they mustn't jeopardise the run.

Matthew and Ikey are each moving from doorway to doorway when the sound of running footsteps up ahead warns of the approaching soldiers. Matthew's only option is the cottage, where he shelters in the porch, but as he bursts into the home of one of his neighbours he is confident of immediate assistance.

William Gibbs quickly rushes one of the kegs upstairs and out of sight, whilst his wife uses the other as a stool hidden under her voluminous skirts as she bathes her baby by the fireside.

Matthew watches from the window as the soldiers run across the side opening at the bottom of the slope, some turning into the lane where they hide. He looks back at Ikey and sees that he is panicking; then, horrified, he sees the glint of a blade.

Ikey is trapped in the porchway and the hot-head has drawn a knife. Matthew watches as he barges again at the solid door. It is no use, it is locked against him and will not budge. He turns back towards the soldiers, his eyes glaring.

Matthew curses, "The damned fool!" The stupid idiot will bring the full force of the law down on them. He turns to William Gibbs. "I'm sorry, but I have no choice. I have to create a diversion."

Free of the weight of the kegs, he waits for the two soldiers to pass his doorway. Swiftly he moves away from the house and down the slope away from Ikey's hiding place. He stumbles, catching their attention. Have they noticed whose house he has come from? He cannot be sure, but he is certain they are now both after him.

"Stop! Halt or we fire!" Their voices echo in the night air.

Matthew runs, turning at the bottom of the slope away from the direction of his home and the other soldiers. It has worked. He hears them behind him. Now his only hope is to be rescued by one of the householders on the cellar run. Round a bend in the road he sees lights in the cottage on his left and bursting through the door he locks it behind him, crying, "Dowse your lights quickly."

Mary James jumps up and snuffs the candles and as Matthew pulls heavy curtains across the window, Mary's husband lifts the rag rug and levers up a flagstone. Not another word passes between them. Matthew almost falls through the hole into the cellar below and as the flagstone is replaced, shutting out the sound and the last remnants of light from the fire, the darkness swamps him.

Choked with anxiety, he listens intently. He hears only his heart thumping and feels a hot searing pain in the fore of his left shoulder as he tries to control his breathing. He does not remember ever using this cellar before. It smells stale and musty. He feels around for some sign of an exit. Moving around the walls, his fingers touch rough and smooth, damp and slimy patches but nothing significant, until he loses his bearings. Then he hears heavy footsteps, doors being opened and banging closed, loud voices muffled from the room overhead.

If only he had a light. Frantically he stumbles about hitting his fingers against some shelving. He feels up and down and along the shelves, but they are empty. Maybe they are hiding the exit. He pushes gently, lifting at the same time. Something squeals and he shudders at the thought of rats, but he can get in behind now and his hands move swiftly from stonework to wood to metal.

It is a rust-flaked bolt, and it scores his fingers as he tries to draw it back, but it is jammed fast. He wiggles and turns the knob, working it loose, aware all the time of the scraping noise, until it suddenly frees and shoots through with a jolt.

He eases the door open. Blindly he goes to pass through but stubs his foot against what turns out to be a step up. Once through he drags the shelving back against the step and with relief closes the door against it.

Anxious to move on he attempts to cross to the opposite side of the room, bumping into a table as he goes. He runs his hands over the surface and finds some wax candles and a tin box. He prizes open the tinderbox and, after fumbling about a bit, he manages to light one of the candles. Gradually his eyes focus; at last he can see. On the table there is also a lantern, which he lights with the candle.

It is a tiny, irregular-shaped room, on a higher level than the previous cellar. The exit is above his head. Slightly to one side of the table there is a trapdoor, but who is above it? Because he has lost his bearings he isn't sure of the direction in which he is moving, which side of the cottage he is now on. Anyway, a gentle tap is his only choice and so he taps and waits. There is an answering tap. Thank God! Someone knows he is there, but nevertheless no one lets him out. He daren't knock again for there has to be a reason for this lack of response. All he can do is wait. The silence is unnerving, but at least he has a light now and he can see there are no rats. The village must be crawling with soldiers and he wonders if Ikey has got away. He thinks then of Violet and whether Dryer will take this opportunity to interrogate her and her mother. He hates the thought of them being together for any reason at all. He feels so helpless trapped as he is, but he has no choice.

As soon as Dryer realises that the coastguards have been sent on a wild goose chase, he knows that something big is going down in the cove. He summons the Coast Fencibles and gets to the beach in time to see the cutter in the light of his flare, her sails filling with a steady wind as she tacks her way back out into the Channel. "Damn, damn, damn!" he curses to himself, they've done it again.

He sends the soldiers to search the derelict buildings but keeps a low profile himself. He cannot show his face at the Cove House Inn and have them all witness his anger and frustration, and if he enters any of the cottages he has to have good reason, or they would be justified in accusing him of harassment.

The soldiers report back to him of the fugitive chased and almost immediately lost to sight and he feels justified in searching the cottages in that area, but nothing incriminating is discovered. He guesses it has been yet another diversion to draw the soldiers from the real culprits and their spoils.

Now he wonders if Annie could offer any clues as to who is involved. If anyone should be prepared to help him she should.

He bangs on her front door and Annie's mother

timidly opens it with several small children hanging onto her skirts and another slightly older girl with a baby in her arms standing just behind her.

"I'd like a word with Annie please, Mrs Shaddick," he says authoritatively.

Mrs Shaddick turns to the older child. "Go and fetch your sister, May," and turning back to him she asks, "Is something wrong, Mr Dryer?"

"Nothing to concern you, Mrs Shaddick. I just want a private word with Annie if you please."

With that Annie comes to the door. Surprise and confusion and then pleasure show in her face. "Go on in, May, you're letting all the heat out," and she steps outside, closing the door against her family. "This is an honour," she exclaims, then she sees his stern expression, "or am I in the doghouse?"

"Neither, Annie, I want you to tell me what you know about the run that took place tonight." He sees the light fade from her eyes.

"Run? I don't know what you're talking about. I don't know nothing about no run."

Annie is susceptible to both his charms and his threats, but which will be most effective? She appears to be disappointed that he isn't there just for the pleasure of her company. He decides gentle cajoling will be his best approach. She will only dig her heels in if he tries to bully her.

"You must have some idea, Annie. You've lived here all your life."

"All the more reason to watch my tongue."

"But there's a lot of money to be made here; a good seizure could line both our pockets."

"Look, Mr Dryer, you know as well as I do that I could do with the money, but as true as I'm standing here I don't know nothing about no run."

"Where are your menfolk then?"

"I don't know," she snaps, "I'm not their keeper.

75

They're probably down the Cove House. That's where they usually are of an evening. Why don't you go round there with your questions?"

"I was hoping you'd be more helpful, Annie. I thought we were on the same team, you and I."

"Well, I'm sorry Mr Dryer, but I can't tell you summat I know nothing about, can I?" she reasons and then adds, retreating, "If that'll be all, I've the children's supper to get."

"Fair enough, Annie, but if I find out you're hiding something from me, don't be surprised if I show a different side to my character."

Annie looks back at him. The veiled threat obviously angers her. "I don't know why you come to me in the first place. Why don't you go pester the Allen family? Or are you afraid they'll take you for a fool? Violet Allen knows more about that business than ever I do. Go and ask her your questions." She swings back into the cottage angrily and slams the door in his face.

He stands for a moment deliberating. Is Annie just being spiteful or is she trying to tell him something? It is an excuse to see Violet, but one that will anger her menfolk if they are there. But if nothing else he will ascertain their whereabouts. It is worth the loss of face just to see her.

He calls for two of the soldiers to follow, but orders them to stand back and only approach the cottage if summoned.

Violet and her mother both jump as the urgent banging at their door echoes throughout the cottage. "It's all right, Ma, I'll go," she says.

Her heart lurches and thumps. Whatever has happened? Is someone hurt? Could it be Matthew, or her father? Have they been discovered?

As she opens the door she gasps to see Richard Dryer standing there; she flushes and instinctively steps back into the passage. Swiftly he steps in after her. Her voice trembles as she says scarcely above a whisper, "What is it? What's wrong?"

"Just routine enquiries, Violet. Are your father or brothers at home?"

She hesitates, but she has to admit it, "No, Sir, they are not, only myself and my mother."

"Do you know where they are?" he asks softly.

"No, Sir, I don't, I'm sorry." She leans back against the wall for support. "I thought you were coming to tell me there'd been an accident."

He moves nearer. "No, Violet, nothing like that. I just wanted an excuse to see you."

The heat rises in her. He is doing it again. He stands so close that her face is tilted up at him, and she is aware of the pulse at her throat. Nervously, she swallows. She puts up her hand to hold him at bay. "But you promised … You shouldn't come here. Matthew, my father, they'll think badly of me. You must go … Please … you must go."

"Don't push me away, Violet. I can't bear it."

Suddenly he takes her in his arms, trying to kiss her lips. She struggles and turns her face away, but he kisses her cheek, her ears. She throws back her head and his lips brush her neck. Her body is tingling with desire, despite her attempts to reject him.

Although she tosses to and fro, she cannot elude his kisses as, inadvertently, she moves her head to an angle where their lips meet. She struggles, his muscles hard and strong against her, holding her tightly, pinning her against the wall of the passage. He lingers there long enough for her to know the mutual surge of passion that flows between them.

She pulls away but aches with longing for him.

"My mother will come," she whispers. "Please go. You are a devil to deal with me so."

"Forgive me, Violet, for you are responsible for my weakness. Don't pretend you don't feel anything, for I know that you do."

For God's sake, she is weak herself but she has to be strong. She has to resist. "It is no pretence, Mr Dryer." She sticks up her chin. "Besides, I trust you'll allow me to know what 'pretence' brings you to my door?"

Suddenly looking stern, he says, "I am sure you are well aware that there has been a consignment of goods landed in the cove this night and my business is enquiries in connection with the smugglers and their cargo." Then his face softens. "However, my personal business is more pressing."

Audaciously he steals another kiss, but Violet's fear of discovery gets the better of him and she slaps his face. "If you don't leave right now, Mr Dryer, I'll call my mother and expose your true motives."

"All right, I give in." Despite the mark beginning to show across his face he smiles at her feeble attempt to control the situation. "I don't want to get you into trouble, but you'll see. You'll warm to me, Violet, in spite of yourself. You cannot control your destiny." He turns from her then and beckons to his soldiers.

"Goodnight, Miss Allen," he says.

She watches him stride back down Brandy Row with the two men in tow. More soldiers are waiting down by the chapel. He leaves her in turmoil and with no way to vent her feelings. The nerve of that man! And she is none the wiser. Where are her menfolk? Where is Matthew? Why is she always piggy in the middle? What should she say to her mother?

She closes the door, tidies back her hair and

smoothes her dress, then goes through into the parlour.

"The village is swarming with soldiers, Ma. It was Mr Dryer at the door asking questions. I didn't say nothing, but I didn't learn nothing neither." She hopes her voice sounds normal.

"Well, he wouldn't have to be here asking his questions if he knew something, would he? Don't you worry, Vi, we'll know soon enough if there's trouble."

She sinks into her chair, relieved that at least Dryer is gone. She takes up her sewing but cannot put him from her mind. She may be able to distract him from the smugglers, but the last two occasions spent alone with him are proof enough that she definitely is not able to keep any control. He is so daring where she is concerned and so strong. He is audacious and bold and his passion overwhelms her. Is it so wrong of her to find pleasure in this?

With anyone else she would have been encouraged to use her charms to the smugglers' advantage, but it is not only her who thought it too risky to try that game with Dryer. There is too much tension between him and Matthew to consider that again.

Despite her mother's reassurance she is more fearful with each hour that passes. Time is going on and there is still no sign of the men, with the village swarming with soldiers. There is no alternative, though, but to sit patiently with her mother and wait.

Matthew has remained for some time now with nothing to occupy him but the sounds of a diligent search in progress overhead. Dust falls from around the trapdoor as a heavy piece of furniture is dragged across it. Discovery is surely imminent. But the trap must have been well concealed because eventually the activity dies down and he relaxes. After waiting some time in absolute silence he taps again. This time the trapdoor is gingerly lifted and three children look down on him. He recognises them as Nick Way's children and is relieved that he now knows where he is.

He whispers up to them, "I mean you no harm. I am hiding from the soldiers. Do you know where they are?"

"They have gone now. They woke us up and frightened my sister," says the boy. "We have been watching them, they are searching across the road at the moment, but it is safe to come out."

At last! He snuffs the candle, climbs up onto the table in the light from the trap, hands the lantern to one of the children and then hauls himself up through the hole. The eldest child is a pretty girl. "Follow me," she says and she takes him up through the house to the attic, her brother and sister close in tow. "You can go through three attics in that direction." She points. "I have to stay here with my brother and sister. The doors aren't locked against you that way, but you'll have to tap at Mr Seaward's house to be let down and then he will show you the way. I hope the soldiers haven't got me Pa."

"Don't you worry, sweetheart, we've got too many friends like you to hide us from the soldiers. He'll be home soon, you'll see." He pats her on the head, then climbs up onto a small stool, presumably there for that purpose, hauls himself up into the roof space and she passes up the lantern.

"You nippers have been a great help. I'll look out for your Pa and tell him how you helped me. You go on back downstairs now and make sure there's no sign of the trapdoor. I'll see you get this back," he adds, indicating the lantern.

He creeps through cobwebs and along the rafters of three attics. He must move as far away as possible from the point where he has vanished, before he can show his face again. At Mr Seaward's he taps again, but this time the response is quicker.

The old man has already retired for the night and comes to his aid dressed only in his nightshirt. The chamberstick trembles in his hand as he lights the way through his house and down into another cellar.

Matthew thanks him, "I'm sorry I interrupted your sleep, Mr Seaward."

"No problem, son. Glad to be of help. I'm not much use for anything at my age, but I don't want that Dryer getting the better of we, no more than you do. Good luck," he says and he lowers the hinged door.

Matthew shivers, glad of his fustian jacket and warm moleskin trousers. He hates the dark, damp, airless cellars, with the risk of flooding at high tide and, despite his lantern, as soon as the trap falls he begins to feel entombed again. What if he cannot make himself heard next time? What if the folk are all upstairs? By tomorrow they may have forgotten all about him. No, keep calm, Father will make them search and Violet will surely miss him. Is Violet worried for him? Is that Dryer sniffing around her? God, he has to get out of here.

Whilst the villagers are alerted to the smugglers' plight by the soldiers rushing hither and thither and banging on doors, Matthew has no choice but to pass through four more cellars, one of which is hardly more than a tunnel. Then again he finds his exit to be up through another cottage. He listens, holding his breath, for any sign of life. Are they muffled voices he can hear? It does not sound like soldiers stomping about anyway. He knocks gently on the trapdoor. There is silence. He knocks again. The trapdoor is drawn back and a familiar face peers down at him. Relief washes over him and he grins.

"Why, Matthew, my lad, come on up," and a friendly arm hauls him out into a well-lit parlour.

Blinking in the unaccustomed glare, he recognises Jack White and his family sharing a supper of bread, cheese and ale with his fellow smugglers. Playing cards are tossed aside and his father and several others, Robert Allen and Violet's brothers among them, are ready to take up the cards should the soldiers knock.

His father pats him on the back and Matthew asks him, "Where is our share of the crop?"

"Not here, but hidden away well out of sight – have no fear. But what sent you off course, my lad?"

"Bloody Ikey Shaddick, that's what," says Matthew with feeling. "He'd only drawn a knife with soldiers just about to lay hands on him in possession of two of our kegs of French brandy." He slumps into a chair. "I ask you, if that's not asking for trouble?"

He runs his fingers through his hair, feeling tired and dirty. "I played the hare and ran off to draw them and it worked a treat, but they were too close for my comfort. I only just lost them, risking both the houses of the Gibbs family, where I left my loot, and the James family, and also the secrecy of the cellar run. I knew 'twas a mistake involving Ikey Shaddick in our plans. We'll not do it again, for I'll have my way next time."

"What happened to him?" asks Violet's father.

"I haven't got a clue. I had just the one plan to lure the soldiers away. 'Twas bad luck he fell against a locked door, but 'twas asking for trouble to pull a knife. He may have run to the Gibbs' house as soon as the soldiers were after me, who knows? I only know he means trouble, that fellow, and I don't want him bringing it down on us."

"No, you're right, Matthew," says Jack White, "'tis too risky, we'll not be including him next time, rest assured."

They remain chatting together quietly until convinced that the soldiers have been recalled to the castle barracks. Then in ones and twos they leave for home. Their spoils will be collected when it is safe.

Matthew speaks to Robert Allen before he leaves with his father. "Please tell Violet that I've gone home and we're all safe, I know she will be worried."

"Of course I will, lad. It's always the first question I'm asked as I go in the door. You go and get a good night's sleep. I'll see you at sun up."

The following day Dryer is still angry at being so easily thwarted. They have managed to outwit him again by sending him on a wild goose chase, but they will not get the better of him forever. He'll show them somehow that he is not a man to be trifled with. That Jacky Sparrow is useless. He has never offered him any reliable information, just enough to make him appear helpful. These rogues have run rings around him long enough. Is there no weak link to their organisation? He will have to work harder on Annie. She is his only chance. She knows things about the locals; if he gets her talking, maybe she'll let something slip.

Annie is ripe for flattery and he can charm the birds from the trees if he puts his mind to it. Gradually her trust grows and she forgets to be guarded with him. Over the weeks he learns of the bitter enmity that exists between the islanders and the inhabitants of Wyke Regis, with their rival claims on the Fleet. She speaks of how, in past years, fights had often broken out over salvage or wreckage claims.

He makes a mental note of this. Maybe this will be the weakness that will ultimately let them down, but in the meantime he will have to content himself with more frequent shore patrols, more intelligence work, assessment of contacts, friendships and family relationships, and a concerted effort to get Annie on his side.

In May, Susan White and Thomas Atwool are married. Annie and Susan have been close companions since they were little, and she is pleased for her friend; but the event only serves to increase her own longings. It is a joyful affair and Annie is thrilled when she catches Susan's bouquet. Could it be possible that she is next for the altar?

Susan hugs her friend. "There you are, Annie, you'll be next."

"I doubt it, Susan. The man I love don't marry girls like me."

Susan whispers, "Well, he has been quick enough to sample your wares. What would happen if you fell?" Susan nods at Annie's stomach. "Would he obey our customs do you think?"

Annie whispers back, "Probably not."

"But surely he wouldn't desert you? That would make him even more unpopular."

Annie hides her mouth behind her hand. "I would feel a bit safer if only Matthew Stone would forget about providing a home and get on and marry that Violet."

"But why? Everyone knows they are betrothed,

they've been walking out for so long now."

"That may be, but I am certain there is something between her and Richard and I am not going to let her get away with it."

Thomas Atwool interrupts them. "Come on, Susan, we have to lead the procession now."

"Yes, go on, Mrs Atwool, they are all waiting for you. Congratulations, Tom. You make a fine couple."

Annie is arranging the flowers in a vase in Dryer's kitchen when he walks in.

"My word, where did they come from?"

"They are Susan's wedding posy. When she tossed them at the end I caught them and I thought they'd brighten up the place a bit."

She takes them through into the living room and places them on the table. "I didn't want to share them with everyone else at home. Besides, they look so much nicer here on your lovely polished table."

Their reflection, soft in the polished wood, enhances the beauty of the blooms and Dryer smiles his appreciation as he comes in after her and sits down. He has been very kind to her lately, but she knows in her heart that he is only using her.

She sits down on the floor beside him and removes his long boots. She loves the manly smell of the leather. He strokes her hair appreciatively and as she massages his feet she remembers Susan's words. If she was to become pregnant would he obey the custom of the island? Probably not. She looks up into his face. No, he is not a man to be forced against his will into an unwanted marriage, but he looks so tenderly at her now. Surely he wouldn't just desert her.

She smiles up at him and then looks away. It is,

after all, her only hope that he may be swayed because of his loneliness. She rests her head against his knee.

On the 8th September 1831, King William IV is crowned and a rumour soon spreads through the village that free beer is to be given away at the Verne. However, as the day progresses the normally quiet and subdued men of the island are transformed into bawdy groups of undisciplined fools.

Throughout the previous month, the people of the poorhouse suffered an outbreak of measles. The high fevers and delirium of the inmates induced fits and additional shag is called for, to be used as sheeting for the victims of this highly infectious disease.

Violet and her mother attend the Thanksgiving Day service, held 'For the mercy of the Lord in preserving us from the chelous measles', but their prayers are obviously ignored because in the first week of September her mother falls sick and Violet becomes increasingly worried. Her mother delivered the cloth to the poorhouse herself and must have contracted the measles. On the night of the Coronation she is rapidly getting worse.

There is no doctor resident on the island and so Auntie Sarah acts as both midwife and nurse, administering her herbs and potions, using ancient recipes passed down from previous generations. It is towards her cottage that Violet is heading, frantic with worry; she has disobeyed her absent father in order to ask Auntie Sarah's advice and obtain some kind of medicinal remedy to reduce her mother's fever.

It is a foggy evening and darkness falls early. As she stumbles along the cobbled street she hears the echo of her footsteps behind her. The air is cool with the damp and she shivers nervously. She has not been out alone at night for months and has for some reason a feeling of foreboding about her, on this silently shrouded night.

She hurries on with her head down, fearful of encountering some of the drunkards about, owing to the celebrations at the Verne. She heard a couple of disturbances on Mere Common earlier and is tense, all her senses straining for the faintest light or sound.

Breathlessly, she reaches Auntie Sarah's cottage. She knocks but no one answers and so she tries the door. The cottage is empty. Violet hesitates, then taking a little bottle from Auntie Sarah's medicine cupboard she puts it into the deep pocket of her cloak.

As she is leaving a woman calls to her from a neighbouring window. "She be gone round Barth Comben's in Castletown. His Missus is having a baby."

"Will you tell her, when she returns, that Violet Allen has taken some of her camomile, for me Ma's worse; and could she come and see her tomorrow, please?"

"Aye, I will child. Goodnight."

"Goonight," says Violet, and she turns from the house and into the square. Should she go herself and tell Auntie Sarah? She doesn't want to interrupt the birth of the Comben baby. She pauses. In the distance, in the direction of the Castletown track, she hears the regular sound of footsteps resounding in the swirling mist. Thinking that it is the midwife she makes towards it with relief.

As the thickening fog threatens to engulf her she can almost visualise ahead the gateway into Hell and knowing there are few homes, as yet, in Castletown her caution is increased. Apart from the old Portland Castle which is set back on her left, well off the beaten track, there are only a couple of inns that serve the sailors, the staff quarters adjoining them and the jetty, which is used by the fishermen and for the regular shipments of stone.

She has no way of knowing who is approaching and before the figure, who carries no lantern, materialises she thinks it prudent to keep out of sight. Her heart thumping, she darts into the opening beside the Castle Inn and covers her lantern with her dark cloak.

The figure passes by unaware of her. She recognises him in the glow from the inn window as Richard Dryer and is glad she has taken the precaution of concealing herself, for he is obviously on duty and she doesn't want to give him an excuse to question her.

Unveiling her lantern she creeps out of her hiding place, her courage returning as the footsteps die away. However, she is right outside the Castle Inn door when it bursts open revealing inside a noisy revelry, and out stumble two dishevelled, bearded sailor-men. They lean against each other for support and, having closed the inn door behind them, they stumble down the steps and virtually fall into Violet.

She gasps with fright, instinctively backing away, her eyes fixing on them warily.

The men obviously cannot believe their good fortune and, having already felt her against them, they take on smiling, leering expressions and, arms outstretched, lustfully lunge towards her. "What have we here, Silas? A tasty little wench, I'll be damned."

She cries out as her back comes up against the wall of the inn and in a panic she turns to run. Twisting her ankle on a protruding stone she falls and drops her lantern. The glass cracks, the spirit ignites; her eyes fall on the crumpled glass-and-metal object. She screams as the flames lick close to her cloak but one of the men, taking advantage of her distraction, is in an instant upon her.

Fear constricts her throat. "Please don't." There is hardly any sound. She tries to push him off her but she is too weak to make any impression on the man. She beats at her assailant's head and pulls at his hair but he is unmoved. She takes her weight on her hands to try to slide away from him and feels a searing pain in her palm. She gasps and screams in agony.

But the folk behind the heavy doors of the inn are themselves making such a row that they hear nothing. She has never in her life been so terrified.

The man's body is heavy, pinning her down. His filthy hands grope at her breasts whilst the other man stands over her, laughing gruesomely. Her hand closes over the large sliver of glass that is the cause of her own injury. The smell of him revolts her, and as his knees force her legs apart, she shudders and before she even registers the thought, the glass slashes at his face.

He howls like an animal and rises up onto his knees and with all her might she stabs at his chest. He slumps back over her, still supporting himself with his hands each side of her, but his breathing is laboured and a stupid, stunned expression is on his face. She cringes as his blood drips onto her dress, the weapon still protruding from his shirt-front, and then screams in terror as he collapses upon her.

His companion pulls at the heavy body, straining to see what harm has been done, and when he realises he curses angrily and strikes her round the head. She gasps in pain. For a moment blackness swamps her, but then the man is knocked off his feet as someone flies out of the darkness and butts him in the chest.

He is winded and she watches in awe as he receives a hard blow to his jaw, sending him staggering head-first against the wall of the inn, and with knees buckling he collapses awkwardly upon the inn steps.

Violet struggles to breathe. She still cannot move under the weight of the first man and is covered in his blood. Panicking she tries to free herself. Then the person who has defended her comes to her aid and through the dim, hazy light shed from the pub window she recognises the dark features of Richard Dryer.

He uses his boot on the man who lies across her and then gently he helps her to her feet.

"Oh, Violet," he cries, "you poor child." He smoothes her hair, then gripping her arm and taking her weight against him he hurries her from the scene.

As the relief of having his protection soothes her, she begins to weep. In between her sobs she says, "They attacked me … he tried to ravage me … they'll follow us." She grips his arm tightly. "I was so scared."

"Shush, be quiet, Violet, we must hurry away. They are in no fit state to follow; you have no fear of that."

"Whatever am I to do?" she whimpers, "I have no one to turn to. Ma is too ill to understand." If only she hadn't gone to Castletown, if only her father and brothers had been there she would not have been out at all.

"Shush, don't worry, I will sort it all out for you." He encourages and helps her to go faster. But it is hard, because the shock is affecting her. She is stunned and slowed, compared to the quick reactions of her prior panic, and not much more is said until he tries to turn her towards his cottage.

She hesitates as a new fear grips her. "No," she

whispers, "I must go to my mother, she is ill and I have to give her this medicine." She tries to divert him, but he resists. "Please, don't abandon me here," she whispers. "Won't you help me to my home, Mr Dryer? I am fearful those men will come and catch up with me and my ankle isn't half hurting."

"I have no intention of abandoning you, but look at the state you are in. If you came back to my cottage I could tend to your hand and clean you up a bit."

"No, Sir, I cannot. I have to get home with the potion."

They set off again towards Brandy Row, but although he has given in to her, still he continues to question her decision. "But whatever will your mother say? Your father will surely be very angry with you. Why are you out alone?"

"Because my mother was getting worse and I had to fetch the medicine and also I wanted Auntie Sarah to come. For I was all alone and frightened for her, and father and the boys are working."

"Working? I haven't seen them for days. Where are they, Violet? They are neglecting their duty to you. You should not be forced to take all this on your shoulders. Don't they care about you and your mother?"

"You don't understand, they know nothing of this, they are abroad on a fishing trip," says Violet.

He falls silent. What is he thinking, she wonders, as they continue past cottages, past Matthew's house and past the chapel. But then she shudders, beyond caring if he believes her or not. She just wants to be home and to know that her mother is all right and to feel safe in her bed.

Whilst Dryer supports her she can feel his cheek in her damp hair, his arms strong about her, and despite the danger of discovery she feels safer with

91

him there than without him and gratitude wells up in her.

Then he whispers into her hair, "I can't stop thinking of you, Violet. Don't you care just a little bit?"

It would be so easy to say 'yes' at this moment but, exhausted though she is, she says quietly, "Mr Dryer, how can I not be grateful to you, after tonight? You have done me a great service and I will always be beholden to you."

Finally they reach her home, and Dryer can see in the light from her window that she is in pain from both her ankle and her hand. He draws her into shadow and takes up her hand, gently putting it to his lips. Even in the darkness she feels his eyes on her and a warm tingling sensation up her arm. She draws back her hand slowly, not wanting to offend him. "I have to go, it's not safe."

"But what will you tell your mother, Violet?"

"Shush, I don't want to worry her. She mustn't hear. She is that ill that if I change and wash and bandage me hand she'll know no difference. Thank you so much for helping me, Mr Dryer." She pauses, "I can't thank you enough, but you'd best be going now, I'm sure I'll be all right now I'm home, thank you, Sir."

She opens her front door, then turns again to him. "Goodnight, Mr Dryer," she whispers.

"Goodnight, Violet," he whispers back.

As Violet closes the door on Dryer, her faculties seem to return to normal. She rakes up the fire and when it glows with heat she puts the kettle on to boil. In the meantime she soaks her clothes in cold water and bandages her hand. Having removed all evidence of violence she then goes up to check on her mother. She is sound asleep but soaked through with perspiration.

Violet rushes downstairs and brews the camomile. Then returning with the infusion, she wipes her mother's brow and, lifting her head gently, turns her pillow over so it is cool against her face.

"Ma," she says, carefully waking her. "Have a little drink of Auntie Sarah's medicine."

Her mother with some difficulty swallows the potion. She does not fully wake up and Violet easily settles her again for the night. Then she returns to her own room. She cannot sleep; her ankle and her hand are really hurting now. The fearful numbness has left her and her whole body feels bruised and aches. She cannot get comfortable as she tosses and turns, haunted by those horrible drunken faces. She smells again the beer and smoke, feels the chill, damp air swirling around her, the greasy hands going over her body; and then she can see the face of Richard Dryer. How he has changed in her eyes. She wanted him to hold her; she even wanted him to take her to his cottage, to lay her in his bed, to tend to her hand.

For months now she has felt the excitement of knowing that he is watching out for her. She likes to dwell on the hold she has over him and on the other secret desires that are stirred in his presence. At first she tries to deny it to herself, fearful of the consequences. She succeeds in avoiding him, but still she feels his eyes on her. On the beach, she might turn and catch a glimpse of him watching her from high up on the cliff tops. But it doesn't anger her. She likes it.

Could it be that she is in love with him, despite it being wrong? Surely the exhilaration that she experiences whenever he is near would have died by now, if it was just infatuation?

A relationship with him would be forbidden by her family and friends, they both would be shunned, but here she is, considering just that. Surely that only serves to show the depth of her emotions, for although she knows it is madness, still these feelings persist.

Is it only her concern for Matthew that prevents her from going to him? Her secret longings make her feel guilty, but there is no denying that it is not the same since she has met Richard Dryer. It is not just a matter of familiarity either. Matthew has been away for several days now; she should want him with the same intensity, but she does not. It is Richard she now yearns for. Where is Matthew when she needs him? What would have resulted if Richard had not helped her? She cannot bear to think of that, it is too terrible.

She tosses and turns throughout the night and is glad when the dawn finally breaks.

Dryer reluctantly leaves her and returns to his cottage deep in thought; he is almost certain that the man that Violet has stabbed is dead, and fears what that will mean for her. He needs to be alone to think this situation out.

At dawn his bed has not been disturbed. Exhausted, he has fallen asleep in his favourite chair, and having finally succumbed for a couple of hours, he awakes late but with a new purpose in mind.

He has devised a plan that should protect Violet and keep her safe forever, and one that will serve that Matthew Stone right into the bargain. Although in parts it goes against his conscience and he has yet to find the courage to put it into practice, his reasoning is almost plausible and he is therefore quite hopeful of the outcome.

CHAPTER 5 *(September 1831)*

THE CONSEQUENCES

The following morning, to Violet's great relief, her mother is much improved. Her fever has reached its height during the night and she is considerably brighter when Auntie Sarah arrives.

"How's your Ma, Vi?" Auntie Sarah asks with concern.

"Oh, she's much better this morning, Auntie Sarah. Come up and see her. I think it is your medicine did the trick. I hope you didn't mind me helping myself?"

"Course not, me dear. I've brought her some calf's foot jelly. She can have a little now we've broken the fever." Auntie Sarah goes to follow her upstairs. "But, my dear, have 'ee heard about the murder in Castletown?"

She halts on the stairs, as a sinking sensation ices through her. Murder! She swallows … but it wasn't like that. What are people saying? She turns back to Auntie Sarah, a look of shock on her face. She finds her voice, for surely Auntie Sarah will expect some response, "Murder?"

"Oh my dear, didn't you know? I'd have thought it would be all round Portland by now. A sailor by the name of Silas Jones were stabbed outside the Castle Inn. They reckon 'twere a woman involved. His mate were with him. They probably fell out over the wench," she says.

Will Auntie Sarah notice the sudden flush of

95

colour in her cheeks? A knot of fear is tight in the pit of her stomach. She cannot hide her bandaged hand, but if Auntie Sarah notices anything she makes no comment as she follows Violet upstairs.

Violet's mother is considerably cheered to see her friend and she leaves them discussing the gossip. She rushes downstairs and out into the backyard. It is chilly outside and she shivers as she tips out the pink cold water in which her dress and shift have been soaking. The blood has soaked through both materials where her cloak did not meet at the front. Her cloak is not too bad and the few marks don't notice after she has washed each spot with special care. Her dress is a dark pink colour anyway, but her shift still has a tell-tale patch that looks fawn. She takes some lye and scrubs at it some more.

It had been too easy, surely he couldn't be dead … but then there had been a lot of blood. Why hadn't she realised that at the time? Her knuckles are sore and red as she scrubs away at the damning evidence. They were drunk and about to abuse her. What else could she have done, she acted in defence of herself, but if everyone is saying it is murder she could be hanged!

She becomes more and more distraught as she thinks about it. That other man saw her and could recognise her again. The more she dwells on it the more scared she becomes of leaving the house. The cold of the yard has soaked into her and her fingers are hurting from the icy water.

She hears Auntie Sarah come down the stairs and call "Goodbye" to her mother but she does not come in from the yard until she hears the front door close. She is afraid that, seeing the bandage, even her mother might suspect her.

Once sure Auntie Sarah has gone she goes inside and is trying to warm up by keeping busy in the kitchen, when a sharp rap at their door gives her a start. She hesitates; she daren't go to the door. Keeping out of sight, she peeps through the living room window, but she can only see the back of a man's frock coat, whoever it is, standing in tight to the building. She begins to shake. The man knocks again.

Her mother calls out, "Who is it, Vi?"

She has to answer; "It's all right, Ma. I'm just getting it." She opens the door a crack, keeping her toe against it, but gladly lets the man into the passage when she recognises him.

"Oh, thank heavens 'tis you," she whispers urgently. "I am so worried. What shall I do? They're saying the man was murdered."

Richard Dryer removes his hat, and looks gravely at her, saying, "Go in and sit down, Violet, I want to talk to you." He follows her into the living room and waits until she is seated in the nearest chair. "I am afraid the man that you stabbed has died and the other sailor will be able to identify you. Although it was in self-defence it will be your word against his." He pauses and looks down on her with compassion. "I have not slept all night thinking about this and as I see it, there is only one course of action left to you, but you have to be prepared to agree. You need me to give you an alibi." He puts up his hand to prevent her interrupting him. "Violet, I have a proposition to put to you, but I don't want you to say anything for a moment, just sit quietly and listen."

He continues, carefully, "I am the only person, other than the drunken associate of the dead man, who can connect you with the incident. I am willing to say that we were together that night at my house but I cannot do so without jeopardising your reputation. Unless you are willing to return my

97

affections in the manner I would wish, and consider accepting a genuine offer of marriage, it is not possible for my alibi to be taken seriously."

She is stunned. "But you know I cannot … What about Matthew? … And my parents, they will never accept you."

"At present they are not my concern. My main worry is your safety and keeping this matter to ourselves."

This is a nightmare. She gets up, moving slowly, but her mind is racing. She goes to him, looks up into his face and takes up his hands in hers, "Can't you just tell them the truth, that I was attacked and that you helped me defend myself?"

"The truth is not that simple, is it, Violet? The man was already dying when I arrived on the scene. I did not actually see what happened and we don't know what the other fellow is going to say, do we? It wouldn't bear close scrutiny and could you stand the interrogation?" He pauses, watching her carefully.

"I want to help you, but I think it best if you were nowhere near the scene of the crime. The men were known to be excessively drunk and are not local people. It was foggy and dark and I am sure he'd never recognise you again, but even if he said that he did, no one would take his testimony seriously and he'd have an impossible job proving it against my alibi. I am an officer of the crown and my word carries a lot of weight."

She releases his hands angrily. "You are prepared to tell a falsehood nevertheless," she cries.

He takes her by the shoulders as if to shake her, but his voice is breaking up as he says, "Only to save you from harm, because I care so much for you. Violet, I can provide well for you. You'll not want for anything."

Her mind runs back again and again over what has happened. "But I was seen at Auntie Sarah's. I left a message with her neighbour; they know I was out last night."

"Did you say you were going round to Castletown?"

"No," she hesitates. "I asked her if she could get Auntie Sarah to call and see Ma in the morning."

"Well, there you are then. No one knows you changed your mind … It will be all right, I promise you."

It is tempting to feel safe, to imagine that his love protects her, but it is wicked to consider hiding the honest facts about the sailor and cruel to betray Matthew's confidence so easily. She longs to accept this way out, but will she ever be able to trust Richard again after he has manipulated her in this way?

"Violet, I'll protect you if you'll marry me. They'll take the word of a respected government official against a drunken sailor. You've only got to tell your mother that you've been seeing me and that it's in your mind to marry me. You do feel something for me, I know that you do. I wouldn't want you otherwise. Has Matthew Stone set a date yet for your wedding?"

She is ringing her hands in her apron. Could it be that Matthew did not love her as much as she thought he did? "Well, no. But …"

"No buts, Violet. He cannot care for you the way I do. If he did you'd have been wed long ago." Dryer turns away from her.

Matthew might even hate her if he knew what she was capable of. How can she possibly think straight in the midst of this nightmare?

Still Dryer persists. "The fact is that sailor could have you convicted of murder. As the daughter of a suspected smuggler you might have difficulty convincing them of your innocence, but that is the chance you will have to take if you admit to what actually happened."

She sinks back down into the chair. The situation is hopeless. He kneels down at her side and takes her hands in his.

"You know in your heart that I love you and that for as long as I live, I will care for you. You know that, don't you, Violet?"

Matthew will never forgive her and her parents and friends will shun her. But what choice does she have? After a long silence she says, "All right, I'll do it, I'll marry you." She gives a deep sigh. "I'll do anything you say."

"Oh, Violet, thank God, you won't regret it, I promise you." He pulls her up out of the chair, and she falls exhausted into his arms. She buries her head in his coat and weeps with defeat. His arms are about her and his strong body supports her as she sobs defencelessly. Why has he done this? Will she ever forgive him? Although it seems to be the only way open to Dryer, the tired defeat of her acceptance to his proposition, and her distress as she sobs in his arms, tears at his heart.

He hates to see her in such anguish, but knows she will never marry him any other way because her parents and friends will disown her. This could be his only chance and although he sees himself as devious, contriving such an underhand trick, and manipulating her in this caddish way, he convinces himself that he has her best interests at heart. She must never regret this decision. He will see that she never does.

He strokes her hair to soothe her, loving the feel of her slight body warm against him. A feeling of triumph sneaks through him, vying with the guilt.

He hasn't won yet though, they have a long battle ahead and a feeling of unease takes over.

Violet's mother hears the voice of Richard Dryer, then Violet's wafting up through the ceiling. There is an urgency in the conversation that gives her cause for concern but she is too ill to move and is forced to wait.

When eventually Dryer has gone and Violet is sufficiently recovered to go and check if her mother needs anything, Mary Allen broaches the subject cautiously; "I heard Dryer downstairs earlier. What were that all about, Vi?"

Perhaps her mother can tell she has been crying. She looks away not wanting to worry her. "He were just enquiring after your health, Ma."

Mrs Allen laughs weakly at that, "Come now, Vi. I'm too old in the tooth to fall for that one. You surely don't think I'm that daft do you? Come and sit down and tell me what's going on. If you can't confide in your old Ma 'tis a sorry state you're in."

It is no use. She has to tell someone or she will go mad, "Oh Ma, I'm in a dreadful fix."

"If that Dryer have laid a hand on you he'll be thrown off the island." Her voice is sharp at the thought.

"No, no, Ma, it's not like that, really it's not. Although he says he wants me, he has behaved like a gentleman always. Last night he saved me from the threat of two drunken sailors. He wants to help me but I don't know what to do. I have done something dreadful."

"Whatever are you babbling about? I don't understand what you're on about."

"I've killed a man ... Ma." She begins to cry again, "I didn't mean it, I just panicked ... but he bled so much he must have bled to death."

"Oh my God, Vi! Whatever have you done!"

"The man, Silas Jones who's been murdered, Ma ..." she sobs, "I did it. 'Tis me they're looking for."

"Whatever are you saying, child? ... For heaven's sake, Vi, tell me from the beginning, what happened?"

Between her sobs she explains everything. Her mother listens in dismay. Then she holds out her arms to her. "Come here, child. Don't take on so."

She sits down on the bed and her mother holds her close. "Those men were devils to try and abuse and violate you in that way and you were justified in defending yourself." She pats her shoulder gently. "They were bullies and deserved what they got. Somehow we'll sort it out, we must ... somehow."

"I never meant to kill anyone, Ma," she sniffs. "I was that scared I panicked. I thought I was going to die myself."

"I know that, Vi, and I understand about that, and I am quite sure that any defenceless young girl would have panicked just the same, but what is all this nonsense about accepting Dryer's offer of marriage? Have you taken leave of your senses?"

"Ma, he won't help me if I don't."

"But that's blackmail!"

"He doesn't see it that way, Ma, he says the alibi won't work unless we say we've been walking out for some time ... and if it doesn't work, I could be transported. Ma, I couldn't stand that, I'd rather die."

"Some people would rather die than wed a man they don't care for, Vi," says her mother watching her carefully. Violet looks away and then back at her mother.

"But I do care for him, Ma." There, she'd said

it. "If it weren't for Matthew, I'd have wed him anyway."

"I knew there was more to it than met the eye," says her mother nodding in acceptance of the truth.

"I know he's a Kimberlin and an enemy to the free-traders but I cannot help myself. I've tried to get him out of my head, but he's always been in the back of my mind since I first set eyes on him. I felt right from the start he wanted me and it excited me more than anything."

"I've never seen such a willing lamb to the slaughter. But if that is how you really feel, what's bothering you?"

The tears well up again. "Matthew," she says. "I cannot bear to hurt him. He doesn't deserve it."

"That may be so, but 'tis better to start off by wedding the right bloke. A man like Dryer could drive a wedge between husband and wife that will cause more pain than you could handle. He will always be there, tempting you to sin if you are not sure of your love. That is what you have to think about, Violet. A mistake now will hurt Matthew far more in the long run."

"I love Matthew too, you know that, Ma, but I want Richard more. I am so confused and frightened." She brushes away the tears.

Her mother passes her a hanky from the embroidered sachet at her bedside and Violet dabs at her sore eyes and then blows her nose.

"Have you told him you love him?"

"No, I would feel like a hussy. He thinks I am accepting his proposal for an alibi, but I think he knows the effect he has on me, 'tis something I can't hide." She looks away again. "Only you know the truth, Ma. I just don't know how to admit it to Matthew, or to Father for that matter." She pauses, "They will never forgive me. The whole village will hate me. All Matty's relations, my own father and brothers, all Annie Shaddick's family … they'll all hate me … and Richard. 'Tis a miserable situation."

"I will always be here for you, love. I cannot go against your father, but I'll always be here if you need me, Vi. This is something you have to be very sure you want to take on though … it is not going to be easy. Matthew will be torn apart, but he is a good catch, a strong character and a handsome enough young man and he'll have no difficulty finding someone else … He's young. He'll get over it, you'll see."

"I couldn't bear it if he hated me, Ma. It would be dreadful."

"He couldn't hate you, Vi, I just know he couldn't."

"Don't, Ma," she sniffs, "you're just making me feel worse."

"I don't want to do that, but you have to be clear in your mind what you are going to say when the men come back. You have only got a few days to decide."

"I really don't know what I'll do, Ma. I'm going to need you to help me work it out." She wipes the tears from her eyes.

"I think the best thing is to keep it simple. We cannot tell them about the sailors attacking you, it would be best to keep that between ourselves. Just start off by telling Matthew and your father that you have fallen in love with Dryer, that you still love Matty, but that you are 'in love' with Dryer. There is no sense beating about the bush. Men like to have the facts straight down the line and we shall have to wait and see how they take it." She ponders a moment, adding, "I'm afraid that if they make trouble, Dryer will turn nasty and he'll get them in the end with the smuggling."

"I don't think he would act out of spite, Ma, but it might be a good idea to let them think that he would. They might think first before they do anything they'd be likely to regret." Violet blows her nose in the handkerchief. She is tired of struggling with the problem. They will just have to wait and see and she will have to put up with the consequences.

When talking to Annie later that day, Dryer feigns concern that the murder incident is not being investigated very carefully. "Not much seems to be happening with regard to investigating the murder that everyone is gossiping about."

But Annie is not at all surprised, saying, "Portlanders don't care in the least about the death of a Kimberlin. It was probably just another argument between two drunks, who aren't worth bothering with anyway."

Dryer smiles wryly, for if Annie had any idea of the truth she would adopt a very different attitude.

"I hear tell the victim was a sailor by the name of Silas Jones and he was found in a pool of blood at dawn, at the side of the Castle Inn."

It is obvious to Dryer that when the other sailor came round he had dragged his companion out of sight, then realising that he was dead he'd fled from the scene and returned to his vessel in a panic, deciding to keep mum, in order to save his own skin.

It is up to him though to try to put the frighteners on this man. He cannot risk the possibility of him identifying Violet. He decides to enlist the help of a lieutenant of the Portland Coast Fencibles, encouraging him to believe that the crime was the result of an argument between two people the worse for drink. He also suggests that they board the ship and report the incident to the captain.

The following morning, Violet paces the living room in agitation. Where is he? Why hasn't he come to let her know what is happening out there? Surely he knows how anxious she is?

Then she sees him pass their window and hears the knock at the door. Thank God. She lets him in. "What's happened? What have you heard? How could you leave me so long without news?"

"Calm down, Violet. I have been working on your behalf. Go on through and I'll tell you."

He follows her into their parlour. "I have managed to discredit the rumour of a woman being involved and the accepted theory is that it was a disagreement between two sailors. Please sit down, Violet, and relax."

"I can't relax. How can I?"

"You don't have to worry any more. I went with Lieutenant Lano to the quay and we boarded three vessels. I was able to recognise the man, but I didn't identify him. His captain was very anxious to appear helpful, but not surprisingly his ship has already set sail."

"So the man has gone back to sea then?"

"Yes, Violet. The ship has sailed. You are much safer now."

"Thank God."

"It is important though that you carry on as normal. Hiding away will only cause suspicion," he says.

"But I am too frightened to go out. What will folk think when they see my bandaged hand?"

"Violet, the only man who could have identified you has fled. With my alibi, you have nothing to fear anymore. Besides I will come with you and you won't even need to speak. I'll do all the talking."

Eventually he convinces her that it will be safe to venture out to get water. "I can help you carry the water pails back. Leave your yoke behind, we can take a bucket each, and then you won't need to use your bad hand."

Although she is reassured by his presence, as she feared their mere walking together is sufficient to fuel the gossip. Curtains twitch and conversations halt as they walk along together.

Annie Shaddick is in the Square. She is already acutely aware of something between them but has been unable until now to point a finger. She jumps at this opportunity. "Talk about when the cat's away, the mice'll play," she says loudly to a group of women at the well; but they quickly disperse under the cool, belittling gaze of Dryer.

"Have you nothing better to do than idle around here gossiping, Annie? I would have thought there was plenty to occupy you back at the cottage."

The knife twists painfully in the wound as Dryer skilfully turns the tables on his domestic, and Violet watches with some satisfaction as Annie tosses her head in the air before stomping off with the buckets, back to his cottage.

For the next week they spend every spare moment together. Richard is eager to make his intentions public knowledge and Mrs Allen is cautiously allowing the situation to be tested by public opinion. Violet and her mother dread Matthew's return as the village gossips wait with bated breath.

On the day they are due to come home, Mary Allen suggests that Violet and Dryer should spend the day away from the cove. "You both need time together to talk quietly away from prying eyes," she says, but she hopes that it will enable her to break the news more gently, in their absence. In any event it will safeguard the men against interruption as they beach with their illicit cargo.

Violet wants to run away. How can she face them all? She is glad to accept her mother's suggestion and an hour later they are walking south, in the direction of the Beale. It is a typically damp September morning, but when the early mists clear and the sun breaks through it will be a beautiful day.

Silently, they follow the dry stone wall up Lankridge to the cliff top path. The diffused light is already touching the long grass heavily laden with dew. It glistens like tiny lanterns, swaying in the breeze.

While they walk, Violet tries to untangle her thoughts. Her face looks strained. There is so much to worry about: the death of the sailor, Richard's proposal, Matty's reaction, her father's attitude, and her future loyalty.

How can she betray the secrets of past generations? Surely Richard cannot expect that of her, but then neither could she betray her future husband's trust. From this day on she must turn a blind eye to anything connected with smuggling. Dryer continues walking silently by her side.

They reach the path that borders the quarries and turn along it, disturbing a rabbit which runs ahead of them, its white tail bobbing and flashing before disappearing between the large slabs of rock on their left. Violet stops dead.

"What's wrong?' asks Dryer with concern.

Violet remembers the warning words of the fortune-teller who said to beware of danger and death. What if it was true? She says, "It's a bad omen."

"What is?" asks Dryer.

"I don't want to go on," Violet turns back but

feels Richard grab her arm. "We can't go that way."

"Don't be silly, Violet, there's nothing there."

"I'd rather go back, you see they're unlucky. Everyone on Portland knows, it means a disaster," whispers Violet.

"What does?" exclaims Richard, "a little rabbit!" He looks amazed.

"Hush, don't say it. You mustn't say it."

Seeing her distress he does not pursue the matter, but does as she requests. They turn back, silence between them again, and divert up over Royal Common instead. The haze is lifting and the West Bay is now on their left as they backtrack. Violet notices Mr Stone's lugger as it makes towards Chesil. At least the men are home safely. They will soon know the worst.

Her face is troubled as the thought of Matthew stabs at her mercilessly. He will be so hurt that she has been hiding her feelings from him and now she has decided to insult him in this way. How will she ever be able to face him again? She diverts Richard eastward across the common, but not quickly enough. He has noticed her sadness and also the vessel.

As they walk across the isolated common land, he takes her hand in his. Violet stares down at the stunted turf at her feet, but is not seeing it. She is only aware of Richard now, with his hand holding hers, and the thought that he is soon to be her husband. They come to a large flat slab of rock and they rest a while.

"Violet, why did that rabbit frighten you so? It couldn't harm you." He is genuinely puzzled.

"No one on Portland likes them. They're dangerous; there are always accidents in the quarries, 'cus of their burrows weakening the pit sides. The quarrymen will down tools if they sees a coney and go home, and if you see them in Chis'ell

109

it means they're fleeing from the sea flooding over Ham. No one ever says their name on Portland 'cus they're a bad omen."

"I see," he says, "but if accidents occur it's got to be coincidence. You can't blame the, er ... the wildlife if the sea floods Chiswell. They shouldn't frighten you, not a harmless animal."

"I'd rather not talk about it, please," she pleads. "We've trouble enough without making it worse."

"Violet, do you really feel that hopeless? When all I want to do is look after you and make you happy." He looks at her so sadly that immediately she regrets her words.

"Oh, I didn't mean it like that ... I really need your help and I'm very grateful to you and although I know I shouldn't go against my family and it's wrong of me to deceive them, I want to marry you ... but ... well ... I'm just so worried about hurting Matthew"

"Matthew, always bloody Matthew!" he shouts. "If you love the damned fellow that much, go on back to him. Risk being arrested for murder, or being transported and if you should get away with that, accept being a fisherman's wife for the rest of your life, but remember, they are all breaking the law and if ever they get caught, they'll be imprisoned, or transported, and then you may just as well be a widow." He gets up and stalks off.

Violet is stunned. Now she has hurt his feelings. She didn't want to upset him either. How could this big mature man be so vulnerable? He is truly jealous of Matthew. She jumps up and clambers down after him.

"Richard!" she calls. "Richard, wait. Please wait. You have got it all wrong." Suddenly aware that she has the power to hurt two people, she has reached a decision. At the foot of the rock, she stands and shouts to him, "No, you are wrong. Please don't be angry with me. It is guilt that I feel, not love. I feel guilty for hurting Matthew because I realise now that I am no longer in love with him ... for if I was ... how could I be in love with you?"

He stops dead and turns.

"Yes, Richard ... I really do believe I am in love with you."

She runs to him and he takes her in his arms and swings her around. He holds her so tight and kisses her so hard that she is left gasping for breath. "You have no idea how much that means to me, my darling," he whispers in her ear, "I have longed to hear those words."

"It is true, Richard. I love and need you more than anyone else in the whole world."

They kiss again and then stroll along holding hands in the sunlight. Seagulls cry as they soar above them and a tiny skylark rises from the ground ahead, luring them away from its nest, its high-pitched melodic song reflecting the happiness of their mood. Violet feels so much easier now that at last she can be honest with herself and they actually laugh together for the first time.

Some of the barriers between them are gradually crumbling. There are still many obstacles ahead, but at least she is no longer fighting her feelings. Somehow that now seems more important for her peace of mind.

For a short while they can forget the storm that is brewing down in the cove. High above the rest of them, they can pretend that it cannot touch them there, that nothing is amiss, at least until they return together just before teatime.

When they arrive back at the cottage, Richard insists

on facing Violet's father, but whatever her mother has said has done nothing to calm her father's fury. As they enter the small living room together, the atmosphere of animosity is almost tangible.

Her father jumps up, red-faced and shaking with anger, and before Richard has the chance to say 'Good evening' he demands, "Who the hell do you think you are, marching in here as if you own Violet? You haven't earned the right to enter my home uninvited."

"Forgive my impertinence, Mr Allen, but I am with Violet and hoped that as her guest I might be welcome in her home."

"In that case you are misinformed and I would appreciate it if you would leave this instant."

"I was hoping that Mrs Allen would have explained my intentions regarding your daughter and that you would be prepared to give me a chance to prove that my proposition would greatly benefit Violet's future."

"This is contemptible. What do you mean by this ridiculous proposition, imposing your will on an innocent child, turning her against her family and friends and even her betrothed? You should be ashamed of yourself. A man with your breeding should set an example to simple folk." Without giving Dryer a chance to reply, he continues, "Violet is barely eighteen and easily impressed by your gentlemanly ways, but what you suggest is impossible. I won't allow it. She is wedding Matthew Stone, whether you like it or not." He emphasises this last remark by pointing angrily at Richard, but he remains unshaken.

"I am sorry you feel like this, Sir, because I wished to avoid any unpleasantness. I have only Violet's happiness at heart. I believe it is me and not Stone whom she loves and I know I can offer her a more honest and stable way of life than Matthew can." Boldly he takes hold of Violet's hand.

"You miserable land shark, you have the nerve to talk about honesty after the underhand manner you have wormed your way into her affections as soon as our backs are turned."

Dryer wipes some of Violet's father's spittle from his face. "You can think what you like about that, Mr Allen, but Violet is a grown woman and quite capable of deciding for herself and she has accepted my offer. Ask her yourself."

Her father turns to her. "Well, what have you got to say for yourself, young woman?"

She has been speechless until now and her throat feels tight as she tries to form the words. "I don't want to hurt you, Father, but 'tis for the best."

"For the best! For whom, I'd like to know? Have you forgotten about Matthew, about all your plans?"

"No. How could I?" A feeling of nausea sweeps over her, "Please try to understand, Father, I have good reasons for changing my mind. I am very fond of Matthew, but this is for the best."

"You had better be damned sure of those good reasons, because if you are determined to go through with this you can leave this house right now. I am finished with you. You have brought shame to the family name. Go, Violet, if it's for the best. Go now and don't come back. I don't want you in this house ever again. Do you understand?"

"Oh no!" Her mother starts to cry. "Don't be so hard on her, please. It's not her fault."

"Be quiet, Mary," he says. "Go on, Violet, choose. It's him or us. It's as simple as that." Her father has miscalculated. He is sure that his little girl will not have the courage to walk out with the Kimberlin.

Violet is shocked and dry-eyed. She cannot

believe what she is hearing. She knew it would be bad, but not like this. She has never seen her father so angry. Tom is comforting her mother, while the other two boys just stand there with their mouths open. She turns towards Richard and silently walks out.

She walks by his side, past Matthew's house, as if in a trance. It seems that, far away in the distance, she can hear a voice calling, "Violet, Violet". It is Matthew, she knows, but she walks on as if she'd not heard. She cannot cope with such a painful confrontation, now. She feels sick with misery and shame, filled with sadness, confusion and guilt.

On reaching his home, Richard opens the door and lets her in. Violet sits in the cold living room while he lights the fire and puts the kettle on to boil. When he returns she is still in the same unnaturally straight-eyed, stiff-backed position that he'd left her in, and he is suddenly worried that the shock has been too much for her. Violet has been so very close to her family and although she has said she is in love with him, he is still a stranger to her in reality.

He sits down by her feet and takes her hands in his. He speaks softly to her. If only she would cry. Slowly she turns her deep blue eyes on him, and as he pleads with her, he gently penetrates the invisible barrier that is separating her from reality. The tears gradually well up and he holds her close, yet again.

The poor girl has done nothing but cry with every contact I've had with her, he thinks. How much of her pain is he actually responsible for? It is, after all, her decision in the face of her father to walk out with him. Surely that must mean something? After a while she composes herself and he goes to make them both a drink.

She drinks it down. Then, helplessly, she looks at him. "Whatever are we going to do now? They will never forgive me, you know. It's not 'cus of Matty they're cross. If you were another boy from the island, they'd say, 'All's fair in love and war', and forget about it; but you're a foreigner, a Kimberlin, and it's that what's making them all mad. Last time a girl from here said she wanted to wed a bloke from Wyke, they stoned him with pebbles out on Chesil when the couple tried to meet and dragged her back to the island. So nothing could come of it. They'll hate me more than they do you, if we marry, 'cus I'm betraying them all."

He stands up and walks to the fireplace. "We could always move away."

"Oh no!" She jumps up at him. "I'll not leave, you can't make me leave. They'd never forgive me, if I left with you." She grips him by the shoulders, "Please don't make me leave here. You've forced me to betray them. Isn't that enough?"

"Forced you? What do you mean? I haven't forced you to do anything."

"Yes you did. You said you wouldn't give me an alibi if I didn't marry you."

Removing her hands from his shoulders, he says gently, "I said no such thing. I said the alibi would not be taken seriously if we were not committed to each other." This is the truth, but he'd also implied that he would not help her unless she accepted his proposition, and this is why the guilt still tears at him. Will she believe his nobler motives?

"I love you, Violet, so much that I have gone against all my principles to cover up the fact that you killed that sailor. You know in your heart that I love you and I believe that you care for me too. You have said as much, or are you playing games with me just to save your skin?"

She stares up at him and all he can see is confusion in her expression. He cannot bear it. "You don't have to marry me, Violet. I can't make you," he says, defeated. "We need only to keep up the pretence for a while and then we can call it off if you prefer and you can go back to Matthew."

"It's too late now, the damage has been done. I will just have to learn to live with my guilt. I'm sorry if I misjudged you … but it's all been said now and I can't go back. I didn't think me Pa could turn against me so easily. I want to stay here though, I want to stay here with you and maybe one day win them round."

Relief courses through him. He has given her a way out but she hasn't taken it. They have cleared the air and he feels more honest. They can fight this together.

"All right, don't worry, I don't want to leave either. I like it here and, strangely enough, I like the people. They have strong characters and I don't blame them for hating me for stealing you from them, but they're going to have to get used to the idea. I'm here to stay and I'll not compromise. They will have to come round and accept that Smallmouth doesn't exempt them from the way of life set down by the government. They have to step in line, like the rest of the country. I know that if they could, they'd cut the umbilical cord that ties them to Britain and float off and become a Channel Island, but they cannot and submission is inevitable sooner or later."

He has forgotten that Violet does not understand half of the words he is using, but she obviously understands his meaning because she warns, "Don't let them lull you into a false sense of security. You may be led to believe that they submit but you'll never conquer a Portlander's spirit; they will never let you."

She smiles at him then and he holds her against his broad chest and strokes her hair. "They'll get used to me in time, Violet. We'll be all right, you and I." He kisses her forehead. "Come on, you are exhausted. I think it's bedtime."

Her face suddenly flushes. Is she remembering the last time she was in his cottage, when she came to hang the curtains?

"But where am I to sleep?" she asks.

"Well, I have only the one double bed. There is nowhere else." He cannot help grinning, but then he adds, "I won't touch you, if you don't want me to, until we are married, but we can sleep in the same bed. It will be nice." He smiles and holds out his hand to her and she follows him upstairs. Why did he say that? How the hell can he stop himself?

Shyly she removes her clothes. He sits down on the edge of the bed, and with his back to her he also undresses. But he cannot contain himself and before she is in the bed he turns to catch his first glimpse. She is exquisite. Her summer-tanned skin looks rich and supple against the white of her chemise and her slender legs are perfect. Her breasts are firm and rounded. He can see the shape of her nipples, pert against the fine muslin, and his lips long to taste and caress them. Not noted for his self-control, he is already finding it hard to remain on his side of the room. He is not fully versed in the customs of the island and Violet has given him no indication of her wishes. Now he cannot bring himself to ask.

He watches her, now completely naked, lift back the covers and get into his bed, surprised that there is no hesitation in her actions; she lies there watching him.

Self-consciously he finishes undressing and puts out the lamp, leaving just the chamberstick making seductive, flickering patterns on the walls and casting fascinating shadows on their faces.

Violet lies with her dark hair spread out on the white pillowcase and before getting into bed he bends over her and kisses her mouth. Her mouth is sensitive to his; her arms go around his neck. She is so responsive it is too much for him. He pulls the blankets back and kisses her beautiful body, her breasts, her stomach. She writhes with passion at each touch; she wants him, there is no doubt. His whole body aches for her and she lies there in sweet abandonment.

His heart and hands are gentle and loving, but his muscles are hard and athletic; her body is soft and yielding. He touches and caresses and kisses until there is no turning back. He delays, wanting the moment to last forever, but feels her pulling him into her, her body arching with passion. She cries out as he enters her, but she clings to him, loving him. He must have hurt her but she kisses and holds him tightly, her body moving rhythmically in tune with his own.

It is bliss; he closes his eyes and kisses her mouth, her neck, and her skin so smooth. Ripples of joy run through him. He feels the tremors of joy running through Violet and her gasps of pleasure thrill him. She belongs to him now and forever. He relaxes, hugging her to him, whispering, "I love you", nuzzling into her hair. He basks in the smell of her and they lay wrapped in each other's arms until finally they fall asleep.

It is Annie Shaddick who wakes them the next day. She has, as usual, let herself in and is raking out the ashes when Dryer enters from the stairway door.

"Good morning, Annie," says Dryer, unusually

bright for the beginning of the day.

"Morning, Mr Dryer," she replies, still on her hands and knees.

"Morning, Annie," says a female voice, as Violet follows him into the room.

Annie jerks up her head. She brushes her hair from her face with the back of her hand, and in doing so writes a black coal mark across her already black expression.

"What's she doin' here?" she shouts, as if he owes her an explanation.

"We are to be married, Annie. So I am afraid I will no longer require your services." The double implication of that remark infuriates Annie.

"You are welcome, of course, to stay until you can find another position."

"I ain't doin' no scivying for the likes o' her. She can do 'er own dirty work." So saying, she throws down the brush and pan into the grate and stalks out of the cottage. Angry tears fall as Annie makes her way home. Why does that Violet always get what she, Annie, wants? She will never forgive them for this. She thinks with determination, I'll get even with 'em one way or another.

CHAPTER 6 *(September 1831)*

MATTHEW

Matthew has eagerly looked forward to seeing Violet again. Whilst away he's longed for the sparkle of her eyes, her mischievous smile. In France he bought her a present and on the day that he returns home he burns with anticipation. Then he sees her, walking past his cottage by the side of Richard Dryer. It is a strange Violet, who seems in a trance and who does not respond to his desperate call. Something is very wrong. He hurries to her home to speak to her father.

Violet's brother Bob opens the door to him and appears uncomfortable as he stands aside to let him in. Matthew walks into the living room. He sees Mary Allen's red-rimmed eyes. He looks from face to face and hears Robert Allen saying, "Sit down, lad, we've something to tell you."

They pity him. "I'd sooner stand, thank you, Mr Allen. What's happened?"

Violet's mother leaves the room, tearfully, before the explanation is completed. Five minutes later Matthew strides from the cottages. He has to get away from them all, from the humiliation and from the eyes that wait for his reaction.

He walks across the scooped-out beach of the cove, towards the rocks under the cliffs of West Weares; and there in Hallelujah Bay, where the driftwood collects in the crevices and pools between the seaweed-capped rocks, he sits and stares at the horizon. Gradually the anger surfaces through the pain. The realisation that he has lost so easily the one thing that made his hard work worthwhile is unbearable.

He jumps up. Gone is all control as he grabs a large piece of timber, re-sculptured by the sea, and brings it crashing against the rock. Again and again he smashes the driftwood against its natural anvil until finally it, and he, breaks down. No one witnesses his desolation.

Having sat for almost two hours with his head in his hands, he sees in the distance a female figure carefully picking her way through the rocks towards him. The setting sun casts a golden light in her curls – his heart sinks – it is Molly. She approaches cautiously.

"Hello, Matty." She stands a distance from him as if scared to come any closer. "We've been looking for you."

"Who has?" asks Matthew, with just a glimmer of hope.

"Hannah and me," says Molly. "Hannah went towards the Bound Stone, so I came towards the Beale." She pauses awkwardly, and adds quietly, "Are you all right?"

'No, I'm not', are the words that scream out inside him, but instead he snaps back at her, "Of course I am, Moll. I just wanted my own company for a bit, that's all."

Molly hesitates, "I'll be going on back then, I just wanted to find you and see you are all right." She turns sadly, to retrace her steps.

"No, wait, Moll. Don't go, come and sit awhile. I could do with a kind face and a good ear for a spell." She was only being thoughtful. He cannot hurt her feelings.

Molly is quickly by his side, pleased to be of

comfort, she kisses him gently on his cheek. He puts his arm about her. "You're a good pal, Moll. I'm glad you came to find me. I just can't understand it; she must know what this is doing to me." His voice breaks up, his head and shoulders sag.

"I dunno, Matty, really I don't. 'Tis like she've been bewitched, it don't make no sense at all. I thought that Dryer'd mean trouble, he always did take a shine to our Violet right from the start. She'd say to me how he'd make her feel strange with his staring, but I never thought he'd get the better of her, never."

"I really counted on us getting wed. It never entered me head anything like this could happen. I were sure she loved me. She said as much often enough."

"I know Violet loves you, Matty. It makes you wonder if Dryer has some sort of hold over her."

"What do you mean?"

"Well, I was thinking about the gossip."

Matthew lets out a faintly exasperated sigh, "What are folks saying now? I don't hold much with gossips, Molly."

"Well, it was to do with the murder of that sailor. 'Tis said that a woman were involved, and I wondered if maybe Violet knew more than she let on. I know it sounds daft but it is the only thing that has happened recently that is out of the ordinary."

"That's ridiculous, Molly. Violet is not capable of hiding anything so dreadful, she is too gentle and honest … Besides, I'm sure she'd never marry against her will, she must want to wed Dryer, and it's that fact I cannot fight. I tell you, Moll, I were going to get into me boat and leave forever for France but it's no use doing that; me Ma and Pa, Hannah and Johnny all need me. Times are hard and likely to get worse. Anyway, I can't leave the island, it's my life, I know nothing else, and why should that damned Dryer have it all his way? I belong here, not him, but I'm scared, Moll ... I'm scared that if I stay I'll kill him."

This thought effectively shuts out all others and they both sit in silence as the implications ripple through their minds. Then, painfully, he continues, "If Violet still wanted me she'd have let me know somehow. I can only assume she's made her choice. If she has decided ... that's it, he's won." A sob shudders through him.

Molly puts her arm round him and he fights for control. "He's not going to take everything though, I'm not giving up my home and family as well and I'll run rings round him with the free-traders. He's not going to get away with everything, I'm going to make sure of that."

"I don't blame you, Matty. There ain't no-one on the island as won't be on your side. He'll have to take on other work just to make ends meet; he won't be just feeding himself now, will he? ... Maybe they'll leave."

"I hadn't thought of that. Every time he suffers so too will Violet. Oh, God help me. Is there nothing I can do?" He buries his head in his hands. How is he going to face the contemptuous pity that will greet him from his and every other family in Chiswell? He couldn't up and marry someone else, just to save his face. No one could fill her shoes. Would she even be jealous if he did see someone else, when there was no girl on the island who could give her reason to be so?

He shrugs his shoulders and fists away the tears. Why should this have happened to him? What has he done to deserve it? If only he could wake up from this nightmare. But it is reality; he saw with his own eyes his Violet walking alongside another man.

It is true that Violet has been different ever since Dryer settled here, her moods have been more exaggerated and now he knows why.

"When I was in France I bought her a present. I was so looking forward to giving it to her and now I probably never shall." The sobs come freely now. "It is the first gift I have ever bought her. I should have been more generous. It's all my fault," he says to himself, "I should have been more attentive."

"You weren't to blame, Matty," says Molly, gently squeezing his arm. "You haven't done nothing to reproach yourself for. I'm her closest friend, and I can't understand what's got into her. It's best you forget her, she doesn't deserve you any more. I just can't make her out."

He lets out a deep sigh, "You'd best be getting on back now, Moll. I'll be along shortly, and don't worry, I'm fine." He fabricates half a smile and fondly she squeezes his arm again.

Then he watches her depart, stepping from one stone slab to another with the front of her skirt held high, showing off her remarkably slim ankles. On another occasion the observation would have made him smile, but it causes him now to become more pensive.

How long will he be able to remain sane, watching Violet with Richard Dryer day in, day out? But what choice has he?

He returns eventually to his parents' cottage.

At dawn the following day, he sets off along Chesil with a mule and cart. He does not wish to witness the first flush of rumour and innuendo. He has business with the firm of Gundry's at Bridport, where he is to purchase rope and nets, and also at Richard Roberts' Linen Mills at Burton Bradstock where he will, on his return, buy sailcloth and sacking, twine, cheesecloth and canvas for bags, and if he has enough money some flax hemp, or silk for Hannah and his mother. It will keep him occupied for a few days, at least.

The large slab of rock that forms the backcloth to Matthew's exit gradually diminishes in size as he approaches the ferry at the end of the causeway. Luckily it is a calm day and the crossing is routine, although Mowbray, the mule, does not appreciate it very much and he has his work cut out to keep the animal calm.

The road to Bridport runs all along the coastline, which throughout its length is caressed and plundered by the moody ocean below. Inland, small villages huddle protected from the north wind by the dependable undulating Dorsetshire hills. These are dotted with sheep, larger, Matthew notices, than those bred on Portland. In the shelter of the many copses that cap the rounded hills, and often tucked in the folds of verdant green, nestle the shepherds' huts.

He could have been born to that; it would have suited his temperament as well as anything. The solitude and the gentle nature of that way of life would be very comforting, especially now. He urges Mowbray forward; a little encouragement does wonders with the animal. Its jaunty step would have been a great stimulant to him a week ago. As it is he is glad only to leave the island; the unpleasant thoughts of what it all means to him he cannot jettison however hard he tries.

The coast road is very potholed and crosses numerous hills and valleys of very steep gradients. They pass on by Moonfleet, and through Abbotsbury, Swyre and Burton Bradstock. He is very travel-weary and strokes Mowbray appreciatively as finally they trudge alongside the river Brit, which takes them up the last stretch of road into Bridport itself.

Darkness has fallen. He makes for the inn called the Buck and Doe, where he stayed on his last trip, when his uncle brought him along to show him how to deal with the merchants on the islanders' behalf. He should feel proud, for it is an honour to be chosen for this task. It would be very easy to exploit the fishermen who have entrusted him with their money.

Instead he is just relieved to rest his aching limbs in a comfortable chair by the fireside. The bread and cheese and pint of ale are brought over to him by a barmaid who attempts to flirt with him. He does not respond to her advances, but although he is tired he is pleased to have someone to chat to after his long period of meditation during his journey.

She is a pretty enough lass but she soon realises that there is no penetrating that barrier and, when called away, she does not afterwards resume her efforts. However, she remains intrigued with the handsome face and those distant, wistful eyes.

He retires early to his room, which is clean and functional. He sleeps heavily, but then he is falling … falling … and he awakes with a jolt in the unfamiliar surroundings. He hears the sound of cartwheels and voices outside his window and a dog that is whining at the side door of the butcher's shop opposite. He pulls on his breeches and washes at the washstand in the corner of the room. Has he overslept? Out on the landing a grandfather clock strikes seven and he relaxes.

Downstairs a girl is removing the tallow from the candleholders, whilst talking all the time to another girl who is whitening the hearth.

"Our Emily's baby's got pneumonia and it's only three and a 'alf months old. She'm really worried and me Ma keeps goin' over and tryin' to help but she keeps moanin' 'cus there's no warmth in the farm cottage and they'm all sleeping in one room to keep warm, all six of 'em; Luke don't like it 'cus me Ma says 'e shouldn't 'ave left mill jus' to get cottage 'cus farm labourers don't earn no money and there were work for the kids at the mill."

The young girl at the hearth has completed her task and removed to the front doorstep to repeat the procedure.

"I 'spec' Emily 'ud tell Ma to leave'm alone if 'tweren't fer the little nipper bein' so poorly. An' her so scared o' doin' summat wrong in carin' for it." She pauses to concentrate on hooking out an obstinate lump of wax, and then continues on in a new vein. "What about that young man who 'rived las' nite? Betty says 'ee's come from Portland. They'm a rum lot over there I heard tell, but 'ee's a bit of all right, I reckon. You seen 'im, Ruby?"

She looks round for her companion's comment, but her eyes meet Matthew's, who stands quietly in the doorway. Her cheeks flush crimson as her hand goes quickly to her mouth with a gasp. "Oh! Beggin' your pardon, Sir, I'll be out o' your way directly." She immediately finishes her task in silence and hurriedly leaves Matthew to sit alone at the enormous refectory table, where a breakfast will shortly be served on the scrubbed wooden surface.

Later that morning, as he approaches Gundry's premises, which lie to the west of Bridport, he reflects on her comments with a smile. Ah well, at least someone thinks I'm worth a second glance, he muses.

He rolls up outside the huge iron gates of the factory and the cartwheels clatter on the cobbles. A young boy of about eight years takes charge of the mule and cart and Matthew strolls into the main building. A large man immediately comes to greet him in a business-like way, although obviously involved in the practical work of the factory with his shirt sleeves rolled high above his elbows and all clothing kept tidily in check under a large canvas apron.

He shakes hands and Matthew introduces himself. "Good day to you, Sir, I come as a representative of five fishing families from the village of Chiswell on the island of Portland and I have a large quantity of rope and nets that I have authorisation to purchase, at the right price of course."

"Ah, my dear Sir, you have come to the right place. Why, our rope is the best in the world. You don't get better flax or hemp than that grown in the Marshwood Vale, and you just come and see our new machine."

He follows the owner of the mill past the great bales of raw hemp, that look like a mixture of horsehair, straw and dried grey weeds; past the young girls who soften the hemp by washing out odd fragments and cleaning the sticky surface; then the children who comb the raw hemp, separating the tow from the dressed hemp or lint; and finally the rows of women who spin the slivers of dressed hemp onto bobbins at high speed to emerge as yarn, and the men who are twisting the yarn into twine or line.

The owner is explaining, "The twine is polished, that is bathed, brushed and dried so as to get rid of its whiskers, wound onto a reel which when full to capacity is called a ran." Two boys hurry past with a 'ran' apiece. "Then it's sent out to be braided into nets by outworkers, but now I can put it through this little beauty."

He proudly takes Matthew up into a large loft

to see the 'jumper' loom, which is hand-operated by a man who is really concentrating on his task. The net moves slowly in jerks as the hooks move in, collect and tie their knots. Then it flows down through an opening in the floor to where the women are waiting with scissors and twine to make perfect any flaws, their hands moving like lightning.

"Soon I'll have a machine for every type of net we produce," says Gundry, with pride. "But at the moment the smaller, finer-mesh nets are made by the outworkers."

Matthew is fascinated. It is the first machine he has seen and he is very impressed and glad to have something other than Violet to think of. The mill owner is saying how the Bridport Mills supply the Newfoundland fishing fleets and, even more important, how his ancestors supplied Drake's fleet and had watched with pride as they defeated the Armada off Portland. "Six score proud galleons defeated by the smaller and swifter ships of Drake."

The two young lads have laid down the 'rans' by the machine for the operator, and rushed back past Matthew to fetch some more, when one stumbles at the top of the loft steps and disappears with a shout and a crash to the floor below.

Matthew and the owner rush to the hole in the floor. The boy lies at the foot of the steps, holding his ankle and groaning in agony. The owner, who had appeared a kindly enough man, shrugs; "Get off home, boy, you're no use to me with a broken ankle."

"Yes, Master," says the lad, who can only be six years old. He tries to stand up but cries out in distress and a young woman rushes over to help him.

"Can't you see he can't walk?" she snaps at Gundry.

Matthew, surprised at her disrespect, listens with interest for Gundry's reply.

"Of course, and if he can't walk, he can't work and I don't want him under my feet. He's dismissed and if I have any more of your cheek, you'll lose your job to someone else too. I've a business to run, not a nursery."

The girl bites her lip, "I'm sorry, Master, but 'ee can't walk all the way 'ome to Chideock, it's too far."

The pace of the other workers has slowed noticeably as they listen, which makes the owner more angry. Matthew glances around at the apathetic little faces and their ragged clothes. Some of the children have no shoes and many are too thin to be healthy.

"He's got all day. If he takes it steady he'll be home by dark."

"He's only six years old and 'e's hurting bad. I'll 'ave to take 'im."

"You'll lose your pay if you do, girl," snaps the owner.

"Look, I've a mule and cart outside. I could take him for you, when I'm through here, and I'm sure Mr Gundry will be able to take the lad on again when the leg is healed," intercedes Matthew carefully.

"Oh, thank thee, Sir. Your kindness is unusual." She scowls at Gundry, and grabs Matthew's hands and squeezes them and shakes them hard. "Dory will show you the way, and me Ma'll feed you for your trouble. Thank thee, Sir."

"Enough!" snaps Gundry. "Get back to your work. There's been enough time wasted. Boy, go and wait outside in the gentleman's cart."

Finally they load the rope and nets, and Matthew hands over the agreed amount of money;

but before they leave, the girl rushes out with two 'rans' of twine.

"Would ye mind taking these for me Ma. Save us carrying them 'ome tonight?"

"No, surely not," says Matthew and taking them from her, throws them up alongside the boy on the cart.

"What's your name?"

"Matthew … Matthew Stone. What's yours?"

"Eliza Hodden, and that's Dory. Thank thee for helping me. I know you're from Portland and 'tis taking you out of your way and I'll not be forgetting your kindness."

He had intended continuing his journey to Burton Bradstock and stopping there for the night, but one more night at the Buck and Doe won't hurt. Besides, this gives him something to think about other than Violet. He says 'Goodbye' as the girl returns to her work and they set off towards the village of Chideock.

The boy sits silently behind him on top of the nets and watches his ankle swell. The lump seems exaggerated on his spindly little leg, and every now and then he grunts with pain when the cart lurches over a stone in the road, bravely trying hard not to cry out.

Mrs Hodden is sitting braiding nets, which are laid across the kitchen table. In one hand she has a wooden needle and in the other a lace, which gauges the mesh size. The twine is wound on the traditional 'Bridport cross' laid beside her. She jumps up horrified when she sees Dory sitting on top of the cart as it draws up outside her cottage.

"Whatever's 'appened?" she exclaims, rushing out to Matthew.

"It's all right, the lad fell down the loft steps at the mill and may have a broken ankle. It could be just a sprain, but it needs attention to reduce the swelling."

"And who might you be?" she asks bluntly.

"I just happened to be buying nets at the time and offered to give the lad a ride home. He couldn't walk the two miles and your daughter was very concerned."

"Well, thank you for your trouble." Her tone changes when she realises that he is not connected with the mill, and she seems eager then to be hospitable. "Would you care for a sup of ale before you go or some soup and tea?"

"I would be grateful, Ma'am, I've not eaten since breakfast."

"Oh my dear, come in and sit yourself down."

The cottage is small but clean. Mrs Hodden notices the glance Matthew gives the wobbling table as he sits down. "I've no man to do the handiwork about the 'ouse. He were drowned in a fishing accident five year ago, so excuse the wobbly table, it comes from dragging it outside in summer to do braiding in fresh air."

"I could fix it for you if you've some tools."

"Oh, I've got the tools all right, me hubby were a carpenter. They're out back in the shed. Go and have a look. It's a sad waste."

Matthew wanders down to the shed. It is odd, but although all this is most inconvenient it is, nevertheless, an illuminating experience for him. It is strange that unlike the Portlanders these people automatically respect a travelling man, and he really likes being addressed as 'Sir'.

He opens the shed door and is amazed at the neat, orderly kept store. Although coated with dust, the tools have all been kept as the man must have left them: immaculately stored in rows, some in special boxes, larger tools hung on the walls; screw top tins of graduating size, cleverly fixed to the ceiling of the shed, containing every size of nail, tack, screw, nut or bolt. He selects what he needs and returns to the cottage.

"Your husband must have been a skilled craftsman, it's obvious just by looking at his tools. They are kept beautifully."

"That 'e was, me ducks, 'e always said a bad workman blames 'is tools, and that 'e could never do."

Matthew is only too glad to be doing something with his hands. They have been idle for long enough. He turns the table upside down in the middle of the kitchen floor and in just a few minutes has planed off the base of the legs until they are all equal in length. He then strengthens the joints at the top with diagonal supports. Mrs Hodden and the boy watch him, impressed with the tidy way he works, sweeping up afterwards and returning the tools to the shed. Her reward to him is a tasty meal upon the finished article.

Matthew feels sorry for the family. Although they all work hard, and therefore live quite well, he cannot help thinking how it could have been if the husband had survived. He doubtlessly would have had a thriving business in operation by now. It is certainly very unfortunate.

He realises that Mrs Hodden is enjoying fussing over him and he and the boy are firm friends by the time he is ready to leave. Although they appear reluctant to say 'Goodbye', they do so and wave him off on his way.

He is saddened as he looks back at them. Life can play such cruel tricks and yet that little family is fighting back. He might yet have to fight for the family he wanted. The only problem is, there is only one person he can imagine spending the rest of his life with and she has deserted him.

By the time Matthew again rolls into Bridport the monotonous rattling of the wheels of the cart have made him feel very weary, and the thoughts that tear relentlessly at him have only served to deepen his despair. He tries to walk off his melancholy mood.

Under normal circumstances he would be feeling well pleased. He had done a good deal with Gundry, and Mrs Hodden and the boy were full of gratitude. It was a simple task mending the table; he often has to repair the lerret and enjoys the work immensely. Then there was the little maid who was so timid after her untimely declaration. She was, as the islanders would put it, 'a pretty bit o' muslin' and he was flattered. Nevertheless no other feelings were stirred and that too saddens him. Violet has spoilt him for all other women.

A sudden swell of determination takes hold of him. If a woman like Mrs Hodden with two children can carry on without her man, then he can carry on without Violet. No one else will do; nothing less than his Violet will make him a wife. Dryer's Violet he won't fight for. He doesn't want Dryer's Violet; she is different. He wants his Violet back and he can wait. He'll wait forever if necessary.

The next day he completes his purchasing at the Linen Mills at Burton Bradstock. He's decided against buying silk, there are cheaper sources; instead he buys cheesecloth for the women. It will come in handy for shifts or petticoats. He doesn't know much about such things but he is sure it will be fine.

He'd had mixed feelings about going back home, but now he aches just to see her again. The regular glimpses of the wedge-shaped rock basking in the sea on his right seem to be teasing him all along the way and make his progress seem exceptionally slow. He looks a solitary figure as he completes his journey along the causeway just as the sun is going down, but he is glad to be back with his family and friends again now.

CHAPTER 7 *(October 1831 – July 1832)*

WOMEN IN PARALLEL

The pleasure Violet feels from at last being in the company of Richard is tarnished by the attitude of her father. Night after night she finds herself standing in the front window staring hopelessly at the back of her home. There is no sign of life and she is desperately worried for her mother. Her father, once at his work, will be able to forget about things but her mother will be left alone to cope and to fret. She wants to see for herself that her mother has recovered from the fever and she needs to talk to her about her marriage.

Richard is determined that they should be married as soon as possible with or without her parents' consent. "We'll go to Scotland if necessary. Nothing will stop me making you my bride."

He gives her a form. "I want you to take this to your mother and ask her for their blessing. But make it clear that whether or not they consent, we will be married one way or another."

She does not want to pressurise her mother but, desperate to see her, she decides to go one morning when Richard is at the harbour and the men are at work in the cove. She can take the form with her and collect her clothes and bits and pieces too.

Defiantly, she puts on her cloak, bonnet and boots, and leaving what has become her sanctuary she goes down the slope, turning right into Brandy

Lane and then left up to Brandy Row towards her parents' home.

She passes a group of children playing 'jacks' with pebbles on a comparatively smooth part of the cart track. She ignores the whispering and sniggering, but she cannot ignore the sharp nick of a pebble as it hits the back of her calf. Another hits the wall, and another skims past her ankles. She does not react, however; she will not give them the satisfaction. She bites her lip but still she does not turn round. The children are laughing now, but she is out of range of their aim as she reaches her parents' cottage. She opens the door and is quickly inside the home that has always been her refuge. She turns from the passage into the living room and there, with arms outstretched, is her mother.

"Oh Ma." She runs to her and hugs her.

"Oh Vi, I've been so worried for you and I miss you so much. How are you?"

"I'm fine, honest, Ma. There's nothing for you to worry about." She sees the tears welling up in her mother's eyes. "Oh Ma, don't cry. It's all right. They'll all forget sooner or later and I am happy, Ma."

Until she'd walked out with Dryer, Violet had hardly ever known her mother to weep, or even to laugh. The most that she offered was a smile, which had always seemed a façade behind which many different thoughts and emotions were concealed.

"But it's all my fault, Violet. I should have told your father everything, right from the start. He's so bitter about it all and I know he partly blames me." Tears run unchecked down her hollowed cheeks. "I have never gone against him before and he cannot understand it."

Violet does not know how to comfort her; she has never seen her so upset. "Ma, I am sorry to give you all this worry. Pa'll come round in time. You wait 'til I give him a little grandson; he'll soon change his tune. He always did have more time for the boys; he never really bothered much about me."

Her mother pulls away from her. "Oh, Violet, you're so wrong. He worships you. He has done ever since you were the tiny baby that he held in his arms, just minutes after you were born, when he kissed the top of your head and declared that you should be named Violet because of your deep blue eyes. It's breaking his heart, Vi. Please forget about this marriage and come home."

She pauses and walks away to the front window. Staring out to sea she continues, "I never told your father about the killing of the sailor because I thought he'd be so angry with Dryer that he might make you publicly admit killing the man, saying it was self-defence, rather than sentence yourself to a marriage against your will. I even thought he might get violent with Dryer and thus there would only be more trouble."

She pauses again and looking round she studies Violet carefully, "So, like we agreed, I told him that you are in love with Dryer." She searches her face. "It is the truth though, Vi, isn't it?"

"I've told you, Ma, I cannot help myself. I love him more now than ever." Her voice is soft but very positive.

Her mother moves closer, "But you still have feelings for poor Matthew, haven't you? It's not too late if you want to make it up. The folks round here don't care about the murder, they've already forgotten about it, but hurting Matthew will be like a scar on their minds forever."

"No, I'm sorry but it is too late, Ma. I belong to Richard now, and I'm determined to marry him. He thinks at the moment we are living in sin. He doesn't care if I give him a child or not, he only cares for me and he wants to do things properly. He won't wait until I am with child. That's not proper in his eyes. He has asked me to give you this form. We need your consent for us to marry here, but Richard says he'll take me to Scotland if you won't sign. Please sign, Ma, it means so much to me."

Her mother takes the form from her. "Your father will never accept him, married or not."

"But what about you, Ma? Will you make your mark?"

"I cannot go against your father, Vi, but if he'll sign, I will too."

"Try to persuade him for me, Ma. I'll leave the form here and I'll call back later on in the week, when the men are at sea. I had better get on. I'll just go upstairs and pick up some of my clothes."

Up in her bedroom she again becomes melancholy. It has all changed so quickly. She had never thought of living somewhere else. That sort of thing gradually develops and is not normally thrust upon one in this way. She touches her quilt and remembers the hours of patience that went into making the patchwork and the many hours as a child she lay with her rag doll in her arms, unable to sleep because of the roaring wind and sea and the angry rain lashing at her window. She can picture now her mother creeping into her room to light the warning candles and how she lay watching the flickering light until she heard the latch on the front door and knew that all were safely home.

Then again she remembers the scene where she had watched Richard leaving their house and saw in the same instance Matthew and his father right on his heels. So much has passed since then. She would never have believed that her life could become so very complicated. She collects her most important possessions and the majority of her wardrobe together and ties them all up into a bundle.

Downstairs her mother is waiting for her. "Violet, do you remember that bale of grena velvet that came over in May? Well, I want you to have it. You can make yourself a nice outfit from it. 'Tis too bright a colour to be of any use to me, and 'twill keep you occupied and maybe help to keep your mind off your troubles."

Violet takes the gift gratefully, "Thanks, Ma, 'twill be the last time I profit from the free-traders, but I'll do you proud with it, I promise." She tucks the material under her free arm, adding awkwardly, "I'd best be getting back now, Ma. Please try to talk Pa round." She kisses her mother's cheek.

"Don't come out, I'll go on back quietly." She pops her head round the door to see if the coast is clear, and luckily there is no one about.

She deliberately has not mentioned the children to her mother, and now she sees they have gone somewhere else to play. Her parcels are heavy and awkward to carry and she feels cumbersome, but her relief is premature.

She turns into Brandy Lane and sees at the top end a group of boys lounging against the wall. She grips her parcels and as she draws nearer she notices their pockets are bulging with pebbles. Her heart thumps. One is tossing a stone from one hand to the other and as he does so, he stares insidiously at her.

Her pace slows. Another, at the sight of her, begins sharpening a penknife menacingly whilst the tallest wears a lecherous grin that strikes fear into her heart. She freezes. Images of that terrible night in Castletown flood her mind and panic banishes rational thinking. She cannot endure that again.

She turns to run back the way she has come,

but her exit is blocked by a group of children at the other end of the lane. Both groups are closing in on her. She is trapped.

The first stone hits her forehead. She crouches against the wall trying to use her bundles as protection. The pain is sharp as stone after stone hits her, again and again. But they will not make her cry out. She utters not a sound and remains quite still because the fear of what these boys are thinking, of what they are intending, hurts her even more. She is at their mercy. As they grow closer their aim is more accurate and each blow more powerful and her stubborn, proud silence is difficult to maintain.

Then the stoning stops and a voice says, "Kimberlins ain't welcome 'ere; neither are common sluts such as the likes o' thee."

Someone pushes her to the ground and catches hold of her hair. "Anyone got any scissors?"

"I got a penknife, Ikey."

"That'll do," says Ikey Shaddick, and he takes it from the lad.

Amongst the boys are Annie's younger brothers and she recognises most of the other youngsters and cannot believe what they are about to do. She drops her bundle and grips her hair, which Ikey is pulling hard, and as the bundle falls her clothes are shed at the boy's feet.

"Oh, I say, look at this," says one boy, holding her lacy pantalets up against himself and ridiculing Violet. The others quickly take to this sport and within minutes they are prancing around in her clothes, putting on airs and graces, hooting, jeering and taunting her.

It is hard to say which feels worse: the previously deadly, silent animosity, the violence, or this. She is devastated. Her scalp is sore from her battle with

Ikey, where the tugging causes sharp pains that bring tears to her eyes, but then the pulling ceases. He does not release her but his attention is drawn temporarily to her underwear. Their tug-of-war is for a moment forgotten as he laughs and joins in with their mockery of her.

She slumps helplessly in the dirt clutching her bale of velvet, frightened to move a muscle and hoping they'll soon tire of their cruel sport. She doesn't notice Richard standing transfixed with anger at the top entrance into Brandy Lane. Suddenly, like a mad bull he is in the centre of them taking hold of Ikey by the scruff of the neck, at the same time locking his arm around his back, and forcing him to let go of her hair and drop the knife.

"Call your hoodlums off or I'll break every bone in your body," he says through his teeth.

Ikey yells in pain as his arm is yanked back further and he cries, "All right, boys. Take 'er stuff off." Another yank on the arm, and he adds, "And go 'ome."

The boys sheepishly remove the garments and throw them in a pile next to Violet.

Dryer waits until they have dispersed and are all out of sight, except for Ikey, whom he has deliberately detained. Then he says menacingly, "If I hear or see any of your scum near her again, I'll kill you." He puts his boot in the small of the lad's back and propels him forward with such force that he falls face down into the dirt. He quickly scrambles up Brandy Lane and is gone.

The silence is pronounced. Richard lifts Violet to her feet, they gather up the torn and dirty clothes and he helps her home.

Once inside, it is Violet who breaks the silence. "They were throwing pebbles at me, and they were going to cut off my hair with a penknife." Her voice sounds weak even to her and she trembles. Richard is looking horrified as she sorts through her clothes.

"It is lucky in a way that I dropped my bundle or I might be bald." She smiles nervously, to herself.

"Rather your clothes ruined than you, my love." He puts his arm around her. "Forget about your clothes, sweetheart, we can replace them. I just cannot understand their mentality."

"No, it doesn't matter." She shrugs, "I can wash and mend them. It doesn't matter at all … Look what me Ma gave me." Her voice is strangely light.

"What is it?" Dryer is frowning in a distracted way.

"It's a length of velvet material. I thought I could make it into a bridal gown for our wedding. Isn't it beautiful?" She is smoothing the rich, dark burgundy pile of the material with the palm of her hand.

"Yes it is. It will suit you very well." He strokes her hair. "Violet, you are so brave and I love you so much." He touches her tenderly at the nape of her neck and puts his head close to hers.

He holds her tightly to him for a few moments and then says softly, "Let me see what they have done to you." Gently, he unbuttons the front of her dress and, easing the material, gradually exposes her slender shoulders, badly bruised. He lets the dress fall to the ground and kisses the angry marks that are beginning to stand out on her pale skin. Then he buries his head in her hair, "Oh my sweet innocent love, I am so sorry. How can people be so wicked?"

"I'm not harmed, Richard, it is just a few bruises." She smiles, but it is a nervous, shaky smile and he sits her down in the armchair that is beside them.

He goes into the kitchen, returning with a pot of arnica ointment. Gently he applies the balm to her tender skin, soothing away the pain and cooling the inflammation. He strokes and kisses her and holds her close, her body trembling against him.

"I'll get you something to make you feel a little better." He pours her a brandy. "Here, drink this. You'll feel better in a minute. You just sit quietly for a while."

She sips the brandy, feels the strong flavour hit the back of her throat, and is conscious of a burning sensation as it journeys down towards her stomach; but even when the goblet is empty the heat has done nothing to alter her pallor.

She is shivering now and Richard decides she'd be better off in bed. He carries her with ease up the stairs and gently lays her on his bed. She closes her eyes, trying to shut out all thoughts of what had happened, and he covers her with the bedclothes, staying by the bedside until she falls asleep.

His compassion changes to anger as he descends the narrow stairway, at himself as well as at them, for he should somehow have stopped this happening to her. He has never experienced such anguish. He is convinced he is under the shadow of a very bad omen, doomed to trail sorrow behind him wherever he goes, and yet he never meant to hurt anyone.

He will make it up to her. One day she will benefit from his love and she will be happy. Until such time he will protect her. He will use his power as a government official to safeguard her, until she becomes strong and proud again.

An hour has passed when suddenly he hears her crying out and he rushes upstairs to her side. Her arms are defensively protecting her face and she is shouting, "No, No! Please, stop it," and threshing about in the bed, and then, "Oh no, the blood, it's everywhere."

Dryer takes her in his arms and says, "Violet, it's all right. You're safe, I'm here with you. You've nothing to fear, no one can hurt you now." He keeps reassuring her and rocking her gently. Holding her close, he can feel her tense body slowly succumb to weeping. Every silent shudder causes a sharp pang of guilt to remind him that he is as much to blame as these stupid, clannish islanders for Violet's desperate unhappiness.

The next day Violet's mother calls and hands her the form. "Your father has signed your form, Violet, but he asks me to say that he washes his hands of you. He has signed you over to the Kimberlin. He said for me to tell you that, 'You've made your bed, now you must lie in it'."

"Was he so very angry, Ma?"

"Yes, he was angry, but more hurt than anything. I just hope one day he will be able to forgive you. I have made my mark too. Just prove us all wrong, Vi, and be happy."

"I will, Ma ... I will."

Over the next three weeks the banns are read in the church and Violet works on the velvet gown she has designed. It has a tight corsage laced over with red satin ribbons, which show off her white lace chemisette underneath. The cloth is of excellent quality, soft and warm. It is ideal for an October wedding.

Richard takes her on a great adventure to Dorchester and buys her some square-toed, flat-heeled black shoes and her first ever silk stockings, and she covers her bonnet in red velvet, decorating it with artificial flowers.

For hours on end she practises writing her name so that she can sign the register. Richard has shown her how to form the letters and has promised to teach her to read and write properly after they are married.

When Richard had applied for the post on Portland he had been warned that preventive men in coastal stations were forbidden to form close relationships with local girls, lest they became too familiar, or even married into smuggling families. It therefore comes as no surprise when he receives a communication from the Commissioner of Customs in London.

Dear Sir,

It is with great consternation that I am told of your impending marriage to a local girl on Portland. I implore you to reconsider your impulsive decision. Your position as a Customs Official should be forfeited if you proceed with these plans.

Yours, etc.

Undeterred, he hastily draws up a quick reply:

Dear Sir,

It has for a long time appeared to me quite absurd that the official view should actually encourage young customs officers to have carnal knowledge of village women and escape their responsibilities when numerous illegitimate children are born. If you want good men in the service you must trust their judgement when it comes to their relationships with women. Otherwise you will end up impotent, with scoundrels representing the service.

As I have no intention of becoming celibate, and I have

already decided on the person I wish to become my wife, you may accept my resignation. I will await your instructions on the appointment of my successor.

No doubt it will be some time before you find a willing and suitable replacement and I am at your service until such time.

I am obediently yours, Richard Dryer.

Knowing that he has them over a barrel, he puts aside his irritation and proceeds with his wedding plans. He has hired a gig to take them up to St George's Church at Reforne. Violet would have been married at the Methodist chapel but it is too near home under the circumstances and she is entitled to marry at the only Church of England church on the island.

Of those folk who watch them defying tradition and travelling together to the church, not many think any good will come of their union. An old lady in the Square prophesies doom to all and sundry.

Susan Atwool asks her what makes her say such things, and she replies, "Aven't thee heard o' thic ole' rhyme ...

'Married in wyte, you'm chosen right,
Married in green, ashamed to be seen,
Married in grey, you'll go far away,
Married in blue, love ever true,
Married in yella, you're ashamed o' your fella,
Married in black, you'll wish yersel' back,
Married in pink, of you he'll aye think,
Married in red, you'll wish yoursel' dead."

... And in't she in enuff trouble as it is, without wearin' a dress red as blood?'"

"There's another ole rhyme that don't bid well," says another voice.

'Monday for wealth,
Tuesday for health,
Wednesday the best day of all,
Thursday for crosses,
Friday for losses,
Saturday, no luck at all.'"

Whilst the gossips tarry, the gig continues up through Maidenwell, Fortuneswell, and on to Yeates.

Violet has told her mother the time and date of the ceremony but knows that she will not be able to attend against her father's wishes, and this lies heavily on her. But as they climb higher, the white ribbons fluttering on the gig, she watches the clouds scudding the sky, their shadows chasing across fields and over dry-stone walls, reckless and free, and her spirits lift. She will not be shackled by guilt or doubt, she will win them round – she has to.

Then she spies Molly making her way up the steep footpath over Lankridge. She must be on her way to see John Pearce. Their paths draw closer as the gig approaches the sharp bend near the top of the hill. Molly stops and their eyes meet.

Violet grabs Richard's arm. "Stop a moment, I want to talk to Molly."

He reigns in the horse and Violet calls to her, "Molly, won't you come celebrate with us? We need a witness and it would mean so much to me if it was you."

Molly looks from one to the other of them. "I'm not dressed for no wedding, Vi," she says, her voice cold, her eyes looking away.

"Of course you are, that is your best frock and bonnet and I'm sure John won't mind a bit if we borrow you for a few moments."

Molly turns. Violet can see that Molly really

wants to, they had been such close friends for so long, and although they have been avoiding each other, she knows it has been only for Matthew's sake. She sees Molly falter.

"No one else need know, Molly. The verger will be the other witness. Please, Moll, you are my closest friend."

Molly smiles then, "You know how I feel about poor Matty, but if you are sure you want me after all that has happened, I would like to be there for you, Vi … I'll follow on behind you, shall I?"

"No, Moll, you can sit on the tailboard and be my maid of honour." They laugh, and Molly hoists herself up and they set off again jauntily to the church.

It is a short ceremony and after the duties are performed, Richard is told he can kiss the bride. Molly watches as they embrace and then Violet sees the warmth in her eyes and hopes it means that she is forgiven.

Molly and the verger watch then as Richard signs his name with a flourish. He hands the quill pen to Violet. She carefully and neatly forms the letters of her name, Violet Mary Allen, and proudly lays down the quill for Molly to add her mark alongside that of the verger.

Molly raises her eyebrows at her signature and they both smile their old familiar smile and she is glad, for Molly really has forgiven her. If only it wasn't for Matthew her parents might even have been more understanding. The guilt begins to gnaw away at her again, and her heart aches for Matthew's sake, but then Richard is kissing her, Molly is hugging her and it is all over.

Molly smiles, congratulates them both and then, saying 'Goodbye', runs off to tell John what has delayed her.

Violet and Richard leave the church and spend the afternoon riding around the island in the gig. At the Beale they walk hand in hand along the cliff top above the rocks which, it seems, are being pummelled by rejoicing waves. The seagulls seem to cry out their congratulations from the lighthouses, and from the stone-stepped gables and chimney stacks of the crofters' huts.

They do not return home until darkness has fallen. At the doorway Richard carries his wife across the threshold, and their special day is nearly over.

Annie is being sick and is off her food. Her mother keeps nagging, saying, "'Tis no use pining fer thic Dryer. You'm too late, 'e's 'ad 'is nuptials now an' cast you off like an old boot. You were too willing, that's your trouble; 'ee were a man as needs to fight fer 'is woman. If you'd a belonged to someone else you'd a been all right."

"Ah shut up, Ma. I'm ailing, not pining, and who are you to be giving I advice. You weren't playing hard to get I know, with ten kids to show for it."

Mrs Shaddick stays silent. It is the day after the wedding and Annie's mother greatly fears the real reason for her eldest being so pale and sickly. She fights against her better judgement and asks Auntie Sarah to give her something for a bilious attack.

Annie wanders along the beach, leaving her mother to manage the chores. She cannot even help with gutting the fish, her stomach is so weak, and so she avoids the groups of women thus employed.

After a fortnight her taut and swollen, tender breasts confirm her worst suspicions, but her sickness is wearing off and she resolves to say nothing. Nevertheless her mind dwells on the new life growing inside her and she begins to get pleasure from knowing that she carries Richard's child. It is a marvellous secret and Annie begins to plan for her baby.

As soon as she feels able she joins the women gutting fish; it is the best way to mix with the menfolk and she wants a husband as soon as possible. She has always got on well with William Stone and because he is older than the other men she has less competition.

William is Matthew's uncle and the villagers are all amazed when Annie and he become close companions. His name has never been linked with a girl's before and he, too, is getting to like the idea. He shares a cottage with his mother but she is getting too old to care for him. He definitely needs a wife.

He thinks himself fortunate that a young buxom woman like Annie should enjoy his company, for she is now over the first few weeks and has a healthy shine to her hair and eyes, and roses in her cheeks. No one would have guessed her secret and even her mother has now dismissed the notion.

One cold night after she has spent the day washing and cleaning for William, Annie decides to make her move. William, still a bachelor at the age of thirty-six, is a willing victim of a seduction that ends with Annie sleeping with him in his bed all night. The next morning she is up early as usual and returns to help her mother with the boys. From then on William is treated to unrivalled passion, until one night Annie whispers her news, "I am with child."

William looks at Annie with raised eyebrows and his mouth agape. "That is wonderful news, Annie."

"Are you pleased, Will?"

William grins at her. "I am over the moon."

"We will have to make plans to be wed as soon as possible."

The next morning Annie and William go hand in hand to tell William's mother their news. She is sitting knitting in her rocking chair.

"We have some news, Mother." William pauses significantly. "Annie is with child."

"You mean I am going to be a grandmother!"

"Yes, Mother, and Annie and I are going to get wed."

"Well, I never thought I'd see the day!" Tears of joy brim her eyes, "That is wonderful news, son." She turns to Annie, "Congratulations, Annie, I am very pleased for the both of you."

Annie bends over and kisses her mother-in-law. "Thank you, Mrs Stone. We are both very excited. I am sorry to be rushing off but I must hurry home and tell my own folk."

Moments later, when Annie enters her parents' living room, she can hear her younger siblings upstairs screaming and laughing and she finds her mother waiting for her.

"What time do you call this then?" her mother asks, looking at the clock on the mantelpiece. "I have been waiting for you to get here so that I can deliver the laundry."

"Sorry I'm late, Ma, but I have some news." Annie pauses expectantly.

"Well, spit it out then, I just said I don't have all day."

"Well," Annie pauses again to build up the suspense and then grins. "William and I are going to make you a grandmother."

Mrs Shaddick looks puzzled. "What! Do you mean to say you're with child?"

"Yes, Ma, we are expecting a baby and William and I are to be wed."

"Well, bless my soul! You didn't waste much time did you!"

"Well, William is no spring chicken and I do want children of my own, so why hang around."

"Your Pa is going to be thrilled, and your young 'un is going to have plenty of aunts and uncles to look out for 'en, but you've got your work cut out now planning for a wedding and all."

"I know that, Ma, but you are pleased for me?"

"Of course I am, maid, but I hope you will still be able to help me with the young 'uns occasionally."

"You know you can count on me, Ma, besides I will only be just around the corner."

Annie hears footsteps coming down the stairs and the twins followed by little Lilly enter chattering noisily.

"Will you nippers shush a moment? Your sister has something to tell you."

"What is it, Annie?" asks Joseph, curiously.

"I am going to have a baby."

"Are you? A real baby?" asks Janey incredulously.

"Yes, a real baby. What do you all think of that?"

"It is good, Annie. I think you are very happy."

"Yes, I am, and you and Lilly are going to be aunties and Joseph will be an uncle."

"But we are not old enough!" says Janey.

"Yes you are, but you will still be able to play with the baby."

Lilly shouts, "Hoorah!" and starts to clap her hands and they all join in dancing around the room merrily.

Once all the family members have been told, the wedding plans are announced. Annie lives between the two homes until they are married. Then she moves in with William and his mother. William is a well-built man with a quiet, introverted nature and Annie knows she has made a good choice. She likes him and he is easy to please and does his best to please her in return. When the baby is born she will insist that it is premature and William is too naive to suspect anything amiss.

Annie is filling her pails at the well when Susan Atwool joins her.

Susan puts her hand on Annie's shoulder. "I hear congratulations are in order."

"Yes." Annie smiles proudly and strokes her stomach. "I hope it is a boy. It will be so good for William."

"You ought to ask Auntie Sarah, she can usually tell at a glance."

"I think I would prefer it to be a surprise."

"I shall have to watch out because there must be something in the air."

"Why, what do you mean?"

"Well, I hear that Violet and Richard Dryer are also expecting a happy event."

Annie frowns. "Who told you that?"

"Well, it is general knowledge now, but it may have been Auntie Sarah who let it slip."

Annie cannot hide her anger. "That is typical of her, stealing my thunder. I was so enjoying the novelty of having something newsworthy happening in my life and then she has to go and spoil it."

Annie is disappointed and frustrated at this, but her fury is absolute when Violet's baby is actually born prematurely on the twelfth of June and she is still waddling around waiting. Ikey enters the cottage while Annie is babysitting for her brothers and sisters. "Guess what I've just heard." Ikey looks smug.

Annie sighs. "What have you just heard, Ikey?"

"That Violet Dryer has just dropped her sprog."

"What!" Annie jerks round.

"Saw Auntie Sarah coming from their house this morning and word is she has had a boy." Ikey grins maliciously, knowing that his sister will be upset at the news.

"Well, I'm glad you are back, 'cus you can look out to the kids." Without giving Ikey a chance to argue Annie storms out to confront Dryer. She will waylay him in Brandy Lane.

As she leans against the stone wall at the corner of the lane, shuffling her feet in agitation, she ignores the strange looks thrown at her from the fishermen who pass by. They obviously think it strange, a heavily pregnant woman standing around as if waiting to waylay someone, but what business is it of theirs? Eventually, just as Annie is feeling desperately tired, she is rewarded by the distinctive sound of Dryer's footsteps. As he approaches, she sets off slowly so that their paths will meet.

"Good evening, Annie."

"Evening, Mr Dryer."

Dryer nods, intending to pass on his way with just a polite greeting, but Annie persists, "How are your wife and child?"

He is surprised at her sudden interest, as they have avoided each other since Violet moved in with him, but he answers her cheerfully. "They are well, thank you, Annie. We are naming the baby Joshua. He is premature but doing well all the same."

"It is unfortunate for me that my baby is now overdue, for it is very tiresome carrying in this heat."

"I am sure it must be, but it shouldn't be long now surely?"

"It certainly shouldn't. It's two weeks past already and the baby is very large apparently." She lowers her voice, "I conceived several weeks before my marriage," she pauses. "You especially should understand my meaning."

At first embarrassed at being told such intimate details, he then feels decidedly uncomfortable. "I'm sorry, Annie, but I don't understand. What are you trying to say?"

"I hope you will be giving me a strong, healthy son, Mr Dryer." She has stepped closer and spoken clearly and with emphasis. "The life within me is as much a part of you as it is me, Sir. It has been my secret until now and I trust it will now be ours alone."

He is stunned, his first reaction disbelief. "I don't believe you, you would have told me before."

"'Tis true, Sir. You'll see when the child is born."

"Well, why the hell didn't you tell me?" In trying to avoid shouting at her, his words come through gritted teeth.

"I didn't know for sure 'til it was too late, but don't tell me it would have made no difference, for I know that's not so."

"Well, I had a right to know, difference or not!" They both stand intent each upon the other. Gradually he realises the implications: not only the difficult position in which he has stupidly placed himself, but also the problem he has left Annie with to solve alone.

"Poor Annie," he says gently. "I will help with the child. I'll not deny you your rights."

"I'll not need anything from you, ever," she replies vehemently. "I am happy with a good husband. The child may be yours, but no one will ever know and you'll have no legal rights. It will be William's child as far as anyone else is concerned and some day you might regret not giving him your name. I will get satisfaction from knowing I own something you'll be

156

unable to claim." She sticks up her chin. "It pleases me to have such a secret. What would your precious Violet say if she were to find out?"

"Please don't be bitter towards Violet, Annie. I can't help loving her the way I do. Like you say, you've a good husband in William and it is wise to count your blessings, rather than be unhappy over things that cannot be changed." He pauses and studies her kindly.

Annie, uncomfortable with his sympathetic gaze, shuffles her feet and says, "Auntie Sarah says it will be a boy and if she is right I will call him Benjamin."

"I wish you well, Annie, don't ever forget that. I'll always be here if you need me." He looks up and down the deserted lane and then kisses her on the forehead before going on his way.

She watches him out of sight, then, brushing away a solitary tear, she too goes about her business. Life is strange, but he does have some feelings for her after all. It is that moment that Annie most vividly recalls during her long labour and when the pain is at its height, and her mother-in-law has been gone ages trying to find Auntie Sarah. She keeps saying to herself, "He'll be there if I need him," over and over again.

When the child finally emerges, Auntie Sarah puts him into Annie's arms. "I was right, Annie, you have a bonny boy."

Annie studies her baby. He looks like a true Portlander. No one would guess he was Dryer's. "He is beautiful, isn't he? We have chosen the name Benjamin for him and I think it really suits him."

"You have a little cuddle while I tidy up and then I will wash him and call William to come and see him, shall I?"

Annie replies sleepily, "Thank you, that would be lovely."

The labour had lasted all of six and twenty hours and the last stage took the longest, but Annie is delighted. It doesn't matter that she will be confined for some time to recover her strength and mend her stretched muscles. The baby is the first important thing she has ever owned.

His first cry is strong and healthy, and his indignant arms flay about unsure of this strange environment. His skin is dry and peeling. She remembers Auntie Sarah telling her mother how it was a sign that Lilly had been overdue, and that was also why her soft spot was almost closed over.

Ben's is the same, but Auntie Sarah makes no comment as she takes the child and washes him. Then she wraps him in a white sheet, gives him back to Annie to nurse for a while and calls William to come and see them both. Annie is exhausted but sublimely happy. She hands the baby to William, "He came sooner than we expected, dear, but he's a bonny lad all the same."

William beams with pleasure and Annie relaxes as he carefully takes him and rocks him nervously against his broad chest. That is the last thing she can remember because in minutes she is asleep.

When later she awakes, William's mother says she should put the baby to the breast to encourage the milk to come in. He doesn't seem to be hungry and after several minutes of suckling each side, he falls asleep contentedly. Annie brims with pride as Mrs Stone gently takes him from her and lays him back in the bottom drawer of the chest which serves as his little cot.

He will soon be demanding his feeds and she is thankful that, by helping her mother care for a large family, she has learnt enough to make her a competent mother. She looks forward with confidence now to caring for the child.

Her mother and Auntie Sarah both visit regularly, but soon she is doing things for herself, the baby, William and his mother, knowing that it is her job to make these people into a real family where she and Benjamin will feel secure.

CHAPTER 8 *(July 1832 – August 1835)*

WARNING SIGNS

At first, Violet lacks confidence with her baby but it isn't long before an instinctive bond develops between them. She loves the feel of his tiny fingers against her naked breast and the pull of his eager suckling makes her feel sleepy with contentment. Richard watches them tenderly as Violet does up her camisole and puts Joshua in his cradle to sleep.

"What are you going to be doing today?" he asks Violet.

"I was planning to do some shopping later, but I could pop out now if you are going to be here for a while and you could watch Josh for me while he is sleeping peacefully."

Richard smiles, "Are you sure I can be trusted with such a precious charge?"

Violet pretends to doubt him. "Well, I don't know, but he is fast asleep and I intend to be very quick." Then she smiles.

"He will be fine, do not fret, and if he should wake I shall just rock him."

"I have no intention of being long. Hardly anyone gives me a pleasant word anymore. Some still pointedly ignore me, and some are openly rude and snide, so no one is likely to delay me."

"I'm sure it won't go on forever, if we can just ride out the storm they will come round eventually."

"Don't worry, I have hardened my heart to their insulting behaviour. I am determined to prove to all

160

of them that we need no one else as long as we have each other."

"Auntie Sarah pays them no mind, but nobody would dare to criticise her. Anyway I think she has a soft spot for you," says Richard.

"I really value her visits, especially missing me Ma so much. She is popping round this afternoon, so I had better get on."

Later, just as she is leaving the chandler's in Castletown, she closes the door, turns and swings straight into Matthew. She has until this moment been successfully avoiding him, but now suddenly thrown together she is overcome with shame and embarrassment.

"Matthew," she gasps. "How are you?" The look of hurt in his eyes is unbearable.

"How do you think?" In the confines of the doorway he towers over her. "It's been a long time," he says, and he strokes a stray lock of her hair back into place, then he adds, "but nothing's changed."

"I have changed, Matthew, becoming a mother has changed me." She looks up into his face, her eyes brimming with tears. "I'm sorry," she says softly, blinking them away. "I'm truly sorry."

She is aware that they are the subject of covert glances. "Please try to forgive me." She turns quickly from him and walks on, unable to bear his scrutiny. She cannot allow herself to look back. The tongues will wag again now.

Matthew, having watched her out of sight, sighs heavily and strides on into the chandler's to purchase his linseed oil.

Violet wipes the tears away. It would not do for Richard to notice her sadness.

She crosses Mere Common fighting off

161

memories of past times with Matthew. He hadn't deserved the way she had treated him. She had behaved badly, but she loved them both. Something had made her need Richard just that much more, she couldn't say why. It may have been the excitement. Richard excites her in the way of forbidden fruit, for everyone knows the preventive man is not supposed to marry a local girl, but it is more than that: he excites her physically too. She knows that he wants her far more than he wanted Annie and is convinced that Richard needs her far more than Matthew had done.

She sweeps back her hair, remembering how everyone had assumed that she and Matthew would marry; how she had felt obligated, despite her uncertainty. She had feared then that they were taking each other for granted and, measured alongside Richard's overwhelming desires, the doubts had torn at her heart. Although it had made her appear selfish and cruel, the power of Richard's love had been too strong for her to resist. If she had been in the wrong she had been punished for it. She thrusts back her shoulders and hurries on. Their front door is ajar and she rushes in, giving Richard an enormous hug.

"What's that in aid of?" he asks smiling.

"I just needed a cuddle, that's all," she says, loving the feel of him against her.

"You must pop out more often, that bit of fresh air has done you good. You've really got roses in your cheeks."

That evening they sit together over a reading lesson and as Richard watches her he congratulates himself on the progress Violet is making. As her reading and writing improve, so does her speech and grammar. She is losing the hard 'r' and her voice is becoming as lovely as the rest of her. He had never taught anyone before, but watching her in the lamplight, struggling with concentration to form a word, with puckered lips and puzzled eyes, and seeing the pleasure of success illuminate those deep eyes of hers and spread into a smile is worth more to him than anything.

He worships Violet to the extent that it has even dulled the blade of his sword against the smugglers. He will have to harden his heart to deal with those scoundrels, for he fears that once again Chiswell is a happy hunting ground for the free-traders and it is his responsibility to put a stop to it.

In the meantime Joshua is developing into a bright child and losing his baby ways. The days are full of questions and they both find him very entertaining. Perhaps because of his lack of playmates he becomes interested in the birds. His attention is first drawn to the noisy seagulls that squabble and screech and make him laugh, and the little sparrows that chatter all day long in their backyard.

One afternoon Violet is out walking with him along the cliffs when they see a hoopoe. She knows they visit the island sometimes but she has never before seen one. It is smaller than she had imagined but very colourful. They are so close she can see its large crest of orange feathers tipped with black, and its small, round black eyes.

"That little bird has flown all the way from Europe, Josh. Isn't that clever? It must be hundreds of miles." Violet laughs as Joshua sees it and waves his arms around excitedly.

For several days afterwards Joshua is imitating its characteristic cry. She gives him scraps of stale food to feed the sparrows in the yard, but one day to her horror she finds a jet black raven glaring down at them from the chimney stack. Its stooped position and evil black eyes give it a threatening pose.

The bird could swoop down and peck his eyes out. She grabs Joshua up into her arms and, clutching him to her, she rushes indoors, but the raven returns day after day until Violet is convinced it is another bad omen. She can only vaguely remember the words of Madame Christabel, but clear in her mind is the warning of danger and death.

She stops Joshua from feeding the sparrows, but still the bird persists. She cannot tell Richard, he would think her foolish, but she has to tell someone and eventually she confides in Auntie Sarah. They go together to the back door and there, sure enough, is the bird.

"It gives me the shudders every time I see him. It's like he's trying to tell me something bad is going to happen," says Violet.

Auntie Sarah eyes it suspiciously, but putting a lightness in her voice she says, "Oh aye, that there's a raven. Those birds don't stay any place for long, they change their haunts as the mood takes them."

"'Tis strange he never seems to come when Richard's here," ponders Violet.

"He won't be perched in thy yard long, never fear." Auntie Sarah pats her on the shoulder reassuringly as she speaks, but Violet remains uneasy nevertheless.

Richard has no patience with her when she responds to the superstitions of the islanders. Instead he tries constantly to instil in her more rational fears, spending hours with her talking about the harm smuggling has done and begging her to look at it from all sides.

The night after Auntie Sarah's visit they are sitting by the fireside. Richard sighs. "These fishermen are running rings round me, but I don't know what more I can do."

"You are not doing so badly," says Violet. "You and the coastguard men on the 'Sprightly Cutter' have discovered their spoils quite a few times."

"Well, thank heavens for that. At least I am justifying my presence in some small way, but we never seem to be able to trap anyone claiming it!"

"Well, at least we get a percentage of the crop."

"But it is not stopping them, is it?" Richard sounds exasperated.

"I don't think you will ever stop them, sweetheart. Many would starve through the winter months on Portland without the free-traders' help."

Violet is content just to watch the flickering lights of the fire dance across Richard's serious expression, but he is determined to make her see reason.

"I know you think there's no harm in it, but you're wrong. People get involved so deeply there's no turning back." He gently takes her hand in his. "Some men get to enjoy the excitement of fooling the authorities, others enjoy the power they hold over more subservient men, and become sadistic. Many of these men are ruthless killers and it is people like the Chiswell smugglers who enable them to operate."

She watches as he shakes his head. "A hungry man who steals from a wealthy man to feed his family may be morally justified, but the habit is hard to break. Need turns to greed and fear of the consequences turns a man into a cornered animal; he will do anything to save his own skin."

Violet comments defensively, "But it's never been like that here 'cus everyone always accepted it. Even old Taggart got his due for turning a blind eye and no one ever came to no harm."

"Maybe not, but surely you can see that there cannot be exceptions. It is wrong and it has caused terrible violence in some areas. It has to be stopped." Violet makes no comment. What does he want from her?

"Violet, what about the ruthless gangs that operate runs right up inland, who depend on the co-operation of local people, and 'safe houses'. What happens if an innocent bystander accidentally gets involved? They'll stop at nothing, you know, to prevent anyone jeopardising their organisation. They terrorise innocent people, who only turn a blind eye because they are scared of reprisals against other members of their families. I have heard of customs men and informers being tortured, having ears and noses cut off, limbs broken or burnt and even being buried alive."

He is just trying to shock her, "Well, I don't recall hearing of anything like that."

"That doesn't mean that it doesn't happen though does it, Vi? Believe me, Violet, whole villages have been terrorised in the past. The women, even young girls have been raped and their homes plundered, where the ruthlessness of the smuggling gangs so terrified honest folk that they were outnumbered and defenceless against them."

The fire collapses, sending a puff of smoke into the room, but Violet doesn't stir. She wants it to die down so that they can go to bed and Richard will forget about the smugglers.

"I was told of one case where an unfortunate riding officer, a family man with five young children, came by chance upon a smuggling gang. To prevent him going for help they hamstrung his poor horse and left it crippled. It died in agony. They then took the officer with them until they could decide how they might teach him a lesson."

"He was repeatedly beaten and abused, bound and gagged until, covered in blood, he was hidden in a coffin. By the time they eventually decided to take him to France and dump him there, the poor man had either suffocated or died from his injuries."

She sits open mouthed; she doesn't want to hear this. She doesn't want to think about it. It is too horrible, the poor fellow, but however Richard puts it to her she cannot compare those evil men with her family. "But things are different now, and besides, it was nowhere near here. Our men don't go killing folk."

"Don't expect me to fall for that, Violet. This coastline is notorious for wreckers. Your men are no different from anywhere else. If it wasn't for the authorities, the coastguards, the revenue men and people like me, times wouldn't have changed. They'd still be up on the cliffs with false lanterns drawing the ships onto the rocks, and clubbing the survivors as they struggled ashore, robbing the dead and looting the wreckage."

"Oh no," says Violet, "I never believed 'twas true."

She'd heard the old stories of nights dense with fog, of the donkey wandering along the cliff top with a lantern tied to its tail to imitate the motion of a ship at sea and thus lure unsuspecting vessels onto the treacherous rocks below; but she had refused to believe such nonsense. She knew that no ship's master worth his salt would ever be tempted to steer towards a light.

The picture of the donkey was amusing enough, but she had seen what the sea could do once it had a ship at its mercy. She had seen for herself the panic and sheer terror of the crew and passengers, often children among them. Her family had always been proud of the many acts of courage shown by the local fishermen in their numerous endeavours to save lives.

There are two sides to every story, but many would have starved through the winter months on Portland without the free-traders' help and so she just prayed that nothing would ever go wrong there.

She wishes Richard would put aside his anger; she hates it when he makes her feel obliged to defend her people. "Let's just be thankful it's not so bad nowadays, my love." She smiles tenderly, looking deep into his eyes. "Let's not quarrel." She takes his hand saying, "Come on, the fire is almost out. I think it is time for us to go to bed."

Richard has on numerous occasions joined forces with the coastguard men on the 'Sprightly Cutter' and discovered crops of contraband, but has been unable to trap anyone claiming it.

This is acceptable as far as the customs officials are concerned, as long as he justifies his presence in some way. He is awarded a percentage of the value of the crop. Although he knows the fishermen are running rings round him there is nothing he can do about it.

However, in the spring of 1835 a run of bad luck hits the island. The Portlanders are tired and hungry after a long, hard winter, where men have been laid off at the quarries and the weather has immobilised the lerrets. The spring tides and mellow weather following the March winds have turned the beach into a hive of industry, but the fishermen's joy is to be short-lived.

Richard, out on his regular patrol, is surprised one morning to see three rabbits on Mere Common.

He immediately thinks of Violet and smiles to himself. Then two men, one coming from Chiswell, are killed in two separate incidents within a week of each other, the latter of the two being thrown into the sea from the quarry at the Beale. This makes him question his own certainty that Violet's superstition is a load of rubbish.

On the twelfth of May the weather turns yet again. Richard notices the great grey shadow that looms ominously from the south-west, its forerunner being a sudden squall. He can see from his cottage window that the fishermen far out at sea after the mackerel hardly have time to draw in their nets before the character of the sea is transformed into an angry physical fury of strength. He dons his waterproofs and, with many other villagers, he runs through the beating rain to the shoreline to help pull in the tossing, tumbling lerrets. As the wind whips the surf into a bubbling, swirling broth he can see the men are rowing hard for the beach.

The first crew to draw near to the shore are the Gibbs brothers. Old Jabe attaches a line to his web-footed sea dog, unique on Portland and bred for this very purpose, and it dives into the sea to try to reach the lerret. It is swept back a couple of times by the thrashing waves, but with determination the third time it manages to reach the boat and the men catch hold of it and haul it on board. They tie the line to the front of the craft and the shore-men heave together to pull it in. They are jubilant for they have a catch to be proud of.

"There bain't nothin' like the calm before a storm for a good catch o' mackerel." They make a fuss of Skipper and are laughing and patting each other on the back when they see two more boats coming in, and go with the dog, to lend a hand.

Visibility is much worse as the torrential rain

obliterates all beyond a few yards and it is then that someone shouts that Matthew and his father are also in difficulty. There is much yelling and confusion. Finally they organise a human chain and Richard, with a rope tied around his waist, plunges into the sea to reach the line thrown ashore.

His feet are unable to stand fast, the powerful undercurrent fighting with the mobile pebbles to topple him; but for the iron hold of the chain he would have been swept away several times. He is submerged and then he swims, and stretching out he grabs the line. Now the strong men heave desperately against the furious waves and the boat is slowly but triumphantly brought in with its catch and five men. Richard collapses exhausted on the beach, saturated and cold, but still the torrential rain beats down on them mercilessly.

Matthew cannot ignore Dryer's assistance; he watches Dryer get up, as his own and Violet's father and the other crewmen show their gratitude, and he braces himself to face the man with his thanks. He cannot bury the jealousy and hatred he feels for his rival but his pride dictates that he too must show his respect for the man's courage. He may well have saved his life. He forces himself to suppress the confusing conflict within and shake Dryer's hand, but no words pass between them. They understand each other perfectly.

A sense of victory is in the air as others gratefully acknowledge their rescuers and Richard turns to help again as more are struggling to beach their small crafts. The wind howls louder and the rain lashes into his face. Then a hush falls over the gathering. To everyone's dismay, they realise that a considerable distance from the shore there is another lerret fighting to reach the safety of the beach.

Richard can just make out two of the crew

trying to pull the catch back over the side and it is obvious that they are in grave trouble. The other two men are rowing hard when a loud clap of thunder, like a roar from the God Thor, heralds the disaster. With half her catch weighing down the lerret on one side, a huge wave strikes the boat and it overturns. The men are thrown all ways.

There is a gasp of dismay from the onlookers. They watch helplessly, knowing that the crew are too far out for salvation. In minutes they are swept out to sea, only to be returned ashore at the ocean's whim.

"Whose boat was it?" Richard hears someone shouting.

"'Twas Alex Shaddick's." Matthew pauses as the wind sucks his breath away, "And William and Jonathan Stone, and Joseph White were with him," he adds in despair.

"Poor Annie Shaddick! That's her father and her new husband." The man shakes his head in sorrow. "There's some widows made this day."

Dryer stays among the relatives and friends and watches the shoreline for nearly an hour, knowing it to be a futile gesture. The ocean shows no mercy, and ten days later a memorial service is held in the chapel.

Richard and Violet attend the service and they are both relieved to find their presence there acceptable. The mutual need for compassion draws the community together, all emotion concentrated on supporting the grief-stricken. Not a soul wastes a moment in unnecessary spitefulness towards them.

Mrs Shaddick has to be physically supported by her two eldest boys, whilst Annie appears to be in a trance. She dare not cry as her face will go all blotchy and she has no veil. She sees Violet is there with Richard Dryer and cannot help resenting her presence. If that Violet were to cry the tears would no doubt enhance her wretched beauty, she thinks jealously.

After the service, May and Rose, the two sisters of Jack White, are weeping audibly as their friends offer their condolences, and Annie's mother again breaks down.

Annie cannot bring herself to comfort her mother, because the lump in her throat is hurting her so and she knows that if she stays any longer she too will succumb to her own grief. She leaves quickly and unobtrusively, but her sudden exit does not go unnoticed by Violet.

It is obvious that she wants to be left alone and, in any case, she would not welcome Violet's compassion, but as the slow-moving file of people leave and Violet steps out into the sunlight she turns to her husband. "Poor Annie, she'd just made herself a family with William and young Benjamin and then last year his Granny died. And now this. 'Tis a sad thing. I do feel for her, Richard."

"We all do, my dear." He takes her arm, "But she'll get help from every able-bodied man around and she's a survivor. She'll be all right and the boy is a strong, healthy lad."

They walk on together, relieved to leave behind the mourners. "I'm so lucky that in all the years our ancestors have fished off Deadman's Bay we've never lost a soul. Not even in the great gale in 1824. Yet some families seem to get all the bad luck."

"Oh, I don't know, I think everyone gets equal portions of good and bad. It's just that some people get it spread evenly throughout their lives and some have to suffer it all at once. We have to make the best of things and usually those who suffer a great deal of misfortune enjoy equal amounts of good to compensate."

"But sometimes it is so hard to have faith when everything seems against us, especially when we are all alone and have no one to turn to for support." It is Annie and Mrs Shaddick she is thinking of as she speaks.

"That's why I think we are lucky. It is not always easy to understand the will of God, but he tells us that in everything there is a reason and it seems to me that we have found something wonderfully good out of something that at the time seemed essentially bad."

"I didn't know that you were religious, Richard," she says, surprised at this revelation.

"I'm not, in the pious sense; but I do believe in God and in the forces of good and evil. I have seen my fair share of bad luck, and now I wish to make the most of my share of good fortune, of which you are the greatest part." He hugs her more closely to him, and she smiles back at him feeling optimistic. Surely their fortunes can only improve.

Annie has left Benjamin at her mother's home and, knowing that she will have to speak to her younger brothers and sisters before Ikey and Bill return with their mother from the chapel, she summons all her strength of will to conceal her grief.

As she walks in, the unusual silence strikes her as very strange. As a rule, when left unattended the fighting and squabbling can be heard from down the street. The house is a mess, the children seem dazed and hardly register surprise at the sight of her, but the bewildered little ones continue to play with Benjamin.

She does not know how she finds the strength to

organise them, feeling so bereft herself, but life must go on and somehow she has to make them see that too.

Although they all do as she asks, they will not stick together for long. They will be arguing over the chores next week and nothing will get done the week after that, unless she keeps a close watch over things. She chops up some vegetables that she salvages from the rotten selection left in the larder and boils them up to make a soup. The main problem is going to be feeding the boys, who are growing fast; Bill and Ikey are eighteen and nineteen years old and have huge appetites. At least with a big family there are plenty of willing hands.

It is only May and Eddie who've gone to school. The older ones never did, and cannot read or write. They were too old by the time the British School in the High Street was founded. But May and Eddie have already learnt to read, so now maybe the twins can take their place. It will keep them out of mischief and she can look after Lilly sometimes, along with Ben.

"May, I am afraid that you are the one who will have to hold the family together. I know you are only thirteen but you are so good with the little ones. Ikey is too wild and the boys will follow his example if we are not careful. Eddie and the two younger boys, Tom and Henry, love messing around with the boat; they've been doing it for quite a while now. It is time they put their skills to good use. They will have to lend a hand with the fishing. If Eddie takes charge of the boys and you stay home and help Ma, then Joseph and Janey can take your places at school." She smiles at her younger sister. Skivvying won't come easy to her; she had set her sights higher.

May is about to protest when their front door

opens and the return of Ikey, Bill and her mother interrupts them. Annie helps her mother up to bed and leaves May to dish out the hot broth for the rest of the family. She tries to get her mother to take a little too, but is unsuccessful and she fears the worst.

"Come on, Ma. You've got to fight this or you'll be ill." In spite of her own pain, she tries to appear strong.

"I don't care, I just want to die," moans Mrs Shaddick, her face almost buried in the pillow.

Annie feels despair run through her. She is finding it hard to keep her own grief in check and cope with her own difficulties, without having to contend with the burden of both households. "Don't be stupid, you've a family downstairs. We all need you."

"I can't help it, Annie. You're strong, but I've always had Alex, we were childhood sweethearts. I had you before I were sixteen. I can't imagine life without 'im and he's never coming back, never. I just know I'm going to die." She groans, "I want to die. I can't face it, Annie, I feel so weak." She cries helplessly into the pillow. "There's no strength left in me." Her voice is filled with despair. "Please leave me be. I just want to be left alone."

Annie, feeling a mixture of alarm and compassion, decides to leave her mother for now and, closing the bedroom door, she goes downstairs to take Ben home. She is greeted with ten spoons scraping on ten nearly empty bowls.

"Thanks, Annie," says Ikey. "Ma hasn't been able to cope these last few days. You don't fancy moving back here do ya?" As usual Ikey's sudden thought is blurted out, on the spur of the moment.

"I can't, Ikey. There isn't room enough, besides the rent's paid on our cottage until November." She picks up Benjamin, feeling torn between her two families. "I'll help all I can, but I want to keep me own cottage now I've got one. I'll call in tomorra and see how Ma is. See ya." She tries to sound confident and cheerful.

"Well, thanks a lot," says Ikey sullenly. "Pull up the ladder, Jack, I'm all right!"

That is the last straw. Annie turns on him, "Look, I lost William as well as Father and I've got Benjamin to think of now. Just let me get over my own grief, will you, Ikey, and try not to think only of yourself all the time." She cannot stop the words tumbling out, but it does Ikey no harm. What she says is true. She does need time to adjust to the situation and he is only thinking of himself.

She marches off holding Ben tightly to her. When she finally settles him for the night, she feels dreadfully lonely. She sits by the fire, in the old rocking chair that William's mother always sat in. She is knitting a coat for Ben and as she rocks to and fro, she feels like an old woman. At twenty-four she feels older than her own mother and the tears fall unchecked onto the black lace of her dress.

Within a month her mother has died pining for Alex Shaddick. She has virtually starved herself to death and has left much bitterness in her passing. Annie is forced to move back in with her brothers and sisters and it is a wrench to leave the cottage that has become her home.

She takes the best of the furniture with her and makes a little money on the things that become surplus, but it will not last long and she knows that money is going to be a big problem.

Another worry is Ikey and Bill. They are both drinking far too much and Annie can see that they could be the family's downfall if they do not pull themselves together. Although they still work hard, as the need for money becomes more desperate so does the need for ale. It is a vicious circle, and neither is man enough to break it.

Unbeknown to Annie, their drunken abuse at the Cove House Inn is put up with by the locals for a time, but patience is wearing thin. Finally it snaps, when they are both involved in a brawl there and John Motyer has to call out the Coast Fencibles to regain order. Several of the villagers are hurt and after that it isn't only Dryer who will stand no nonsense; John Motyer will not serve them if he thinks they have already supped enough.

Because of this, Dryer keeps an especially close watch on them. This could be his breakthrough; this weakness in their characters will surely lead to their undoing. He can see that they are likely to become desperate and therefore reckless and in the event he wants to be prepared.

One night in August he is particularly keen when he sights what appears to be the Shaddick boat. It is some distance south of the position of the revenue cutter on which he is patrolling with the customs men. They immediately give chase in the moonlight, and are gaining on them when they round the headland below Blacknor Fort.

The revenue cutter is in close pursuit and yet when they too pass the headland the small craft has vanished. It is an unusually clear, moonlit night and the sea is not too choppy; all that can be heard is the lapping of the ripples at the water's edge. It is uncanny. The boat couldn't have disappeared.

A light is pointed in the direction of Mutton Cove. Perhaps they are hidden in the shadows of the huge rocks, but they can see no one. However,

Dryer has observed an oval black opening in the cliff side. It is obviously concave by the shadows played across it from the moon.

"Is that a cave I see there, Sam?"

"'Tis that, but you'll never pilot a lerret through those rocks, 'tis too dangerous."

"Well, that boat's gone somewhere, unless it was a ghost ship. I reckon there's the answer."

"Well, I can't take 'er in any closer, I'm sorry."

"Look, just anchor a while and I'll take the dinghy in as far as I can. I can't come to any harm and it's worth a try. Please just bear with me a while."

"All right, Mr Dryer, but I reckon they went on round tight to the shoreline."

Richard goes in alone equipped with a lantern and a pistol. As he manoeuvres the little craft through the channel between the rocks, it occurs to him that it would have been more prudent to come with one of the crew and as he comes closer to the black hole a chill runs through him. There could be any number of cut-throats holed up in this cave.

The boat begins to struggle against the changing tide, but he rows straight into the cave, stows the oars and holds high his lantern, keeping his pistol handy but out of sight. There in the farthest recesses of this dark cavern are the huddled forms of Tom and Henry Shaddick.

As Dryer stows his pistol, a voice from the cutter calls, "You all right, Mr Dryer?"

"Yes, I'm fine. I've found something. I'll be with you in a minute." He then lowers his voice. "What the hell are you two kids doing out in a boat at this time of night? I thought it was your older brothers."

The two helpless faces stare back at him, wide-eyed with fright. "We had to, Mr Dryer, May's worried sick we won't have enough rent money if we don't."

"Don't what?" asks Dryer quietly.

They remain silent. "Come on, or do I have to search the boat and the cave?" He lifts a grappling hook but he can tell from their faces that he's won.

"We were on a 'pick up'," says Tom dejectedly. "These." He pulls a rope attached to several tubs of spirits and lets it go again; it is fixed to their boat.

"You've obviously used this cave before," says Dryer.

"Aye, in good weather and bad. We've not much time, we'll have to move soon or we'll be left high and dry, as the tide drops," says Tom. "You have to time it just right …" His voice fades. "'Tis a difficult thing to judge."

"Well, son, you were unlucky tonight. I wouldn't have attempted it if the sea hadn't been fairly calm."

"We'd better make a move soon or we'll be marooned, Sir. We're ready to take our medicine, 'tis a fair cop," says Tom conceding.

"No, wait awhile," he pauses, reluctant to do his duty. They are both so young. "I'll have to confiscate the contraband but you stay put. No one knows you're here, except me, but in return I want your word you'll not do this again. Your brothers knew that if they were in the Cove House Inn I had them taped, but I would not expect you youngsters to go in their place. They're too clever by half, but leaving you youngsters to carry the can is cowardly.

"You may not think it now but it was lucky that I was the one to discover you. It's just not worth the risk, boys; you can make the money you need fishing. Let your brothers give up the ale or do their own dirty work. Do I have your word?"

"Yes, Sir," they both reply in unison. "It's just, Ikey'll be livid," adds Tom.

"You leave Ikey and Bill to me." He is transferring the 'slung load' to his own boat as he speaks. "Listen carefully; I'll be going on round the Beale with the cutter and into the harbour." He turns the boat carefully within the cave, "You go quietly back to the cove the way you came, and say nothing of this to anyone." Dryer then paddles back out through the entrance of the cave on a receding wave and rows hard to join the 'Sprightly Cutter'.

"You were right, they must have kept tight to the shore and carried on round the Beale, but this is what they were after." Dryer wonders what Violet would think of him covering up for the boys, as he secures the tender astern with a painter. Then they set off full sail ahead, in the opposite direction to their quarry.

Tom and Henry cautiously emerge minutes later and pull hard towards the cove. They are exhausted when they finally pull the lerret out of the water and up the beach. "All that flaming work for nothin'," grumbles Henry breathlessly.

"What would 'ave 'appened if Dryer had told on us?" Tom is panting as they upturn the lerret. He sits on it and rests a moment. "He could've. It would have been good for him, and after what we did to Violet that day, with all 'er clothes, we deserve to be punished. You'd think he'd have wanted to get his own back, wouldn't you?" says Tom thoughtfully.

"We'd have been pressed into the Navy, most likely," speculates Henry, and he comes round the boat and joins his brother. "I bet if it had been Bill and Ikey he'd have seized 'em with pleasure," adds Henry. "They couldn't have put up a fight, they'd have been cornered just like us."

They sit in silence for a while. "What'll we tell Ikey?"

"Dryer said to say nothing, but we'll 'ave to tell 'im the truth. We can't use that cave any more," answers Tom. "Dryer will be sure to 'ave words with 'em anyways."

"Come on then, let's get it over with."

The two boys go directly to the Cove House Inn, where they know their brothers can be found, somewhat ashamed at losing a valuable crop but also a little confused about their loyalties. On entering the inn they find it to be filled solely with their own kind and are soon explaining quite openly to the fellow smugglers of Dryer's leniency.

"You damned fool boys, there were twenty kegs in that crop," says Ikey angrily, "and now Dryer has a hold over us."

"He did have, and he could've used it, but he hasn't now, has he? He's no proof we was there in that cave. He didn't have to let us off, Ikey, he were armed with a pistol and we was well and truly trapped."

"Ye, but he'd have looked a proper fool if he'd have come out wi' you two whippersnappers."

"He didn't do it for that, he did it for us. He let us off 'cus we've no Ma or Pa and 'cus you 'n Bill be drunk ha'f the time and he felt sorry for us."

Tom is knocked off his feet backwards with a blow across the side of his jaw from his angry older brother, but before another brawl ensues, Matthew and his father step in and Mr Stone speaks severely to Ikey.

"Now you look here, lad, you've got a responsibility to your family and I suggest you start by pulling yourself together. There weren't no couple in Chiswell that worked harder'n your Ma and Pa to keep you kids in clothes and, if nothin' else, 'twere summat they were proud of. We've all felt at some time or other that things is against us. We've all done our share of smuggling and foolin' Dryer, but he's just doin' his job and as I see it he's been more'n fair wi' your two lads here. I reckon if it had been you and Bill, t'would have been a different story, 'cus of late you've been nothin' but trouble and to have you both drafted into the Navy would have been a blessing.

"Nevertheless, it weren't and I should let it be a lesson to you before you go shouting your mouth off about any devious plans you think Dryer may be harbouring. All men aren't tarred with the same brush and I reckon our Dryer is a very unusual man and not to be underestimated by any one of us."

The silence that follows that lecture could be cut with a knife. Ikey jerks himself free of Matthew's hold, throws back the last of his pint and says to his brothers, "It's time we were leavin'."

They go to follow Ikey out, but then he turns back. "Though why the hell you're speaking up for him, when your own son's been stabbed in the back by Dryer, makes me think you must be mad." They leave then and Ikey slams the door behind him as he goes.

Mr Stone can still hear their discontented muttering from outside as he looks around. "Well, credit where credit's due, I say."

Matthew says nothing.

CHAPTER 9 *(November 1835)*

THE RAVEN'S DEPARTURE

Violet is busy darning socks and thinking quietly to herself that the tide is changing towards herself and Richard. She looks up at her husband as he sits relaxing beside the fire, his handsome features bathed in the light from the flames. She is certain now that they had been right to go against public opinion. She loves him so much and she decides to tell him how she suspects that people's attitudes are improving.

"You know, just lately I have noticed a change in folks' manner towards me. It is only the odd 'Good morning', but when folk are civil it makes a big difference."

"I know what you mean. I think it is since the storm and I was allowed to help bring in the boats. Since then folk have seemed more respectful to me as well." Richard sucks on his pipe.

"Well, by all accounts you did risk your own life saving Matthew and his father and their crew."

"I did have some help. It wasn't all my doing."

Violet smiles at him, "I know, sweetheart, but it must have made them all realise that you are not all bad."

"I think me letting off the young Shaddick boys has also influenced opinion. They all know that it would have been a different story if it had been the two older boys. That Ikey and Bill seem to be going from bad to worse. I hear that the ill feeling of the locals at the Cove House and the Castle Inn has driven them out to find other pastures, and now they regularly leave the island to tour the Weymouth quayside inns and taverns."

"That's a bit of a mixed blessing don't you think? Folk hereabouts say there are any number of scoundrels lurking over there, drinking their brandy, gambling their wages and taking whatever whores come their way."

"I agree. Already Ikey and Bill can be gone for several days at a time and return with empty pockets and the worse for liquor. It is good to see the back of them, but their drinking only seems to be getting worse."

Violet shakes her head, "I don't know how Annie puts up with it."

"I am sure she makes her feelings known, but what can she do? I fear it won't be long before they encourage their cronies back over here with them."

"I don't know, the ferry crossing has always been a bit of a barrier and in the past has put off those lads from Weymouth. They seem to find enough to entertain themselves over there."

"Well, I think I am getting near to a breakthrough as far as they are concerned. I believe that their drunkenness will be their downfall."

"Let's hope so." Violet dreads a showdown between Richard and Matthew or her father and brothers and while he is preoccupied with Ikey there seems less danger of that. Her only fear is that Ikey and Bill, whose escapades have gone from bad to worse and who have alienated all who come in contact with them, will be too treacherous for Richard to outwit.

Ikey has found solace with a skinny little wench

called Maggie, whom he discovered at a harbour-side bawdy-house. Maggie becomes a regular companion and tonight she is leaning against him caressing and occasionally kissing him. At the same time Ikey and Bill are drinking with some crewmen off the Jersey packet boat and Ikey starts to brag about the enormous profits the Portlanders are getting from smuggling.

Ikey knocks back a large mouthful of his drink. "This is a very good drop of brandy, I must say."

"I can get you some better stuff than this from the Channel Islands at a knock-down price if you are interested." The sailor lowers his voice. "Our commander on the 'Countess of Wessex' turns a blind eye to any extras we care to conceal in our cabins, if you know what I mean."

Ikey laughs. "No thanks. We've got a good little business going ourselves on Portland."

"But aren't you worried about the new coastguards being so full of zeal?"

"We never do bother too much about the waterguard or the land sharks. We can always lure them in a different direction if we need to, because everyone involved is related on Portland and 'tis easy to pull the wool over the Kimberlins' eyes. We free-traders easily outnumber the gobblers."

Bill draws Ikey to one side as the serving girl turns up to refill their mugs. "Ikey, don't be so free with the information. It is because we keep ourselves to ourselves on Portland that we have always been so successful, but we don't want all and sundry knowing too much. As it is, we have only been included ourselves lately because our family is so hard up."

"Ah, shut up, Bill, you always have been frightened of your own shadow. They are just like us. No harm in bending the law a little. 'Tis not like we are criminals."

"That is not the point, Ikey, your big bragging mouth is likely to be a danger to us all."

"Rubbish! There's no one here man enough to beat us at our own game, Bill, besides there ain't anyone here sober enough to care."

The serving girl finishes filling their mugs and goes on to the next table and Ikey and Bill return to their seats.

The second crewman leans forward confidentially. "If you want some extra cash I know where you can get five shillings or more as a bearer, but if you're prepared to be a batman you could earn yourselves twenty shillings plus a dollop of tea, probably worth a further twenty-five shillings."

Bill gives Ikey a warning look. "No thanks, we've no need to go further afield."

Ikey laughs and shakes his head. His brother is too cautious by half! "I'll let you know if I ever need to take you up on it. At the moment I've got my hands full. We've already got a run of our own planned off Deadman's Bay at high tide on 8th November."

Maggie is listening and thinks to herself, that information is worth a bob or two.

As Bill fears, Ikey is to be proved wrong, and he is not the only one who pays the price of his indiscretion. Through Maggie, detailed information of the landing in November, including times and date, reaches via the grapevine the ears of Adam Kinson, the leader of a notorious smuggling gang. Inevitably he and his men plan to seize the contraband by force.

Miles inland bearers are eager to join what they think is a routine run. The batmen are soon prepared, with blackened faces and clubs at the ready to dissuade anyone from interfering. They set off as darkness falls, stopping en route at a 'gentleman's' house for refreshment, provided at Kinson's expense. The more ruthless batmen, in addition to the bats or clubs they use, are also armed with pistols and other weapons and will not hesitate to use them if the need arises.

At around eleven-thirty at night, the large rabble of undesirables converge at Swyre and have the long trek across Chesil ahead of them.

At this time the landing party are guarding all approaches to the landing spot, and stretch from the Cove House Inn to the outer limits of Chiswell. Whether prepared with a lerret at the ready, grappling hooks or spout lanterns, all have a duty to perform. The area of water that lies before the Cove House Inn is where the silent, stealthy men are to meet the freighter.

It is as if time stands still whilst they endure that dreadful waiting, all senses straining and muscles so tense that their hearts lurch and thump within them.

Bill alone anxiously glances towards the mainland. The others concentrate their sights to the sea, but all the time wary, listening for Dryer behind them. Then the flink out at sea is spotted and answered and the ship's boat struggles ashore, almost over-laden with goods.

The Chiswell men are now intent upon their tasks. It is a good sea, choppy but nothing a decent seaman couldn't handle, and they peer into the darkness for sight of the vessel as she pulls her weighty cargo inland. Nothing can be seen, until just detectable in an instant of moonlight, there she is a fair way out, but all is well.

It is in that sudden break in the clouds that Bill

observes, far in the distance, men and horses with muffled hooves silently and slowly progressing towards them. The whole convoy appears to him like a deadly, nocturnal reptile stealthily crawling over the ridge and he panics. He runs from shadow to shadow, his body bent low, searching for Ikey. He is brought to the ground, stumbling over the foot that Ikey has stuck in his path. He is furious. "For Christ's sake, Ikey."

"Shush, what you panicking about?" whispers his brother.

"I've seen about forty men coming along the beach. They'll be here in about twenty minutes and we'll be caught with our pants down."

"I know, I spotted them, I'm not stupid," says Ikey, through his teeth.

"But they're a big gang, Ikey. We'll not stand a chance," whispers Bill in desperation.

"It'll serve 'em right," says Ikey defiantly, "making me look foolish. It's about time they all had some problems. Why should the Shaddicks get 'em all?" Ikey is smug.

Bill cannot believe what he is hearing, "You did it deliberately?"

"I told you, it serves 'em right."

"But they'll know it was you," Bill says, trying to make him see sense. "You've got to warn them."

"They won't suspect me if I'm here with them, will they?" argues Ikey.

"Well, who else could it be?" demands Bill. "They're not idiots."

"Look," says Ikey, his eyes piercing those of his brother, "you go back and keep your place. 'Tis too late for heroics, what's done is done."

"You're a bloody fool, Ikey. We need this crop as much as anyone. You're cutting off your nose to spite your face."

"Ah, shut up and do as I say, you sound like an old woman."

There is no point in arguing with him, besides there isn't time. Bill cannot think straight but he knows he cannot stay there and watch what is about to happen. A tight ball of fear is knotted high in his stomach as he runs from the scene.

What am I doing behaving like a miserable coward? He enters the cottage quietly and sits down, his head in his hands by the remnants of the fire.

Annie, who sleeps like a cat on nights such as these, hears the sound of someone entering the cottage and is down the stairs in an instant. As the latch lifts on the stairway door, Bill's heart thumps. Annie enters the room, and he starts to his feet.

It is obvious to Annie that something is wrong. "Whatever's up with you?" she asks with concern.

"Nothing," snaps Bill, his brows lowered guiltily as he wrestles with the problem.

"Don't lie to me, William. Summat's 'appened. Where's Ikey?"

"On the beach still," he mumbles.

"What you doing 'ere then?"

"Oh Annie, you wouldn't understand," he groans. He leans his arm against the wall and presses his head into it.

Annie is frightened. She grabs him and pulls him round to face her. "Look, you tell me what's going on or I'll take Da's whip to thee."

Fear has made something inside her snap, and Bill is made aware that she means what she says. He answers dejectedly, "There's a gang coming to take the crop. It's a valuable crop and half of Chiswell are on the beach. 'Twill be a fearful fight, and what's worse is, it's all 'cus Ikey were bragging. He knows they are coming and he don't give a damn."

"Oh my God!" Annie falls silent, her mind in

turmoil. No wonder Bill is deathly white.

"Look, forget about Ikey for the minute, Bill. She pauses in thought. "We've got to stop them landing the crop without it being known on the beach, or it'll be a pitched battle." The thought hits her, Dryer'll do it. She turns quickly to Bill. "You stay put, I'll get help."

She lights her lantern, quickly wraps herself in her cloak and rushes out.

Violet is reluctant to leave her warm bed to answer the urgent banging at her door, but her mouth drops open at the sight of Annie, for beneath her cloak she can see she wears only a thin night-gown.

"Is Mr Dryer at home, Violet? 'Tis urgent."

"I'm sorry, Annie. He's not. What's wrong?" She draws her shawl more closely about her as the chill night air swirls in.

"Can I please come in and explain?" she asks.

"Of course, I'm sorry." Violet stands aside for her to enter and gladly closes the door against the cold.

"There's going to be a bloody battle on the beach tonight, 'cus a gang of Kimberlins is on its way to steal the crop."

Oh God. Where is Richard?

"I thought if Mr Dryer could stop it being landed we could avoid the trouble, but as 'ee's not 'ere I don't know what we can do about it."

Violet watches Annie pace the room like a caged panther, and tries to make sense of what she's just heard. Their only hope is the candles. "I'll signal a warning to the boatmen. They could turn back. It might help."

She rushes upstairs and lights the warning candles. Her hands shake as gradually the gravity of the situation comes to her. She visualises again the horrible deeds described to her in the past by Richard, and nearly trips on the stairs in her haste to get back down to Annie.

"It's not enough, Annie. We must alert our men."

"But how?"

"I don't know, I cannot leave Josh alone."

"I'll go back, maybe there's time for Bill to warn them." Annie leaves in haste and speedily despatches her brother to the scene, but everything is destined to go wrong for it is already too late.

The boat had been about to beach as Violet lit the warning candles and the men are too busy with the contraband to notice the danger signals. They are all working in silent harmony when, at the clink of a bit, someone spots the Kimberlin gang closing in on them and then pandemonium breaks out.

The outsiders easily overpower the Portlanders, who are unarmed and completely unprepared for this turn of events. Whilst the takeover is bloodless, angry words are exchanged and a very bitter fury is barely kept in check.

Richard Dryer has no knowledge of the run and is out on his horse that night. It is his habit to go quietly on foot patrols in the village of Chiswell, but he also makes use of the revenue cutter on occasion and sometimes he might enjoy a good gallop along the cliff tops surveying the sea from various points all around the island. It is a dark, cloudy night with a strong southerly breeze.

Dryer slows his horse to a trot as he moves with the wind at his back towards Royal Common. From this vantage point he notices the warning lights and his suspicions are aroused. He then imagines, in an instant of moonlight, that he sees a convoy of animals and men moving slowly towards him, southwards along the causeway. Seconds later his opinion is confirmed as the moonlight reveals the secrets of the night and he sees Chiswell smugglers and inland distributors working, as he believes, in harmony.

He instantly spurs his horse to a gallop and descends Lankridge at speed. He hurtles down the hill and into Chiswell. There is no time to lose, but his heart sinks when he realises that the signalling light comes from his own cottage. How could Violet betray him like this? His chest tightens with pain and, disregarding his duty on the beach, he leaps from his horse and bursts in to confront her.

"Why? You little traitor," he shouts. "How could you betray me like this?" His throat is so tense it hurts.

"What do you mean? I were only trying to help me menfolk." He sees the terror in her eyes.

He cannot bear this. "Against me?" he cries. "Don't you understand, even now?" He grabs her tightly by the shoulders, annoyed by the look of panic on her face.

"No … No, you must listen to me. It's you who don't understand," she pleads.

At the report of a gun they both freeze. Then he pushes her aside and rushes out without a backward glance. She reels and falls to the floor, her head striking the corner of the dresser. She tries to call to him, but darkness floods the room. Her lips barely move; her thoughts fade until there is nothing but the swirling pain.

Violet shakes her head and tries to focus. She feels nausea swamping her, but Joshua is crying. She has to get up. She moves unsteadily up the stairs and lifts him from his cot. Blood trickles down her face as she wraps him in a blanket; she brushes it away with the back of her hand, wincing where her skin is sore and bruised. Pain pulses in her head. She has to go to the beach but first Joshua has to be safe. As she leaves the house in panic, fear is like a tight ball within her. She rushes to her mother's cottage, there is no time to explain. She calls loudly as she enters, "Ma, come quickly, it's me, Violet."

As her dazed and perplexed mother descends the stairs, she pushes Joshua into her arms. "Take him, Ma, I've got to go to the beach. There's trouble and Richard's gone there in a fury."

She runs then, through the darkness, stumbling and fearful, towards the beach, hearing the noise of the fighting that has resulted from the warning shot.

The dim scene that greets her is confusing, but she dare not go closer for fear of being seen. The shadows of men with heavily burdened animals are turning away from the Chiswell smugglers, the batmen protecting their withdrawal, but Richard is nowhere to be seen.

She watches helplessly, hidden from view behind a partly derelict building. She can see someone lying wounded and groaning. Is it Ikey Shaddick? She cannot be certain. The lump of fear is now in her throat, making it hard for her to breathe.

Suddenly up ahead of the withdrawing convoy she sees someone thrust his mount forward into their path. "Halt in the name of His Majesty's Government." It is Richard's voice. "You will be cut off up ahead by the Dorset Coast Fencibles. You have no escape. They are at this moment …

A shot rings out. Richard slumps and then falls from his horse.

"No!" she screams. Then she is running, regardless of her safety, her heart pounding with terror. Suddenly she is grabbed and held firm by strong arms. She fights and struggles with them to free herself, but Matthew and her father are unyielding. Her desperate cries are clear above the noise and chaos of the scene; her anguish so dreadful, a silence falls upon them. The batmen's horses prance edgily, the men leaning forward in the saddle now trigger-happy as they cover the withdrawal of their fine haul.

Then an officer's command to troops rings out and she hears the clang of swords, the jangle of bit and bridle and a row of flame torches light the scene. She sees then, through her tears, the blue uniforms of the mounted troops. The ruthless gang are trapped by the Portland Coast Fencibles. Richard had not been bluffing, he must have alerted the castle and he'd been playing for time. Please God let him be all right. Don't let him be badly hurt.

Violet holds her breath as the batmen change their attentions to the military stand ahead and the Chiswell men maintain their positions at the rear. She has to reach Richard somehow. What if he were to die, lying there on that cold beach before she could reach him? How would she and Josh manage without him?

Feeling sick with anxiety she is forced to watch and wait as the skirmish takes place close to where he lies so still. The troopers are intent on preventing Kinson and his batmen's escape. Meanwhile many of the men who are on foot abandon their loot and make their escape into the shadows. Some of the Chiswell men repossess what they can and vanish also and a few of the troopers gather together the deserted pack animals.

Matthew and her father still hold her firm, trying to pacify her. Her heart-rending sobbing has ceased, but their fear for her sanity grows whilst she just stares fixedly, willing her husband to move. As the fighting men push their way towards the mainland they can hold her back no longer. She breaks free and runs to where he has fallen.

His crumpled form lies face down in the pebbles, still and silent; and as Violet turns him gently in her arms she can see there is no life left in him. The left side of his chest and half his shoulder ripped bare to the bone. All hope has gone.

She hugs him, agony tearing at her, rocking him to and fro, her face contorting, as an animal howl erupts from her and echoes throughout the shadowy ruins of the beach houses.

She clings to him when they would have dragged her off. "Don't touch me," she wails. "Leave me be." She shakes off a compassionate hand.

No one defies her. Her anguish is powerful, filling those who love her with guilt.

Matthew and her father can hardly bear to witness it, but they stay, facing the wind to dry their tears. They watch over Violet whilst she weeps inconsolably. For what seems like an eternity they stand by as she kisses him feverishly, clinging tightly to his unresponsive body, desperate for some faint sign of life.

Richard's horse shivers and fidgets until finally the sounds of the skirmish diminish and die away. Violet lies, her mind blank, her body as cold as her husband's, as the prisoners and contraband are removed to Castletown and the silence of the night encloaks the remaining suffering few.

CHAPTER 10 *(November 1835 – April 1836)*

JUST ONE LAST LOOK

The villagers now rally around Violet and her family, casting aside the bitter rebukes of the past. Matthew is glad at last to be in constant attendance, but she is not of the same world. For weeks her solitary figure can be seen in that area of the beach, a black silhouette against the wintry white of the pebbles.

People whisper of a ghostly figure seen in the dark of night pacing the ridges and haunting the derelict buildings, until one night someone recognises Violet dressed in a scant nightgown and leads her back to her father's cottage. Thereafter the doors are securely bolted and the family sleep lighter, persuading her back to bed on numerous occasions. Even in her wakeful hours she is merely functioning, enacting what should be painful formalities without releasing the slightest hint of emotion.

The whole community attends the funeral at St George's Church in Reforne. Although it is a tribute to Dryer that he has at last won their respect, the irony is lost on Violet, who behind her veil remains aloof. Even when she removes the black lace that night, a veil remains nevertheless.

Matthew stays close by. He waits and he watches over Violet who, encased like a cocoon in a shield of bitter sadness, seems to have gone into hibernation, but he prays that something will eventually bring her back to reality.

Aware that this type of protection is a fragile

thing, he holds back. He doesn't want to make any mistakes and so he takes his time, treating her with constant kindness, at every opportunity being there to help, but deliberately making no romantic progress whatsoever.

Mrs Allen finds it exhausting looking out for both Violet and Joshua, and when Matthew calls later that day she breathes a sigh of relief. "Thank goodness you're here, Matty. Josh has been playing up all morning. He wants to go out, but I've too much to do and I can't trust Violet with him in her state. Just come and look at her."

"I know, Mrs Allen, I've already seen her. She stared right through me as I passed the window. Perhaps it would help if I took them out for an hour or so. It would do them both good and give you a break."

"Thank you, Matthew, I would be grateful."

He follows her through into their parlour, where Violet sits in the window seat ringing her hands. She is talking to someone, but the room is empty.

"I would not have betrayed you. You should have known I would not have betrayed you … But I was trying to help!" Then she jumps up. "The bird," she shouts, fear in her eyes, "quick, the bird … Shoo! Shoo!" She waves her arms erratically. Her voice, pleading, changes to a higher pitch. "No … No … I was scared." She looks down at her hands, and winces as if someone is shouting at her. "I'm sorry … I'm sorry … but it's not my fault."

Matthew moves and startles her. She says, "Who are you? … Where's Richard?"

"It's all right, Violet, I've come to look after you."

"But I want Richard to come back."

"He can't, Vi. He can't, love." He takes her into his arms, her heartbeat flutters against his chest. She feels frail like a bird and he aches for her.

"Come on, Violet," he coaxes. "Let us go out for some air." She turns her eyes upon him and, quiet as a lamb, walks on his arm to the door. He fastens her cloak around her and calls to Joshua, "Come on, Josh, let's go down to the beach."

Once out in the air, Joshua is happy. He clings to Matthew's free hand as he walks Violet to the beach. Matthew lets him run as they enter Big Ope, knowing he is safe there and that his short three-year-old legs will make heavy going of the deep and shifting pebbles up ahead. But Joshua behaves impeccably for Matthew and despite him being the image of his father, Matthew warms to him. Poor little lad, he's not only lost his Pa but his Ma too for the moment. No wonder he's been playing up. Who could blame him?

As they go he continues to talk gently to Violet, not expecting any response, but trying all the time to reach through to her.

"He's a smart little nipper, your Josh. You should be proud of him."

He watches Joshua collecting different coloured pebbles. The child brings them to show to his mother, but throws them down again when she appears to ignore him. As he turns away, Matthew calls to him, "Josh, do you know how to play ducks and drakes?" He shakes his bowed head. "Come on then, I'll show you."

He holds out his free hand again and Joshua takes it. They go down closer to the water's edge. "Right, that's close enough. Sit down next to your mother, Josh, and I'll show you what to do." Violet and Joshua obediently sit on the shingle.

"Now this is important, because if you can count, you are better at it. So you have to count the jumps each time. Are you ready?"

"Yes," says Joshua, his eyes on the flat pebble in Matthew's hand.

Matthew looks at Violet, but there is no response. She sits silently, her eyes blank, as she stares straight ahead. He flicks his wrist and the pebble flies through the air. "One, two, three, four, five," counts Matthew as the pebble skips the waves. Joshua claps his hands and Matthew throws another.

"One, two, three," Joshua echoes, clapping again as the pebble disappears. "Let me, let me now," he squeals. He picks up a heavy pebble and throws it. It falls short of the sea and he looks disappointed. Then he tries again and the pebble falls behind him. Matthew laughs and then so does Joshua.

"It takes lots of practice, Josh, so we'll just get used to throwing as hard as we can today, but be careful you don't hit your Mama."

Joshua's pebbles are reaching the water by the time they decide to leave the beach and the child is exhausted. Matthew promises to take him again and again, until he can do it properly. All the time Violet has sat in silence. Matthew squeezes her hand, content just to have her close again. If only he could break through this spell it would mean so much to him.

Mrs Allen has prepared tea by the time they get home. "Thank you, Matty. That made such a difference."

"I want to help, Mrs Allen. You know how much I feel for Violet. The lad was no trouble and I think he enjoyed a bit of attention. He should sleep well tonight. I'll call again perhaps tomorrow, early in the evening."

"That would be fine, give me a chance to get the supper on."

Violet watches people coming and going every day. What are they all doing? Why won't they leave her in peace? Richard knows I only need him. Why doesn't he make them go away? Where are all Richard's things? Who has taken his things? ...

Someone is talking to her. Who is this man? She just wants to be left alone. Can't he see she is busy?

She gets up. She'll ignore him. She draws the curtains and lights the lamps. Can't they all see she is tired? If they won't leave her in peace she will go to her bedchamber.

Matthew and her mother watch as Violet leaves to go upstairs. They dowse the lamps and throw back the curtains. There is at least an hour to go before dusk.

"It's going to take a long time and a lot of patience I'm afraid," says Mrs Allen, shaking her head.

"Well, I've been patient for this long. I'm not going to give up on her now, Mrs Allen."

Day after day Matthew keeps up his vigil. Joshua grows to depend on him and Violet seems to accept his protection and friendship. As Joshua learns to count, so Violet begins to speak again, but it only takes a single nightmare to set her back again. She is treading a fine line.

One night Matthew sits with his father at the bar of the Cove House Inn. Opposite them is Bill Shaddick talking to John Motyer. Matthew's father observes them. "It seems that Bill has turned over a new leaf and taken over as head of the Shaddick household since his brother was wounded," he says quietly.

"Yes, Bill certainly seems to be welcomed by John now that Ikey's been forced to stay at home."

"Apparently that surgeon who come from Weymouth had to amputate Ikey's leg in the end.

He left him some laudanum but the wound's still not healing well and he's in constant pain."

"Well, you can't blame Bill for wanting to keep out of Ikey's way. Now that he's unable to get his hands on sufficient grog to drown his sorrows, he must be more morose than ever."

They fall silent then and listen as the other two men chat, and they overhear Bill explaining how Richard Dryer had seen him only minutes before he was killed and had sent him to Castletown to alert the troops.

Matthew interrupts them, "You must have been the last person he spoke to then, Bill."

"I s'pose I was," says Bill.

"Can you remember what he said exactly?"

"Can't say that I can, but he didn't say much of note." Bill takes another drink. "He was in a right temper at first and his horse nearly ran into me. He demanded to know what I were up to and I told him about the Kimberlins coming to steal the crop. Then he says something about his Violet."

"What? … Think, Bill, what did he say about Violet?"

"I can't rightly mind, but 'twere summat like 'My God, I misjudged her.'"

He misjudged her? What did he mean? …

"Why weren't you on the beach with the rest of us then, Bill?" asks Mr Stone.

"Well, to be truthful, I panicked … Ikey has often bragged to strangers in Weymouth and when I saw the Kimberlin gang I knew it was Ikey's fault. I tried to make him see sense, but when he wouldn't budge I didn't know what to do for the best … and I ran away. 'Twas Annie made me go back to warn our men. She'd already tried to get Dryer's help, but it was all too late. Violet had lit the warning candles, but even that was useless."

Of course, the betrayal … "Worse than useless for Violet," says Matthew as realisation comes to him. "Bill, I want you to do something for me. It might go some way to make amends for your brother's stupidity. I want you to go and tell Violet what Dryer said."

"Oh, I don't know about that, Matthew, I heard tell she's losing her mind. I don't want no crazy woman going for me."

"I'll come with you, Bill, she's used to me; besides, she is getting a little better every day. But I really think you can help her."

"All right, I'll go with you, but if she acts weird I'm off."

They meet up the next evening and go together to Violet's cottage. Bill takes a deep breath and knocks on the door. When Mr Allen answers his knock he removes his woollen hat, he opens his mouth to speak, then closes it again and looks sheepishly at Matthew.

Matthew says, "Bill has something to say to Violet, if you don't mind, Mr Allen."

"What about? I don't want her upset."

"It's something that Dryer said to him that I think she should know," says Matthew.

Bill looks uneasy, but Violet's father says, "Come on in then." They follow him into the living room.

"I'll go and get 'er for you. But don't expect too much, she may not recognise you. Sometimes now she seems almost like the old Violet, but then another day she's gone again. We've been worried sick about her."

Bill looks even more uncomfortable and Mr Allen takes pity on him. "Sit yourself down, lad, you may be in luck, she's not been too bad today."

Mr Allen leaves the room, and Bill turns to Matthew. "She's lucky she still has both her parents to turn to after all she put them through."

Violet's black figure enters from the stairway door. She looks from Matthew to Bill, "What's wrong? Pa said you wanted to see me." Her voice sounds flat.

Matthew reassures her, "It's nothing to worry about, Violet, but I thought you should hear what Bill has to say." He nudges Bill.

"Aye." He pauses ... "I've had it on me mind for some time, that you might wish to know something that your ... er ... late husband said to me on the night of the ... er ... accident."

Violet sinks into the nearest chair and Bill is not sure if he should continue, but Matthew nudges him again.

"I don't want to upset you by reminding you of something that may well be painful to you ... so if you'd sooner I left and kept it to meself, I'll do as you bid."

Violet's face shows a glimmer of life but it does not show in her words. "I should wish to hear anything he said that you can remember."

Bill takes a deep breath and then speaks slowly, "Well, you see, Annie had sent me back to the beach to warn the men, when there was a shot. It fair made me jump and I stood froze and listened, only to hear the sound of horse's hooves approaching from behind me on't cobbles, and racing along at a terrific pace come Mr Dryer out of the darkness and almost fell off 'is 'orse when it rears up at me at the bottom of Brandy Lane.

"'Where the hell do you think you're going?' he says to me. 'Well,' I says, 'I were going to warn the men about Kimberlins coming to steal the crop, but I fear I'm already too late.' Well, Ma'am, he looked kinda stunned, and puzzled like, in a right taffle, and then he says, 'My God, my poor Violet, I misjudged her … Will she ever forgive me?' Then after hesitating a moment he says to me, 'You must go directly, as fast as you can to alert the bluecoats. There's a chance we can prevent the rogues getting away with it. Quickly now, run,' he yells, and he rode off down towards the beach."

Bill pauses, "Well … you know the rest." He feels his face reddening and wishes he hadn't said that. He continues quickly, "I'm sorry … It weren't much, but Matthew felt that you would want to know."

Violet has turned a deathly white, but it is as if the veil has lifted at last as she looks up at Bill and smiles. Matthew will never forget the look of love on her face as she says, "Thank you, Bill. Thank you so much for coming, it was something that has been troubling me, and you have put my mind at ease."

Bill turns his hat over and over in his hands. "I'm glad." He pauses. "'Twas Matthew made me come. I weren't sure what to do, but I'm glad I come now." He hesitates, searching for words in the silence of the room. "I'll be on me way then, Ma'am … Good day to thee," and he backs out of the door. Matthew follows and sees him out.

When he re-enters the room, Violet takes both his hands in hers. "Thank you, Matty," she says, and for the first time in years he sees warmth in her eyes.

From that day on Violet has some peace of mind, even if she does feel in all other respects quite numb. Richard did not die believing that she had betrayed him. It is small comfort compared with the enormity of her loss, but it is important to her.

Gradually she improves, her parents force her

to eat and she keeps going only because of Joshua's need for her, but she is unaware of the harm she is doing to the child. Now she can see how wilful and desperate for attention he has become, for he does the strangest things.

One day she is walking with him along the beach, deep in thought as usual, and he keeps going too near to the water's edge. Several times she runs to catch hold of him and drag him to safety as the pebbles at his feet are sucked away by rigorous waves; another day he climbs up onto the walled surround of the well. She catches hold of him just as he slips. He is getting known as a little daredevil and Violet seems to have lost control of him, but his constant antics finally break through her reverie. No, she must not give up; she has to keep going for his sake.

After Christmas, she makes the decision to return to their cottage. It is a painful step initially, for every corner holds raw reminders of Richard, but although the memories are distressing and she fears the nightmares, she needs her independence. Besides, the cottage cannot stay empty, even though they have kept up the rent. It will be re-let if it is not occupied and she couldn't bear that.

Her mother goes with her to air the place and they are very busy that first day. Violet cleans out the fireplace on her hands and knees, while her mother sweeps the floors. They are soon both sneezing and laughing.

Water has to be fetched for the copper and boiled up ready for all the scrubbing and cleaning, and the larder needs restocking. While Mrs Allen is inside making up the beds and generally tidying, Matthew's sister, Hannah, takes Joshua with her to fetch the water.

Matthew has already collected driftwood for

their fire, but it needs to be chopped and stacked. Violet decides to start with chopping up the wood and she steps out into the yard eager to get on, but is immediately arrested by the strange, staring black eyes of the raven. She stops dead in her tracks and shudders, feeling the creeping, prickly sensation of fear and superstition moving bone by bone up the centre of her back.

As Madame Christabel had warned, the bird had also been the harbinger of death and she stares back hypnotically, not daring to move. Whereupon the raven puts its head on one side, looks for a second or two, then turns carefully and takes flight. Violet sighs and relaxes and then makes a start on chopping the kindling.

Violet is making up the fire under the copper in the scullery when there is a knock at their front door. Her mother goes to answer it and is pleased to see Auntie Sarah there.

"Come in, come in. We are just boiling up some water and then you can have a cup of tea with us," says her mother.

"I heard thee were moving back in, Vi. I am so pleased to see thee looking so much better."

"Thank you, Auntie Sarah, I do feel much better."

Auntie Sarah hands her a large cake tin. "I have brought thee some dough cake. It will go well with a nice cup of tea."

"That is very kind of you and much appreciated. Ma has given us some food and has been tidying up for me. We brought a little water with us, but Hannah has gone off with Josh to get some more. He is so keen to help, bless him."

Mary Allen goes into the scullery to get some plates and cups. While her mother is out of the room Violet decides to confide in Auntie Sarah.

206

"Auntie Sarah, you remember I showed you that big black raven back in September."

"Yes, I remember. Thee was worried about Josh out there feeding the other birds."

"That's right. Well, I also felt that it meant that something bad was going to happen. I didn't tell you at the time, but when I went to the Reeve Fair, Madame Christabel called out to me to have my fortune told. I tried to get away, but before I could stop her she foretold of danger and death and I could not help thinking that the bird was the harbinger of death."

"And tragically she turned out to be right. I'm so sorry, Violet, I had no idea." Auntie Sarah puts her arm around Violet.

"Well, the first thing I see when I get back here is that evil bird waiting for me in the yard. It put its head on one side, looked straight at me for a second or two, then turned and flew away, but it was as if it had wanted just one last look. It was so strange, almost as if it was Richard's eyes on me; as though the bird possessed his spirit."

"Well, it seems to me that the prophecy has been fulfilled and hopefully that will be an end to it and thy life will settle down again now."

Violet's mother enters with the cake on plates and the teapot and they all sit down to eat.

Violet has been back only a few days when one evening she comes across the locked casket in the Davenport and, immediately filled with curiosity, she sets about finding the key. It has never been deliberately hidden from her and she soon discovers it in one of the drawers underneath some paperwork. She has not previously given the casket much thought but because it belonged solely to

Richard it is now more precious to her and she feels compelled to discover its contents.

She unlocks the casket and lifts the curved lid. Inside there is a smaller box that reveals one of a pair of pistols. She has seen its mate often because Richard invariably took it with him, but there are other things, and one is a pocket watch that is engraved. She holds it in the glow of the lamp and a chill goes through her as, slowly, she reads the words, 'To dearest Richard, everlastingly yours, Martha'. Who in heaven's name is Martha? Richard never mentioned anyone from his past.

She fingers more quickly now through the other items: a penknife, buttons, a ring, a receipt and … a letter. She goes hot and cold as her shaking fingers carefully open the two sheets of notepaper. They are two hastily written notes written in the same hand. She holds them unsteadily under the lamp and reads them.

My Dearest Richard,

Oh, how I miss you. I cannot believe your father could be so hateful! It is not as if I am an atheist. I know our religions differ, but I love you and that is all that matters to me.

My father is very sad. He cannot understand why his Lordship does not consider a Vicar's daughter good enough. I know he feels insulted that your father will not permit the wedding. However, I must see you. I trust Sadie will deliver this note to you; I cannot say what I have to tell you in a letter. I have to see you. Please meet me by the tithe barn Wednesday night.

Your own true love, Martha.

The second sheet is dated nearly a year later.

Dearest Richard,

I do not want to know why you did not meet me. I felt sure you'd send for me, but you did not and I was heartbroken. I have to tell you that I am very ill.

I was so deeply hurt by your cruel treatment of me, which forced me to leave my home and go to Sherborne to live. Richard, I had no one to turn to, even my father would not have understood; but now I am desperate. I must see you, I have something terribly urgent to tell you and I fear it will soon be too late.

If you have any feelings for me, take pity on one who worships you. I am at the Castle Lodge. Please come soon.

Your true love, Martha.

Violet is not jealous, for this all happened long ago, but she is hurt, for until this moment she has thought of Richard as hers alone.

Tears well up in her eyes and some fall onto the receipt. She wipes her eyes and dabs at the receipt and then takes it out and holds it under the lamp. It is a death certificate and is marked 'For the interment of Martha Mead and child.' The cause of death is cholera, and it is dated only two weeks after her second letter.

Oh ... poor Richard. She must have been carrying his child and he couldn't have known about it until it was too late ... How could he ever forgive his father?

This is obviously why he left his home. No wonder he had seemed so bitter and aloof when he first came to the island. But why hadn't he told her about Martha and the baby? He shouldn't have felt guilty; it wasn't his fault if he didn't know about the child.

If only he had shared this with her it would not be so painful for her now. He had known everything there was to know about her, although he'd never been certain of this. For some reason he had always imagined that she still cared more for Matthew, and this was evident when he actually believed she had betrayed him in favour of the smugglers. If only he had trusted his instincts.

She remembers again the night that he pushed her aside and rushed out to his death. He wouldn't listen to her and he'd left her to such anguish and pain. She feels sick at the memory. Feeling fainter by the minute, she does what Richard would have done and pours herself a large brandy. Then she sits, too exhausted to produce another tear.

She wonders if Joshua's grandfather is still living and, God forgive her, she hopes not. She has no desire to trace him. Her child's paternal grandfather was obviously heartless and would certainly have no wish to proclaim Joshua as his grandson. If this Martha had not been good enough, she would be at an even greater disadvantage.

She replaces the items as she found them in the casket and, locating the missing pistol, she places it in the velvet niche beside its mate and locks the boxes. Having returned them to the davenport, she pours herself another large brandy. Then she attaches the two keys with ribbon and hides them in a crack in the wall, just below the big oak beam over the fireplace. She does not want Joshua finding the pistols, or for that matter the other items.

She takes her cup of brandy and goes up to her bedroom. Slowly she undresses and climbs into bed. Then she sits in the moonlight and sups the remaining contents, enjoying the strange sensations that result from her inebriation. Finally she slips into a deep sleep.

When she awakes the following morning the sun is streaming into her room and Joshua is standing by the bed staring at her, puzzled. It is the first time he has found her asleep, she is usually up long before him. She turns to him guiltily and a sudden pain shoots across her eyes. She feels thick-headed, but this is no use as she must rouse herself and feed the poor child. Unsteadily she gets out of bed and Joshua observes her strange behaviour with a curious expression on his face.

"Go and play, Josh, while I dress. I won't be long, I just overslept."

This is no use at all. It's the last time I drink brandy like that. Ashamed, she resolves to pull herself together. There is much to be done in the cottage. It is no use wading around and floundering in her troubles; and so the daily routine prevents her from slipping into a decline. Its regular pattern forms a stable platform on which to build a new life and although it all begins in a purely mechanical fashion, it is at least a beginning.

Several months have passed when a customs official calls on Violet with some comparatively good news.

"Good day, Mrs Dryer, my name is Joseph Talbot, I wonder if I may come in. I have some news that is very much to your advantage."

"Please do step inside."

"I have been instructed to inform you that due to the bravery of your late husband and the part that he played in the capture of the contraband last November you are entitled to a percentage of the value of the goods seized."

Violet sits down in the chair immediately behind her. "I had no idea I was entitled to anything."

"I can assure you it is a portly sum of money. The seizure was a sizeable one, and at the auction, a sale by inch of the candle, the proceeds were unusually high owing to the good quality of the crop."

"Well, thank you very much for letting me know. How do I go about claiming this money, Mr Talbot?"

Joseph Talbot draws out some paperwork from his bag. "You will need to sign this official form, but I have the money in the form of a banker's cheque on me and can give it to you now."

Violet puts her signature on the form and he passes her an envelope. "Thank you very much, Mr Talbot. Can I offer you some refreshments before you leave?"

"That is very kind of you, Mrs Dryer, but I have other appointments organised for today."

"Well, it is very nice to have some good tidings for a change."

"I am pleased to be of service. Good day to you." Violet shows Mr Talbot out and then hurries to her mother's cottage. She calls out to her as she enters, "Ma, come quickly, I have something to show you."

Her mother comes in from the scullery wiping her hands on a towel. "What is all the excitement about?"

"Ma, there is a sum of money in this envelope and I am afraid to look to see how much is in there."

"What do you mean, a sum of money? Where did it come from?"

"'Tis the proceeds due to Richard from the sale of the contraband."

"Well, about time too."

"I feel uneasy accepting it because of the dreadful circumstances in which it was earned, but I really have to, for Joshua's sake as much as my own."

"Well, 'tis no use looking at it, get the envelope open and let's see what is in there."

"You open it, Ma." She thrusts the envelope towards her mother.

Mary Allen tears open the envelope, draws out the cheque and passes it to Violet without looking at the amount. "It is your cheque, Vi," she says, smiling with encouragement.

Violet looks at her mother and then down at the cheque. "My God, Ma, 'tis for sixty-four guineas."

"How much?"

"Sixty-four guineas, Ma, that is nearly what Richard was earning a year. He was getting eighty guineas a year salary and twenty guineas for the upkeep of his horse." Violet starts to laugh and grabs her mother and spins her round in a circle. "'Tis a godsend Ma. It means that I don't have to sell Caraway after all. I enjoy so much riding up on the common. I feel free up there and it is where Richard and I spent some of our happiest hours." She shakes her head determinedly, "No, as long as I can pay the horse keeper and the blacksmith's bill I am not going to sell him."

Violet's mother puts her hand up to her head, "Oh dear, I am feeling a little dizzy after all that spinning." She sits down in the nearest chair to recover her balance and then continues, "That's wonderful news, Vi. I have been wondering how you are going to make a living for yourself and Josh, and that horse is a means to an end."

"I know, Ma, it means that in addition to the chamomile, arrowroot and cuckoo pint, and other herbs and lichens that I gather for Auntie Sarah, I can also get a good price for starchmoor by selling it in Weymouth.

"Well, with that and your sewing you should be able to manage well enough, I'm sure."

"I have thought about promoting myself as a seamstress, by placing a card in old Reg Flew's shop window. I know you have passed on a lot of customers to me, but it is time I set up a business of my own."

Mary Allen is quick to encourage this plan as it is important for Violet's state of mind for her to be kept busy. "That's a good idea, Vi, and when you go over to Weymouth with the starchmoor, why not place cards with your contacts over there?"

"I will, Ma, that's a good suggestion." Violet ponders for a moment. "Josh will need schooling very shortly and I am going to make sure that we have the money for it."

CHAPTER 11 *(May 1837)*

THE BEATING OF THE BOUNDS

The village has an air of spring about it. Seven years have passed since the last beating of the bounds have taken place, and the islanders are looking forward to Ascension Day when they enjoy their traditional celebration. It is the custom that a procession of Portlanders pay an official visit to the spot along Chesil where the Bound Stone is situated to check that it is still in its rightful position and that all is well.

No one knows when the first monolith was erected, but as one has perished another has taken its place. It is up to this boundary that the islanders jealously guard their ownership, for beyond it they have no rights to wreckage or anything else that might be washed ashore.

Violet has not taken part in any of the celebrations on the island since Richard's death, and Molly tries to persuade her to take Joshua to the beating of the bounds ceremony.

"I am really looking forward to the ceremony. It seems ages since we had anything to celebrate."

"Everyone seems to be talking about it. I don't remember such excitement, not since King William IV was crowned." Violet's mind goes back to the event when free beer was given out at the Verne and she was attacked by the sailors. She looks pensive.

Molly tries to cheer her up. "Vi, you should

come too, it has been more than two years now. It is time to leave off your mourning costume."

"Oh, I don't know, Moll. I have grown used to it, besides I have nothing else that would suit."

"Come on, Vi, that is no problem for you. Next time you go to Weymouth get yourself some nice cloth and we can make up something for you together. Just think how Josh would enjoy it."

"It would be a bit of fun for him 'tis true. He is getting quite big now that he is five. He could do with some new breeches as well."

"Well, there you are then, and I will help you make a new bonnet," she says decisively, looking forward to having some fun with her friend.

After much thought, she and Molly set about making a gown of rose pink poplin, which she decorates with white satin ribbons. To go with it, Molly has helped her make a pink straw bonnet and they stitch white roses underneath to set on her hair.

She begins to dream a little of dancing herself, like in the old days, but fears she might be left out like an old maid. Nevertheless, however anxious she may feel she cannot disappoint the child and so she is determined to be happy and gay for his sake. She makes him a new pair of breeches and smiles to see how splendid he looks.

But still after all their efforts she fears that she lacks the confidence to wear the outfit. She has become used to the image of herself dressed in drab clothes and is disturbed by the notion that people may think she is being disrespectful to the memory of Richard. Whilst everyone else is enthusiastically making their own arrangements, she remains undecided.

The day preceding the event is full of preparation. Driftwood is collected and taken out on carts and a huge bonfire built, which is to be lit as darkness falls. Jacket potatoes are pre-baked to be put into the fire and warmed; hams are cooked, cheeses prepared and all liquid and solid refreshment is made ready to be conveyed on the shoulders of the menfolk the following day.

Two of the locals are observed arguing about the simplest way to convey a great plank of wood to the spot. Having decided it will be lighter by half if they cut it in two, they do so and carry half each, much to the amusement of the other helpers, whilst John Flann the common crier rings his bell and announces the details of the ceremony to all and sundry.

It is into this atmosphere that an unfamiliar figure appears. Her gig comes to a halt at the well and she asks Letty White to direct her to the home of Matthew Stone. Letty's curiosity is immediately aroused, and in minutes the grapevine is buzzing with folk unable to guess the identity of this apparently independent young woman.

On the day of the celebration, Violet returns from a ride on the common and notices the gig outside the Stones' cottage. She thinks little of it until, whilst she is collecting Joshua, her mother mentions that an attractive young woman has been asking for Matthew. She is not sure whether it is the way that her mother puts it, but she is for some reason irritated by the information.

She makes no comment, but setting her hat carefully in place and teasing her hair a little in front of the hallway mirror she thanks her mother for caring for Joshua and they say their farewells and leave.

She walks past the Stones' cottage, not even glancing at the gig and holding onto Joshua's hand so tightly that he is unable to pat the pony as they pass. She ignores his puzzled frown and walks briskly on, at the same time trying to plan what to prepare for their luncheon.

She was surprised to find herself quite looking forward to the event and earlier that morning she even felt a little excited, but the presence of this strange woman has spoilt it for her. If it was not for Joshua, who has been full of eager, impatient questions all morning, she might have decided against going, but she cannot disappoint the lad and so after they have eaten they both dress up in their new clothes. Joshua is ready first and Violet hugs him to her.

"My word, Josh, you look a proper little gentleman."

But when Joshua sees his mother, dressed ready and looking so young and beautiful, his mouth drops open and his eyes shine with love and admiration.

"That is very pretty, Mam, I have never seen you looking so nice."

She smiles and kisses him, blinking away the tears. Her love for him brings such joy and yet the poignant memories still hurt so.

They make a pretty picture as they walk side by side down Brandy Lane on their way to meet Molly. Joshua begins to skip happily at Violet's side but his mother's grip on his hand tightens as again they pass the pony and gig.

"What's wrong, Mam? I was only going to pat him."

"Nothing's wrong," she says, adding quickly, "Look, there's Auntie Molly."

She releases his hand and he runs ahead to greet her. Then together they join the meandering procession of Portlanders all strung out in family groups throughout the length of the causeway, the men heavily burdened with cider barrels and all kinds of food.

It is good to see so many people taking part in the ceremony and Violet feels secure knowing that she belongs here among these people and on this island. Whatever else she may have lost, she is still a Portlander. She may be just another pebble on the beach, but it is the best beach in the whole world and she loves it.

By the time they reach the Bound Stone, Joshua is tired out. They sit down wearily on the winter ridge and listen as some of the old boys who have brought fiddles and mouth organs start to play. Other folk join in, singing along as they settle themselves around the great mound of sticks and driftwood that promises later to be a spectacular bonfire.

Some children are playing tag and running hither and thither between the small groups of adults and Violet recognizes young Benjamin Stone amongst them.

Annie is with the Atwools, who are joining in the singing, and although Violet can see she is thoroughly enjoying herself, she also notes how she constantly keeps a sharp eye on her son. He is quite an extrovert for his age and is well clothed and obviously well cared for. Unlike Joshua, he has the look of a true Portlander. She feels a few tugs at her sleeve. "Can I play too please, Mam?"

"Yes," Violet concedes, "but don't stray too far so I can't see you."

"No, I won't," he cries excitedly, and off he runs again. Molly and herself are seated behind the general gathering and have a fine view of all the goings on. She watches Matthew and his family settle in a spot lower down the shingle and notes his attentiveness to the stranger, who is elegantly dressed with a very trim figure. There is much laughing among the group and that is what draws Molly's attention.

"Why, there's Matty and Hannah, I didn't notice them there before, did you? Let's go and join them." She is getting up, but Violet catches her arm.

"I'd rather not just yet, Mol, I can see Joshua playing better from up here. Stay a while longer. We've got all day, we can join them later."

Molly at first appears puzzled but then it is as if something has dawned on her and she says, "They haven't even noticed us." She sounds peeved. "Too busy entertaining their guest, it looks like," she adds.

Violet says nothing.

Then the familiar bell is heard, heralding the approach of John Flann, the common crier, followed by the island's dignitaries and the two little boys who are taking part in the ceremony. Violet stands up and calls to Joshua and whilst the children join their respective parents, he too runs to her side.

It is then that Matthew notices Violet and as she turns to sit down again their eyes meet. He smiles and nods acknowledgement, mouthing "Vi" as he does so, and she blushes and smiles in return and then sits down in readiness for the ceremony. John Flann rings his bell again and as the colours are hoisted it begins.

"Oh ye … oh ye … oh ye! We are gathered here on this Ascension Day to bear witness to the beating of these our bounds. Let the position of the Bound Stone be checked to be truly affixed in its proper location since time out of mind."

Having established its location as correct the two boys are asked to lay themselves over the Bound Stone and, by strokes applied to their backsides by the rector with the reeve staff, are forcibly impressed with 'the location and importance of these our bounds that they might be witnesses thereto in years to come.'

The ceremony is then concluded with a short service conducted by the rector, after which, with almost indecent haste, the fiddlers strike up and the dancing begins.

In a dip where the pebbles have thinned and sea pinks grow in the compressed silt of past centuries, many feet now skip and dart, skirts swish and sway in time to the music, and Violet can feel the rhythm setting her feet a-tapping, she is itching to dance.

The setting sun casts long shadows amongst the dancers and the beautiful tones of the sky are made doubly so by their reflecting in the waters of the Fleet. Someone puts a torch to the fire and as the tinder-dry wood crackles and spits, the gathering lets up a cheer.

Again Joshua is off to join the other children, the elders are yarning and smoking their long churchwarden clay pipes, the non-dancers are eating and drinking and in all everyone is entertained.

Violet is distracted from observing Joshua because of Matthew, finding it hard to take her eyes off him. She has never seen him looking so smart in all the years she has known him. He is wearing a new silk shirt and his breeches and plush coat are also new and a deep shade of blue that suits his light curls handsomely.

Celebrations are few and far between and Matthew is obviously intending to make the most of this one. Their company are full of hearty laughter and gay conversation, and as Violet watches them longingly she is reminded of the happy, carefree times they enjoyed before Richard had become part of her life. People keep approaching them with greetings and introductions and a great shaking of hands and patting on backs.

It would be churlish not to join Matthew and his friends and when Molly again mentions doing so Violet braces herself for the confrontation.

They are all standing near the bonfire and call out greetings as they approach. Matthew is offering the young lady a baked potato that he has warmed in the fire, at the end of a spiked implement on which are impaled two more.

He turns to the two girls. "Ah, just in time." His broad smile at once welcoming them, he points the spike in their direction that they might help themselves to the remaining two. They are reluctant to remove them immediately for they are obviously very hot, as the visitor is tossing hers from one hand to the other, but as others are waiting their turn, they do likewise, which starts Molly off giggling, and soon all three of them are laughing merrily.

Matthew passes the spike to his father and turns to Violet. "Vi, Molly, I'd like you to meet Eliza Hodden from Chideock."

"How do you do?"

"I'm pleased to meet you, I'm sure," reply Vi and Molly respectively, both unable to shake hands owing to the hot potatoes.

"I've known Vi and Moll since they were babies. They're like sisters to me." Again their eyes meet and Violet flushes, remembering when they had been much more to each other than brother and sister.

Matthew continues, "I met Eliza the first year that I went to Gundry's to buy fishing hose for the Chiswell men and each year since she has been a friendly face on my visits there, but what a surprise when she turned up yesterday out of the blue. You could have knocked me down with a feather."

Eliza laughs. "I thought you'd be pleased. I'm so glad you weren't offended."

"Offended!" exclaims Matthew, incredulously, "I'm honoured, truly. No one has ever paid me such a compliment."

A young girl interrupts them by offering a large tray of cheeses and Matthew cuts off a wedge of Dorset Blue Vinny and divides it up for the girls. Then they all have a swig of cider to wash down the cheese and potatoes which, having cooled sufficiently, are now just right.

Violet becomes more and more pensive as she eats and listens to their happy chattering. "I think I'll take some food to Josh, I won't be long."

She has not seen Matthew flattered by a woman before, but what really rankles is the way he is loving it. And to suggest they have always been like brother and sister is ridiculous. Although maybe she is being unfair, because that was how she has treated him ever since she came under the spell of Richard … Perhaps he said that deliberately to upset her. But no, it is not her who is uppermost on his mind; it is the delectable Eliza who, it seems, has cast a spell on him.

She finds Joshua but he is not hungry, he is too excited to eat and she is pleased that at least he is enjoying himself. Then she sees her mother and father nearby. They have been watching over him, having not long arrived.

"You go on back with your friends. We'll keep an eye on Josh 'til he's worn himself out and then I can take him home and put him to bed for you. I'll come and tell you when we're ready to go back."

"Oh, I'll not be stopping long myself, Ma. That's all right."

"Oh yes you are. You go and enjoy yourself and make the most of it. You look lovely, Violet, but do let's see a smile. It makes such a difference to those eyes of yours." Violet smiles self-consciously. "That's better, love."

"Thanks, Ma, I would quite like a bit of dancing, but don't go back until I kiss him goodnight."

"We won't," says her father. "You go on and enjoy yourself. We'll see you later."

She turns back to the bonfire, from which heated pebbles have begun to spit viciously from the embers. Some of the driftwood settles and caves in a little and a myriad of sparks and tiny red stars shoot up into the smoky rufescence directly above the fire.

The dancers are bathed in the warm orange glow of the firelight and there in the middle of them are Matthew with Eliza.

She feels her heart sink. They make such a picture of togetherness that Violet can sense the whispered comments, nudges and nods where others are noticing too. She realises that she also is the subject of much conjecture and although feeling lonely and unhappy she resolutely joins her friends.

John and Robert have arrived by this time. Everyone being neatly paired, she is the odd one out, but remembering what her mother has just said she smiles brightly and joins in the happy badinage. Soon Matthew and Eliza rejoin them breathlessly.

"Oh, I did enjoy that," cries Eliza.

"Me too, although I am not quite so light on my feet as you, Eliza. It's been a long time since I did any jigging about. It sure does work up a thirst. Where's the cider jug? Anyone else want to wet their whistle?"

"Yes," says Vi, quickly. "Please," she adds, "I'm dying for one."

As he passes it to her their hands touch and Violet is reminded of the first time their hands touched over a pebble. It seems many years before, and had led to her first kiss. She drinks, deep in thought.

What is the matter with her? She has seen Matthew daily since Richard's death and yet not seen him. Her heart is like an old clock on the mantel that has stopped for half a decade and then, with just a nudge, has started ticking again. The cider jug is empty. He is watching her.

She says, "I'm sorry, it's empty."

"I'll fill it again in a minute." He brushes it aside, "Would you like to dance, Violet?"

Not Vi, but Violet. He whispers her name with a kind of reverence. It is as if no one else is there.

She takes his proffered hand and it is like a dream, his hands firmly about her waist, his warm body weaving and touching hers in time to the music, their cheeks brushing. She has not until now realised how she missed the warmth of this physical contact. Confused images fill her thoughts. For an instant it could be Richard who holds her, but no, it is Matthew. He spins her round and round and his strong arms catch her again. His eyes are on her and many eyes are on them. Her cheeks are flushed and her heart racing. His eyes are only for her and she knows Eliza is not on his mind. At last she feels alive again.

The dance is too energetic to talk at the same time; one minute they are facing each other and the next he's turned her and she can feel his breath in her hair. She wants this moment to go on forever but the music stops and the magic is gone. They return to the others and she watches his attention go straight back to Eliza. The doubts tear at her heart. Why is he playing with me so? It is cruel.

She sits down next to Molly and Robert, and Molly says, "You looked lovely together, Vi."

"I did enjoy it. I haven't danced in years," she replies.

"You two make a fine pair, but Matty won't stay

a bachelor forever," says Robert. He stands up, adding, "It's time you forgot the past and started fresh, thinking on the future."

Violet watches as Robert, Hannah, Matthew and Eliza again join the dancers and her eyes fill with tears. It is then that she realises that she is jealous.

"I do believe he has lost his heart to Eliza," she says to Molly sadly.

"Of course he hasn't, Vi. He's just being gentlemanly, she's his guest. He could have had any girl on this island in the last five years and you know it. Don't you think after all this time it's a little obvious who he really wants?"

Violet is surprised at the impatient tone in Molly's words. "Well, he's never said as much and I can't blame him after what I did, Moll."

"Mam." Joshua runs up to her out of the semi-darkness, her mother and father close on his heels. "Goodnight, Mam. I'm going home with Nana and Grandpa."

Violet kisses him. "I'm feeling very tired with the dancing and all, and it's such a long walk back, I think I'll come with you."

"There's no need to, Vi, I can manage. You stay and enjoy yourself."

"Yes, please stay, Vi," adds Molly.

"No, really. My mind is made up. I have had enough for today. Come on, let's be off." She takes Joshua's hand. "Say my farewells to the others, Moll, and enjoy yourselves … I'll see you tomorrow. Bye."

They are soon leaving the dancers behind and as they distance themselves from the warmth of the bonfire, the chill of the night air fans Violet's flushed cheeks and dries away hot tears that are on the brink of falling.

As they trudge along and Joshua chatters away about all the salient parts of his day, Violet thinks

226

she hears her name being called. She turns but can see nothing. But there it is again and turning once more she can just make out the figure running towards them, his white shirt sleeve waving in the air. He is calling for her to wait.

"I'll take Josh home like I said, you go on back, Vi. It's Matty, he wants you."

She stops still as her parents and Joshua continue on their way. 'It's Matty, he wants you' echoes in her head as Matthew breathlessly reaches her. He bends over double, breathing in great gasps. "I didn't think I'd make you hear," he gasps. "Where do you think you're going at this time?"

"I was going home to put Josh to bed."

"But why, Vi? The evening has only just begun and your Ma said she'd do it for you."

"How do you know?" Violet is surprised.

"Molly told me," he admits. "She also said that you were unhappy." He comes closer to her and puts a finger under her chin, lifting her face to look him in the eyes. "Is it true?"

Her eyes brim with tears and she closes them, squeezing the tiny droplets through her eyelashes.

"Oh Vi, don't." He kisses her eyes and tastes the salty tears. He kisses her tender cheeks and she raises her lips to his. They join together in a kiss charged with emotion, Matthew breathless from his running and Violet sobbing with relief.

"Oh Violet, it has been so long. I can't stand it." His arms enfold her and he squeezes her so tightly. He is broader than she remembers and she feels so safe in his arms, just the two of them concealed within the darkness of the night; the gentle waves breaking down below them on the edge of the beach, the fiddlers' music wafting to them on the breeze and the little shafts of light at Chiswell, like another world, in the distance.

They sit down on her cloak and Matthew takes her hand. "I love you, Violet," he says gently. "You know I have always loved you." He pauses and then coaxes, "Tell me what it is that is making you so unhappy?"

"How can you ask that?" Violet feels she is making a fool of herself. "It must be obvious," she says, trying to hide her vexation.

"But it's not," he cries. "Tell me, is it something I have done?"

"'Tis not right to tease a body so with your philandering." She sounds peevish, but she cannot help it. She wipes away her tears.

"Who, me?" Matthew exclaims with mock indignation.

"You have been toying with me. I believe that you are trying to punish me for hurting you. That you are going to become betrothed to Eliza because you cannot forgive me for what I did to you."

"Eliza?" he cries. "You are jesting."

"It is not funny. You should have seen yourself. You looked quite besotted."

"Well now, I should never have acted that way if I'd thought this would be the result, now would I?" he says with a gentle kind of wickedness that is quite maddening.

"What do you mean?"

"Why, that it would make you jealous."

"I'm … I'm not jealous but she is a very attractive girl and to come all this way to visit someone must mean something."

"Well, I'm not saying she is not fond of me and she came all this way to bring me a very fine gift."

"A gift?" she says. "What kind of gift?"

"The most magnificent collection of carpenter's tools you could ever wish to see, and I must say I am most flattered by her kindness."

Violet cannot help feeling irritated by his cheerfulness, but in her heart she cannot believe that he loves this woman. "Do you love her?" she asks, forcing the question out.

"I just told you, Violet, I love you."

"But you can love two people at once. I know because I did."

"Not the way I love, you can't." Then he realises the implication of what she has just said. "Anyway, what do you mean, did?"

"I did, Matty. I loved you and Richard to distraction, I was just compelled to do what I did."

"Now? How do you feel now? I have been by your side ever since he was killed, always there to be relied upon and trusted, but never loved. I really need to be loved, Violet." He grips her tightly by the shoulders. "Don't you understand? I cannot live in the shadow of another man. I need the love of a whole woman and I cannot compete with a ghost." His tone is urgent, "I know what I want, but do you?"

"Yes." She puts her hand up to gently touch his face. "I believe I do now and I'm sorry it took so long for me to realise it."

She kisses him tenderly on the lips and he responds, stirring in her powerful feelings of passion long suppressed, but she is still uncertain and she pulls away again, "I know you think I'm silly, Matthew, but I must know for sure about Eliza. Why is she here? Do you mean anything to her?"

"She is just a friend, nothing more, I promise."

"Are you really certain?"

"Absolutely." He nods his head.

"I couldn't bear to watch you both together. I see now how I would feel if I were to lose you forever."

"Maybe you are feeling something of the pain that I felt, seeing you constantly with Dryer."

"I'm so sorry, Matty." Her eyes fill with tears, "I can only beg you to forgive me. I have been punished for my sins."

She closes her eyes and lays back her head in the crook of his elbow. He kisses her, caresses her lovingly, gently and then with more urgency and passion.

For Matthew, after years of longing for her; watching her with Dryer, imagining their first time together when it should have been him and Violet; then the terrible feeling of inadequacy that burdened him after Dryer's death, when nothing he did seemed to matter to her; after suffering all that time and controlling his turbulent heart until this moment, he is overwhelmed. His heart races and his hands tremble. No one is near, and he is lost in a wonderland of sensuality.

But Violet gently restrains him. "Matty," she whispers, "someone may come and, besides, we have a whole lifetime ahead of us. Let's wait 'til the time is perfect."

He simply cuddles her then, and Violet could fall asleep she is so warm and relaxed in his arms. Then she thinks again of Eliza. "Matthew?"

"Mmm?"

"You'll have to tell Eliza about us."

"What do you mean?" Matthew can hardly disguise his amusement.

"Won't she be upset?" asks Violet, concerned.

"I doubt it," he says smiling.

"But how can you be so sure?"

"Because she is being married next week and is leaving with her husband for the Americas."

"What? You rotten devil!" She pummels him with clenched fists.

Laughing, Matthew catches hold of her hands and traps them against the shingle above her head.

"A desperate situation calls for desperate measures," he says, grinning wickedly. Then lowering his chest onto hers to stop her writhing, he kisses her deliberately and forcefully and she succumbs to his kisses again willingly.

They do not return to the dancing but meander along the causeway, down by the water's edge. He tells her how he had been determined to remain a bachelor in the hope that some day they could be together again, for he could not imagine his life with any other person.

Violet tells him how she had been almost sick with apprehension at the thought of joining in the celebrations today. But she knows now that, despite her loneliness, it was the fear of rejection that had made her hide away from him, feeling safe behind her mourning clothes.

They both enjoy the intimacy of these confidences and the long-remembered warmth of the other's embrace, and savour a peaceful and fitting end to a magical day.

Eventually he takes her home and she invites him in for a nightcap. Her mother has put Joshua to bed at their house and so the cottage is empty. It is the most natural thing in the world for Matthew to stay the night, but he cannot bring himself to sleep in Dryer's bed and so it is not to be.

He kisses her goodnight and they part, Matthew with jaunty steps and whistling gaily and Violet soon snuggled up in her goose-feather bed. For a while excitement keeps her mind alert but then she sleeps fitfully. In her dreams she is still distressed, torn between her disloyalty to the loving memory of Richard and her newly aroused, rekindled love for Matthew.

CHAPTER 12 *(May 1837)*

HEARTSEASE

When Violet awakes the following morning she feels a sudden chill of fear as she sees Joshua's empty bed. Then she remembers he is still at her mother's and the reason why brings a sleepy smile of contentment to her face. She stretches lazily, thoughtful of all that has happened, and closes her eyes to doze a while; but as she drifts in and out of sleep it is Richard and not Matthew who enters her dreams.

He is sitting on the edge of her bed with his back to her, as she remembers him on the first night they spent together. He turns towards her but before their eyes meet, he disappears again.

Her mind is still playing cruel tricks, but somehow it makes her aware of what she has to do. Before her relationship with Matthew is common knowledge there is someone she has to talk to and there is no time like the present.

It is routine for her to saddle Caraway and ride up over Lankridge to Reforne, but she does not. She wants to walk so that she can think. She picks wild flowers for Richard's grave as she goes.

It is nearly dawn, but no one is about and with cheeks moist with tears she lets the memories flow, filling corners of her heart that have fought to keep them at bay for the last two years; she relives the most painful and joyful of those moments.

A cock crows as she passes the old rectory, but it could be a thousand miles away. She does not hear it, nor does she notice the ducks quacking and quarrelling as they squabble over the early worms just a stone's throw from the church gates.

When she reaches the churchyard she discards the dead flowers of her last visit. She fills the pot with fresh water from the pump and arranges the wild hyacinths, red campion, cuckoo-pint and mayweed, and places them carefully in the same spot. She has planted violets and purple heartsease because Richard said these reminded him of her. The heartsease is now in flower.

She kneels down and closes her eyes, and in a whispered, hesitant prayer, she begins ... "Dearest Richard, there has not been a day that has passed since our parting that I have not thought sweet things of you ... I know you are watching over me and Josh, for even now I still feel your presence all around me."

She pauses, struggling to untangle all the things she wants to say. "Although it was hard for me to take the criticism of my family and friends ... I was sure in my heart that the joining of you and me was a destiny we could not avoid. It was so right and true for us that even though we hurt poor Matthew so, I could never regret my love for you; only the cruel injustice of having to choose between two good men both of whom I loved ... and still love." Her voice wavers.

She inhales deeply, her eyes huge with tears, but resolutely she continues: "There were times when the memories I had were so painful to recall ... that it was self-torture to think of you. There were such depths of despair that I could have put an end to it all ... flown with the raven away from the real world ... but for Josh I had to be strong and this somehow led me through the bad times ... until I was able to cope from day to day."

She pauses again, running her fingers through the grass, touching it as if gently running her fingers through his hair. Her voice drops to a whisper. "But it's not a comfortable feeling belonging to no one … I feel lost, like an autumn leaf tossed on the breath of fate, wondering with each new day what the future holds for me and Josh, and still bearing the burden of guilt for my treatment of Matthew."

A tear drops and trickles down her hand as a slight smile touches her lips; "It was such a release to know that I was forgiven and still wanted by Matthew … that my feelings of love have not been completely buried for good … that I need him to hold me again in his arms."

She thinks for a long time. The lump in her throat hurts her so, it is painful to speak. "I just want you to understand that it will never lessen my great love for you … if I could change anything I'd turn back the clocks to that moment when you tore from the cottage … I'd stop you; cling to you; beg you; anything to prevent you from leaving me to such anguish and despair … but that cannot be." A deep sob prevents her from continuing and she blinks away more tears, biting her trembling lip to gain enough control to continue.

"You never told me about Martha and the child, I don't know why, but I sometimes hope that you are reunited with them and … in that way you will find it easier in your heart to understand the new hope I have found in Matthew."

The tears run freely down her face as she strains the words through the tight constriction in her throat. "I was yours body and soul until death us did part, for 'twas only the hand of God that could have come between us. Pray for me, my darling. Come to me and let me know you understand … for God has decided to give me another chance for happiness … and like a hungry child I clasp it with both hands, fearful of being robbed a second time. I'll always love you and I need to know … that it's all right with you … that you understand."

Feeling spent, she remains sitting there, silently. Someone else is moving carefully among the gravestones, discreetly keeping away from where Violet sits with her head in her hands. They tend their grave and depart, leaving Violet to stillness and solitude until a sudden flapping of wings brings her back to reality. It is the raven and there upon the lead roof of the church is another. Its rapid flapping wings have frightened her, but it seems he has found his mate at last.

"Oh, thank you! Thank you!" The soundless words shine from her bright, watery eyes and she knows it is all right. That he has freed her imprisoned heart to let her love again and she weeps exhausted tears of gratitude.

Annie noticed most of what went on at the beating of the bounds ceremony and was amused to see Violet so disconcerted. She has never felt any interest in Matthew, even though they are almost the same age, and now that Richard Dryer is dead Violet poses no threat to her. But she knows that vulnerability so well, and she is quick to recognise it in Violet.

She saw Violet leave early with her family and she also saw Matthew's reaction when he discovered that she'd left. Annie is burning with curiosity as to what next transpired, but it is several days before the gossip finally reaches her ears.

She watches the departure of Eliza Hodden with a group of other women whilst gutting fish, and someone mentions the handsome gift she has given to Matthew.

"I don't suppose it'd be no use to 'er, lugging it all the way to the Americas 'n 'er marryin' into money over there into the bargain," says one of the older women.

"It'll certainly come in handy for Matthew now he's setting up home with the flighty Mistress Violet."

"Is that a fact, Tilly?" asks Annie, surprised.

"Got it straight from Molly Byatt. They's gettin' hitched in August."

"A bit sudden isn't it?" asks Lotty.

"I'll bet that'll be a shindig," says the older woman.

Lotty looks up and with the back of her blood-stained hand pushes a greasy strand of hair out of her eyes, tucking it expertly over her right ear. "She don't deserve Matthew Stone the way she jilted 'en first time. Once bitten twice shy, I always says." Annie smiles; Lotty is a plump fisherwoman on the lookout for a husband.

"Well, I think that boy o' hers could do with a father and if anyone deserves a family 'tis Matthew. And let's be honest, there's no one who can hold a candle to her round here. She were that broken-hearted when her man were shot I thought she were a goner but look how she's come through. She used all her ability to advantage and runs a good business with them Weymouth shops," says Tilly with admiration.

"That's typical o' her. Portlanders are not good enough for the likes o' Madam and her fancy clothes."

"You're just jealous, Lotty."

"Well, what if I am? 'Tis hard enough to get one good looking man hereabouts but two's just down right greedy."

They all laugh at the indignant expression on Lotty's face and proceed to list the available men in the vicinity, along with all their assets and their shortcomings, and when one of them happens along just after his name has been mentioned they all go into even more raucous laughter, which has the poor innocent completely baffled.

"Women!" he exclaims, stalking off in an embarrassed huff, which just makes them shriek the louder.

Annie has changed since she's had Ben to care for and she no longer bears any malice towards Violet. Ben and Joshua have become close friends, often playing together, and she is prepared to let bygones be bygones. She has even asked Violet to make a smock for the child.

But this is a juicy bit of gossip and Annie cannot wait to mention her news that evening to Bill. No one ever tells Ikey anything. He has no interest in anyone's problems but his own and is usually in an alcoholic stupor and beyond comprehension anyway, but at the mention of Violet his ears prick up.

"What's that you sayin'?" he growls from his corner.

It is so rare to get a word from him, Annie jumps with surprise.

"I thought you were asleep," she replies.

"Well, you were wrong then, weren't you?" he mumbles crossly. "What were that you were sayin' about that Dryer's whore?"

That angers Annie because it is as much a slur on herself as it is on Violet. "There's no need fer that kind o' talk, Ikey. If ya can't be civil keep a still tongue in ya head." She carries on dishing out the supper things and Bill gets up to help.

Ikey isn't going to let it drop. "Stone's never daft enough to wed that slut after Dryer's had her first, surely?"

"Everything that goes through your mind has to

come out dirty, doesn't it?" says Annie with distaste.

Ikey pulls himself up from his corner. "What you defending her for? You were never what you'd call bosom pals, were you, or did you and she make up a Dryer threesome?"

Annie lashes out, knocking him off balance back into his dingy corner, and Bill moves in between them.

"Stop it, both of you."

"If he doesn't watch his foul mouth I'll leave him to rot in Hell." Annie's face is contorted with anger, and Bill takes her by the shoulders, trying to calm her.

"No point in taking it out on me 'cus you're a frustrated old widow woman," Ikey yells back.

Annie tries to brush Bill aside as she shouts over his shoulder, "You can talk, look at the mess you've made of your life. How many sons do you think you're man enough to father?"

She immediately feels guilty for being so spiteful, but Ikey is quick to growl, "You bitch! At least I won't be bringing bastards into the world."

Annie struggles with Bill to get back at him, but he holds her firm. "Stop it fer Christ's sake you two. Annie, how low can you go?"

"I'm sorry, Bill. He brings out the worst in me. Look at him. He's evil. There's not an ounce of good left in him. I don't think the gangrene stopped at his leg, it's gone on rotting and decaying to his very soul."

Bill leads Annie away into the scullery and out of earshot. "Just take no notice, Annie. He's to be pitied, but not bated. You'll only end up hurting yourself, if you let him get to you."

"I know, Bill, I'm sorry. I just dread what he's going to come out with next, maybe in front of the kids. He's lost all reason. I'm also fearful of you leaving us," she whispers.

"Oh, I'll not be going for a long while, and soon Ben will be at school and you'll be free during the day." He nods in the direction of the other room. "He'll have to look out for himself then."

"I'm afraid he'll set the house on fire one day smoking and drinking all the time, he rarely knows what he's about and he's dangerously unsteady on that leg of his."

"It's no use thinking the worst all the time. He'll simply have to get used to it and accept it. He'll settle down eventually."

"Can't you get him to go out more, Bill? It would do him the world of good to get out in the boat. He'd feel mobile again."

"He'd be all right in the boat but it's getting him there. He won't be stared at."

"Well, how about getting him to go at night? It'd be like old times for him and he could do a bit of fishing," suggests Annie. "Couldn't you persuade him?"

"It's not a bad idea. I'll suggest it when he's in a better mood. Like you say, it would keep his mind busy and give him a bit of exercise into the bargain. It might even make him easier to live with."

He takes a plate of food over to Ikey, who scowls angrily back at him, and he cannot help feeling that he doesn't deserve the concern they feel for him. He also suspects that fishing is insufficient enticement to get Ikey back into harness and that the bait would have to be far more tempting. But he doesn't want to think about that and on hearing the others come in for supper he joins them at the dinner table.

The smocking that Annie has ordered for Ben is taking Violet a long time, and having watched the lad playing with Joshua at the beating of the bounds she fears that she may not have allowed enough for a month's growth.

This plays on her mind and when the garment is nearing completion she decides, to be on the safe side, she'll call round to measure the child.

She knocks on the door and a voice calls for her to enter. She opens the door and steps inside. She has never been beyond the front door before and is uncomfortable in the oppressive heat and darkness. "Annie?" she queries, as her eyes grow accustomed to the shadows.

"Annie ain't here," says Ikey, struggling up from the gloom of his corner.

"Well, she asked me to do this smocking for Ben, but I need up-to-date measurements to complete the garment." She holds out her work as she tries to explain to Ikey. "Anything that Ben is presently wearing will do as a guide," she says. Ikey looks blankly at her and she sighs, he is in no fit state to comprehend. She will have to come back again. There is little point in wasting her time with him.

She makes to leave but jumps as he snatches hold of her arm. A foul smell of bad teeth, stale spirits and tobacco wafts over her. She stands quite still. He is drunk and therefore unpredictable.

"That's a very dainty piece of needlepoint, ain't it now?" he says, wavering slightly as he speaks.

"Thank you," she says warily, still standing motionless.

"Our Annie don't have the lightness of touch fer that kind o' work." His speech is slow and deliberate. "She don't have slender, ladylike fingers like these."

He strokes the sensitive tips of her fingers. She shudders, drawing away.

"What's the matter, maid? Aren't I good enough to touch the likes of thee?" He draws even closer to her and as he speaks his breath is directed into her face.

She freezes in fear, though she wants to hurl herself from him and his odour. Ikey shakes her. She turns her head away.

"Aye, I'm not good enough for you, am I? Don't like the way I smell. You walk into my home, bathed in fresh lemon soap and dressed up to the nines, and I'm not good enough to look upon thee."

Violet tears herself from him. He is blocking the way to the door. She backs into the darkest corner of the dingy room. He follows, as if savouring the look of fear on her face. And now she remembers the sailors at Castletown.

Still he comes, his shabby figure lurching and swinging towards her, his wooden leg tapping noisily on the flagstone floor. He does not take his eyes off her as he thrusts aside a heavy wooden chair with one hand.

She puts out her hand to stop him, frightened to speak lest she make matters worse, but he hits it aside and, taking her jaw in his right hand, he forces his mouth down on hers. His left arm goes around her waist and he jerks her body tight to his own. He is strong. She struggles but he holds her tighter.

She yanks his hair, beats him with her fists, then manages to lift her leg and bring it down hard on his good foot. His mouth gasps on hers and he doubles up in pain. She pushes past him. He overbalances, falling heavily to the ground.

He lies there, helpless on the bare flagstones and, to Violet's dismay, he begins to wail. He is a pathetic sight, a dirty bundle of old rags. She senses his terrible frustration and, disconcertingly, is filled with pity. She feels ashamed for hurting this wretched man's pride.

She tries to make amends. "I'm sorry, Ikey, but

you shouldn't have trapped me." She is contemplating helping him up, but his next words banish all thoughts of that.

Unable to bear her patronising tone Ikey goes for revenge in the only way he knows how. "You're sorry," he scoffs. "I don't want your pity." He wipes a dirty sleeve across his nose and then, his body twisted awkwardly, he rests on his elbow preparing to play his trump card, "You think us Shaddicks are not good enough for the likes o' thee." He looks smug. "Well, a Shaddick was good enough for your husband. He didn't turn his nose up at our Annie, until you came along. 'Twas him put her up the spout. Why else did you think she was in such a hurry to find herself a husband?"

Violet has never been so angry in the whole of her life. "How dare you talk to me about my husband. He was worth ten of you. You're not fit to even speak his name. It was you who played the biggest part in the raid that led to his death; and that," she points to his wooden leg, "is the Lord's justice. 'Tis no more than you deserve."

Ikey is livid. "Why you little witch …"

"What if I am a witch?" she threatens. "If I am, I put a curse on you, you're evil." She points down at him with an intense look in her eyes, and she can see the flicker of fear cross his face as he shrinks from any power she might have. "Don't you ever lay your filthy hands on me or mine again, or I won't answer for the consequences." She turns and stalks out of the cottage, her face flushed with anger and hurt as his words echo in her wake.

Violet cannot bring herself to tell anyone of the incident with Ikey. He is a spiteful, vengeful villain. How dare he say such things! But his words hang in the air to taunt her. First she discovers the secret of Martha and the child and now this. Is her life always to be so painful? She goes over it in her mind again and again.

It is true that Annie spent a lot of time alone with Richard before Violet moved in with him … at a time when Richard was most vulnerable … The two babies were born close enough for it to be possible, considering that Joshua was premature … but how could he? With Annie Shaddick of all people! It would mean that Benjamin and Joshua are brothers, not cousins. How could they keep that a secret? Jealousy sears through her. But could she really blame him? She wouldn't have anything to do with him then, because of Matthew.

If it was true, no wonder Annie stalked off when Violet first moved in … but why didn't she confront Richard, if it was his child? Why didn't Annie demand money from him for the baby? Maybe she did … No, Richard couldn't have known. He could never have hidden that from her, surely? But what if he had kept seeing Annie … what if he had needed both Annie and herself? No, it was out of the question. How dare Ikey make her think these hateful thoughts? She would not give credence to his insinuations by putting them into words herself. She could not bear to think of the repercussions if this became public knowledge. She was not thinking only of herself in this, she was determined to protect Joshua from any scandal.

If Ikey spoke the truth, Annie had obviously gone to great lengths to protect Ben from her guilty secret and Violet had no wish to stir up ill feeling by bringing it all out into the open. That evil Ikey would have to go and spoil things for her, just as her life was taking shape again. She hated the thought that Ikey had the power to disrupt her peace of mind. At any moment he could decide to spread his nasty gossip, true or not, and blacken Richard's name, hurting her and Joshua. Her only consolation was that if he spoke up, Ikey would besmirch his sister and Ben too. But would that restrain him?

CHAPTER 13 *(May – August 1837)*

IVORY SATIN AND WINE VELVET

As May draws to a close the village is humming, it being the first month of the fishing season for the seine crews, there is much work to be done. The fishermen are filled with renewed enthusiasm; like calves being let out to pasture, they are in high spirits and for Matthew it is combined with the joy of being reunited with Violet. There is no one happier. Everyone is now aware that at long last they are together again and the general opinion is one of approval that the wrong is righted.

It takes Violet a long time to break it to Joshua that she and Matthew are getting married in August. He is starting school in September and it seems a lot for the lad to accept all at once. But once she has broached the subject she is pleased at how readily he accepts the situation.

"Will he be coming to live with us, Mam?' he asks.

She hugs him. "Would you like that, Josh?"

His brow wrinkles. "We don't have a room for him though."

"No, Josh, he will sleep with me in the big bed."

He looks at her, his head on one side, and asks, "Don't you mind, Mam?"

"No, Josh, he will help me to care for you, and make us into a proper family. It will be much better."

"Will he be my Papa then?"

"Well, he would like to be, if that's all right with you?"

He considers carefully. "Yes, I would like that."

She smiles, but silently in the days that follow, she prays. Her marriage must be as good for Joshua and Matthew as she hopes it will be for herself. She has to make it work for them all. In the meantime there is a great deal of work and preparation to be done. Molly calls to help her.

"It will be so different to my first marriage, Moll. This time we will be married in the chapel. Joshua has been attending Sunday school there and he has already told the minister." She laughs, "He told me that he was so excited he just couldn't wait."

"It's going to be grand, Vi, a proper wedding just like you deserve." Molly counts the names of the guests. "Do you realise there'll be nearly sixty couples following you, two by two, after the ceremony … someone will have to warn the neighbours." She laughs, as Violet raises her eyebrows.

"They'll love it," says Violet. "As long as we don't all call at once on the same household. Ma's already planned the wedding feast and she can't wait for the following day when everyone calls on me for the bride cake and to toast us for the future."

"What about your gown?" asks Molly.

"I am making it myself and it is to be kept secret, but I could do with your help on the handmaidens' frocks, for you and Hannah. Ma has fitted Joshua for his page-boy suit, with some wine velvet she had. She has spent hours embroidering undergarments and sewing to fill my linen chest. She keeps saying, 'If you care for the under part and keep it neat, the top will be sure to keep so.'" She mimics her mother and they both giggle.

"What are Matthew's mother and Hannah doing?"

Oh, they've been frantically busy making lace for all the trimmings."

"Then I suppose we had better get started too."

Violet is grateful for her brothers' help when the new bed arrives. Then, of course, new pillow-slips and a bolster have to be made and embroidered. How will she ever manage? But she is amazed at how many nimble fingers want to do their bit towards this wedding.

She begins work on her gown. The task is so enjoyable that the hours fly by. Her only fear is that it will not be completed in time. Her mother helps to keep her clients happy with the dressmaking and early in August everything is prepared.

When the day of the wedding dawns the weather is kind rather than generous but the atmosphere in Chiswell is animated. All the women are dressed in their best bonnets and frocks. There are smiling faces everywhere.

The procession to the chapel is long and impressive, and on her father's arm Violet feels like a princess in her ivory satin gown trimmed with Hannah and Mrs Stone's handmade lace at her wrists and throat. She is pleased, for she had seen in Weymouth a piece of fine net lace shown to be the latest style worn as a veil and she has managed to copy the idea. She can see that people are impressed with its novelty and she feels quite bold and mysterious. Several children run alongside the procession eagerly looking for their relations, bobbing and darting from one couple to another until they reach the chapel.

The ceremony, a simple service, is virtually the same as that which had joined her with Richard five years before, but this time the chapel rings to the joyful voices of the congregation. Violet could not be happier knowing that the majority of the Chiswell folk truly rejoice that she and Matthew are finally married. She sees no one who could mar her day and fortunately is unaware that in the Shaddick household someone still harbours ill will towards her.

As the ceremony is concluded and the couple appear in the porch the sun finally breaks through the clouds and congenially smiles down on them. Violet throws back her veil, revealing the happiest of faces framed by the honeysuckle and dog roses set in her hair and matching the posy she carries. There are gasps of admiration all around. She looks at Matthew, standing tall and assured at her side and beaming with pleasure at the sight of all their friends, and she feels so very proud of him.

The onlookers descend upon them, throwing rice, and Violet throws her flowers towards Hannah and Molly. She is thrilled when Molly catches the bouquet with a shriek of delight. There are shouts of 'Kiss the bride' and a cheer goes up as Matthew eagerly responds and she feels that warm glow of happiness surge through her. Then the procession sets off in a buzz of elated chatter and a confusion of arms and rice and laughter.

Joshua, somewhat unimpressed with all the fuss, has spied Ben sitting on some steps at the edge of the roadway. He is watching with interest, as the hullabaloo drifts off in the direction of the Mere. Joshua calls to him.

Ben's eyes light up. "Hello," he says, simply. "Aren't you going with them?"

Joshua thinks it looks more fun to play with Ben and shrugs, "I can't see what all the fuss is about. What you doing there anyway?"

"I was picking up some of the rice. We could

feed the fish, see if they'd rise to it," suggests Ben, thinking that a far more amusing pastime.

Joshua looks interested. "I'll help you." They gather up handfuls of rice and stuff Ben's generous pockets.

"I daren't put it in mine, Ma'd kill me." He brushes his hands together to shake off the dust. "There, that's enough. Come on."

They follow in the wake of the procession but on Mere Common they cross over to Castletown and make their way to the jetty, nattering like two little old men.

It is high tide when they reach the jetty and the weight of the water slops heavily against it. Their small bodies and the darkening sky behind them are reflected back from the depths of the water just beneath their feet. But seeing no danger they run recklessly from one side to the other dropping their handfuls of rice and watching them slowly sink.

Violet asks, as the procession winds its way from cottage to cottage, if anyone knows where Joshua is. "Don't you worry," a guest reassures her, "he's just dawdling a bit with his young cousin Ben." It is as if a dark cloud descends over her, as she thinks again of the venom that Ikey spat at her. She supposes they will be accepted as second cousins now that she and Matthew are married, for William had been Matthew's uncle. They will be related in the eyes of the villagers now, after all. She can't help wondering what people would say if they suspected the boys were half-brothers.

However, reassured that Joshua is following on behind, safe and happy, the intrusive thoughts of a drunken Ikey are dispelled by someone else offering their congratulations and another glass of metheglin. Although she accepts graciously she cannot help wondering how she is going to last the afternoon if she is obliged to drink at every place they stop.

It is soon time to move on again but Violet, asking again for Joshua, decides she can go no further without him. When no one seems to have any idea where he is she begins to panic. "But where could he have got to?"

"He can't have gone far. He was last seen with young Ben Stone and someone has gone to his house to see if they've gone there," says Matthew.

"I just thought he'd be content to stay with your Johnny and the other kids in the procession. How could I have been so stupid?"

"It's not your fault, Vi. I thought he'd be enjoying all the fun too, not wandering off by himself. You'd expect a nipper of that age to want to keep near his mother."

"He's always been adventurous. I should have put someone in charge of him." She becomes more and more agitated.

"Look, please don't blame yourself, it will spoil our wedding day and they're probably just playing quietly somewhere together. It's no use getting in a tiz." Matthew gently pulls her to him, soothingly rubbing his hand up and down her arm.

John comes panting up the lane, "They're not there," he says.

Violet gasps, "Something's wrong, I just feel it in my bones. They're only five years old. We've got to find them." Immediately a search party is organised and the wedding procession fans out in all directions.

Joshua and Ben hear the shouting as they sit on the dusty jetty. Joshua stands up, turning towards the common. "They're looking fer us," he says.

"Gosh, your suit is covered, Josh," Ben says with concern. Joshua looks down at his beautiful new suit all covered with dust.

"I forgot. Ma'll be mad with us … All the people there, and all. Come on, let's hide." They run, their stout little legs pounding back along the jetty and down onto the pebbles below.

"They're coming," whispers Ben urgently. "Let's get into that lerret with the nets in and hide underneath. Quickly or 'twill be too late." They both run and conceal themselves before the men come into view.

The lerrets, led in rows, pulled up high onto the dry pebbles of the small strip of beach out of reach of the tide, are inert, not inviting further investigation; and the searchers, expecting some cry of recognition from the children, pass by.

Violet decides that she and Matthew should go straight to her mother's and there the waiting begins. The womenfolk hand around plates of food.

Violet is unable to think straight, she can only hear the spoons chinking, chairs scraping and the clock ticking, the strange sounds that dominate a tense atmosphere seeming so loud above the muffled voices of the guests. She has images of her child getting lost and being frightened as darkness falls and then, even worse, she can see him balancing precariously on the edge of the well and then falling.

"Matty, can someone check the well, please ask one of the men to check the well."

"Don't worry, Violet, every nook and cranny will be searched." Matthew tries his best to reassure her, and sends Bob off to double-check the well, but one by one the men return with no news.

Annie Shaddick arrives in a state of agitation,

but neither can put the blame on the other for their child's disappearance. Finally, after two agonising hours have passed, Johnny Stone comes tearing along, "We've found them," he shouts triumphantly.

The women surge out into Brandy Row to see Thomas Atwool marching along with one under each arm. Violet and Annie rush forward, tears of relief in their eyes.

"Oh, thank you, Tom. Wherever were they?" asks Violet, taking Joshua into her arms and squeezing him tightly to her.

"They've been hiding from us. That's why it took so long. In one of them lerrets they were, on the quay in Castletown. They'd hid themselves under some nets." He hands Ben to Annie. "If it weren't fer a bit o' his wine-coloured velvet showing out under I'd never o' found 'em." He indicates Joshua's outfit.

"I'm grateful, Tom," says Annie, hugging Ben to her. She turns to Violet, "I'm sorry, Violet. I hope it didn't spoil your wedding day."

Violet turns away holding Joshua tightly to her, "No, of course not, I'm just relieved they came to no harm."

"Come and join us in a glass of mead, Annie." Violet hears Matthew inviting Annie into her parents' home. Matthew squeezes Violet's hand. "I think you could both do with one, don't you?"

"Thank you, I do feel a bit shaky, I'd appreciate that," says Annie.

Matthew hands them both a cup of mead, but even the relief of having Joshua safe, the joy of her wedding day and the love of her family and friends cannot oust the bitter feelings caused by the Shaddicks and Ikey's painful insinuations.

Violet's mother sits the boys down in plain sight with a plate of cake each. No one reprimands them;

252

they are all too relieved to be angry and the children look so tired and dirty.

Then Violet's father suggests they all drink to the health of the bride and groom, which needs no second bidding. Several of the men contribute to the gaiety with their own personal tribute to the happy couple and there is much laughing and passing of bottles and jugs, inside and outside the cottage, where half the village folk have congregated laughing and singing and saying good luck to them both.

Eventually Joshua is put to bed upstairs after Annie and Ben have left. Robert Allen bids the rest of the villagers goodnight and closes the doors, leaving only the close members of the family.

Violet's mother brings in a great bowl of punch, saying, "All must drink to the good luck of the young folks just on the threshold of a new life together."

Each in turn takes a drink from the bowl. With each sip, more caution is thrown to the wind and the celebrating goes on long after Violet and Matthew have left.

They walk arm in arm together, up to the Cove Cottages. It is a pleasant, starry night and their footsteps in perfect time with each other echo in the night air.

The cottage is as clean as a new pin and Matthew feels so proud of Violet. Their new bed looks as inviting as any bed he has ever set eyes on. She has polished the brass until it shines and the fresh white bedding, plump with swan's down, reminds him of a picture he has seen in one of Johnny's books of three little cherubs nestled in a cloud.

'At last', he thinks as his body sinks into the feathery mattress. He watches as Violet undresses, fascinated by every tiny move she makes, savouring the long-awaited moment when they lie together. Her body is so slight, it is perfect.

"Violet, you are lovelier even than I imagined." He reaches over and takes her hand, drawing her closer. He puts out his other hand and gently he touches her face.

She smiles, sliding, naked, under the covers. His hands move slowly over her as she nestles against him. Her skin feels so soft, so sensitive.

"You feel nice," he whispers.

"So do you," she speaks softly into his ear. "You are so strong and yet so tender." She kisses his neck, his temple, his mouth.

"God, I love you so much it hurts," he cries, holding her tightly to him. He wants this moment to last forever, and as their bodies entwine, desire surges through him.

But their lovemaking is not of a frenzied, passionate kind, more a leisurely savouring of what the future holds. A gentle taste of milk and honey, the silky meeting of warm, supple skins and the exquisite bouquet of their bodies and fresh linen, tempting and appealing; their racing heartbeats contradicting their slow body movements, in a kind of controlled responsiveness, both wishing to prolong the sensual ecstasy of the other's loving embrace.

Later, as they lie in each other's arms they can hear the occasional reveller making his meandering journey homeward.

"What a wonderful day," says Matthew.

"We'll never forget it, that's for sure," says Violet.

"No, we won't. It was a shame the nippers wandered off like that. I hope it didn't spoil it for you."

"No, of course not."

"I can't imagine whatever got into them."

"They were probably just bored with the wedding, and when they realised they were unsupervised they took advantage," says Violet.

"I think Josh wanted attention basically, and he got it from Ben. Annie said that Ben told her Joshua was afraid you'd be cross because he'd got his clothes dirty."

"That's ridiculous," protests Violet.

"It sounds to me like an excuse to justify their hiding from us all," says Matthew. "But we are going to have to make sure nothing like this ever happens again." He wraps his arms around her affectionately.

"They'll both be at school soon. That should keep them occupied and out of harm's way," says Violet. "It was a lovely day, Matty," she adds softly. "Everyone was so nice."

"Yes, they were; helping to find the boys, and all those generous gifts, and John bringing all that extra beer. We would have run out if he hadn't."

"It was smashing, and now I'm Mrs Violet Mary Stone. It does sound strange."

"Not to me it doesn't. It's music to my ears." He smiles to himself, wrapping his arms more tightly around her, thinking how happy he is feeling.

"Talking of gifts, I had almost forgotten I have something for you too." Matthew gently eases himself from their embrace.

Violet looks up at him in dismay, "But Matty, I have nothing for you."

She looks so sorrowful that Matthew adds, "Well, it isn't really a wedding present as such because I bought it for you a long time ago, but I think you'll like it and find it useful. But we can leave it 'til the morrow now," and he snuggles back against her.

"Oh Matty, don't be so mean. I can't wait till morning now you've awoken my curiosity." She sits up and tugs at him. "Please can you not show me now?"

He has longed to give her his gift for more than five years, yet to make her wait just one night still seems to him too cruel, and so he relents.

Violet watches him in the moonlight as he puts on his nightshirt. When he goes to fetch his gift she sits up and straightens the bed covers and then lights the bedside lamp.

He returns with a huge parcel. Hannah has gift-wrapped it for him and secured it with a large satin bow and now Matthew watches, anticipating her pleasure as Violet undoes the ribbon and begins carefully to unfold the paper.

He is not disappointed. He has always known the meticulous French workmanship could not fail to enchant her.

"Oh Matty, it's exquisite." Her fingers trace the pattern of inlaid mother of pearl, caressing the smooth satinwood, before lifting the lid and exploring all the different compartments: for her scissors, pins and needles, cottons and silks, bodkins, thimbles, everything she could possibly think of.

Her eyes shine as she looks up at him, "It's so beautiful, Matty, thank you so much. Wherever did you find it?"

No longer feeling any bitterness, he tells her how he brought it back with him from France the day she walked out on him and that he had kept it for her ever since, determined that one day they would be together once more.

Her eyes huge with tears, she says, "I really don't deserve someone as kind and good as you are, do I?"

"I wouldn't have waited all this time if I thought

that, would I now?" He kisses her forehead and the scent of her soft skin entices him to bed once more. Gently he lifts the sewing box and, putting it out of the way in the corner of the room, he swiftly returns to kiss away her salty tears.

His lips hunger for the taste of her; his body feels her warmth; he feels her tension ease and an urgent passion take its place that makes his heart pound as they kiss, touch and move with fluidity. He feels her desperate desire as she clings tightly to him with such slender arms and he loves her again and again until the thrill and fire of mutual desire leaves both of them exhausted.

Matthew is brought near to tears when Violet whispers, "I love you so much," and he knows that she really means it. He cannot imagine ever being happier than he is at that moment, but a few seconds later she whispers again, "Do you think the corn dolly that Molly gave us will work?"

"What do you mean?" he asks.

"It's a fertility charm," she giggles.

"Oh, I hope so," he says with feeling. "More than anything now." He kisses her, "I finally won the thing most dear to me today, but a little nipper … well … that would be extra special."

CHAPTER 14 *(June 1838 – May 1844)*

THE END OF AN ERA

The Princess Victoria is crowned Queen on 28th June 1838. The following month Violet gives birth to a little girl. They name her Rebecca after Matthew's grandmother, but they all call her Becky. She is remarkably like Violet with her baby blue eyes and dark, fluffy, fine hair, and both Joshua and Matthew are fascinated by her.

Joshua spends much of his time rocking his old cradle and dangling the coral rattle that Matthew has bought until eventually she falls asleep. It is he who first entices a smile from her and then excitedly runs to fetch his mother, trying in vain to get her to do so again, but it is not long before she is smiling and gurgling for him all the time.

Violet loves to watch them together. At last Joshua has someone to cherish, and he becomes the child's constant companion. She thinks Matthew must be the perfect father; he is so proud of all of them but never makes more of his Rebecca than of Joshua. He works long, hard hours, determined to make life easier for her and their family, and although folk may have thought him stupid when he bought one of the derelict buildings on the beach, he has proved them all wrong. Once he had patched it up it enabled him to start a boat repair service and it is this that keeps him busy in the winter when the other fishermen can only repair, oil and re-tar their own lerrets, or make new nets. He goes from repairing to building, which is far more lucrative, and Violet is glad that he finds the work a pleasant change.

In January 1839 the Ferry Bridge is completed and on the 30th it is opened in grand style. Matthew is one of those who have been instrumental in getting the project started, and with his father is privileged to be included among the marchers.

They set off from the King's statue in Weymouth. There is a detachment of the dragoon guards, Weymouth town band and the tenants, landowners and responsible committee. Matthew and his father are with the committee members. Among the Portland families eagerly awaiting them are Violet, Joshua and the baby on the Portland side of the bridge. They all follow the procession to the Portland Arms for a sumptuous event, and afterwards the troops go through a variety of military manoeuvres and sword exercises which enthral Joshua and the other children watching.

Later that evening, after the children are in bed, Matthew sits in his winged chair and Violet sits on a cushion at his feet, her head resting against his knee as they chat quietly in the firelight.

"'Tis the end of an era, and I think 'tis sad in a way."

"There's no doubt but what 'twill make a tremendous difference to us. Trade is bound to increase because there is more work available here with the stone quarries than in the rest of Dorset. People are sure to come searching for jobs. Did you enjoy the ceremony, Vi?"

"I did and I was very proud of you. I couldn't stay the whole time because Becky was fractious but you should have heard Joshua when he got home. He was so impressed with the troops he now says he wants to join the military when he's older."

"Children all have such dreams. He is only six, he'll have changed his mind by the time he's a young man, I'm sure."

"Probably," says Violet, not quite so sure. "They grow up so fast 'tis hard to imagine. I don't think I like the idea of more strangers settling on our island though, Matthew. The children see enough bad behaviour from the sailors and foreigners over to Castletown without these Kimberlins actually moving in permanently."

"I can understand how you feel, Vi, but we couldn't have stayed isolated forever. Sooner or later we would have had to improve our access to the mainland and now we must accept all that that entails. It will bring good things as well as bad, and we should benefit in the long run."

Violet soon sees that Matthew was right. With the opening of the Ferry Bridge, trade with the island is made so much easier that with it comes prosperity but, to the consternation of the true Portlanders, their population explodes.

Throughout the hungry forties men come looking for work in their droves and, having found success, their families follow. Despite her fears, Violet knows that these families are all prospective customers of hers and the germ of an idea begins to grow. She is too busy caring for her children and Matthew to put her plan into practice immediately, but as time goes on and the children become more independent she is sure she can make her idea into a successful venture.

Six years have passed when, in the Spring of 1844, on an unusually mild and wet morning, Violet has been waiting for a storm to pass over and is then in a great hurry, rushing to complete her shopping so that she might also finish another order before the children come home from school.

There are many Kimberlins abroad in Castletown and the chandler is extremely busy. She waits impatiently for her turn, relieved that those ahead of her are quickly despatched. She makes her purchase and hurries on her way.

Seeing her haste, several gentlemen step off the pavement to allow her to pass. This means stepping into the mud created by the carts and wagons transporting the stone, which make deep channels and ruts in the roadway, but they do not seem to notice this as they raise their hats to her, at the same time eyeing her up and down.

Violet nods her thanks and smiles without really taking notice of them. After all, 'Kimberlins' are just foreigners, not island folk, and these men should make way for a woman, it is only polite. Besides, it is her island, her birthright.

Then one man steps from left to right just as she does, effectively barring her way. Immediately agitated she says, "Excuse me, would you allow me to pass?"

The man grins knowingly and makes a great scene of bowing and humbling to her as he steps off the pavement, making her feel foolish. It is obvious he wanted her attention, but he says nothing; he just looks insolently at her. It is unnerving and the face and situation feel familiar. She pauses but then continues; there are many tasks to complete before noon and she does not have the time to contemplate the motives of a lunatic.

However, in the days that follow she notices the man often. He is always hanging around in the shadows. She does not like him, his familiarity makes her feel ill at ease. She cannot understand why he has singled her out for this treatment and on the occasions that she sees him first she takes steps to hide from sight.

One morning in May, whilst shopping, she is surprised to see a sale notice in the doorway of Miss Bennett's haberdashery. It is an attractive building situated on a sunny corner, with bow windows each side of the doorway and baskets of flowers hanging from under the porch. She stands on the steps and reads the sign carefully. Apparently it is a closing down sale.

She goes in to make her purchases. Inside is a real treasure trove of all the things young ladies like to do. There are pieces of handmade lace, collars and cuffs, guipure and all shades of silks and ribbon, mantalets, tarlatan and tulle, and shelves of colourful materials. She pores over the costume patterns and accessories: the hat pins, gloves, evening bags and ornamental flowers. It is a wonderland for a woman with heart and hands as willing as hers.

The sun pours in onto the shining mahogany counter, and Miss Bennett is saying, "Will that be all, Mrs Stone?"

"Oh, I'm sorry. Yes, thank you very much."

"That'll be three and four pence ha'penny, dear, please."

She counts the coins into Miss Bennett's rounded pink palm. "Miss Bennett, would it be impertinent of me to enquire as to why you might be selling off all your wares?"

"Not at all, me dear, 'tis no secret. I've had an offer too good to turn down at my time of life."

She tries to keep the deflation from her voice. "Oh, I see, someone has already bought the shop."

"Bless you my dear, no. 'Tis an offer for my hand, I mean, holy matrimony."

"Oh, but that's wonderful." Violet's excitement is taken for delight on behalf of Miss Bennett's good fortune.

"I know, I know, 'tis amazin'. He's a sea captain as hails from Cornwall, and he's been askin' me this last month to set up with him. Well, I were takin' me time afore I gives 'en 'is answer, to be sure it were bona fide. But sure as eggs is eggs he do keep comin' back wi' the same. Well, I mean to say I got to be careful how I plays me hand. I can't afford to be too cautious at my time o' life, can I dear?"

"Well, I think its wonderful news, and I am very pleased for you. How soon is the wedding to be?"

"We hope, if all goes well, 'twill be Lammas day."

"Well, I shall surely be in to see you again before then. Best wishes for your preparations. Goodbye, Miss Bennett."

"Good mornin' to you, Mrs Stone, and thank you."

Violet closes the door behind her and crosses over to the other side of the road to stand back and take in the overall impression of the business. She is filled with inspiration, but then a stealthy movement catches her eye.

It is that wretched man again; he must be following her! She feels sick with confusion and fear as he approaches her. She cannot take her eyes off him. Who is he? What does he want from her? Then he steps back into the shadows as someone turns the corner.

"Violet, what a lovely surprise. I haven't seen you for ages."

Relief washes over her, the merry words preventing her from panicking. "Molly, how lovely to see you." Her voice is trembling but she has to keep talking, "How is John?"

Molly chats away, oblivious of the knot of fear in her heart. Violet stands so that although she faces Molly she also keeps the man within her view.

"I've so much to tell you. You'll be thrilled when you hear." Molly is enjoying the suspense before she blurts out her good news.

Violet tries to respond normally, wanting to hide her agitation from both Molly and the man. "Come, tell all then, don't stop now," says Violet.

"We're getting married!" exclaims Molly, bursting with joy.

"Oh Molly, that's wonderful." She squeezes her hand with affection. "When?"

As she listens to Molly she watches the man slink off down the main street. Even though he is now out of sight she still cannot relax. She wants to tell Molly about him but she can see that her friend is bubbling over with excitement and after all, what is there to tell? No one would take her seriously; they would say it was just her imagination.

Not wanting Molly to think that she is not pleased for her she pushes aside her fears. She smiles and jokes, "What brought the old trout round?"

"Oh don't, Vi. She never did come round, Old Nick got her first."

"Oh, that was dreadful of me, Molly. I'm sorry, we mustn't laugh; we've all got to get old sometime."

"I know, but it was a happy release for John and me, all the same."

"True. Oh Molly, I am so pleased for you. You and John have been so patient when it has been obvious to everyone that you belong together. Do you know yet where you are going to live?"

"Well, 'tis a long story, but to be brief, John has inherited the mill and bakehouse, with twenty perch of land adjoining. His parents got the main dwelling house and the farm." She smiles and puts on airs.

"I'm soon to be married to a man of some considerable property." They both laugh.

Violet says, "You deserve it, after waiting all this time, Moll."

"That's not all though, Vi, his grandmother also left him three roods and forty perch in 'Snalterfield', four acres two roods and fifteen perch in Grove, several undivided quarter parts of quarry land and several penny rents in 'Drakes Wear' and 'Hynds Wear'. The old trout had strips and fields all over the place, 'twas a sizeable estate."

"My goodness, Molly, you really are going to wed a wealthy man, you won't be wanting to mix with the likes of us soon."

"You know better than that, Vi. John was only saying yesterday that we should pay you a call."

"Well, I think that's a grand notion. You and John must come and have supper with us to celebrate. I know Matty would love it, and we have so much to talk about."

"That would be lovely."

"How about tomorrow evening then?"

"Why, thank you kindly, Mistress Violet, we would be delighted." They laugh, both remembering the last time they were fooling around and putting on airs.

"I must go. I have been much longer than is usual and the children will soon be home for their lunch. It's been lovely seeing you again, but we can have a long talk tomorrow."

"I'm really looking forward to it, Vi."

Molly says farewell and waves her hand as she continues up the hill. Violet, alone once more, completes her shopping in haste, fearful of encountering the stranger again. Distractedly, she makes a few extra purchases in preparation for a special supper the next day.

Once at home she will not think at all of the man. He must be a halfwit. She is not sure if menace is intended by him or merely imagined by herself and so she does not give credence to her fears by voicing them to Matthew.

She spends the whole afternoon cleaning and tidying the cottage, and then hurriedly prepares the supper table. It will have to be cold fish pie and some bread and cheese tonight. There are some tarts to follow if anyone is still hungry. She will spend the morrow baking to make up for it.

When Matthew comes home she wants to hold him tightly to her and never let him go. She wants to tell him of her fears and of the man who haunts her quiet moments. But surely she is overreacting; surely it is just her vivid imagination. She listens as he talks to the children. She feels warm and safe, her fears allayed, and instead she tells him of Molly's visit.

"Guess who I bumped into this morning?" Violet waits as Matthew sits in the armchair and slowly pulls off his boots. "Matty, go on, guess?" She leans over the back of the armchair.

"Molly?" he asks, with a grin.

"Oh, how did you know?"

"I didn't. I only had to look at how pleased you are to know it must be someone close that you haven't seen for some time. So it had to be Moll. How is she?"

"She's fine, but you'll never guess what else."

"They're not getting married?"

"Yes," says Violet gleefully. "Isn't it grand?"

"Whahey! 'Tis about time," said Matthew. "That is good news." Rebecca climbs up onto her father's lap, attracted by his good humour.

"I knew you'd be thrilled, and I've got another surprise for you." She pauses, for effect ... "I've asked them to supper tomorrow."

"That is good news, Becky. We'll have a decent meal for a change." He laughs, tickling Rebecca and making her squeal excitedly.

"Why, Matthew Stone, you ungrateful devil!" Violet threatens him with the wooden spoon and he ducks down laughing heartily at her indignation. Rebecca immediately joins in, trying unsuccessfully to tickle her father with her tiny hands.

Violet leaves them to call Joshua to the supper table.

Later, whilst she eats and listens to their carefree chattering, she smiles. She is right to ignore the stupid man. He is obviously half-rocked, and what sort of threat can he be?

After supper, when the children are tucked in bed, Violet cheers up. The time is right to broach the subject of her new idea.

Taking Matthew a mug of his mother's pansy wine, partly to sweeten him up and partly because he deserves it, she sits down in her favourite spot on the rug at his feet and rests her head against his knee.

"Matty, how are things at the boat yard?"

"Very good at the moment, Vi. Even though we're still busy getting the boats seaworthy after the February storms, a lot of the blokes are so pleased with our workmanship they've come to us to build more."

"That's wonderful … How much have we put by now then, Matty?"

"Well, I reckon given the monies owing to us … I reckon I can afford to get me a new roof and a better furnace."

Violet then feels guilty, and falls silent for a while, whereupon Matthew senses there is something on her mind.

"Vi," he says quietly, "what are all these questions in aid of?"

"Oh, 'tis nothing, just a silly notion of mine, nothing important."

"Come on now, spill the beans. You don't fool me."

"Well, 'tis a long story, and I know you'll think me a silly thing, but it did seem a good idea at the time."

"Let me be judge of that, you just tell me what's on your mind."

"Well, I went to the haberdashery today, and there are all manner of things in that little shop that I could make good use of, with the dressmaking … and your Ma, well she'd be overcome with all the lacemaking bits and bobs. Oh, Matty, 'tis a lovely little place and 'tis to be sold."

"You want to go on a shopping spree, Vi? You know I don't mind, you can turn a fast profit with your eye for fashion. You can buy what bits and bobs you like, my love."

"Oh, Matty, you are so sweet and generous but …"

"Well, what's wrong?" Matthew looks puzzled. "I really don't mind what you buy, Vi. I know you'll be sensible."

"But … but Matty … I was wondering if we might buy the shop."

"The shop!" exclaims Matthew. "Good grief, Violet, I might be doing well but we are not made of money."

"I know, I know, it was just a silly idea," she says, trying not to sound too disappointed. "It was just that … as I stood outside, I could just picture a model in the window dressed with one of my costumes and … and displays of lace dotted about and some bonnets and straw hats on stands each side … It would have been such fun planning it all out and all the stock would be really cheap and would be worth a mint to me." She pauses, but her mind runs on excitedly. "The living quarters would make a wonderful work area, with fitting room and sewing room and stock room." She pauses again, "I had it all planned out in an instant."

"Violet, haven't you got enough to do with the children and the housekeeping and all the dressmaking that you take on now?"

"Yes, but I am always having to turn work away, and if it was really successful there would be an outlet for my mother and your mother's lacemaking, and maybe Hannah could help me in the shop taking orders and fittings. It could be good for the whole family, Matty. There are shops like it in Weymouth, why shouldn't we have our own here on the island? More and more people are coming here to live, now we have the bridge, and instead of going to Weymouth they can come to me."

"I can see you have given it a lot of thought, and I admit it all sounds marvellous, but it would be such a lot of work for you and it is not as if we need it. I provide well enough for you, don't I?"

"Of course you do, I know that. I just got so excited when the idea came to me, 'cus I know I could do well with it. I just know I could. It seemed such a good opportunity, if only we had enough money."

"Yes, well, that's another matter. Did you ask how much Miss Bennett was asking?"

"Lord no, Matty, I could do no such thing without talking to you first. Whatever next?"

"Well, it's bound to be more than we have."

"Well, I was coming to that. You see I have been putting a bit by each time I go to Weymouth and each time I complete an order here and it must be a pretty penny by now."

"What do you call a pretty penny then, Vi?"

asks Matthew, a little taken aback.

"I don't know exactly, I got bits and pieces of monies all over the place." She feels a bit guilty at having a secret from Matthew. "You see it was going to be for Christmas presents and birthday surprises and such like, but it has quite mounted up."

"Come on then, let's see how much it is," says Matthew, smiling.

There is some in a jar in the pantry; some under the mattress in her bedchamber; some more in the davenport in a secret drawer, that she discovered quite by chance one day when she was polishing the inside; and she knows there is another packet that she got some time ago for starchmoor, but she can't remember where she has put it.

This makes Matthew laugh. "Violet, you are impossible."

Together they count up the coins. "Why, there's nigh on forty-five guineas altogether, and you haven't counted the amount for the starchmoor."

"How much do you think Miss Bennett will want for the shop, Matty?"

"I have no idea, Vi. But 'tis no use guessing anyways. The best thing to do is go and ask her outright."

"Oh, Matty, would you? Would you really?"

"Well, don't be getting thy hopes up. There's no harm in asking though, is there?"

The following day Violet cannot concentrate on anything. She spends the morning on the common collecting arrowroot, and dreaming and planning her new project. When her basket is finally full she returns to the stable yard feeling well pleased with herself. She crouches low to clear the doorway, riding straight into the stable as usual, when out of the shadows steps the man, spooking the horse and causing Caraway to shy and neigh, creating confusion in the confined space of the stall. She freezes.

He touches her skirt. "Remember me?" He smiles, displaying gums and barely three crooked, blackened teeth.

She can hardly breathe. That voice. It is the same voice! Her mind races. He is one of the sailors in Castletown. She grips the reigns. Caraway jerks. She turns the horse in the stall, pinning the man momentarily against the wall. She hears his cry of pain as the horse treads on him. She kicks her heels urging the animal back out into the yard.

He yells after her. "You will remember, I guarantee. I'll make sure you never forget."

Thomas the stable boy is crossing the yard. She flings herself from the horse. "Take him, Thomas," she shouts and runs, heedless of the mud splashing her skirts, praying that his injured foot will prevent his pursuit of her.

She is in a dreadful state of agitation when she reaches home. Thomas may not have heard the man shouting after her, but he must have noticed her distress. Did he discover the man in the stable after she had left? What if he told Thomas that she'd killed a man so long ago?

The horrible memory of that Castletown incident fills her head with nightmares. She cannot believe that after twelve years this animal should return to haunt her. Does he intend to harm her? To reap revenge for what she did? Or is he going to expose her as a killer, a murderess? She isn't a murderess; she had only been defending herself … But who will believe her?

They are expecting Molly and John for supper that night. How is she going to hide her guilt and her fears from them all? Maybe she should tell Matty of his threat, but what would her loving husband and friends think of her if they knew what she had done ... of what she was capable? She cannot tell them, they will despise her.

When Matthew comes home that evening, he brings the news that the shop is to go for three hundred and thirty guineas. Violet pretends to be excited. She is busy preparing the food for their guests, and hopes that Matthew will assume that that is the reason for her distracted manner. They do not, however, get down to discussing the matter until after they have all eaten their fill.

Rebecca is upstairs asleep and Joshua has excused himself to go off out with Ben somewhere. Matthew, Molly and John are settled in comfortable chairs ready for the best parlour gossip, glasses of sherry wine and mugs of beer. Violet is clearing away the last of the crockery; she is stiff and tense as she tries to play the part of cheerful hostess.

"That were the best meal I've had in an age, Violet," says John sincerely.

"Me too," adds Matthew, dryly. He is smiling and expecting some reaction from Violet, but she is not paying attention.

"You must let me have the recipe for that ham and apple pudden, Vi. It was delicious. I have to start collecting tips, because I'll have a hungry man to feed shortly, too."

"'Tis one I got from Auntie Sarah, but 'tis very tasty, don't you think?" says Violet over her shoulder as she carries out a pile of plates.

John speaks clearly and the sound carries through to her, "It were all very appetising, and much appreciated, I'm sure." He has eaten most heartily and obviously puts great store by his food.

As Violet puts the plates down in the scullery and begins to clear some pans away she suddenly freezes with fear, for there is a shadowy face peering in at her through the window. With sheer panic her hand loses grip on the pan she is holding and it drops with a loud echoing clang on the flagstones. It is that horrid man again! Her heart is thumping. He knows where she lives! The face disappears immediately, but the sight of the man frightens her so much that it leaves her trembling; she puts her hand up to her forehead to steady herself. Keep calm, she silently urges.

Matthew comes through to see what has happened and picks up the pan for her. She brushes aside his concern and, taking his arm, hustles him back into the parlour. She does not want him to notice how shaky she is, and draws them into conversation again.

She sits down next to Matthew and takes a large swig of her sherry wine, and then she looks up and smiles at everyone, "Sorry about the bang, but nothing's broken. By the bye, I have been meaning to say how much I liked your straw bonnet that you were wearing yesterday, Molly." She forces herself to keep up the pretence, smiling away and smothering her fears.

"John's mother made it for me, for a birthday gift. They have a ready supply of straw from the farm, and 'tis a simple thing to fix it with field flowers."

Violet passes a significant look to Matthew, whereupon he grins knowingly back at her.

"What is it?" asks Molly, looking embarrassed.

"'Tis a long story, Molly," says Matthew. "Vi, you had better explain to John and Moll what it is that's on your mind. In the meanwhile I'll refill your tumblers."

When Matthew eventually sits down again the story has been fully related.

"So what do you think?" he asks curiously.

"Well, if you have the amount necessary I would say 'twas a bargain not to be missed and just the thing for our Violet." John sounds enthusiastic. "What do you think?" he asks Matthew.

"I think so too, but the problem is, although we have just enough, Violet wouldn't have anything left over to run the business with."

"That wouldn't matter, once you've got the premises you could sell stuff and just have a commission to start off with. I could get John's mother to sell some of her hats and I am learning to make them too, so I would be able to help keep the supply going if you wanted me to," suggests Molly enthusiastically.

"Well, that would be marvellous, Molly, 'tis what I was thinking when you said John's mother was making them. I know I could sell them and I could make costumes to match."

"My mother and Hannah would surely help with their lacemaking. I must say it does sound possible, because there is some stock to be going on with, and you still have some material put by to make a few things," reasons Matthew.

He looks at Violet but she does not seem to be listening. "Vi, are you all right?"

"Yes, I'm sorry, I was deep in thought day-dreaming of it all," she lies. She cannot rid herself of the image of that man peering at her through the scullery window. She shakes her head to dispel the thought. Whatever it is that that man wants she is not going to let him spoil her golden opportunity, a dream of a lifetime. However apprehensive she might feel, she will not let Matthew believe she has any doubts about the shop.

"I was just saying that with some help it would be possible." Matthew studies her carefully as he speaks.

"I know I could do it, Matty. I would work really hard, you know I would, and it would be a good investment for Becky's future too."

"Well, maybe tomorrow I should go and make her an offer. What do you think?" He looks at Violet.

"What do you think I think?" She laughs, getting up and going to him. "I think you are wonderful," she says, giving him a big hug and a kiss on the mouth.

Molly then speaks up diffidently. "Vi, I have told John Motyer that when we are married I will be giving up my work at the Cove House Inn … and he has already found a replacement for me. It would be my pleasure to help you set it all up … if you'd like me to."

Violet can see that Molly is shy about offering her services. "I would be very grateful for your help, Molly, and it would be lovely for us to work together, but we can't count our chickens just yet, we have to agree the sale with Miss Bennett first."

Matthew is surprised at the note of pessimism in her voice now, considering how she had been so certain of success before, but although he is determined to get it for her if he possibly can, he simply says, "We must just wait and see."

The rest of the evening is spent playing cards, joking and drinking and discussing John and Molly's wedding plans.

CHAPTER 15 *(May 1844)*

TWIST OF FORTUNE

That night Violet tosses and turns, unable to sleep. The sound of Matthew's regular breathing makes it seem worse. He is so untroubled, so content. How can she tell him what she has done? She has no one to defend her now that Richard, her only witness, is gone. She doesn't know where to turn; she cannot live in terror of that sailor and his threats.

In the early hours she awakes in a cold sweat to find Matthew looking down at her with concern. Has she been talking in her sleep? Her face is wet with tears.

"What is it, Vi? Tell me all about it." He holds her close to him, "You have been crying and saying, 'I haven't killed him. He's not dead,' over and over again." He rocks her gently for a while but still she remains silent. Then he holds her from him, looking into her face, seeking out her gaze. "I think it is time I knew it all, don't you?" Gently, he coaxes her. "Start at the beginning and tell me exactly what happened."

She lies there fearful of forming the words, but she knows now that she has no alternative. Once she begins to speak she sees it all so clearly, unlike the moment when it had happened. But still she finds it hard to believe that she actually slashed at a man's face and then stabbed him so seriously that he died.

As she talks she feels the burden lift from her

shoulders, but at his silence, fear and apprehension fill her. She waits for his reaction, terrified that this will end their happiness. How could he love someone who is so wicked? She looks up at him, at his serious expression and she closes her eyes to shut out his judgement of her.

Finally he speaks, "How could you keep this from me for all those years? Why could you not tell me?"

Oh God, please don't make him be cross.

"I am so sorry, Violet, that I was not there when you needed me. I'll make it up to you, I promise."

"Oh Matthew." She stretches up her arms for him to hold her. How could she have ever doubted his trust? Relief washes over her, wave after wave, and with it the tears come at last. Tears that have been building up, it seems, forever. She can rely on Matthew to help and defend her, she is certain. She clings to him, feeling safe with his strong arms tightly clasped around her.

Everything makes sense to Matthew now, the gossip of the past and the trick of fate that threw her into the arms of another man, "Just you let me get my hands on him. I'll teach him a lesson he'll never forget."

A new fear grips Violet. "Matty, please don't try to handle him alone. If anything goes wrong you might be killed, but it would be just as bad if he were to die because you would get the blame and I couldn't go through it all again. Either way, I just couldn't bear it."

"Don't you worry; we'll find a way to trap him so no one will get hurt."

"But how? What can we do? We cannot go to the authorities. I have no witnesses to prove that I was acting only in my defence. You weren't there when it happened and he was. It's my word against his."

"Leave it to me, love, and don't you worry about a thing. It will be all right, I promise you."

"I just don't know what he's after, hanging around all the time. He's so revolting, he terrifies me." She shakes her head sadly. "I just don't know what it will take to get him to leave me alone."

"He'll make his move soon, I'll be bound, and then we'll see exactly what he wants and we'll be ready for him. Don't you fret."

The following morning Joshua and Rebecca leave for school and Violet is tidying up the cottage, when out of the corner of her eye she imagines that she sees someone stealthily pass by the window. Her heart starts to thump for she is all alone, she goes to make sure that the back entrance is secure and returns to the parlour to check out of the windows again. There is no sign of anyone.

Suddenly an arm tightens around her neck, dragging her backwards as she is grabbed from behind by the villain. Unable to breathe, she frantically pulls at his vice-like grip, but as she struggles he brings a knife close to her face. Faintness and nausea overwhelm her. He must have felt her resistance diminish with her lack of air because, to her great relief, he suddenly loosens his hold. She gasps for air.

"Don't you make a sound; it would be a shame to scar such a pretty face. You know me now, don't you?"

She feels his breath in her face, his lips touching her ear as he speaks. "This time the tables are turned, for I'm the one with the weapon and you are going to do as I say." His grip tightens again and she struggles against him, but he is stronger than he looks.

"I've been watching you and I know you and your husband are nicely set up, thank you. Now I'm just a poor sailor and I don't see the justice in the likes of a murderess living the life of the blessed when myself, I work like a navvy and barely eat enough to keep a sparrow alive."

Her fear and the smell of him makes Violet heave. It takes all her self-control to stop herself from vomiting.

"As I see it, you owe me a debt of silence that you can well afford to pay. You wouldn't want your handsome new hubby to hear all the truth about you, would you now? So here's what you gotta do."

Still holding her firmly with his right arm against her chest, he switches the knife into that hand, its blade pressed at her throat, and with his left hand he produces a felt purse from his pocket and dangles it under her nose.

"You put sixty golden guineas into this pouch and I'll be in the stable to collect it tomorrow at noon, and you come alone. If you're not there by five past, I'm going to the Peelers to tell my tale. Then it'll be your husband next. Savvy?" Her heart sinks as he twists her round to face him.

"Now don't you utter a sound 'til I'm long gone or it could be your last." He pushes her away from him and is gone in an instant.

She runs to their back door and retches violently and then she slumps against the wall feeling faint and sickly. Forced to wait until her heaving stomach and her heart rate are normal again, she has time to collect her thoughts. This man has devastated her life once before, she will not allow it to happen again. She must find Matthew and tell him.

The following day, noon is fast approaching as

Violet, her heart pounding, reluctantly makes her way to meet the sailor. Having rehearsed over and over what Matthew has told her to say, she walks in cautiously.

He is already squatting there in the empty stall next to Caraway's and he stands up impatiently. "Took your time, didn't you?"

"You said noon," she answers boldly.

"Give us the gold," he snaps.

"First, I have to tell you, there'll be no more. I have no more," she says firmly.

"This'll do me fer the time being, ducky. We'll not be docking here again for a year or two." He goes to grab it, but Violet bravely puts out her hand to stop him.

"Don't think that every time your ship docks in the roads you can come to me for funds because you'll be disappointed. This is the one and only time you benefit from my hard work."

He grabs hold of her hand, "Who is laying down the law here, lady, you or me? I said give me the gold, or I will get my desserts some other way." His eyes fill with a look of lust and the horror of the attempted rape comes flooding back. She cannot hold out any longer and trying her best to control her trembling she immediately passes him the pouch.

She watches warily as triumphantly he shakes out the gold coins into the palm of his callused hand. His eyes glint at the sight of them; then they glint again at the sight of her. She backs away slightly, her courage failing her.

"How about a nice big kiss for your partner in crime then?" He grins, almost drooling where he has so few teeth and she inwardly cringes.

She must pull herself together for he won't be so cocky in a minute. Defiantly she sticks out her chin and replies, "That was not part of the bargain."

Mercifully there is a sound in the yard and he is distracted. Violet holds her breath. Maybe he will not think it wise to tarry after all. He freezes and listens until a seagull takes flight, wailing mournfully. He has the gold in his hands and his good humour returns.

"So long then, my beauty. This'll see me through to the next voyage, so fare thee well until we meet again." Obviously he is risking discovery the longer he dallies and thankfully he decides to forgo the kiss.

He bows himself out with the cheek of a highwayman, but as he turns into the sunlight a large seine net falls from the sky and encompasses him from head to toe. Matthew shouts down from the stable roof, "That'll teach you to lay your hands on my wife, you scurvy creep."

The sailor is bending, attempting to unsheathe his knife from the back of his boot and Violet stands quite still, frozen with fear, but Matthew is upon him and thrusting Dryer's pistol into his face. He says, "If you come near me or mine again I guarantee you'll regret it."

Violet watches, her heart thumping as Matthew disarms the man and discards the blade. The sailor struggles but Matthew twists him roughly in the netting, like a spider with a fly, then he tosses him towards her brothers who, dressed in the uniforms of the Dorset Coast Fencibles, are waiting for their turn.

They obviously enjoy ridiculing this intimidator of women, now reduced to a coward. They jostle and jeer at him, then finally they yank on the mesh and the man is toppled with a heavy thud. Matthew is by this time joined by his father and father-in-law, dressed as officers of the Court Leet, and young

Thomas, the stable boy, and John Motyer.

He alters his tone sarcastically. "Allow me to introduce you to Captain Manning of Portland Castle." Then addressing John Motyer he says, "This man, Sir, has been threatening and trying to blackmail my wife."

Still she watches from within the safety of the stable as her brothers roll him along until he is all trussed up, covered in dust and laid before the phoney Governor. They prod him to his feet.

The man hangs his head as John Motyer speaks to him with the authority of one responsible for law and order on the island. "Mr Stone has explained to me the circumstances whereby his wife was forced to defend herself from you and your shipmate's unwelcome advances and which led to the death of your companion."

"She killed him," he mutters, his head still bowed.

"However," John Motyer continues, ignoring his protests, "I do not feel you were free from blame in that incident and you are certainly guilty of extortion here today."

"But she murdered my mate." He glances up for a second, but then thinks better of it, bowing his head again and mumbling, "She shouldn't get off scot-free. 'Twas her, she killed him."

Violet trembles, his accusations piercing through her, like the murderous shard she used. But John Motyer will not be shaken. "As I see it, she was an innocent girl and you and your so-called mate accosted her. In my opinion, he got his come-uppance. Furthermore, I suggest you hand over your ill-gotten gains and leave this island forthwith. If you ever return you will be immediately placed under arrest for extortion."

He turns to the officers. "Gentlemen, would

you be so kind as to extricate this scoundrel, confiscate the gold and escort him back to his vessel where he is to remain until the ship departs."

Her brothers, as the three bogus officers, take charge of the man.

Violet cautiously emerges from the stable and Matthew immediately goes to her side and hugs her.

"Captain Manning, I'd like to present my wife."

"How do you do, my dear?" He takes her hand and presses it to his lips, as her brothers frogmarch the man out of the stable yard. Once they are out of earshot Violet sighs with relief. "We did it, we really did it," and she throws her arms around Matthew.

He holds her close. She still feels weak at the knees.

"I told you we'd sort him out," he says and then he kisses her. He is so brave and kind, the tears well up but they are tears of relief. They are all brave and kind and they have all taken dreadful risks just for her.

She turns to John Motyer. "Thank you, John," she says, squeezing his big hand in hers. "You were really convincing."

"I think it was the beer belly that did the trick, I have a portly, stately appearance you see." The innkeeper rubs his hands over his well-rounded shape and they all laugh.

"I hope your brothers are as convincing when they hand him over to the ship's captain." Matthew looks at Violet with an expression that warns it's not over yet.

"So do I. I hope they don't meet any real officers en route as well, 'cus that'd really put the cat among the pigeons," says Violet, still worried.

Her father comes up behind her, "Don't you

283

worry about those boys, they can look after themselves. They've faced enough officials in the past and always managed to pull the wool over their eyes. Those Kimberlins are no match for my boys, rest assured."

Violet hugs both fathers, "Thank you both of you, and you too Thomas, you were all wonderful."

"You weren't so b-b-bad yourself, Missus," he stammers self-consciously. "He were quite a nasty p-p-piece of work that sailor. Took a lot o' p-p-pluck to face him like you d-d-did."

"I couldn't have done it without knowing you were all there to help if he got violent. But, thank God, it's all sorted out at last. I feel so relieved it's over."

She puts her arm through Matthew's, "Let's go back to Ma's to wait for the boys."

They have not been back at the cottage in Brandy Row for long before the boys come home jubilant. It had gone like clockwork. The ship's captain was easily duped and they had left him chastising the man.

On their return they exchanged the uniforms for their own clothes, in the alleyway at the back of the Castle Inn. This meant that they did not risk passing the castle garrison twice, and their mother who met them there returned the uniforms to the fort in her delivery sack with the rest of their order.

"It went like a dream, Matt. You should have seen the poor sod. He looked that dejected. The captain looked at him as if he was a troublemaker anyway, so I wouldn't want to be in his shoes for the next few months."

"Ma took the uniforms back to the fort. 'Twere a bit of luck still having those alterations. If our Ma hadn't had that other order for the rector she'd have returned them and it would have been too late."

"Well, it just goes to show that when families stick together, problems are so much easier to solve." Violet smiles, "Thank you so much for helping. God knows how many times he might have come back for more and more each time. You have made it possible for me to sleep easy again and I am so grateful."

"Of course we'd help you, Violet, no Kimberlin ain't getting the better of we." Tom obviously speaks for all three brothers for they are nodding their heads in agreement. "Just give us a shout and we'll be ready any time to lend a hand," concludes Ted.

Violet puts the kettle on the fire to boil, and by the time the tea is brewed her mother is back home and all are able to relax completely once more.

Violet hugs her mother; it brings back memories of old times. She sits with her on the settle and they drink their tea, and Violet tells her of their plans for the shop before the sailor turned up and put everything in jeopardy. She fears that she is too late to go ahead with them now, but nevertheless they must all keep their fingers crossed.

When Matthew approaches Miss Bennett with the offer of a cash sale as soon as possible, she is delighted.

"I couldn't wish for no one better to take over me little shop than your Missus, young fellow. She's as bright as a button, that one, and I'm sure 'twill suit her needs just perfect."

"I am sure you're right, Miss Bennett, but we were concerned that someone else might also be interested."

"No, Sir. I've not had any other enquiries, and I

am prepared to accept your offer of the askin' price here and now. Like I said to your wife, I am in haste to join me new hubby in Cornwall and 'tis good news to me that I've a buyer so soon."

Matthew looks around him and is impressed with the place. "I am very pleased for you, Miss Bennett, we are obviously both eager to get the matter sorted. If you could arrange a meeting with your legal agent as soon as possible, we can set the wheels in motion." He holds out his hand to her. "I'll look forward to hearing from you; you have my card?"

"Yes, my dear, don't thee fret, I'm as eager as you to get things settled. I'll be seeing thee shortly. Goodbye now." She shakes his hand cheerfully, and he sets off to tell Violet the news.

Within a fortnight Miss Bennett has moved out and the place is theirs. Violet and Molly really have their work cut out. Violet has decided to keep the shop open and overnight she has dressed the window just as she had imagined. Matthew has brought all her sewing equipment up to the back room, which has been cleaned in readiness, and it is arranged that Hannah should serve the customers, whilst Violet does the fittings. Molly is the first customer, because together they are making all the wedding dresses.

When the shop opens the following day it takes everyone completely by surprise. Regular customers are astounded to see the transformation, and as the news travels by word of mouth many curious ladies make incidental purchases as an excuse for finding out 'what that Violet Allen is up to now'. The business does very well because of this and soon the orders are pouring in. Molly is quick to learn; she has not had much opportunity to practise her skills with the needle but, with Violet doing the more tricky parts, her trousseau is coming together nicely.

Matthew surprises Violet with a new sign to go above the door, dated 1844 and naming his wife as proprietor; he has in bold letters painted 'Fortunes Corner' across it.

Violet is that proud as she watches him fixing it in place, "What a good name, Matty, I hope it bodes well for us." Then she notices the carefully hand-painted violets. "How lovely, you are clever and so thoughtful."

"I cannot take credit for the flowers, 'twas Josh suggested that, but they look nice don't you think?"

"I think they are very dainty, and you are more clever than I ever thought: 'Fortunes Corner, Fortunes Well'. It does have a jolly ring to it, doesn't it?"

He hugs her affectionately, "I thought so, but I suppose I had better get back to work and see if I cannot make my own fortune. I can't be having folks saying I'm a kept man."

"They'd never dare, Matthew Stone, and you know it." She laughs, and they part until supper-time.

Molly's wedding is a great success. The joining of a Top o' hill man and an Underhill girl would previously have been frowned upon, but it is a sign of the times that such an obstacle has eventually been overcome. The wedding feast has been prepared by John's parents in the garden of their farmhouse, and after the ceremony everyone assembles there for the festivities.

Violet's mother is chatting quietly to Violet. "I must say, Molly has more guests at her wedding than I have ever seen before."

"Well, John is a Pearce and it is the largest clan on the island and John's branch of the family is one of the more prosperous."

"By Portland standards I would say that this is a society wedding."

"Mmm, I think it is." Violet lowers her voice. "I have heard that there are more gold sovereigns under the mattresses in Southwell than anywhere else in Britain."

Mary Allen laughs, "I can well believe it to see the evidence here today. The wedding feast is like a banquet, and all the guests dressed in their finery make a grand sight."

"It is a wonderful opportunity for us to promote our business. I have overheard Molly on several occasions telling people that her trousseau has all been made by 'Fortunes Corner', and she has already introduced me to some people who have made enquiries."

"That is wonderful, Vi, but I am not surprised. Molly looks gorgeous in her beautiful gown and the handmaidens all look stunning, especially little Becky who looks such a pretty little poppet in that outfit."

"I know, I am so proud of both of them. Josh is looking so grown up and he is being so helpful going around all the guests offering them top-ups of drink."

Matthew joins them with a glass of mead for each of them. "Have you seen all the gifts piled up and laid out on display over there?"

"I know, it is amazing, and I am so pleased for Molly. She has not had an easy life, and she deserves a great big helping of happiness at last."

Matthew brims with pride as he stands back with a pint of ale after all the speeches are over. He looks first at Rebecca, his small bundle of joy; she is the smallest handmaiden, and looks a picture in her new frock, her hair a mass of curly ringlets, and she is hopping and skipping, exposing layers of handmade lace and ribbon. Then he observes young Joshua, a tall, handsome young lad just turned eleven and yet confidently chatting to all the guests. Then he finally looks at Violet who is decidedly the most beautiful woman there. He knows that she is on the brink of a very successful business venture and that this wedding is just about the best publicity anyone could wish for. He has given Violet this opportunity and it gives him so much pleasure to see how happy he has made her.

He puts his arm around Violet, "At this moment I am probably the proudest man alive."

CHAPTER 16 *(May 1847 – December 1848)*

LEG IRONS AND HEARTSTRINGS

Preliminary work for the breakwater has already started when one morning in May 1847, Matthew comes home with the news of the Royal Assent to the Act of Parliament.

"Several cottages have to be demolished at Castletown and a gravity railway is to be constructed down the cliff side from the Grove."

"What about the folk who live in the cottages? What's to become of them?" asks Violet.

"They will all be rehoused, Violet, within the month I reckon, because the work is supposed to begin in August."

"I doubt they'll be pleased. Those folk have lived up there for years and they had a lovely view of the coastline and the harbour. 'Tis a shame they could not have found a different route."

"It would have been too costly though," says Matthew.

"I thought as much, money has to come before people these days."

Matthew makes no reply.

By November, railway contractors are employing five hundred and fifty men, constructing not only the new incline but also a railway, to link the piers and jetties at Castletown and the high-level construction railway near the top of Verne Hill.

Whilst the rest of Britain struggles through a decade of famine, poverty and hardship the Portlanders have their own period of prosperity. Workers are now arriving daily from all parts of the country.

"I didn't think it would be this crazy," says Matthew one night after attending a Court Leet meeting. "So much traffic is now using the ferry bridge that it already needs strengthening."

"I knew there'd be problems with all these newcomers," says Violet. "There's been a dreadful increase in cases of drunkenness, assault and indecent behaviour. There was a day when no one locked their doors at night and the children had the freedom of the island," she complains begrudgingly. "That government has a lot to answer for, altering our lives with their big plans."

Matthew sighs. "Our children still enjoy the freedom of the island, Vi. You cannot be watching over them the whole time. Anyway, my love, where would we be without the trade?"

"I can see that it's good for trade, Matty, and I am grateful for that, because the shop is doing really well."

"Well, there you are then; it is already good for our family." He looks at her worried expression and cannot help feeling guilty. "I know, sweetheart, that as a member of the Court Leet you think that I am partly responsible, but it was the decision of the committee."

"Matty, I realise that you and the other members have invested a great deal of your time preparing for the hard negotiations with the government over the purchase of Verne Hill, and I know that you protected, as best you could, the interests of all of us islanders. But you know as well as I do that I am not alone. There have been several mass meetings of folk concerned for their ancient rights. I know you feel that change is inevitable, but like the rest I cannot help my fears.

"I think we got a fair deal in the end. The sum of twenty thousand pounds in compensation has been agreed upon and for the prosperity of this island I think it is worth putting up with a few more Kimberlins. Compared with the rest of Britain we are doing very well on Portland.

Violet is not convinced and her look of concern is evident. She is very proud and protective of her island home and cannot help but comment, "But Matty 'tis the riff-raff that bother me."

He sits down beside her. "Most of them are just farm labourers, who because of the enclosures are unable to graze their animals on the common land, or get bedding, fuel or even catch the odd bit of game anymore. The majority are not riff-raff, love. They're honest workers like you and me, reduced to the brink of starvation and forced to leave their families and travel to where the work is."

"But there are so many, we can't build the homes quickly enough."

"Well, there is so much labour needed in the quarries, and with the plans for construction of the breakwater, the prison and all the homes needed for the staff, we should be glad, for without their labour these tasks would never be completed."

Joshua and Rebecca finish their card game and, preparing to go to bed, come to kiss their parents goodnight.

"Well, I cannot be glad when I'm too afraid to allow the children the same liberty that we enjoyed when we were small. But you're right; we can't do anything about it now so we must make the best of it. I just can't help regretting that Josh and Becky will never feel that special way about Portland that you and I did as children; like we were one big family."

Joshua kisses his mother goodnight. "Ma, I am no longer a child, I am fifteen years old and although I love this island I do not intend to stay here for the rest of my life. I intend one day to join a ship and go to sea."

Rebecca is about to kiss her father but stops still, staring at her brother in horror at what she has just heard.

Matthew is dismissive, not taking Joshua seriously. "We will see, Josh, but you have to finish your apprenticeship with me first and get some money behind you before cooking up some hair-brained scheme."

Violet sees Rebecca's reaction and knows that she too is afraid he will go. Rebecca kisses her father and goes to her mother, and Violet can see there are tears in her eyes.

Violet whispers to her, "Don't worry, Becky, we will persuade him not to go somehow." They kiss. "Goodnight both of you."

By the autumn of 1848, with Christmas fast approaching, Violet is doing brisk business. All the wives are busy making gifts for their families and it is to 'Fortune's Corner' that they come to buy their raw materials. Husbands and sweethearts come to purchase pretty knick-knacks and wealthier clients order new costumes for their loved ones.

Violet is now employing outworkers in addition to members of her own family. She is kept so busy she barely has any time at all to spend with her children. Nevertheless she notices that whilst Joshua is working with Matthew, Rebecca is lonely. She tries hard to occupy the hours helping Auntie Sarah, who is getting too old for traipsing up over Lankridge, and enjoys teaching her the healing properties of the plants that she gathers and how to mix the cures and potions. She helps her mother too, on warm sunny days, taking the washing and laying it out on the beach to dry, collecting the seaweed and shen for fuel and gathering arrowroot and starchmoor to sell to the Weymouth shops. But all the time she dwells on the hurt that Josh and Ben no longer want to make time for her and the fear that Joshua will one day leave them and go off to sea.

One mellow autumn evening she decides to visit Auntie Molly on the farm. As she walks up over the rise she mulls over the many happy hours she has spent with Josh and Ben playing tag and hide-and-seek and picnicking up on the common. She wants to talk to Molly about Josh. About how no one but her seems to notice how discontented he really is. That even though she is kept so busy she can see what her parents cannot. How he is expected to earn his own living now and it is assumed that he will be satisfied in the boat yard, working alongside Matthew. But she can see his reluctance in the droop of his shoulders and the lack of sparkle in his eyes. And one day, she is sure, he will just up and go.

When she reaches the farm there is a pony and trap in the yard. Auntie Molly is obviously entertaining guests. Disappointed, she turns around and wanders aimlessly towards home. She feels let down not being able to confide in her. It would have been so good to unburden and share her fears about Josh with Molly, she is so easy to talk to. Everyone else seems so content and busy with their lives. Why does she feel so lonely and wretched?

A week later, whilst on an errand for her mother at

the chandler's in Castletown, she notices through the shop window her brother sauntering along in the company of some sailors. He is soon out of view and by the time she has completed her purchases and stepped out into the open he is lost to sight. She is filled with curiosity, for surely he should be in the boat yard? She hurries home but does not encounter him until late that night, when she asks who the sailors were.

"They're just some fellows I met on the quayside yesterday, but they've such stories as 'ud set your hair on end. I were that taken with their tall tales I forgot the time."

"They looked to me to be very drabby scoundrels."

"Well, they've seen more life in their two years at sea than anyone could manage in a whole lifetime stuck here on this poxy island."

"How can you say that, Josh? 'Tis beautiful and wild and free. I could not bear to be stuck for days on a stinking ship, with those loathsome louts for my only company." She is scornful of Joshua's dreams, certain that the ocean is not bluer on the other side of the globe and determined to convince her brother that this is the case.

"They have just returned from a trip across the China seas, and were chased for miles by a pirate ship, until they turned and fired a shot across her bows ripping out her topsail and splitting her mast in two. Just imagine it!"

"But Josh, it wouldn't be like that at all, you might be killed and eaten by cannibals," she says in frustration. "The ship might be caught in a terrible storm and sink, we have seen the horror of that enough times ... you could die of starvation afloat in a life-raft ... or catch some mortal disease; or ... or you could be captured by pirates or the press gangs." The more she thinks about it the more dramatic she becomes and the more Joshua laughs.

"You little coward." He sits down near her, "Becky, there's a magical world out there; sun-soaked beaches and dusky maidens, new sights and sounds and smells, and real people with so much blood coursing through their veins, what do they care if they spill a little on the way? Life is to be lived, not endured. I want more out of life than the day-to-day routine, just existing to make ends meet. I want money in my pocket, stories to relate … a life to be proud of. So that when I die, I will be known throughout the world; many people and places will remember me and I will be rich in those memories too."

She sits wide-eyed, on the edge of his bed. He is going to do it sooner or later and she will be left desperately lonely. Her parents are so busy they've no time for her. How can she stop this? Whatever is she going to do? "Josh, please don't leave me." She tries to swallow the lump in her throat. "I couldn't bear to be left here all alone." But she beseeches him to no avail.

"Come now, you couldn't possibly be that lonely left here with all our family, friends and neighbours."

"But everyone is always so busy."

"You know Ben would always make time for you, I would ask him to take special care of you if I did decide to go. But I haven't decided yet, so don't think any more about it."

Rebecca thinks sadly how little time Ben has spare to spend with her. "You know it could never be the same between me and Ben as it is with you, Josh. I could never tell him all my fears and troubles." She is sure that her problems would be laughed off by Ben, who seems to have not a care in the world.

"Have no fear, 'tis just my wild imaginings. They'd never take me on anyway. I've no experience and their next trip is around Cape Horn, which is known to be fearful dangerous."

"Oh Josh, you are cruel. 'Tis so unfair of you to worry me so, I believe you do it on purpose just to vex me."

"Hush thy fretting, Becky; you know I'm all talk. Come now, 'tis nigh ten of the clock, we must go to bed."

"I shan't sleep, and 'tis all your fault."

"Don't make me feel guilty, Becky; I cannot help this restlessness I feel."

"Then you should talk to Ma and Pa."

"They wouldn't understand. But I'm not happy here, you know that. Anyway there's no point because it will be ages before I can do anything about it."

"I hope so, Josh." She kisses him goodnight, saying, "Night-night, sweet dreams," and then she leaves him to his fanciful notions.

Several days pass while, unbeknown to his family, Joshua spends considerable time with his new sailor friends who are enjoying their leave of absence. Having been late for supper on two occasions that week, it comes as no great shock when one night he doesn't come in for his meal. As the evening wears on and there is still no sign of him the family begins to worry.

"I don't know what has got into Josh, he never used to be this thoughtless," grumbles Violet.

"I have seen him with those sailors in Castletown. I expect he is with them again. I am so afraid he is planning to go off with them to sea," confides Rebecca.

"Surely he wouldn't want to leave his family and all he has here to go off to God knows where, risking his life for unknown pleasures and certain danger?"

"But he seemed so excited talking of the tall tales those sailors have been telling him."

Matthew is pragmatic. "'Tis no use us speculating. The lad is growing up. He has to find his feet sometime and we have to be prepared to let him do so."

Finally they go to bed, leaving him free to come home when he is ready. When the following day dawns, his bed has not been slept in and there is no sign of him, and they all become more concerned. Matthew sets off to make enquiries on the quay.

Several hours have passed when a young lad knocks at their front door and hands over a note. Violet's hands shake as she tears open the envelope, with Rebecca standing nervously at her side.

The note explains how he has gone as a deck-hand on the Methodist Missionary Brig bound out with missionaries to New Guinea with Captain Buck. She sailed out of Portland Roads the previous evening and is now well on her way. It is full of apologies for not telling them his plans, but he knew they would have tried to stop him. There is a special message to Rebecca, telling her chin up and it won't be long before he returns with amazing tales to tell.

Violet slumps into the nearest chair and Rebecca fetches her mother a drink. When the reality of what has so suddenly happened gradually dawns on Violet she begins to shake uncontrollably.

Rebecca tries to console her even though she is feeling just as devastated. Eventually Violet recovers some composure and instructs Rebecca to go and find her father and tell him the tidings.

For days afterwards the family mourns the

sudden absence of their son and brother, until finally Matthew decides enough is enough. One evening after an almost silent supper he says, "Right, I've got something to say to both of you. I know 'twas a terrible blow to find Josh had gone off like he did, but there hasn't been a death and it don't do no good for all of us to be miserable. We got our lives to lead and 'tis no use worrying over things we can do nought about. 'Tis time we let Josh worry about himself and we to sorting out our own as best we can. So let's be having a happy household once again. I'm fed up with the miserable faces that greet me. I want to see my happy, smiling ladies again. How about it?"

Rebecca goes to her father and sits on his knee, "I'm sorry, Papa, I just miss him so. I will try to be more cheerful, I truly will." She smiles a watery smile at him and gives him a hug.

"That's better, I do not like to be seeing you both sorried so."

"It's not his leaving that troubles me though, Matty, 'tis the thought of him never coming back to us," says Violet despondently.

"Why, you sillies, the lad has the sea in his blood. No harm'll come to him, you mark my words. Besides, doesn't he have the prettiest sister and the loveliest mother in the whole wide world to come home to? He'll be back, like he says, with tales to tell us and all the other folks hereabouts. You'll both be proud of him. He's on the Missionary ship, isn't he? Taking Christianity to the heathens, he is doing something that is meaningful and 'tis what he wanted."

"'Tis true, he is on a good ship with good Christian values. I couldn't have chosen better myself if I'd a mind." This thought slightly reduces the furrows in Violet's brow.

"Well then, there you are. What is there to worry about? God will be keeping his eye on that vessel, and you don't get higher command than that." Matthew chuckles, and they all start to laugh.

"Oh, Matty. What would we do without you?" laughs Violet.

Matthew ends up with a girl on each knee, relieved that he has managed at last to disperse the mist of pessimism that has hung over the household since Joshua left them.

Rebecca is just beginning to get over her disappointment and loneliness when something else happens to disturb her peace of mind. She is on the beach one rather dismal December morning, collecting up the seaweed that had been washed ashore the night before, when she notices unusual activity about half a mile along the otherwise deserted beach. Curiously she makes her way along in that direction to see if she can make out what the commotion is about. A ship is anchored in Dead Man's Bay and as she draws nearer she can see a flotilla of rafts are landing men onto the great beach, where they stand strangely huddled together in small groups.

She approaches warily until she realises with dismay that it is a consignment of transports. She freezes to the spot, unable to move, terrified even of running away; she cannot turn her back on them, nor can she take her eyes off them. Their guards have flails, which they use on the men to move them forward when they have all disembarked. Shouting words of abuse and pushing and shoving the slowest along, the pathetic convoy struggles towards her. The convicts look half-starved, they walk barefoot with torn and dirty clothes, their ankles bruised and bleeding from the leg irons as they struggle against each other, helplessly trying to find a footing among the shifting pebbles. They look like skeletons. Their heads have been shaved and their thin, hungry faces individually are pitiful, but collectively, eerie and macabre. Eventually they cross over the rise of the beach and are soon out of sight.

Rebecca takes flight. She had heard that the first transports arrived a week ago, but she had no idea they would look so sinister. Thinking that she will never again rest safe in her bed, she runs until she has a pain in her side and a burning feeling in her lungs. When she reaches the first cottages she pauses to catch her breath, and only then does she notice Ben trying to unravel a mess of nets. She approaches him nervously and sits down onto an upturned lerret. She is still panting but the burning feeling is easing now.

He glances up to see who it is and smiles to see Josh's little sister. "Well, this is a surprise. I haven't seen you, Becky, since your Josh went off to seek his fortune."

"I've been very busy helping me Ma, but I do miss him so, Ben." Her voice trembles, "I have just had a terrible fright and no one to comfort me at all." Then she bursts into tears, which completely baffles Ben. He stands quite still, with the netting hanging limp in his hands. He lets it slip to the ground and goes and sits down next to her. "Whatever happened?" he asks, looking at her gently.

"Did you not see the transports?" she mutters between sobs. "There must have been nigh on two hundred of them."

"No, I've not been here long, but they can't do you any harm." He puts his arm round her. "They're always chained together and they'll have an armed guard."

"I know, Ben, but they looked so terrible. I was that scared I nearly wet my breeches."

"Oh dear," Ben laughs, "surely not."

She manages to laugh too, "No, but you know what I mean." She wipes away the tears with the back of her hand.

"Yes, well, 'tis natural that you should be scared; they are criminals and vagabonds, but you do know, really, that they are kept well and truly under lock and key and cannot possibly escape."

He sounds so grown up for his sixteen years and Rebecca is comforted and reassured. "I suppose so, but I didn't expect to see them on our side of the beach. I thought they'd all be landed on the stone quay."

"So did I," agrees Ben. "They must have travelled from the West Country, from Dartmoor or somewhere."

"Why do they have to come to our island, out of all the places in the world?"

"Because we have built the strongest prison fortress out of our magnificent white stone; where else would they choose?" he asks with pride. "Besides it being a very secure jail, it is also ideally situated for the transport ships to Australia. Whatever the reason, you must not fret, for they cannot possibly harm you. The way they will be kept in chains, freedom for them is out of the question."

"I suppose you're right. Anyway, thank you for trying to cheer me up. I do feel much better now, Ben." She smiles up at him, thinking how kind and thoughtful he is.

"I tell you what, Becky. I will stand in for your Josh while he's gone and any time you need a friendly ear, you just come and see me."

She could not have asked for more. "I would like that, Ben, I do miss him so."

They both sit quietly for a while, then Rebecca turns to him and, with eyes still a little tearful, she asks sweetly, "Would you mind walking a piece with me, up to Brandy Row? I do still feel a bit shaken."

It was artful of her, but although Ben may have thought her a crafty little maid he obliges her all the same, and taking her arm in his he escorts her to her grandmother's home. Maybe such a dreadful shock has been worth it after all.

When Violet comes home at the end of her working day, Rebecca immediately tells her of her experience. That night Matthew has to bar all the doors and windows and make sure all is safe before the women will rest easy in their beds.

CHAPTER 17 *(December 1848 – July 1849)*

BEN'S APPRENTICESHIP

As the backlog of work accumulates in his yard, Matthew is working much longer hours and his tiredness is beginning to show. One night he groans as he lowers himself into his fireside chair and Violet is immediately concerned.

"You are overdoing it in that yard of yours, Matthew. You are going to have to slow down or you'll be ill."

"I can't let the blokes down, Vi, we are talking about their livelihoods."

"But if you cannot keep up with the work they may get tired of waiting and find someone else."

"Well, luckily for me at the moment there is no one else."

"But that is not lucky for them, is it? Perhaps you should employ an apprentice." Violet sees the relief in Matthew's eyes and realises then that it was for her he had been struggling on.

"I was afraid that you would want the job left open in case of Joshua's sudden return, but the help of a good, strong lad would be invaluable."

"My main concern is that you don't overwork yourself, my love. I know it will be at least two years before we see our Josh again."

"Well, if you really don't object, it would be a great load off my mind."

Rebecca, who is doing the dishes, overhears the conversation and it saddens her to think that her brother's absence has taken on a look of permanence. She confides her feelings to Ben later that week, and is surprised that he feels so strongly on the matter.

"'Tis no use keeping a job for a man who doesn't want it, not when there's so many around that would give their eye-teeth for the chance of a wage in these troubled times."

"I suppose you are right. I hadn't thought of it like that."

"Becky, you don't know how lucky you are having both your Ma and Pa bringing in money and only you to provide for. How do you think my Ma gets on with all of us to feed and Christmas nearly upon us? Things are even worse on the mainland; people are starving for want of a decent diet. If I was offered an apprenticeship, especially with Matthew, I tell you, I'd jump at it."

Rebecca thinks for a moment. Why not? Ben would be the perfect choice. She cannot believe that she has not considered this before. She must find her father immediately. She picks up her bundle of driftwood and says, "I had better be going, Ben. Ma wants me to decorate our Christmas cake this afternoon."

Ben thoughtfully continues with his work, later going on to the Cove House Inn for a ploughman's and a yarn with the rest of the menfolk who have time on their hands.

On Christmas Eve, Matthew approaches Ben with the offer of the job. "Can I have a quick word with you, Ben?"

"Of course, Mr Stone, how can I help you?"

"Would you like to join me in a pint of ale?"

"I would be very happy with a pint of ale. Thank you, Mr Stone."

Matthew pays for two pints of ale and he and Ben sit at a fireside table. "As you know, our Josh has gone off to seek his fortune and it has rather left me short-handed at work in the boathouse, and I was wondering if you might be interested in an apprenticeship with me?"

"Are you serious?" Ben looks incredulous.

"Of course I am." Matthew studies Ben's reaction. "What do you think?"

"I think it is the best Christmas box I could have wished for and I am so happy to accept your kind offer. I am a hard worker and I am very keen to learn. I will be a good investment for your business, I promise you, Mr Stone."

"I think we can dispense with 'Mr Stone' if we are going to be working together, Ben, it is Matthew from now on. Let's shake on it." They shake hands to seal the deal.

Later that evening after they have eaten, Ben is sitting on the rug beside Annie. Now is the moment to tell her his news. He whispers, "Ma, I have got something important to tell you." Annie looks down at him. "What is it? Are you in trouble?"

"No, no, 'tis nothing like that, Ma." Ben laughs, "'Tis good news, not bad."

"Well, let's be hearing it then, don't keep us in suspense." Enthusiastically, Annie leans forward in the rocker.

"I have been offered an apprenticeship by Matthew Stone." He can see that his mother is quite stunned by his words and, as she slowly sits back in the chair, Ben waits guardedly for her reaction.

Then she puts out her hand and squeezes his arm. Quietly, she says, "That's wonderful news,

Ben. I am so proud of you. You just show them that you're as good as anyone hereabouts and that'll be the best gift you could ever give me."

He knows that his mother wouldn't want him to take charity from anyone, but he is sure he has been chosen because he is the best man for the job, and he hopes that he has given her reason to be proud.

"I know a few tricks of the trade just from keeping my eyes open and watching the other men. I already do my own small repair jobs, but it is the actual building, construction and design that fascinate me, and I am very keen to learn."

"It will do you good Ben to have another string to your bow. There is not much fishing until May now and my brothers can handle that. Anyway, you can always go out in the evenings to keep your hand in when you have finished working with Matthew if you want to."

"It is such a pity that I didn't have the work earlier, because I would have loved to buy you a really special present this year, but all our money always has to go on essentials."

"Don't you worry about that, son. I don't need anything from you. It is enough for me just to have you near. I am so glad that you didn't take it into your head to go traipsing off around the world like that Josh."

The following day they exchange presents.

Ben has struggled to save up enough to buy a new smoothing iron for his mother. He has wrapped it up and tied it with ribbon and now he passes it to her and he watches as she opens it.

He is rewarded by her pleasure and gratitude.

"I hope you like it, Ma. I know the handle kept working loose on your old one and ever since I was there that time when the bottom of it dropped off onto the floor and only just missed your foot, I've been determined to save up enough to buy you a nice new one."

"That is just what I needed, thank you so much, son." Annie gives her son a kiss and then passes him her present. She has knitted him a beautiful, warm jersey and he opens his gift enthusiastically.

"Thanks, Ma, that's just the job." Ben tries it on, "Look at that, a perfect fit."

They watch quietly as everyone else exchanges their presents. After they have all enjoyed their Christmas dinner, Annie uncorks the sherry wine and as they sit together with his aunts and uncles around a huge fire, Ben feels a warm glow in his heart. It will soon be 1849, and the New Year, he feels sure, is going to be a good one. Things are looking up for them at last. Maybe it is their turn to taste the sweetmeats in life. If so, he is eager for his mother to get her fair share.

Ben settles down to his new work quickly and Matthew is content with his choice. They work together well and as the months pass by, become good friends.

Annie's two sisters, May and Janey, start walking out with Jack and Sam Angel, and coincidentally, her brother Henry also begins to dress up for someone.

"What are you getting all togged up for?" asks Ben.

"Wouldn't you like to know."

"Come on Henry, what is the big secret?"

"'Tis none of your business, Ben."

Henry is not prepared to divulge who this person is and Ben becomes determined to find out the identity of the mystery lady. On several occasions he tries to follow him, but somehow Henry always manages to evade him. Until one evening in September when he sees him enter a tiny cottage in Mallams. It is getting 'dumpsy' and as Ben approaches a lamp is lit in a downstairs room. Through a gap in the curtains Ben can just see his uncle and someone who could definitely not be described as a young lady.

She is wearing only a black basque top and lacy red pantalets decorated with black lace and ribbons. Ben's jaw drops in absolute amazement. He has never seen anything like it before in his life, and to his surprise his uncle seems quite at home there in her rather ostentatious parlour. The woman starts to unbutton Henry's clothes and Ben begins to feel decidedly uncomfortable lest he be caught in the act of peeping. However, he cannot somehow tear himself away. The scene enacted before him is having a marked effect on his physical well-being and curiosity gets the better of him.

He stands transfixed; his muscles tense as, impatiently, he watches the woman slowly and seductively remove Henry's top clothes, her hands moving stealthily over his body, sliding down towards his private parts. He can see his uncle's frustration as he tries to kiss her, but she teasingly turns her face away. He kisses her exposed breasts, his tongue searching for her nipple. Then she leads him to a point just out of range of the gap in the curtain.

Ben does not know what to do with himself. He looks around surreptitiously in case he has been seen, but the coast is clear, and he wanders off alone to suffer in silence. When his swollen masculinity has finally lost its potency, he aimlessly wanders in the direction of the Cove House. He has never had reason to be envious of anyone, but now he feels that maybe he knows what is missing in his life.

Skipper greets him as he enters and his Auntie May, who took over as barmaid when Molly left to be married, serves him a pint of ale. He joins Janey and the two Angel brothers at a table near the fire.

Their casual conversation does not interest him and he sits slightly apart, looking around the room at the different characters and trying to picture them with their spouses doing what he has just witnessed. It is an impossible task and he finds himself grinning when his eyes alight on old Jabe Stone, who has hardly any teeth left. He can picture him with a gummy mouthful of his companion, Fat Ginny, who got her name from her favourite tipple.

Janey notices his broad grin and asks him what is on his mind.

"Can't be telling," says he with an even broader grin, which deepens the indentations that exaggerate his warm smile.

This intrigues the friends and they all look enquiringly at him, which makes him grin all the more. If they only knew what had triggered his thoughts. He can still picture Henry, and is amused to wonder what they would think if they could only read his mind. At that moment the outer door swings open and in walks Henry. Ben jumps up and is ordering two pints at the bar before his uncle has a chance to open his mouth. He thrusts one towards an astonished Henry and, patting him on the back, asks with a conspiratorial wink, "Had a good time then?"

Henry eyes him suspiciously, and glances down to ensure there is no tell-tale sign.

"Why? What's it to you?" he demands defensively.

Ben keeps his voice down, and with an air of confidentiality he continues, wickedly enjoying Henry's discomfiture. "I just wondered if it was as much fun as it looked?"

Henry, somewhat abashed at the thought that he's been spied upon, decides to play his own game with Ben. "Now, we're talking man to man here, aren't we? 'Twill go no further?"

"I swear 'twill stay with me to my death," says Ben, dramatically.

Although Ben is sending up the seriousness of the matter, Henry knows that fun is fun but sex is something else. He doesn't know exactly what his nephew has seen but he knows he has seen enough to arouse his curiosity. It is obvious that Ben has not yet broken his seal of boyhood and is eager to taste the wine of Eve's apple.

"I'll tell thee something, what you saw was nothing." He takes Ben away into a small corner of the room and they sit down on a bench and rest their glasses on an upturned barrel. "The other night she had her sisters with her, and you'm never come across such obliging wenches. What they'll do for a florin you wouldn't believe."

Ben's vivid imagination causes something to stir in his breeches, but he maintains his grin all the same. "What do you mean?" he says, beginning to feel decidedly uncomfortable but nevertheless eager to hear more.

Henry winks and knocks his nose with his forefinger. "You just wait and see. I'll arrange everything for you. 'Tis your seventeenth birthday coming up soon, isn't it?" Henry looks smug as the silly grin is wiped from Ben's face.

The birthday surprise is something he would prefer to forget, but however embarrassing his initiation may have been, the cottage in Mallams becomes the source of his further education. He is a zealous pupil and with hearty and persistent endeavour, becomes the most popular student in the establishment, his voluptuous instructors vying with each other for the opportunity to be the one with whom he might put in most of his practice. In short, he is very soon their star pupil.

Ben laps up the flirtatiousness of one, the coquetry of the other, the wantonness of the third and the passionate rivalry that develops between them. He is tantalised and bedazzled. The cottage in Mallams has bewitched him. Its allure cannot be denied.

Eventually, Annie overhears Henry and Tom discussing young Ben in a ribald, smutty way. She listens further and soon realises what is going on at that whorehouse in Mallams.

"Seems Ben's already completely obsessed, he cannot keep away from the place now. He is up there every night."

Tom chuckles, "I don't blame him, that Lily's a right little mover."

"I know, but according to him it seems they are all after him. He can take his pick."

"So I hear. Sadie was telling me he had all three of them the other night. No wonder he is bewitched."

Tom and Henry both burst out laughing loudly. Annie is flabbergasted. She has always wanted him to grow up and be respected as a proper gentleman, just like his father. She can tell by their comments and amusement that her brothers have had something to do with it. Angrily she bursts in on them.

"I haven't worked my fingers to the bone to bring you lot up decent just so as you can go and catch summat from a filthy whorehouse." Her eyes flash fury at them. "How dare you encourage my son to go to that den of iniquity?" The brothers stand aghast at her outburst.

"Well, don't just stand there. What are you going to do about it?"

"There ain't nothing you can do about it now, Annie. Now he's tasted it, he's well and truly hooked," says Henry, frankly. Tom sniggers.

"Bosh!" shouts Annie, and as she yells at him she flicks him sharply round the head with the cloth she has in her hand. She is furious. "You stupid men make me that mad, duped by a bunch of harlots that have served half the sailors in the Roads."

The brothers look sheepish.

"You two are old enough to know better; you both know damn well that those places are to entertain Kimberlins, not our own island folk. 'Tis been proved time and time again that Kimberlins don't honour our women. That's why that place in Mallams has been allowed to stay unchallenged, and you know it."

She paces the room, angrily filling it with her fury, and taking a deep breath she turns on them and demands, "You will not go to that place in Mallams again, not if you want me to housekeep for you; and when Ben asks you why, you will tell him that you have been told that one of the girls is diseased but you don't know which one."

"Come on, Annie, it's not that bad," protests Henry.

"How do you know?" asks Annie with emphasis on each word. "They have been with men, who in their turn have been with women in brothels all over the world."

A sudden chill of fear runs down Henry's spine. He knows that what Annie is saying could well be true. Why, he's even heard that kings have gone mad because of such diseases. He decides that he ought to reassure poor Annie. "All right, Annie. I'll tell Ben what you say. 'Tis up to me to put things right, it weren't anything to do with our Tom."

Annie, although relieved that things are going her way, still cuffs him round the ear for being the culprit. Henry takes it like a man and then grins at her, glad the interrogation is over. "I still think you worry too much … but," he adds, before Annie hits him again, "better to be safe than sorry."

Tom, who has remained silent through most of this, breathes a sigh of relief and goes off about his business, a bit miffed to be caught in the crossfire; but he supposes it serves him right, for he had been having a good laugh at the escapades that Henry described involving young Ben.

Whilst Ben struggles into maturity, Rebecca has been enjoying the more innocent pastimes of others her age, but the most important event that year is the laying of the foundation stone for the Breakwater by His Royal Highness Prince Albert on 29th July 1849. Everyone is saying that the start of the breakwater is a momentous event in their history and Rebecca has persuaded Ben to go with her to witness the ceremony.

At the appointed time Prince Albert and the other dignitaries assemble on a large platform specially erected for the occasion. Ben, Rebecca and some other children have sneaked under the platform for a better view, and there, perched precariously on the rocks, they listen to the speeches.

As the ceremony is concluded, the stone is released through an aperture in the platform, plunging into the sea beneath and sending up a fountain of spray. Rebecca's heart skips a beat as she loses her footing and slips. She nearly slides into the deep water as the huge wave swamps them, but she grabs hold of Ben. They both scream as they are drenched to the skin. Her heart pounds as he pulls her back onto the rock and holds her tightly. It is bliss. She looks up into his face and for a moment she thinks he is about to kiss her. Then he lets her go.

Her wet frock clings about her and she shivers, conscious of her figure outlined by the damp material, her nipples pert and tingling with the cold. Embarrassed, she folds her arms, feeling naked before him.

Ben clears his throat. "Are you all right, Becky? I thought we'd nearly lost you for a moment there." He smiles, but there is concern too in his eyes.

"I'm fine, thanks to you, Ben. Luckily I just grazed my ankle, that's all." She bends down and rubs where the skin is sore, but elation surges through her. He is wonderful and he cares about her. For a second she is sure he had been tempted to kiss her. What does she care if her dress is wet? It will soon dry when they are out from under the platform and in the sunshine again.

Her ankle throbs and she is soaked to the skin, but it is worth it just to be held in his arms for that instant, with her heart madly thumping and goose bumps all over her body.

They clamber back over the rocks and out of the way of the people. Several times he holds out his hand for her as they jump across the huge white slabs, and she doesn't care any more about her see-through frock. Everyone can see she is with Ben. This is the best day of her life.

After the ceremony they go with Matthew to receive the pound of beef that the Prince has ordered to be given to every householder on the island. As they go they tell Matthew how they eluded the officials and found the perfect vantage point.

"It was worth a dowsing to have witnessed the event from such a good spot," says Ben.

"It's true, Pa, we could hear every word and see more clearly than anyone else the enormous stone, with its carved inscription and enclosed collection of coins and newspapers, as it was buried under several loads of huge rocks."

Matthew, who enjoyed the ceremony from a distance, laughs at their cheek. "Well, I think it a fitting end to a decade of change and I am sure that it marks the beginning of a new era of prosperity for all us Portlanders."

Rebecca hopes that her father is right. She looks at Ben, her body still tingling from the thought of his arms held tightly around her, and the moment when he had almost kissed her. She closes her eyes, reliving those few seconds, and makes a wish that he too might feel the same someday.

CHAPTER 18 *(January 1850)*

THE LEGACY

Miles inland Christian Dryer lies on his deathbed, but before the lonely old man passes on, having no knowledge of his son's whereabouts and no other dependants, he wills his fortune to the oldest surviving male blood relation and leaves it for the solicitors to investigate and ascertain who this might be.

His funeral takes place on the 25th January 1850. A bitter wind from the north-east whistles around the little estate chapel and tugs at the sombre clothing of the mourners.

They show their respect to their employer by their presence, but they offer no more than that. All are thinking ahead with hope that the time has come for new life to be poured into the land that supports their families; that new blood will again bring happiness to the home, standing proud and steadfast despite the years of neglect.

The beautiful old mansion set in the river valley, with its surrounding estate and outlying farms and cottages, looks silent, unloved and deserted.

Mr Fairway follows the cart track up from the valley and now has a superb view of the estate from the old Roman road as he starts his long journey to the coast.

He loves this kind of will, which leads to the unknown and often unexpected. It is his duty to investigate and he feels like a Peeler, instead of what

317

he really is, an office clerk in the rut of routine and bogged down with old manuscripts.

It is nearly eight of the clock. The sun's rays are shining through the bare winter branches of the beech trees. There is a frosty crust to the bark and the grassy verge; the sky is pale and cool. On his left in the valley below the tips of the willow trees show orange above the white wall of humidity that obliterates their tall trunks. Nestled in the western corner is Alvington Manor, the contour of the hills protecting it gently from the prevailing winds.

Anyone could love this place. It is a pleasant task he is embarking on. He brims full to the top of his bald little head with his own importance and orders his driver to work the horses harder, impatient for his destination.

Throughout the journey they encounter many wayfarers and itinerants and Fairway is glad of his superior transportation. They pass them by in a cloud of dust, only stopping along the way to rest the horses, take refreshment and pay their tolls.

Travel weary, they eventually traverse the last hill between them and their objective and there before them, like a beached whale, lies the notorious Slinger's Isle.

Unlike the trees and hedges and arable fields, the coastal place of Fairway's destination is in stark contrast. This isolated rock naturally is cold and desolate, exposed as it is to the February chills. Even so, Fairway thinks, it looks as though it has never warmed to people or passion and has never felt anything but coldness, hatred and violence. As the salty smell of the English Channel comes to him on a westerly gust of wind, he shivers violently.

The driver halts the carriage at the toll gate and hands over one and a penny-halfpenny, the levy to cross the ferry-bridge.

The bell rings as the shop door opens. The person entering is accompanied by as much cold air as could squeeze past before the door jangles closed again. Violet glances up from her bookwork and is surprised to see a rather official-looking man standing there with his hat turning round in his hand.

"Good morning. Can I help you, Sir?" She smiles at him.

"I was told that I might find Mrs Violet Stone here."

"Yes, this is my shop, I am Mrs Stone." Violet holds out her hand in greeting and Mr Fairway shakes it enthusiastically.

"I am delighted to meet you, Ma-am. My name is Fairway and I believe I have some exciting tidings for you and your family. Is it possible to go somewhere quiet where I may explain?"

Violet looks puzzled. "Certainly, if you would like to follow me we can talk in the sewing room."

As they enter the room, Hannah looks up from her work.

"Hannah, would you mind looking after the shop for me for a while, please? This shouldn't take long."

Hannah responds immediately and Violet turns again to her guest. "Right, Mr Fairway, what is it that you have to tell me?"

"I understand from my enquiries that you were the wife of the late Mr Richard Dryer."

Violet sits down, poignant memories tearing at her heart. She frowns, confused. "That is correct."

"I also understand that he fathered a son, Joshua."

"Yes, that's right, but could you explain to me please what that has got to do with you?"

"Certainly, my dear. I am a solicitor's clerk, and I

am instructed by the executors of the estate of the late Mr Christian Dryer. I am here to inform you that your son Joshua is the sole benefactor of the Alvington estate: the main dwelling house, chapel, farmhouse and outbuildings, outlying cottages, and some three hundred acres of arable and pastureland. The actual value of monies has not yet been calculated but I can assure you your son is set up for life."

Violet sits there in a stunned silence.

"Can I get you something to drink, my dear? I know this must be a shock for you."

"Thank you … no … I'm fine, Mr Fairway. I'm sorry, I'm forgetting my manners. Please … sit down."

Mr Fairway sits in the chair indicated, and Violet continues. "I am afraid my son is, at present, away at sea … I don't think there is any way we can contact him, for he is with the missionaries in New Guinea and I have no idea when he will return. You see, he left without our consent."

"Well, the best we can do at present is continue with the legal requirements. I will forward to you all the necessary documents, if you could keep them at your bank until such time as he should return. The estate is in safe hands. The staff and servants have run the place for the latter years of his Lordship's life and I will personally take responsibility for things to continue in the same vein."

"Well, thank you, Mr Fairway. I am afraid it has come as rather a shock to me. You see, my late husband and his father were not on good terms and I really know nothing of his family background at all."

"I understand, Mrs Stone, but there is nothing that you have to do. I will handle everything on your son's behalf until he is in a position to instruct me as to his wishes."

"Please allow me to offer you dinner with us this evening. I am sure my husband would be eager to discuss this with you."

"I am very grateful, Ma'am, for the kind invitation, but I really do have to return to Somerset today." He puts on his hat. "However, if he does have any queries concerning the matter, here is my calling card. I can always be contacted through my office address."

As Violet closes the door on the little man, a deep feeling of satisfaction warms her. She has always said that she wanted nothing from Richard's family, but it does seem to be poetic justice that her son, deprived of his father at such an early age, should now benefit from the relationship that has brought her so much pleasure and yet so much anguish.

That evening at supper time, as Violet is dishing up the food, she breaks the news to Matthew and Rebecca. "I had a bit of a shock at work today."

Matthew looks concerned. "What do you mean, Vi?"

"Well, I had a visit from a solicitor from Somerset." Violet is rather relishing her surprise.

"Whatever for?" Matthew is puzzled.

"Well, that is what I mean, it was a bit of a shock. He was looking for Josh and so I had to tell him that he is away at sea. Anyway, to cut a long story short, Josh has inherited his grandfather's estate."

"What!"

"I know, now you see what I mean. It is a bit of a shock, isn't it? There is the main manor house, a chapel, dower house and farmhouse, outbuildings, outlying cottages, and three hundred acres of land."

"Not a bit of a shock, Ma. It is massive!" says Rebecca, her eyebrows raised.

"That is amazing. Well, at least I did the right thing giving the apprenticeship to Ben. It is not likely Josh will be wanting that now, is it?"

"We will all be able to visit him as Squire of the Manor! I cannot wait to see the place," says Rebecca excitedly.

"That will be very exciting, won't it?" Violet smiles.

"Are you sure there hasn't been a mistake?" asks Matthew.

"I don't think so, Matty, Mr Fairway seemed very official and very sure of his facts."

"Well, I don't think we should count our chickens before they are hatched," he cautions.

"I don't suppose we are likely to learn more until Josh comes home from sea."

Rebecca looks thoughtful. "I wonder if that will stop Josh from his roaming. 'Tis a lot of responsibility running a large estate like that."

"That is true. I am not sure I would want to be taking it on myself, but Josh is the ideal person to inherit a fortune of this nature, he has no other ties to stand in his way, and I do think he will look the part, don't you?" Matthew smiles gently as he looks at Violet, knowing that Joshua is the image of his father.

The first person other than the family to hear of it has to be Ben, who is quite amazed when Rebecca eagerly relates her tale.

"Some people get all the luck!" he exclaims good-naturedly. "He will get a shock when he comes home, won't he?"

"I know, I can't wait to tell him. He'll be

stunned, won't he?" says Rebecca, excitedly.

"'Tis a funny thing, don't you think? Josh went off to find his fortune and instead it comes to the island, trying to find him." They both laugh at the irony of it.

"When you go visiting, you'll have maids attending to you. How do you like the sound of that then?"

Rebecca beams. She obviously likes the idea but then she grows serious again. "I hope they're nice people. They will probably think me common."

"Don't be daft. No one could think such a thing. Why, you're the most ladylike lass I know, and I know quite a few lassies." He grins at her meaningfully, and to his surprise she ups and runs off, muttering something about an errand.

Strange, he thinks, as he stares after her. Absently he continues with his work.

Later, in the usual exchange of gossip, he mentions the information to his mother and is surprised at the shocked silence that follows his comments, but is even more amazed at the bitter resentment that shows in the words that follow.

"The sun shines on the righteous or so they say. Perhaps you'd better be going off with the next Missionary ship, Ben, if you want to claim your just rewards. There is no one else in this village as self-righteous as that Violet Stone. The sun shines out of her …"

"Mother!" Ben interrupts her in full flow. "I thought you and she buried the hatchet long ago."

"Be that as it may, I still don't have to like the injustice of it, do I?" She chucks the scrubbing brush back into the pail of water and dries her hands on her apron.

"You're just as much entitled to good fortune as he is. You've always been a better son to me than ever Joshua Dryer has been to Violet. 'Tis so unfair."

"That's rubbish, Mother, and you know it. What would I want with a country estate? 'Tis the sea I love, and nothing would tear me away from this island or from the mother who has cared for me since I were a nipper. So would you want to be rid of me, or what?"

Tears fill Annie's eyes. "Oh son, of course I wouldn't, I only want the very best for you, that's all."

He puts his arm around her, protectively. "Well, you can stop your envying others, for I am the most contented man I know and one day I will make you the most contented old woman on the island. That's a promise."

"You're a good boy," she murmurs, "… a good boy. My life would have been so empty without you." She looks up into his smiling eyes and knows she could not bear a permanent separation. She cannot, however, help feeling bitter that her son should have no claim on this inheritance. He was conceived before Joshua, but Joshua was the firstborn and, more importantly, Joshua was not illegitimate. She knows it would be useless to speak up, and to do so might alienate the villagers who have all along accepted Ben as a Stone and a true Portlander.

Ben himself is unaware of the truth and she could forfeit his respect for her if she were to reveal her secret. She might lose him altogether. She has to bury the past and never think of it again.

Someday Ben will marry and maybe even make her a grandmother. She can imagine herself then relaxing in her rocker with her family around her and thinking back to the seed of love that had secured her happiness after all, which at the time threatened only shame.

CHAPTER 19 *(March 1851)*

'AS YE SHALL SOW,
SO THEN SHALL YE REAP'

As spring 1851 approaches, Violet and her team are busy making up the latest designs for the coming season. Heavily flounced skirts, and wider sleeves ending halfway down the forearm with a sleeve of softer material appearing underneath and gathered in at the wrist, means a lot of material and a lot more work in each new design. With Rebecca's help, Molly is making the open straw hats especially designed for warmer weather. These are very popular at watering places and therefore selling well in Weymouth.

One afternoon Molly notices that Rebecca is particularly dreamy as she works the straw with her nimble young fingers. "A penny for your thoughts?" she offers, curiously.

"Oh, nothing worth paying for, Auntie Molly," she smiles.

"Come now, you can't be fooling me, Becky, there's some young lad somewhere, I reckon, who's a tugging at your heartstrings."

Rebecca's cheeks suffuse with colour at the suggestion, and the twinkle in her eyes tells Molly that she is right.

"Come on, Becky, I do love to hear of a tender young romance a'budding. Don't be a spoilsport."

"Oh, 'tis nothing to speak of, Auntie Molly, he doesn't even know I'm around. He treats me like his baby sister."

"Ah, then you're talking to the right person." She smiles, confidently. "Now, I know how to charm him, but you must be sure 'tis the right fellow that you want. You're very young and this charm is a powerful thing and very sure certain to work."

"Oh, I'm sure. I can think of nothing else. But all the village girls are ogling him, and he's very waggish with them all."

"Well, 'tis easily solved. Here's what you have to do. At twelve of the clock, midnight mind, or 'twill be no use, you have to sprinkle hemp seed in the path of where he do usually walk, so that when he crunches it underfoot and the smell wafts to his nose it will make him turn to you from all other wenches."

Rebecca listens intently.

"As you be sprinkling it you have to say this charm, 'Hemp seed I spread, hemp seed I sow, he that's my true love come to me now.' 'Tis as simple as that."

Rebecca is intrigued. She has nothing to lose, for even if it doesn't work it can do no harm to try. "Where could I get some hemp seed from? Do you think they may have some at Conjurors' Lodge?"

"You don't want to have anything to do with them heathens, pretending to crafty sciences and witchcraft. I don't hold with such goings on. I expect there's some out in the barn, if you'd care to grub around a bit."

"I'll go and see." She jumps up, hastily putting her work to one side, and Molly smiles to see how eagerly she goes off in search of this love potion.

Shortly she returns with a handful of the seeds. "I found some." She shows Molly her treasure happily. Then a thought occurs to her. "Auntie Molly, you won't let on to Ma or anyone, will you?"

"Of course not, Becky, 'tis just between you and me. I promise."

Later that evening Violet is chatting to Matthew. "I am so pleased that Molly and Becky work so well together. Our small team is so efficient that Fortune's Corner has nearly recouped all the money that you provided for the purchase of the place."

Matthew is surprised, "What, already!"

"Yes, well nearly, and I am very pleased because I wanted to repay you as soon as possible. This means that it won't be long before we can afford the new furnace, and so you can start looking out for a bargain."

"I will do, Vi. That is very good news because we can repair the roof in the boat yard and fit the furnace during the better weather." Matthew goes to Violet and gives her a big kiss.

"I told you it would be a good investment," Violet says with a twinkle in her eyes.

The boat yard is also flourishing and by pooling their resources the job is soon in hand. Matthew watches with pride as the new furnace is installed, to the accompaniment of the carpenters hammering up on the roof. Everything is going so well. Joshua cannot fail to be impressed when he returns. There have been so many changes since he left and they have such good news to welcome him home.

That night Ben tells his mother all about the improvements in the boat yard. Annie seems pleased.

"'Tis bound to rub off on you, my son, if ever you wish to change jobs. 'Tis better that you should have worked in a successful business than one that is forever on the verge of bankruptcy."

There is then a commotion outside the front door which, after much ado, is forced open. Angrily, Ikey stumbles in from the cold. "That bloody door be sticking again, can't you fix it fer Christ's sake? It takes all my strength to get in over the threshold these days."

"It means taking the door off its hinges and planing off the bottom, and 'tis too cold at present," returns Ben defensively.

"Well, it's all right for you lot but I find it very difficult, with only one good leg."

"I'm sorry, Ikey. I'll do it as soon as it's a bit milder."

"Don't you worry, I'll remind you soon enough." He hobbles on through to the chimney corner, props his stick against the wall and slumps into his favourite chair with a grunt of pain. "Give us a hand with this here boot. I'm done in, I am."

Ben pulls off his high boot, conscious of the breeches pinned up against his uncle's other thigh.

"I'm not surprised you are exhausted, you do well to get about the way that you do." He has to admire the dogged determination of the old goat even though his hostility never attracts compassion.

"I can't stand to be penned up all the time, besides life ain't worth living without a drop of the hard stuff to take away the pain. I can afford the odd bottle if I make the effort occasionally to take the boat out."

"I do understand, Ikey, I just wish you'd make life a bit easier for me Ma. She does her best for us you know."

"I know that, lad, but it's me way. She'd get a shock if I were any different after all these years."

"Aye, I reckon you're right," says Ben. "It would

have sent me to the madhouse if I had to manage the way you do," he adds.

"Maybe you'd come out with me one night. 'Twould be nice to have a bit o' company."

"I will, as soon as this cold spell breaks."

Ben is amazed that his uncle should be so genial after all these years and has agreed to go with him before he has given it much thought. He only hopes he won't live to regret it. For several weeks Ikey keeps reminding him of his promise. Eventually Ben gives his word that he will go out the next night.

When the time comes there is no moon, and the clouds are low in the sky, threatening rain. This does not deter Ikey, but Ben regrets his foolishness as soon as the lerret hits the water. The sooner they get this over with the better. He sets to with a will, following Ikey's directions.

"What bait have we got?" asks Ben, who left all the preparations to Ikey whilst he put in a day's work at the boat yard.

"A bucket of lugworms and a few herring. There's a conger eel both Bill and I have been after for ages in a crab hole off Church Ope Cove. It's a big, hungry bastard and with your help we might be able to pull 'im in. 'Twill be a good opportunity."

The southerly wind hits them as they round the island, leaving the sanctuary of the Roads. The rowing becomes more laboured but they are still making good progress. Gradually the swell grows more menacing until the boat is rocking to and fro violently.

"I think we should pull in nearer to the shore, Ikey."

"Aye, well, we'll have to be careful here, 'tis rocky."

"Perhaps we'd be wise to give him a miss this

time, Ikey. It looks to be getting a bit rough for the two of us to handle."

"Well, we'm here now, aren't we?" says Ikey impatiently. "We may as well get something out of it." Ikey is determined to have his way, and Ben concedes. "If we drop anchor here, 'tis about the right spot. Pass over the lantern, lad. I can't see what I'm about."

Ben unhooks the lantern and passes it across to his uncle. As he does so he catches sight of a grappling hook. He watches with horror as his uncle eagerly tosses it over the side searching the depths below them for the real spoils.

Angry that he has been duped with such ease, he grabs hold of his uncle. "What the bloody hell do you think you're doing?" he demands. "You know damn well I'd never 'ave agreed to come if I'd known what you were up to."

Ikey shrugs him off. "Oh, shut up your whining and make yourself useful. Here, hang this here lantern back on the hook. I'm gonna need your muscles to get this up and slung under."

"What makes you think I'm daft enough to get involved with this?" Ben nearly chokes as he tries to shout back over the noise of the wind.

"Look, I don't care a fig for your scruples, but if you don't hurry up and give us a hand we might have us a job getting back to the Roads before this storm strikes. Now, are you going to stop grizzling and act like a man or not? There's a dozen tubs of best brandy and all I need is a hand to lift 'em so as to attach 'em fore and aft."

Resentfully, Ben decides to lend a hand. "I'll help you just this once, but don't you ever try duping me again. This is the first and last time you take me for a sucker."

He heaves up the crop whilst Ikey attaches it to

his end of the boat, then moves back down the lerret to hook up his end of the roped casks. "Ikey, you'll have to hold the creeper while I tie it my end or 'twill slip away. Can you come amidships?"

The boat rocks dangerously with the contraband acting as an additional anchor. The rain now beats against their faces and hands as they struggle to secure the other end. Ikey, balanced precariously on his good leg, is standing to take the strain off Ben when suddenly out of the howling wind and rain looms the revenue cutter. The combination of surprise and the wash of the larger craft takes Ikey off balance. Ben lets go his rope to grab him but he misjudges the instability of the lerret, and with all the weight of the crop in his hands Ikey falls against his severed thigh. He cries out with pain as the boat tosses him over the side.

"Ikey!" screams Ben frantically. "Catch hold the rope." His eyes search the grey, heaving mass around him. "Where are you?" He stretches out over the side and yells for all his might. "Ikey! Where the hell are you?"

Ikey lets out a cry as he surfaces, then another wave submerges him.

"Where? I can't see you. Ikey! Where are you?"

"Ben, over here … Help me."

At last Ben sights an arm, then it is gone again … then his hands, beating wildly against the foaming mass … his head shoots up, and goes straight down again … his frantic splashing and gasping is too horrific … then just one hand.

"You're too far off …" He begins pulling up the anchor, forgetting that the boat is also restrained by the crop of contraband it trails.

"I'm anchored here. Hang on, just keep afloat. Take off your coat … I'll get to you."

"I can't!" He goes under again, then emerges

once more, his arms threshing the white surf. "Be … n," he screams, "Be …" but his desperate cry is cut off. Ben cannot hear his last, useless gasps for air.

The noise of the wind is eerie now. The revenue cutter has turned back and is approaching with caution.

A voice hails him. "This is Her Majesty's coastguard. My men are about to board your vessel. I would appreciate your co-operation."

"For Christ's sake! There's a man overboard," shouts Ben. "I need your help." Ben is still frantically trying to locate Ikey to no avail.

"Man overboard!" shouts the officer, urgently. "Man overboard! All hands on deck!"

Five men come to assist. Two of them have lanterns fixed to long poles that they hang out over the water; another is lowered down to Ben in the lerret and they use the grappling hook to try to locate Ikey.

"Take the cutter over that way a bit," directs Ben. "Please. He was there a moment ago."

The hook catches on something and they heave it up to the surface, only to discover the tail-end of the crop.

"Oh shit," moans Ben in despair as he realises his last hope is in vain.

"I'm sorry, lad, but you boys ought to know by now that the risks you take result in accidents like this." He passes the hook to Ben. "Keep trying," he says kindly, as he attaches the other end of the line. It is easier now they are in the lee of the cutter.

They edge forward, scanning the area around the two crafts. "Don't give up," pleads Ben. "We can't give up. He's only got one leg."

"He'll never survive," says one of the coastguards.

They search the area well, but it is fruitless. "There's no sign of him, lad. I'm afraid he's a gonner."

Ben slumps down on the plank of wood that is the boat's seating. His hair is bedraggled, with the rain still beating through the wind. The tight ball of pain in his chest makes it hard for him to breathe as he thinks of Ikey's terror. "Oh God," he groans. "Why did I say I'd do it? Why?"

"I'm afraid we've got to take you in, lad. You've been found in possession of contraband goods." He marks the boat with a broad arrow. "You'd better climb aboard the 'Speedwell' and we'll tow your lerret back to the harbour, where she will be impounded until your case is answered."

Ben protests weakly, "We can't go just yet. We can't just leave Ikey."

"What else can we do, lad? He's gone; he isn't going to surface now. I'm afraid we've lost him. Be a good chap and climb aboard the cutter. We don't want to have to use force, do we, lad?"

CHAPTER 20 *(March – May 1851)*

COURAGE AND CONVICTIONS

"No good came from that Ikey Shaddick when he were alive, and he couldn't even die without bringing someone down with him." Violet is that furious when she hears the news, she does not notice her daughter's reaction.

Rebecca is helping her mother in the shop and hears Mrs Atwool telling of Ben's arrest and resulting summons. Her first thought is to go to Ben, but would this betray her feelings? Instead she listens carefully as the story is related.

"By all accounts he was duped by that uncle of his. Told 'im 'e wanted to do a bit of fishing, so they say, but what with the storm brewing and the 'Speedwell' looming up on them Ikey was apparently tossed overboard and Ben was left caught red-handed with the crop," says Mrs Atwool.

"Poor Ben, God knows what will happen to him now."

Rebecca leaves her mother feeling bereft, knowing that she is powerless, unable to help someone who has always been there for her. But most of all she is angry. She calls in to the corner shop to see if Mr Flew has heard any more news.

"Have you heard anything about Ben, Mr Flew?"

"I have, me dear, I got it from Annie Shaddick

herself. His lerret has been impounded, but he is at liberty until the date of the quarter sessions later this month. Which means 'e'm before the Judge in three weeks come Tuesday next."

"I cannot believe that he was in league with Ikey."

"He weren't according to his Ma, but he were caught-red handed working the crop, and his uncle no longer here to speak up for him. It don't bode too well, as far as I can see."

"No, I fear you are right, Mr Flew. 'Tis so unjust."

She turns towards the boatyard and as she approaches her stomach churns. Ben is still there packing away his tools. Her heart begins to race; if she speaks to him her voice will be charged with emotion. She pauses and as she does so, Ben looks up and sees her.

"Why so shy, Becky, do you take me for a criminal?"

"No, of course not." She hurries forward, anxious to dispel such a notion, "Though I am very concerned for you, Ben. How did you come to be in such a mess?"

"'Tis a long story, Becky. I've told your Pa all about it. You only have to know that my uncle tricked me. He paid the price with his life."

"And so he should, 'tis good riddance. God forgive me, but he deserved to be punished. 'Tis a wonder you didn't lose your own life."

"That's the truth and I thank God for it."

"You know, everyone is talking of the injustice of your arrest, but I've not heard any lamenting the death of your uncle. He must have been the most unpopular man on Portland."

"He had no friends, 'tis true. He never needed anyone. Me Ma did everything for him. If it wasn't for her tending to his every need he might have been forced to be more pleasant to people. 'Tis sad, he never knew what it was to be happy."

"Ben, do you think you will have to go to prison?"

"Even if I do 'twill only be for a month or so. 'Twill soon pass and your father says there will always be a job here for me, which was my biggest fear once I'd got over the first shock."

"But Ben, it's a slur on your good name. Folk like us who know you so well know it's untrue, but folks that don't will be sure to believe you're guilty."

"I know that, Beck, and I'll be relying on you to put them right. Those who dare to slander me."

"I will, Ben, you can depend on me. No one will dare to say a word against you. Not while I'm around anyway."

"Good girl. With you and me Ma on my side I shan't go far wrong." He grins, warmly.

She feels that warmth permeate every part of her body. She aches for his touch. Bravely she asks him, "I know you think I'm just a silly nipper, but I don't want you to go without saying goodbye to me. Will you promise to let me kiss you goodbye, Ben? Please."

"I promise, Becky. I won't go off like your brother did, you can depend on that."

Rebecca spends as much time as she can helping in the boat yard. It is imperative that she should sprinkle the hemp seed before Ben goes to court. For then if things should go badly, if the worst should happen and he is sent to prison, his thoughts might turn to her in his troubles and her love will strengthen him. She had planned to bring about her charm after the May Day celebrations but unfortunately they are still a month away. Besides, the matter is now far more urgent and so she is determined to do it that night.

She goes up to her room early that evening. She washes and grooms her thick, black, wavy hair, and while she waits for the time to pass she experiments idly with some hairpins selected from Fortune's Corner. She stares at her reflection in the vanity mirror, surprised at how these sophisticated alterations have made her appear so much more sensual. She pinches her cheeks, adding a little colour to them, and with her deep blue eyes she is suddenly aware of the likeness to her mother. She is tempted to go downstairs to show her parents how she looks, but decides to wait until a more appropriate occasion. She puts her chamberstick beside the bed and snuffs the candle.

At about half past ten she hears her parents preparing to retire for the night. The bolt is slid across the front door and she hears their footsteps and the creaking of the stairs. She allows time for them to fall asleep and then, having checked through her bedroom window that the moon is still up, she quietly dresses again.

She can hear Matthew snoring and carefully times each step on the creaky stairs with the sound of his snore. Seeing the funny side of this she has difficulty suppressing her laughter, but she manages to reach the bottom without making a sound. Before carefully drawing back the bolt she smothers it in goose grease so that it moves smoothly, then lifting the latch she steps out into the night air.

She exhales deeply with relief. She has made it without disturbing them. Hurriedly she rushes through the village, thankful that there is no one about. The night air is still. As she approaches the beach the gentle sough of the sea is somehow reassuring. She lifts the heavy latch on the boat yard doors and pulls one open leaving it ajar, allowing a shaft of moonlight to illuminate the interior. Then she sits down in the shadows near the furnace, taking comfort from the remaining warmth, and waits for the chimes from the church clock tower.

Her heartbeat seems loud in the silence. Hearing it makes her even more exhilarated. The suspense is unbearable. How much longer will she have to wait?

Then she hears the distant, resonant, echoing sound of the clock chiming twelve times and as the sound lingers in the still air she stands in the moonlight and evenly distributes the precious seed, saying as she does so the words that Molly has told her and that she has committed to memory. "Hemp seed I spread, hemp seed I sow, he that's my true love come to me now." She repeats the chant until all the seed is gone, just to be on the safe side. Then as quietly as she came, she closes the big door and secures the latch.

She strolls back to her home. In the glow of the moonlight it is easy to imagine herself enclosed in the arms of her cousin. The last time he held her was two years ago when she was only eleven and she had felt the tension in his taught muscles, their bodies wet, their clothes clinging. But now she wonders how much longer she will have to wait to enjoy that thrill again? How soon will this charm start working?

Ben is fined one hundred pounds or six months hard labour. As he cannot pay the fine he is detained at Dorchester Gaol.

"Ma, have you heard, because Ben cannot pay the fine of one hundred pounds he has been sent to Dorchester Gaol for six months. 'Tis so unfair.

"I cannot believe they can be so harsh on a lad that age who has never done any harm to anyone."

"Can't we help him, Ma, couldn't we pay the fine for him?"

"Oh Becky, darling, of course we would if we had that kind of money, but we don't, we have only just paid for the furnace and the boat yard roof. There is no spare money left."

Rebecca's concern at the injustice of it is little consolation to Ben. The loneliness is like a painful vacuum inside her; all she can cling to is the memory of a tender kiss planted on her forehead before he left for the mainland and the worst ordeal of his life.

She is drawn to the convict work gangs where secretly she observes the guards, only to find them with their flails, viciously enforcing the law with undue enthusiasm. The prisoners look half-starved, the sweat pouring off them as they labour on the heavy rocks. She cannot bear the thought that Ben is being treated in this harsh way. It is bad enough that the guilty should be abused so, but Ben is innocent.

It seems these men are everywhere in their fustian prison uniforms being used by the government to provide labour for the massive undertakings that they are committed to. In this way they are told that they can earn 'tickets of leave' for good behaviour and hard work. This might reduce their sentence or give them a conditional discharge when they reach Australia. Many are dying in the attempt and yet, because of the publicity given to the project, regular trips of sightseers come from all over the country to gawp at them as they labour.

When Rebecca first sees the Kimberlins with their guides pointing out certain prisoners of special notoriety, she is furious. How can they be so insensitive? What kind of morbid pleasure can they possibly get from this? Are they staring at Ben too? Is he being beaten and abused?

She feels as if time has stood still since Ben left

the island. Everyone else seems to go on as usual with all the business of the day, but something is holding her back. It is as if her whole being is trying to operate submerged in a thick sea of mud. Her parents try to cheer her, not knowing that she will not respond until Ben is returned safely.

Ben is unable to express his anxiety over the court case to anyone, knowing that he has to take the punishment unflinchingly whatever the verdict. How could he further distress his mother or Rebecca by betraying his true fears?

When given six months' hard labour he is filled with despair, unable to contemplate the thought of existing like the men he has seen working in the convict quarries. Never having been restricted in his life before, even as a child free to roam the entire island, he has lived until now untouched by authority and silently he curses the man who has brought him down to this.

Dorchester Gaol is a dismal establishment, and Ben shudders at the thought of his incarceration there as soon as he sets eyes on the building. The cells are divided by corrugated iron partitions and the one he is taken to is a pokey, dank hole furnished with a stool, table and hammock. There is green slime mould on the walls and a musty, stale smell about the place which he is sure he will never, ever forget. As the cell door clangs shut Ben gives a huge sigh.

A voice calls through from the next-door cell. "Morning, neighbour. I am Zachariah, welcome to the pound."

"The pound?"

"Aye, the warders treat us like caged animals here and expect us to eat the most revolting food, knowing we have no choice."

"Well, I am Ben and hopefully I can stick it out for the next six months." Ben sits down on the stool.

"I got nine months' hard labour and I've already done seven. I'd like to think I will make it home to the wife and kids, but I am not well. That hard labour has nearly killed me off."

Zachariah coughs until he almost chokes, sounding to Ben as if he has consumption.

"Well, I don't know how I am going to stomach this. I can't stand being penned in here all day long, I am used to being out in the open air. This is more like solitary confinement!"

"They only take a few of us out at any one time and they have left me here today because I slow everyone down."

"I am going to write a note to me Ma. Do you think the warder will post if for me?"

"Depends which warder you ask. Some are reasonable, but there are quite a few who are real bastards."

"Oh well, it is worth a try."

As May Day approaches, many young girls are coming into the shop for ribbons and bows with which to titivate their Sunday frocks. One of the girls who attends the same school as Rebecca is politely chatting to Violet. She happens to comment on how Rebecca must be missing Ben. It is the first time that anyone outside of the family has noticed their friendship and it suddenly takes on a different light in Violet's imagination. It is obviously the reason for her daughter's introspection. How could she have been so blind?

Rebecca will be thirteen years old in July, she is growing up fast, and Violet must look upon her as a young lady now, not her little girl any more.

Matthew is going to find this even more difficult, especially as her thoughts turn to young men.

Rebecca has always loved Ben, she knows that, but she has until now assumed that it was brotherly affection. It is obviously far more than that. Her daughter is 'lovesick' in the truest sense of the word. It is something that can no longer be ignored.

Had it not been for the hand of providence Violet would have consulted Matthew on the situation, but things suddenly take shape unaided. Someone has sighted the 'John Wesley' as she tacks around the Beale, and the island is soon buzzing with the news, for Captain Buck's family live up on 'Top Hill'. Matthew has rushed up to the shop to tell Violet so that she will not hear it from anyone else and she cries tears of joy and relief that they will soon be seeing Joshua again.

"How soon do you think he'll be home, Matty?" she asks, her eyes glistening.

"Old Jabe reckons they should dock around the seventh or eighth, depending on the weather."

"He could be home by Cow Common Day then?"

"He may well be," says Matthew with a huge smile, happy to see the pleasure on Violet's face.

The door bursts open with a clang of the shop bell. "Have you heard the news?" cries Rebecca. "They've sighted the Missionary Brig at the Beale."

"Yes, we heard," they both reply in unison, laughing and hugging each other.

"I can't wait," Rebecca says excitedly. "Do you think they will anchor in the Roads?"

"I doubt it. Captain Buck will have to stay with the ship until she docks in London. They wouldn't stop just to let our Josh off, would they now?" Matthew grins at them. "We've waited two years, two weeks will fly by. I must be getting back to work.

Will you walk back with me, Becky, and then you can pop in and tell Grandmama all about it?"

When finally Joshua makes his appearance, Violet cannot believe that it is really him: a tall, tanned man standing on the step of the shop, his hand resting on the door handle. As the door opens she slowly closes the drawer of silks. It really is him. He is back at last.

"Josh." Her face lights up.

"Hello, Mama." In a few strides he is hugging her. She blinks away the tears, enjoying the feel of his strong arms around her. Then all the questions begin.

"When did you dock? We have been waiting for you since your ship was sighted off the Beale."

"We arrived at St Katharine's Dock in London on the eighth of May," he grins. "But it took a while to disembark and arrange transport home. London is amazing, Ma, but it is even more chaotic than usual because of the Great Exhibition."

"You look so wonderful. Was it all that you expected?"

"I've had the experience of a lifetime, Ma. You just wouldn't believe the things that I've seen and done."

"We have some tales to tell you too, Josh. I think you may be surprised. But come, I will shut the shop and we can meet Becky from school and go and see Matty and everyone. Oh, I am so thrilled to have you home again, and I am so proud of my big, tall son." She kisses him fondly on the cheek, having to stand on tiptoe to do so.

The villagers pass them by smile to see the prodigal son returned safely and greet them cheerfully, later commenting to each other that they had thought it was a ghost, so like his father has he grown.

Rebecca nearly bowls him over as she runs into his arms after school is out. It is his turn to be shocked. "My word, how you've grown."

"'Tis you who have grown, Josh. You're taller than Pa, I reckon."

The surprise and excitement continues for several days until all the friends and relations are over the initial shock. Joshua misses Ben immediately, and is devastated by the information that is carefully explained to him. He intends to visit Ben as soon as he can reasonably leave his family, but obviously he cannot up and go when they still want him near and have missed him so dearly.

A celebration is quickly planned. Molly and John kill a pig, and there is roast pig meat and a great ham. Violet makes an apple pudding and stuffs and cooks a goose, and Rebecca prepares all the pies and tarts and pastries. They had made wine just before Joshua left. It turned out to be a good year for cowslips and they set aside two bottles for his homecoming. Matthew puts a tap to a new barrel of beer, and with the cider and sherry wine there should be plenty of drink for all.

Soon all the guests are arriving: Matthew's parents, Johnny, Hannah and Richard; Violet's parents and her brothers, John and Molly, Jabe Stone, Thomas the stable lad and John Motyer.

Joshua is in his element, amazing the gathering with his tales of strange happenings as the ship moved in and out among the Fiji Islands. "Whilst we were on one of the smaller islands one of the cannibals was killed and we were all horrified when we realised that his wife was to be buried with him alive to attend to his needs in the next world." There are groans all round. "Did you not try to stop them?" asks Molly, concerned.

"Of course, Auntie Molly, and on that occasion we were successful. But there were many times when we were too late, or the Fijians became aggressive and we could not interfere. They were in real need of Christianity I can tell you."

Violet puts her arm round her son's waist. "Well, you'd hear no complaint from me if you were a convert, for they have been doing wonders on Portland. Many who had been given up as wantons, drunkards and heathens are different folk altogether since the Methodists and Brackenbury have come to the island."

Later, as Violet passes around platters of meat, she overhears Joshua chatting to Richard and John.

"It is hard graft I can tell you, and quite dangerous too. In fact one of my shipmates was washed overboard during a storm, and amazingly he was deposited back on deck by a huge wave. He managed to hang onto some rigging, even though he had a broken arm, until the storm subsided and we were able to help him down."

Violet smiles at Matthew and, lowering her voice for his ears only, she whispers, "You know that I never wanted Josh to go away, but I cannot deny that you were right, it has made a man of him, and given us reason to be proud."

After everyone has eaten and complimented the ladies on the good and wholesome food, Matthew makes sure that all those present have a glass of something with which to toast their pilgrim. With a rat-a-tat on the table, he announces: "I should like you all to raise your glasses and toast 'Our son Joshua'. He has travelled to the other side of the world and back, and has helped in no small way with the spread of Christianity in those outlandish places where many still fear to tread." Matthew raises his glass. "To Joshua."

"Joshua," all reply in unison.

"Now, before we all resume our general chatter and gaiety, I have a surprise for Josh. He doesn't know it but there is another reason why we should raise our glasses to this man who went off to seek his fortune. Please let us all be upstanding for Mr Joshua Dryer, Lord of the Manor of Alvington, in the county of Somersetshire."

All assembled stand up and raise their glasses. "To the Lord of the Manor," says Matthew.

"To the Lord of the Manor," echo the gathering.

Joshua stands with a quizzical expression on his face. He thinks his father must have partaken of too much ale.

CHAPTER 21 *(May – June 1851)*

'LIBERTE! EGALITE! FRATERNITE!'

After only three weeks in prison, Ben thinks he will go mad. This is more like solitary confinement and the inactivity is eroding his spirit. He has not been looking forward to the 'hard labour' side of things, but anything is preferable to this. He has had enough. When the warder next posts his platter of gruel he complains, "Not gruel again! Don't they know how to cook anything else, for God's sake?"

"You will eat what you are given and like it."

"Well, it's not going to do Zach next door much good; he needs building up and it is about time something was done about it. He is obviously in need of some medication."

"And what am I supposed to do about it?" snaps the warder.

"How the devil should I know, you're the warder. Surely there's a physician employed here?"

"Who the hell do you think you're talking to?" says the man, his manner obstructive. "I've come across the likes of you before: peculiar, clannish folk with high and mighty airs and graces. Nothing better than thieves and vagabonds bred on that island, always getting 'em before the beak for smuggling and rowdyism."

"Look, forget about the foul food, I am not asking for special favours. I don't want anything for myself; I just want some medication for the fellow in the next cell before it's too late. Is that too much to ask, for Christ's sake?"

In answer, the warder retrieves the food, spits in it and then returns it to Ben.

Ben tips it through the hatch onto the warder's boots. He knows that he will be made to regret what he has said and done but he no longer cares. The warder grins with satisfaction and slams the food hatch shut.

Ben smiles to himself. Something interesting happening at last, he thinks. I wonder what I've let myself in for? He listens as the warder's footsteps echo into the distance and then he settles back into his hammock to wait.

There is a choke and a splutter from the next cell. "You shouldn't 'ave said nothing, mate. I'll live." His neighbour coughs violently, "Anyway, it ain't your problem. You've asked for it now. That bastard likes to get his teeth into someone and you'll be made to rue the day."

Ben laughs, "It can't be worse than this, Zach. This is a living death to me. I'd rather be worked till I bleed than rot away in here."

"No, Ben, you'll live to regret it, mate." He is interrupted by a bout of convulsions. Hoarsely he continues. "I've been with the work parties ten hours day in, day out and come back collapsing with blistered hands and flail marks across my back."

The following day, Ben is forced to admit that Zach was right. Not because he is placed with a work gang but because Zach is too. The fellow is in a hopeless state and it is obvious to all that he will not see a week out.

The warder is smug. "Enjoyed your trip out, did you?" he asks, as they return at the end of their first day.

"The change of scenery was much appreciated.

My thanks to you for organising it," says Ben, conscious of the raw skin on his palms and ankles but determined not to give the guard the satisfaction of knowing his pain.

They work them in all weathers. Ben is used to that, but Zach's cough is gradually bringing him down. Each bout now causes him to urge and strain his stomach. He is coughing up blood, and he tells Ben that the ache in his chest seems to be burning through his lungs.

Ben is desperately sorry to have been the instigator of Zach's plight and tries to help him, sometimes physically supporting him whilst they work. This only brings more retribution down on their heads and both suffer a severe beating as a result.

"I am desperately sorry, Zach, to be the cause of all this. I was only trying to help."

"I know that, mate, but please don't try helping me any more. Not being funny, mate, but I am much better off without your help." Zach gives a small chuckle which ends up with him coughing again violently.

At night, the sound of Zach's breathing prevents Ben from sleeping. Each laboured gasp adds to the deep sense of guilt that he is dying hour by hour. He fears the silence more than anything. Sometimes Ben calls out if all goes quiet but Zach does not reply; he doesn't have the strength. His return to regular breathing is Ben's only consolation.

Because the men work in pairs, lifting and carrying the sleepers, Ben has to exert himself harder to cover for Zach. He aches, his muscles are so inflamed that any movement is painful, but pain is piled upon pain as the flails rip into the flesh beneath his torn and tattered prison duds. His legs are swelling where the irons cut into his skin; his hands are sore and blistered from handling the rusty rails and splintering sleepers. He cannot bear to think of how Zach must be feeling.

Eventually the rain stops falling and the June sunshine slowly permeates their steaming clothes. The warmth is welcome to the prisoners and seems to improve the tempers of the guards.

Ben begins to be hopeful that Zach will recover. He is not coughing quite so much, but he still looks blanched with weakness. As they are returned to their cells that evening it appears the sun has put some colour back into his frail skin. For the first time since they have been with the chain gangs, Ben relaxes and finally he sleeps with exhaustion.

The next morning, he awakes to a commotion in the next cell. Zach has died during the night.

Ben is chained to a new partner. Not wanting to become involved with anyone else he keeps himself to himself. He cannot endure seeing the pain of others, and fears the responsibility that any friendship might require. He will never forget Zach, nor will he ever forgive himself for the inadvertent part that he played in his demise. He concentrates his thoughts on home, his family and friends. He knows he will get through this, and by looking ahead to the time when he will be free again he can suffer the pain and humiliation of the present.

Thoughts of escape help to sustain him. Visions of the wild sea and memories of the wind on his face, the sweet taste of freedom, tantalising. Images come dancing out of the solitude. Rebecca, lonely, her wide-eyed fears haunting him. He can see his mother, from whom he has inherited his fighting spirit, rocking to and fro, and she strengthens his will to survive. Soon it will all be over and he may well be stronger for it, but he is determined never to suffer such degradation again.

Rebecca follows Joshua everywhere, but the feeling of pride is mutual. He promises her that he will do what he can for Ben, but there is much to arrange before he is in a position to help and he does not want to see Ben until he can go as the bearer of glad tidings. Finally the legalities are completed and he is able to arrange to meet Mr Fairway and the clerk of the County Court in his offices at Dorchester.

Rebecca has begged and begged her brother to be allowed to go with him and finally he gives in, his heart aching with envy at the strength of feeling that his sister has for their cousin. If only someone felt as much as that for him, but Rebecca is still so young and he does not want to see her hurt.

Rebecca is unable to sleep; she is so excited at the prospect of rescuing Ben from his ordeal. She is up before sunrise. Her chores completed, she puts on her new May Day frock and pins up her hair as she had done on the night that she scattered the hemp seed. The most important thing on her mind is to get dear Ben out of that prison, but she also wants him to see her at her best. Satisfied with her reflection in the vanity mirror, she carefully places a small tulle hat covered in tiny flowers among the curls and puts on her new embroidered overjacket.

"My word, you do look a pretty sight," says Matthew, holding out her hands in his. "Let me look at you."

"'Tis only my May Day frock, Papa," she says, knowing full well that it is her hair that has the main effect.

"I know and I thought how fine you looked at the party, but you've done something clever with your hair and it is most becoming like that."

Joshua gazes at her tiny waist, and curvy figure. She is growing up faster than he has realised. "I no longer have a baby sister. You could be the May Day Queen, Becky."

"She'd knock spots off the other girls, Josh, just as your mother always did."

Rebecca smiles. She had hoped that they would like her hair that way, and now she is eager to be off because she cannot wait for Ben to see her new style, or to take with her the news that he is again a free man.

Violet enters from the stairway. She gives Joshua the parcel of clothes that Annie has prepared for Ben. "Bring him home safe and sound," she says. "I hate thinking of the poor lad, lonely and neglected in that prison. He didn't deserve it, just because he trusted that miserable wretch, Ikey."

"I know, Mama, we won't come home without him."

"Why, Becky, Ben will be so pleased to see you, what a picture the pair of them make, don't they, Matty?"

"They're their mother's children, the pair of them. There's no denying that."

Matthew and Violet stand side by side, smiling and waving as the carriage that Joshua has hired bowls off down Brandy Lane, the tassels on Rebecca's parasol fluttering in the breeze.

When the chain gang returns to the prison that evening, Ben is taken separately to see the Governor. Tired, dirty and apprehensive, he waits with the warder outside the heavy oak door of the office.

When summoned, he is frogmarched through the door and the warder is dismissed. Ben stands eyes downcast, ashamed of the dreadful state he is in, a dirty and dishevelled detainee. Although aware of the presence of a young lady and gentleman, he is too ashamed to look them in the eye.

The Governor invites him to take a seat. Surprised, he sinks gratefully into the leather chair to await the reason for his summons. It is not until the man in the cravat speaks that he recognises his voice.

"Ben, we've come to take you home," Joshua says gently.

He spins round, surely he is dreaming? As their eyes meet he jumps up with a sudden burst of energy. "Josh! 'Tis really you. I can't believe it. I thought you were halfway across the world."

"What, when my poor old mate's in trouble?" he grins. "If I could have been here sooner I would have."

The Governor interrupts them. "Mr Dryer has put up the money for your fine in the belief that you are innocent and, after due consideration of the authorities, I am pleased to be able to tell you that you are free to go. I trust this is the last we will be seeing of you, Stone."

"Yes, Sir. I guarantee it." Ben holds out his hand. The Governor hesitates, looking him in the eye for a few seconds, and then reciprocates, saying, "Go and get yourself cleaned up and relieve yourself of the prison uniform. The young lady has a change of clothes for you. They can take tea with me whilst they wait."

The girl steps forward with the parcel and gives it to him. She has been standing there quietly watching him. He takes it and formally thanks her, thinking what a fine young lady Josh is courting. Then something about her smile makes him take a second look. It is Rebecca.

"Becky," he gasps, "I didn't realise it was you."

He is stunned, she looks so grown up. "You look splendid." He wants to hug her but the Governor is showing him to the door.

Rebecca watches him leave and, even though her vision is blurred by the tears she is desperately trying to hold back, she sees the admiration in Ben's eyes and knows that her charm has done the trick. She savours the waiting, wanting so much to see that look and that face again.

The Governor is quite taken with Rebecca himself and dances attendance on them over tea. He is curious as to what Joshua has been up to in the Fiji Islands and thus he is entertained until Ben is returned to the threshold of freedom once more.

The horse chestnut trees that line the avenue taking them from the county town to the port of Weymouth are in full bloom, the huge pink and cream flowers standing firm and strong among the large, rich green, deciduous leaves that dip low overhead. Running parallel with the old Roman road is the new railway, where earlier that day Ben navvied along with the other prisoners.

The railway peters out before they reach the Ridgeway Hill, but it will not be long before they tunnel through, not the way the guards keep pushing them. Ben cannot help feeling compassion for those men left to do the dirty work, even though he knows most of them deserve their punishment.

He has been explaining to Joshua how he was duped by Ikey, until he gets to the part that Joshua already knows from talking to Matthew. It is then Ben's turn to ask questions.

"Anyway, enough about me, it's all over thanks to you. I will never forget this, my friend." He leans over to give Joshua an awkward hug until the carriage lurches over a rut in the road and he sits back down next to Rebecca. "But tell me, how did you eventually make your fortune? I must say I approve." He strokes the leather upholstery of the carriage they are riding in. "This is most impressive."

"'Tis only hired, Ben. I have to admit I returned to Portland rich only in memories."

"I don't understand."

"I found no fortune on my travels, but I have inherited my father's estate."

"Of course, I had completely forgotten about the legacy. I had heard, but you know what it's like, people tend to exaggerate and I didn't set much store by it."

"Well, 'tis true, Ben, and I didn't inherit a load of debts neither. 'Tis a fortune right enough and I cannot wait to see the properties involved."

"Well done, Josh, that's terrific tidings if ever I heard them." He looks at Rebecca with smiling eyes. "What about our Becky then, Josh, I bet it were a shock to you to see how she has grown."

"She's a young lady now, Ben. She will make some lucky chap a fine wife too in a couple of years, I reckon."

"Don't talk about me as if I'm not here," says Rebecca shyly. "I'll have something to say about that when the time comes."

"I think maybe I will too, Becky," says Ben quietly. Then he winks at her.

They both smile and Ben takes her smooth hand in his rough one and places his lips against her soft skin. She tingles from head to toe. This is what she has been waiting for. She studied him in the Governor's office, and although he looked dirty, shabby, miserable and utterly exhausted, with rest and a good healthy diet he will soon be fit again and she feels blissfully happy.

The carriage begins the descent from the top of Ridgeway Hill. Weymouth Bay, the seaside town and harbour and the island of Portland seem to lie at their feet. It is a beautiful sight. The setting sun casts a golden glow from west to east and Portland basks in its glory.

Rebecca rests her head on Ben's shoulder. It has been a long day and she is tired. She knows that Ben must be even more exhausted but he won't care, for his ordeal is over and they'll soon be home.

Ben eases his arm out from under her and she feels him holding and gently squeezing her shoulder. She looks up into his face. Slowly he lowers his head until their lips touch. Can he feel her heart beating? Her lips burn with desire as she kisses him back. It is a proper kiss, not a sisterly kiss, a kiss that promises more. She draws away and smiles. Ben squeezes her arm again. Has Joshua noticed?

Joshua is staring out of the window of the carriage, thinking and planning, for tomorrow he has a long journey ahead of him and his mind is full of all the things he wants to accomplish, now given the opportunity.

Annie is waiting anxiously for the sound of the carriage on the cobbles. She keeps going to the windows of the cottage in case she cannot hear well enough. She must have gone back and forth at least forty times before she is rewarded with the sound of horses' hooves. She is still like a cat on hot bricks even after all these years.

She weeps for joy to see that Ben is still fit and sound in life and limb after his ordeal and he holds his mother in his arms, reassuring her all the time that it will take a lot more than that to bring him down.

Ben thanks Joshua and Rebecca once more for rescuing him, and says goodnight to them, promising to call on them in the morning, after they have all had a good night's sleep. As the carriage goes on up the slope to the coastguard cottages, they close the door on the outside world.

Annie applies balm to his sores and bruises. She has already prepared a sumptuous supper and she mothers him from the moment he steps inside until he is tucked up in his own bed. They both sleep soundly for the first time since he was taken to prison.

The following morning is a clear, warm June day. Ben has decided not to return to work immediately. His mother was right when she insisted that he should rest and build up his strength. He decides to go to the boat yard and make the necessary arrangements with Matthew, and then from there to see Joshua and Rebecca.

As he strolls through Chiswell all the villagers greet him warmly and Ben breathes in the fresh sea air with renewed enthusiasm for his freedom. He has missed this island and its people so much. He has even missed the soulful cry of the blessed seagulls. It is a beautiful sunny morning and he could not be happier to be home. Violet is thrilled to see him again and she hugs him affectionately.

However, Joshua has packed his few belongings into a haversack and is preparing to take his leave of them. "I have to go I'm afraid, Ben, but I will be back and spend some time with you all shortly. There is so much I have to sort out and, to be honest, I am not a little excited at the prospect."

They decide to walk with him at least to the mere. Violet goes with them, as far as the point where the village gives way to the beach, and there outside the boat yard, she and Matthew say their goodbyes. Joshua shakes hands with Matthew and leans down from the horse to kiss his mother lovingly. Tears fill her eyes, but she is proud and excited for him as she stands arm in arm with Matthew and waves him on his way. He sits tall in the saddle just like his father, and as they watch, Matthew is reminded of many years earlier when he had observed Richard Dryer leaving the island for the same destination, and his encounter with Violet.

Ben and Rebecca keep pace with him, chatting optimistically of his future as Lord of the Manor until they reach the causeway and the uneven track along the shingle makes them stumble. Ben falls back, calling his thanks and best wishes. Rebecca trots on a few more yards until breathlessly she falters.

"I cannot keep up with you," she cries. "God go with you, Josh, and come back soon to tell us all about your new life in Somerset."

"I will. You take care, Becky, and look out for Ben. I don't want him getting in any more trouble while I'm away."

"I'll see he doesn't, don't you worry." She pauses to rest, calling out an afterthought: "I hope the people and servants are nice, and they'll make you happy."

"I'm sure they will be. I will write and let you know."

"Yes, don't forget." Finally she cries, "We'll miss you, Josh."

"I'll miss you too, but I'll be back, I promise."

She stands and watches as he weaves his mount along the eastern slope of the causeway. He is nearing a large patch of sea pinks. The terns rise in the air, darting, diving and chattering wildly amongst themselves, angry and frightened as he disturbs their nesting ground. She gazes after him for a few moments and then turns back towards Ben.

Sitting on the beach, his eyes on her, he is watching every move, enjoying his freedom and more than content to be patiently waiting.

Violet turns to Matthew, her eyes full of love. "It's as if time has stood still."

"I know," replies Matthew softly. "It's us all over again." He kisses her fondly on her forehead. "It takes me back twenty years, but a lot of water has flowed through Smallmouth since then."

GLOSSARY

ANKER – Cask usually holding about 8 ½ gallons.

BAT – Stout pole about 6 feet long used as a weapon.

BATMAN – Smuggler armed with a bat to defend contraband.

BEALE – Portland Bill.

BOHEA – An inferior grade of black tea.

BOUND STONE – Stone marking the boundary point on Chesil beach between Portland and Wyke Regis.

COAST FENCIBLES – The Portland Royal Legion formed in 1803 for defence against Napoleon were renamed The Royal Portland Coast Fencibles by George III in 1806.

COASTGUARD – Service introduced in 1822.

COURTS LEET AND BARON – Court established to govern all local affairs. Particularly significant on Portland as it is a Royal Manor.

COW COMMON DAY – 14th May.

CREEPING IRONS – Grappling irons or hooks used for gathering up sunken casks.

CROP – Cargo of contraband.

CUTTER – Small single-mast sharp-built broad vessel.

DAVENPORT – Small desk.

DOWLAS – A coarse linen or cotton cloth.

DUMPSY – Twilight.

FLINK – Smugglers' warning light.

FREE-TRADER – Smuggler's name for himself.

FREIGHTER – Person responsible for buying contraband abroad.

GRENA – Grenadine dress fabric of loosely woven silk or silk and wool.

GROAT – Silver coin issued 1351-1662 equal in value to 4 pennies.

HALF-ANKER – Cask holding about 4 gallons.

KEG – A cask.

KETCH – Vessel rigged fore-and-aft on two masts.

KIMBERLIN – The name for any stranger or foreigner to Portland.

LAMMAS – First day of August.

LAND SHARK – Smugglers' name for land-based revenue officer.

LANDGUARD – Collective name for customs riding officers.

LERRET – A type of fishing boat used on Portland.

LONG OYSTERS – Crayfish.

LUGGER – Two or three-masts with four-cornered sails set fore-and-aft.

MAZEY DANCE – Traditional dance full of turns.

METHEGLIN – Spiced mead.

MILITIA – Non-professional military force employed when needed.

MUMMERS – Village players acting in dumb play.

OPE – Lanes giving access to the beach.

OWLER – Wool smuggler.

PEELERS – Nickname for police founded under Sir Robert Peel's secretaryship.

PORTLAND ROADS – Anchorage.

PREVENTIVE MAN – Mounted customs officer.

QUIT RENT – William II introduced a local land tax to help fund the building of the island's defences. This was 3d for an acre of land and 1d for a house and garden. In return this quit the inhabitants from liability for service to the lord and so it was always known as the 'Quit Rent'. This was distinct from other income from the manor and the tithes paid to the church.

REEVE – Saxon office established for collection of land dues, and recovery of wreckage and treasures washed ashore on behalf of the Lord of the Manor.

RIDING OFFICER – Mounted customs officer first appointed in 1699 to patrol in search of smugglers or hidden or abandoned contraband.

ROYAL MANOR OF PORTLAND – The Saxons established the Manor of Portland with the King of Wessex, later of England, as its Lord.

RUN – A smuggling operation.

SCHOONER – Fore-and-aft rigged vessel with foremast shorter than mainmast.

SHEN – Cow pats used for fuel.

SLINGERS' ISLE – Portlanders used to sling stones to defend the island and a cache of 2,000 sling-sized pebbles was unearthed on Verne Hill in 1936.

STINKIBUS – Foul-smelling spirits which have gone off after long submersion in the sea.

TIDE SURVEYOR – Supervisor of tide waiters.

TIDE WAITER – Customs officer responsible for rummaging ships arriving in port to see that no goods are concealed for clandestine landing.

TRANSPORTS – Convicts.

TUB – A small cask.

TUB-BOAT – Boat used for smuggling small casks.

TUBMAN – Smuggler employed to carry small casks.

VENTURE – An investment in a run.

VENTURER – Smuggler's financial backer.

VERNE HILL – Iron Age hill fort.

WATERGUARD – Collective name for customs men operating at sea.

WEIRS – Wild rough ground on coastal slopes under both east and west cliffs.

WORKING THE CROP – The practice of recovering sunken casks.

YEOMANRY – Volunteer cavalry force.

ACKNOWLEDGEMENTS

I should like to take this opportunity to thank my family, in particular my daughter Nicky, who at the eleventh hour read the story and made some very useful comments; also all the many friends who have, over time, read my manuscript and offered their encouragement and support. Especial thanks go to my writing friends, particularly Margaret Graham whose help and expertise was invaluable. I also received good advice from Hugh Rae (Jessica Stirling) and Iris Gower at the Writing Conference at Swanwick.

This story would not have been possible without the research done by the many Portland enthusiasts, who have written fascinating reference books and articles for the Internet from which I harvested much of the historical information. My grateful thanks go to them and to Dorchester and Yeovil libraries and the curator at the Portland Museum.